HE'D TRAVELED FAR TO MEET TOM HILL . . .
AND NOW THE MAN WOULD PAY.

The half-breed Tom Hill reached for his axe as Laird
kicked the fire. Hot coals, ashes and chunks of wood
scattered as Hill scrambled for his weapon. But Laird was
too quick. With a single leap, he swung full force against
the half-breed, pinning him flat to the ground. Like a
tightly wound spring, Hill burst away, clawing for the axe.

Laird anticipated the move. In a lightning-smooth motion,
Laird swung his fist again, banging Hill's head to the
ground; the motion jarred his teeth, but the half-breed
reached up to gouge Laird's eye.

In response, Laird's knee jerked up to Hill's unprotected
crotch. Pain flashed through the man's body. Twisting
Hill's arm, Laird threw the half-breed flat on his back,
dragged him a foot or so, then pitched him into the scattered
embers of the fire.

In a flash, Laird had recovered Hill's rifle. He stood
over the wounded man, panting as he spoke. "Hill, I've
let you live for one reason: so that Indians will know you
were whipped by the man you persuaded Young Antelope
to capture. What you did hurt others, not just me. Nez
Perce women died of the pox caught from the Blackfoot
who captured us. When I come back to Nez Perce country,
the Nez Perce will tell me where you are and I will hunt
you down and kill you. . . ."

NEZ PERCE LEGEND

MICK CLUMPNER

A Dell/Banbury Book

Published by
Banbury Books, Inc.
37 West Avenue
Wayne, Pennsylvania 19087

Dell ® TM 681510, Dell Publishing Co., Inc.

ISBN: 0-440-06330-2

Printed in the United States of America

First printing—February 1983

To those who love their homeland—and will die to keep it—this book is affectionately dedicated.

Mick Clumpner
January 1981

ACKNOWLEDGMENTS

Eagerly I thank the generous people who not only encouraged me to write this novel about the Nez Perce, but who provided me with the assistance and materials I needed: the Scott Meredith Literary Agency for suggesting that I write the book; Ed Claflin, who made its creation possible; Banbury Books for publishing the story; and the staffs of each for seeing it through.

In addition, I thank Hope M. Scrogin, who edited my rough draft; Marjorie Poleson for the information she contributed regarding William Craig; Helen Storie for sending me books about early Craigmont, the town in Idaho; Valerie Mathis for supplying material about the Bureau of Indian Affairs; Rex Bundy of Western Writers of America for his unflagging encouragement; Dr. Scott Chilcott for valuable information about the Nez Perce Indians; and the many others who, earlier in my life, told me stories that by now are generally forgotten.

My gratitude extends to the officials in the United States Forest Service and the Bureau of Entomology, who sent me into backwoods country with map and compass to check for timber, fires and insect-damaged trees. I appreciate, now especially, the work I have done for lumber and timber companies. Their assignments offered unparalleled opportunity to explore vast, trackless wilderness and miles of unfished waters.

I am thankful, too, for my own memories—of shared campfires and days alone. From them rose the images of how it all must have been so long ago.

M. C.

PREFACE

When it was suggested that I write a novel about an Indian tribe, I wanted that story to feature the Nez Perce. (My first real skill in horsemanship was practiced on descendants of Nez Perce ponies.)

Looking back fifty years and more, I consider it a privilege to have lived and worked in the lands of the Columbian Basin tribes. Having once walked hundreds of miles through this historic country—with only a compass and map for direction and before explorers bulldozed access roads into the timbered wilderness—I sensed the heartbreak the Indians must have felt when they were forced to leave. And farther south, as I traveled through Palouse territory, where herds of Nez Perce ponies once cropped the uncut grass, I sensed, too, what must have been the emigrants' hunger to possess the land.

The story of the Nez Perce Indian tribes will never be fully told. Because the beginnings of their history are lost to even their own tribesmen, recorded tales and revived traditions emerge from hearsay alone.

In the pages that follow, I have interwoven love stories with tales of what is known about the tribes, and again—this time in my imagination—have journeyed through their enchanting land. It is my hope that this novel will stimulate greater interest in the Nez Perce. In their resistance to persecution by those who eventually drove them from their territory, they remain a courageous example for us all.

Mick Clumpner

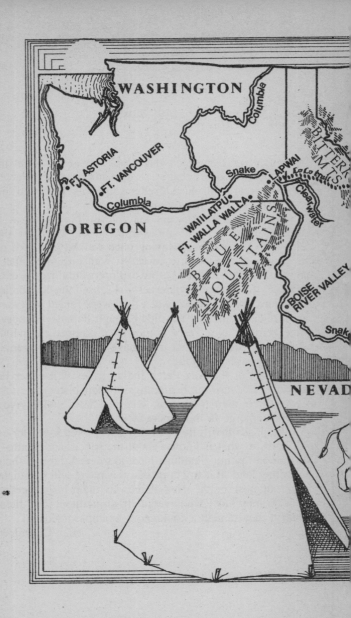

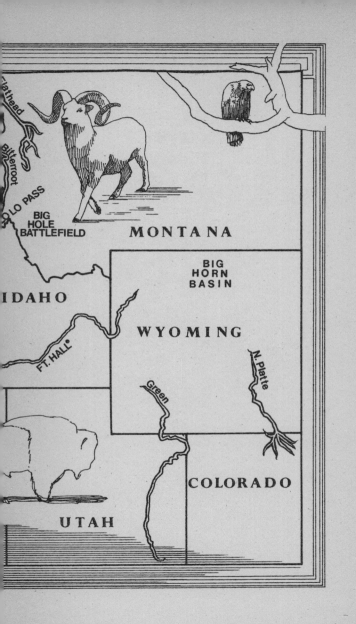

Flathead

Bitterroot

LO LO PASS

BIG
HOLE
BATTLEFIELD

MONTANA

BIG
HORN
BASIN

IDAHO

WYOMING

FT. HALL

N. Platte

Green

COLORADO

UTAH

Chapter 1

The hot Virginia sun poured down. A grim-faced man using a wide-bladed hoe was trying to repair the damage done to knee-high stalks of corn. But patches of earth where wild hogs had trampled could not be replanted. Remaining cornstalks could not be banked with soil. A quiet, deadly fury flowed through the man as he surveyed the damage, then moved next to examine the downed split rails where the hogs had broken through.

A neighbor whom he detested stood before him, his rifle in his arms. "Pa always told us fellers that trouble comes to them as can't handle it." The man with the hoe tried not to listen. The neighbor kept talking. "I figure when a feller takes on a job of fence-building, he ought to do it right. If he don't, critters is bound to get in. Specially when young corn is good eating."

The man with the hoe stiffened. "Jase, you know damn well that fence was built right. Now you tell me how hogs, without help from some human, could knock off the top rail, pull down the stake drove into the ground, and then push or pull through still more to make that gap."

Jase shrugged his burly shoulders, stretched his neck, and close to where the man stood leaning on his hoe, spat tobacco juice that darkened slender stalks of growing corn.

1

"Well, some hogs is purty smart," he drawled. "Seen some that could hide out way past butchering time and show up just when a feller didn't have no gun. Seen some fellers that ain't smart enough to stay away from another man's gal, too. It can get them in purty deep trouble."

Careful not to show his deepening anger, the man with the hoe shifted only slightly before answering.

"If she's old enough and not spoken for, some folks feel it's up to her. You're not talking about Mary Ellen, are you?"

"Bill, how did you ever guess it? Say, maybe if you live long enough you'll figure out how them hogs got into your corn. And if you keep smelling around my girl, you'll figure out how you're apt to get your nose flattened and your neck wrung."

"I don't give a damn what you think, Jase. If I want to see Mary Ellen and she wants me to see her, then by God, it's damn well what we'll do. Now get the hell out of here. I already figured how the hogs got in—saw your big flat footprints in the dirt—and if I ever see you here again or find the fence down and hogs in my corn, I'll come skunk-hunting!" Bill Craig slammed down his hoe and began working furiously to replace the rails and fence stakes. Jase kept at him while he worked.

"You talk mighty big," Jase sneered. "You find it in some book you been reading? Hell's fire, snotnose, it takes more than being able to read and write to do a man's job, and a feller with a limp pecker ain't going to get no woman. Don't get feisty with me or I'll chew off an ear and shoot out one of your purty eyes so you won't look so smart when you go courting."

Craig straightened up, the fence fixed. He was not a weakling, but neither was he a fool. Even with no gun involved, he'd lose a fight here in the corn patch. In a tussle of bull strength, Jase could strangle him or twist him into helplessness.

"If you think you can show me a way to fight without a gun, I just might tangle with you, Jase," he said. "Maybe I can learn something."

The big man couldn't believe his ears. He wallowed his chaw around, gathered some juice and spurted it on Craig's heavy boots. For a moment there was silence. An insult had been made. With it a challenge had been made clear.

Jase's face twisted in a cruel sneer. "Want to take me on right here and now?"

"Lay that gun down," Bill answered, "and we'll get over the fence where we can have some room to tussle."

"Tussle, is it?" Jase scoffed. "It won't be no tussle. You better figure you won't never see my girl again once I'm through with you. Come on, you feisty pup. I'm just the old dog to teach you a lesson."

Jase dropped his gun and placed his hand on the fence as if to vault over. The second he did, Craig picked up his hoe, swung it in a sweeping arc and smashed it against his neighbor's head. The big man slumped down. He made no sound.

Craig cautiously stepped closer. Except for the twitch of Jase's right hand and the jerking of his soil-blackened toes, the body lay still, unbreathing. There was no pulse, nothing to indicate Jase was playing possum. Craig knew the evidence looked bad against him. Striking a defenseless man, enemy or not, would be no one's idea of a fair fight.

Faced with the problem of eluding the hangman's noose, Craig decided to leave the scene immediately. Hurriedly laying the rifle aside, he heaved the big man onto his shoulder and with great effort carried the body to a place in the woods where it probably wouldn't be found for a day or so. Making his way back to the cornfield, he swept all footprints clean and whirled the hickory-handled hoe through the air far down the cornfield; luckily the caved-in skull had left no trace of blood. Next Craig gathered up the rifle, bullet pouch and powder horn and hastened toward his house across the meadow. While he walked he thought, where will I go? What will I need to take with me? West was the answer to where. And at the very least, he'd need food, a blanket, a hand axe, not to mention a few gold pieces. Money was scarce. Gold would get him farther west than anything else and that's right where Craig wanted to be that devilish day: west, and fast.

The Indians in the West knew that white men at the mouth of the Columbia as well as those far to the east were traveling to their homelands and apparently planning to stay. Scattered Indian bands met where their women dug camas for flour. Though some braves raced their ponies, more thoughtful ones among them talked of times to come. They used sign language to converse but were dissatisfied with it. The white man could look at little buglike symbols written on paper or bark and let words come from his mouth as he read them.

Already Indians had horses and weapons, but it was knowledge of the written word that would give them the power that they wanted. Because of this deeply felt need, Chief James of the Lapwai Nez Perce sent for white men from the East to teach his tribespeople to speak and write. The white man's religion would never be all the white man hoped it would be to the Indians—the red men had their own ideas of life and death—but their influence, as well as that of the trappers, would be unmistakable.

While the Nez Perce were thriving—building up their horse herds, learning to speak and write—William Craig had been growing up, unaware that his destiny lay far to

4

the west in unexplored Indian lands. But after the murder of Jase, Craig made his way toward these lands. There, eventual trade with fur trappers took him little by little toward the rendezvous in Wyoming.

Chapter 2

"You know, boys, if I was to take a woman to set up with for a few years, now that my joints are getting a little stiff, I wouldn't pass up a Nez Perce. You been around 'em, Bill. What's your idea?"

"I know the Nez Perce, all right," Craig agreed. "Lived with 'em, hunted with 'em. They're the best of all the Indians I've seen. There's only one thing about 'em I don't cotton to."

"Yeah?" Tom Van Cleve drawled.

"Bet it's because they smell like fish," Alec, the other trapper, put in.

"That's not it, Alec. Sometimes they do, but not always. I'm talking about getting too involved with the Indian women. Since that missionary Spalding taught 'em religion, you can't sleep with one or get her in the bushes unless you marry her. After they got that religion drilled into 'em, even the older squaws won't give in for them purty beads or nothing."

"Hell, a little thing like that don't bother me none," Van Cleve boasted. "I can always find me a little woman of some kind, even if she's old and wrinkled.

"I recollect one time me and old One-Eyed Pease was working north from the Yellowstone and come up on a

7

bunch of Blackfoot. Just a little bunch, maybe half a dozen tepees and not much to eat.

" 'Here's where we sleep warm tonight,' I told Old One-Eye.

"He says, 'Yeah, and you'll wake up with your hair on a pole afore morning, too.'

"The Indians come out to meet us and it was a purty sorry bunch. Anyways, we made the peace sign and went on in after a bit of talk and parleying. After we give 'em the word we was meat-hungry, they killed a dog and we made some plans to kill buffalo meat in the morning. Then I sized up what might be a bed partner. I lets the one that looked interested see I had a good curved sewing needle. Then I pointed to my robe spread out. She knew what I meant right off. That night when we got kind of settled down, she got up to chuck the fire and then found my bed. I was sure warmed up till morning."

Alec chuckled, then waved him off. "Hell, that ain't nothing much. Bill," he said, turning to Craig, "there's apt to be some Nez Perce at the gathering. Got any idea what they might take in trade for a few of their ponies?"

"Alec, it'll be the same old things every Indian wants— guns, powder and lead, with a few extras thrown in. They want guns most," Craig explained. "Old Spalding at the mission tries to discourage 'em from traveling out of his territory to hunt. I'll bet he prayed and snorted when he heard some of his tame Indians was headed to meet trappers at the rendezvous. He wants 'em to settle down and raise crops. All the missionaries and priests are that way, believe in keeping Indians home where they can have hell scared into 'em. I don't like the way things are shaping up."

"You mean out there or back here?" Van Cleve asked.

"I mean all over. We got things going with fellers in

8

Washington who want something done with the Indians besides just killing 'em off. I don't think things will ever get so everybody's happy; we'll have some real fracases in the next few years. You'll see. There's a lot of talk about more people moving into the western country. Jason Lee and his bunch of pilgrims over in the Oregon Valley is saying Americans should move there to keep England from taking over the territory. I think he's right.''

"You been there, ain't you, Bill?''

"Yeah, few times. Easy country to live in if you like warm winters and wet clothes. Hell of a good place for farmers and missionaries.''

Van Cleve and Alec laughed, but not Craig. He pulled on his pipe thoughtfully. In his mind he was picturing the clear waters of the Rogue River, where they had camped on the way up from the Sacramento country. Salmon and trout flashed in the stream, fat deer and elk along the bottoms and in the hills. They had followed the old trade trail over the Continental Divide and camped in a little valley by one of the streams that twisted toward the western ocean. In a few places pine trees loomed so tall they were like the redwoods far to the south. Finally they had reached this place.

"The good times,'' Craig recalled, "come when winter rains stop in the lower valleys and the sun comes out real nice. The Indians around here were kind of easy to get along with, but like all the rest of the redskins, you had to watch your outfit. That's how Jed Smith got caught down near the coast, damn fool careless. He and some of his men figured they weren't in hostile country. I say he was lucky to get out alive.

"Living in Indian country always seems to be a matter of luck; leastways it seems to me that way. I recollect one time me and old Squinch—a trapper I never knew by any other handle—was working beaver along a little flat

9

valley with ponds, real nice place for a few traps. We wanted a deer or sheep to eat but we hadn't shot off our guns because we was in new country and didn't want visitors. I says to Squinch, 'See that woodpecker picking on that snag? If he flies up creek, then I go down. If he flies west, I go east.' Well, the old feller took off over the valley to the west. I picked up my gun and worked my way east and slipped up on a bunch of sheep using a rocky ridge off maybe a mile or so away. I made a circle to get close and peeled my eyes before I got in shooting range. Then I seen 'em. They was three Indians, all dressed up and painted for a good time. Well, I was in a fix. There was old Squinch setting and picking up traps down along the creek——if these fellers wanted hair, he could be bald-headed purty sudden-like.

"I sized things up and figured if they did see old Squinch I could knock one or two off if I was close enough and let him know we had trouble. The bucks were scouting for sign and hadn't reached to where we'd left any. Squinch was working the willows along the creek, staying in the water so as to leave no tracks. Our ponies was hobbled out of sight.

"They was a little stringer of willows coming up from the creek my way. I got close enough for a good shot if they come up around it. Then I saw old Squinch making a set. The bucks hadn't seen him yet but if they crossed the creek they'd ride right into him.

"I ducked down and run to get close to where hell would break loose, got my rifle set and waited. The bucks got suspicious. They stopped and had a parley. It was a long shot, but I held the rifle a mite high and touched her off. Knocked old Three Feathers off his pony. There was a scramble in the willows, and as the two live ones pulled around in a circle, they saw the smoke from the shot. One grabbed for the dead Indian while his partner grabbed the pony.

"Quick as they was, old Squinch had time to make the bank and get in his shot while I was pounding powder and lead in the barrel. Squinch knocked off one and there was another whirlwind. The last one, he was a brave old boy. Jumped his pony right into where smoke from old Squinch's shot hung in the air. I says to myself, 'Good-bye, Squinch!' "

The two men listening smoked silently, each recalling close calls they'd had in past years. Both had heard Craig's story before.

"Squinch was ready for him," Craig went on. "As the pony jumped through the brush straight at him, Squinch swung the trap he was fixing to set and hit the pony in the face. It jumped sideways and threw the buck's arrow shot out of line. Squinch's hatchet took the old boy right in the back and knocked him in the creek. Afore he could get into action, Squinch sunk a knife in him. I tell you, we got out of there quick and took to new country. I always thought if I had gone the other way but what the woodpecker told me, we might have gotten in a fix we couldn't get out of."

Van Cleve was reminded of another story. "Bill," he drawled, "I heard you almost got shot by old Joe Walker when you made that trip down in the Digger country on the way to California. Never heard your side of it. Did he really get mad enough to take a shot at you?"

"He was mad enough, all right. Too mad for me to argue with."

"Well, what happened?"

"Aw, I was just smarting off. Walker had been purty tough across the desert, and when we got to the Humboldt—Mary's River, some called it—we was all feeling purty good, dirty as Digger Indians and lousy to boot. Anyway,

11

here was water and we camped to feed and rest up. I found a place where I could wade out past the muck, all mush banks and duck and goose dirt, slick and slimy.

"After I got sloshed off, I got the big idea to trick old Walker. He hadn't got himself wet yet, so I looked for a place where he could dive in. I found it near a kind of a bank there. With the water all riled up he couldn't see that the muck was just about two feet under. I went back to camp, which was up on a flat away from the mosquitoes. Hell, there was ten million of 'em near the reeds in the water.

"I was putting on my shirt, already had my boots on, when old Walker says, 'Have a good swim, Bill?'

" 'Sure did, boss,' I told him. 'There's a dang good hole you can dive in just down off that little bank. It's cool and nice. Must be a cold spring somewheres under the bank.' "

"Some of the rest of the crowd was getting ready to jump in along with Walker. Ever see the scar on his back? Hell, it must be a foot long. An old buck had slid his lance in and darn near sliced Walker's liver out. Well, Walker puts his hands over his head, gives a leap in the air, and goes into the water like a kingfisher for a trout. Mud and water boiled up and there was a lot of splashing and bare legs kicking in the air till one feller yelled, 'He's stuck!' They jumped in and right there I took off.

"I stayed out of sight after I saw him come out all slimy and blind. When he got through coughing and spitting, he hollered for water to wash out his eyes. Mad? He spit mud and cuss words all together. Oh, he was going to skin that bastard, shoot him on sight. 'Get my gun!' I tell you, if I hadn't been so scared, I would have rolled on the ground laughing. As it was, I took out with my hunting rifle, found a bunch of antelope and killed two. I skinned out what I wanted and took it back to camp." Craig laughed. "Old Joe was still smoking mad, but that fresh meat settled him down. He's a purty good feller, Walker is, and a real fine leader."

The talk shifted once more to women; the coming rendezvous meant just that. Whiskey, of course, and meeting old friends, but first women to relieve the tension. During cold nights spent huddled in fur robes or stretched out by dimming fires, there had been plenty of dreaming. Warm arms, bodies, a tussle with someone who would welcome the brief frantic embraces—that would be paid for in cash or goods, and worth everything it cost.

"Craig, you ever try one of them there senoritas that come over from Spain?" Alec asked.

"Hell, Bill can't sing, let alone play a guitar, or whatever them fancy fellers do under the window," Van Cleve teased.

"You're right about that, Cleve. I just listened. There was good times—and that's in spite of them girls being watched all the time. Those girls are like turkey hens in the spring when they see a young cock strutting around dragging his wings, or in this case dancing the fandango." Craig shook his head, remembering. "It stirs the blood to see fellers stomp their heels and strut while the girls smile and swish their tails at 'em.

"At first we was worried about what kind of place we was in. We come out of the hills expecting to trade—and real thirsty. But when we hit the place they called a city, there was just a few adobe houses and not much—"

"Talk about the women, Bill, to hell with the houses."

"Aw, shut your trap, Alec. Let Craig tell it his own way."

Chapter 3

Craig leaned back before he continued and half-closed his eyes to block out the smoke from the dying fire.

"It was early fall and we wanted to cross through on the way to California if we could. I was the new man in the bunch and Joe took care to tell me not to push things. We weren't there to fight, he said, just frolic and have a good time. So we made sign talk, showed what we had, bowed and scraped and grinned like friendly pups. The men was suspicious as hell until we offered 'em some of Joe's popskull. Then they warmed up real good. We drank some of their stuff too, traded smokes and parleyed. Anyway, some fellers told their women to cook up a feed for us, and 'twasn't long afore we smelled things cooking. Didn't see much more of the girls, though, than just flashes once in a while when they thought we wasn't looking. Even the little kids kept out of sight. They reminded me of quail skittering back and forth."

"Hell with the kids. Tell about the women. Tell about rassling, about squeezing and hugging their soft busts and bottoms."

"I'm coming to that, Tom. I'm telling it my way. Shut up and lay back and listen, or if you can't, go to the brush and take off the pressure."

Craig resumed his story. "The women cooked and we talked and drank with the men and watched our packs and ponies purty careful; they was tied up in the square. I didn't want to get so drunk I couldn't perform when the time come, if it ever did.

"I recollect old Joe winking at me. He says, 'Bill, you take care of the ponies and our packs. I'll have someone trade off with you when the big dance begins.' "

"First I'd heard of a dance. I saunters over to the ponies, gathered 'em up and looked for a place to tie and feed 'em; there was no feed close. An old man come over and makes signs to follow him. He yells at a girl in a 'dobe house and she come out with some grub on a flat plate and a pot of meat and beans. Her little brother carried along a jug and we all went out to a stable where there was hay and grain. The old feller tied up while I unloaded. The girl put down the food and watched us and the boy skittered around the corner and peeked back. The old grampa must have seen the girl ogling me. He said something and she skedaddled out of there, but she looked at me as she left and kind of grinned. Course I winked back.

"After we got the ponies taken care of, the old feller set down and motioned me to eat. He dipped one of the dried-up flat cakes into the pot, filled it with beans and meat and shoved it in his craw. I did the same, but in just one second—whooee! Talk about hot! My tongue and lips felt like fire. The old man cackled and laid back while I grabbed for the jug and tried to swallow beans, meat and water all to once. The kid hung around the corner to watch and then I saw the girl look in the little window."

"Was she purty, Bill?"

Craig nodded. "Purty as the stew was hot—chili, they called it. The old man yelled at the kid to get wine. He disappeared and came back with a jug. Where they got the grapes to make the stuff with I don't rightly know.

16

"After a while I tried to make the old feller understand I hadn't had a bath for some time and I was greasy
and dirty as hell. He grinned, pinched his nose and turned
his head away. We both hawhawed. Then the old man
hobbled off and motioned me to follow him. We went to
his house: clean and cool, built-up place for cooking in
one corner, table and chairs and dirt floor. No women in
sight. In no time, the old feller had showed me water and
cloth with something I took for soap in a bowl. A pot near
the fire was full of hot water; he took a gourd dipper and
sloshed some into a wooden tub, then grinned and went
out. I stripped, cleaned up and put on my cleaner outfit.
There was a looking glass in my pack, along with other
things, and I trimmed my beard a little."

"Don't take so damn long, Bill. Get to the woman,"
Van Cleve grumbled.

"Hold your fire, she's right handy. I went out to
where the stock was and handed the mirror to old Juan. He
grinned like a cat eating fish and bobbed his head, saying,
"Bueno, Bueno," then took off out of sight. I heard
women laughing and talking. Purty soon some came to the
door with him.

"Juan's wife's name was Jovita. She wasn't too old,
real nice-looking—wrinkled some, but a fine, full-figured
lady with black hair, not a streak of white in it. She bowed
and smiled. Then she held up the mirror in front of Rosita,
the girl I'd took a shine to, and brushed the girl's hair
while the girl looked at herself. Next she showed the kids
one at a time how they looked and it was worth the trip to
see how pleased they was. So far as all of them was
concerned, I seemed to be like family. We all smiled a lot
and shook hands. Rosita's was soft and smooth and warm
as a woman's love on a spring night. I was lost right there,
I'll tell you.

"The big dance started in the square after we ate and

squatted around. Some of our fellers were pretty well loaded. I kept thinking of Rosita. Every once in a while I saw her in the crowd. She kept edging my way and I suspected we might get a lot closer once she was out of her mama's sight. When our fellers took to dancing it was more jump, prance, push and haul, not a bit like the natives. A couple young people put on a real good turkey-strutting show. As the women and girls got warmed up, they flipped up their skirts. I kept looking for Rosita, hoping she'd look me up later.''

"And did she, Bill?"

Alec snorted at Tom in disgust. "Any darn fool knows a woman would come to see what a feller with trade goods had in his pouch. Women are all alike. Just wave a little silk or show a little gold and they come sneaking up to see what you got they can use."

Craig nodded, then got back to his story. "When I told Joe I'd better spell Weaver at the barn and let him have a chance to walk around, Walker guessed what I was at.

" 'Don't go to her place,' he told me. 'These people get real jealous if you try to push. If she comes to you, her tail is in the trap. Take it easy and it'll come easy. I seen that gal looking your way. But watch your back, son, because that's where the knife will land if you don't.'

"I went to the barn and told Weaver to go jig with the women if they could stand his smell. He was so hot to get out of there he never questioned why I didn't want to dance. I got out some things—a little bottle of perfume, a comb, a pair of scissors—and it wasn't more than a few minutes afore I heard a squeak on the edge of the side wall next the door. There was Rosita, peeking in and seeing if she could see what lay on my pack. I crooked my finger and smiled till she come in slow and kind of cautious. Then I held up the comb and the scissors and touched

18

Rosita's fingers with mine as she reached for them. She didn't jerk back so I held up the bottle of perfume and opened the top. Rosita came closer. As she leaned toward me I could smell her and I got weak in the knees, wanting to grab her but afraid I'd scare her off. Her hair had a kind of smoky sweet smell, like dried flowers or fruit. When she smiled I knew I had her. I put some of the perfume on her cheek. Her dress was kind of open at the neck and showed her purty valley. I put another dab of perfume there and touched her. Then she put up a hand and smoothed my beard. I stoppered the bottle and gave it to her—the comb too. Once she had 'em both in her hands, I reached for her and pulled her close.

"Rosita's head scarf was of red silk. When it slipped down I couldn't resist smoothing all that soft black hair. She must have liked that fine because the next thing I knew she moved close and bowed her head and we began touching each other.

"Just then a loud yell come out of the square and we heard laughing and shouting. I thought that was the end of our loving for sure. But Rosita took my hand and led me out of the barn, around the corner and down the street to another place, where grain and hay and dried food was stored.

"Once she thought we was safe, she raised her face and we kissed and touched again. There wasn't no holding back on her part, but before we got into the real action there was a big commotion outside and she dropped away from me to look out the little barred window. There was our old Ike, backed up against a side wall with his knife out. He was crouched over and cussing a slim-looking Mexican. The Mex had his knife out too, edging around to jump Ike. I knew this was the kind of trouble Joe didn't want to happen.

"We slipped out the door. Rosita disappeared, and

without thinking, I got between those two gamecocks and held up my hands. A damn fool trick, if you ask me. Ike squalled but I just pointed down the street and when he looked that way I let him have one on the side of the jaw and grabbed his knife as Weaver come running. The Mex looked put out but I bowed and made the peace sign, then held out my hand. He grinned and did the same.

"Near as I could make out after it was all over, the squabble started because Ike had a few too many drinks. When he saw a woman looked like she was interested in a strange man's pants, he got hot and begun pawing her right out in the open. This Mex, her husband, didn't think too kindly of that and he and Ike come down to where they could fight it out. I was plenty upset. Anyway, Rosita was gone and I hadn't really got a taste of her. Joe showed up then. I went back to watching the outfit and Ike come around a little later. He wouldn't shake hands with me till Walker laid it on him for being such a damned fool."

"Did you ever get Rosita?" Alec asked eagerly.

"Yeah, later that night. Joe and me had a talk. He figured we'd stay one more day and night to rest the stock and let the boys get things out of their systems. The little town was getting friendly. Even Joe had lined up a place to sleep with a warm bundle in his arms.

"I was about to doze off there in the barn when I heard a whisper at the window. Rosita was smiling at me and pointing down the street. Luck must have been with me. Newell was still sober enough to take over my job. He grinned and said his turn would come later on. At first, hell's fire, I thought he wanted Rosita, but he said he already had a girl and a place to go after the dance.

"I found Rosita waiting. She didn't have anything on under that long dress of hers and I wanted real bad to see her stripped. She wouldn't go for that. But she did let me make love to her and we spent an hour or two together afore I had to leave. Rosita really liked me,'' Craig mused, remembering. "She cried a little when I left. That sure made me wisht I could talk her language.''

There was a long pause before Alec spoke. His voice was hoarse. "What happened the next night? You and her get together again? Tell us about that part.''

"Let him tell it his own way,'' Van Cleve said harshly.

"Well,'' Craig went on, "Walker figured we better make plans about what to do if there was another ruckus. I was to stay close to the stock. I said I'd saddle up all the ponies and have their packs on early in the evening while everyone ate and got ready for the dance. Joe said he'd holler 'Kentucky' two or three times if things got bad enough for me to scoot with most of the horses. My orders was to head straight west and they'd catch up with me along the trail.

"We spent most of the day sleeping and eating. Once in a while I caught glimpses of Rosita. Old Juan come to sign-talk and we drank his wine. The little kids come around but didn't stay long. Jovita got some goat meat and started roasting it over the coals, then spread sauce over it. Before long I was drooling like a hound at a coon tree with the old coon in sight.

"She hollered and Rosita come in. I thought that gal was purty before but now I couldn't believe it. She wore a high ivory comb in her black hair, glass earbobs that sparkled and that bright red scarf. Her lips were bright red too and her face was a soft smooth tan. God, how good she looked to me. When she smiled I knew if we stayed another day or so, I wouldn't leave the place unless she went with me; it was that bad. I was sure Jovita knew what'd took place the night before but old Juan just kept shoving chili beans and drinking wine, not noticing anything.

"Rosita had picked up a basket and brought back

some eggs. Jovita raised her fingers: one, two . . . When she reached three I nodded my head. Time she figured the meat was ready, she broke the eggs into a bowl and mixed in some broken-up pieces of dried bread and coarse meal. Then she held up a red pepper and looked at me with a questioning grin. I opened my mouth and gasped real funny and it set 'em all laughing. Jovita sliced meat off onto a plate, brought the bowl over to the table and soon Juan and me was eating fine.''

"To hell with the grub," Tom grumbled. "Get to the girl and give us the right details."

"I ain't about to go into all that," Craig replied. "Rosita was too damned nice to tell the likes of you about. I guess I was in love. I couldn't get enough of just looking at her.

"By late afternoon guitars were tuning up for the dance, people were singing and I heard a drum beating a rhythm that started my feet moving. A little boy began to slap his hands in time to the drum. Another feller took it up and pretty soon everyone joined in." Craig broke off. "I thought it was good to be in that town," he added after a moment. "I'd liked to have stayed there and lived with them folks.''

The fire was almost out. Van Cleve got up, dragged in dry branches to fling on the coals. Soon there was warmth and light to cheer the night. As Van Cleve sat down, he was still caught up in the spell of Craig's story of love in that Mexican town. He asked in a low voice, "Did you ever go back, Bill?"

"No, sure didn't. I thought on it a lot, though, while Joe and the outfit made the swing around California and up to the Columbia. But by the time we got there it was too late to head back. Anyway, let me wind up the story.

"When the dance began, Joe got a fellow to spell me with the ponies." Craig drew a long breath. "Boys, I'm

22

telling you Rosita was something to see. Juan, bless his shriveled old soul, led me to her to dance. I saw Jovita smile when he done it. Hell, I couldn't dance, but I could hold her and try. I squared away and we bowed and stomped our feet like prairie chickens on the booming grounds. By God, it was fun. Folks laughed and clapped. Rosita brought up another girl and we bowed and scraped and got acquainted. Old Juan and his friends come around to shake hands and purty soon we was all drinking and patting each other on the back. I had another dance or two with Rosita and was just getting the hang of things when Joe Walker come sidling over.

" 'Craig,' he says, 'you better find a chance to slip out and saddle up. Ike's getting warmed up. The damned fool's looking at that Mex's woman he pawed last night. I wisht I had somebody to take his place, but he's good on the trail and hell on wheels in a real fight. I guess we got to put up with the bastard. Get things ready to go. When I yell 'Kentucky,' you pull out.'

"Rosita saw me go to saddle up and followed me. I stopped what I was doing to hold her and kiss her. Right away she started crying like she wanted more, but all we could do was kiss and touch.

"Somehow I got the ponies packed and tied head to tail. Nobody was on the street when I led 'em out. I tied the lead horse to a post and me and Rosita run back to the granary. We made love and was laying there touching each other—she crying some more without making a sound—when I heard Joe squall, 'Kentucky!' again and again. I grabbed Rosita, kissed her for what would be the last time, picked up my rifle and run for the ponies. Where Rosita went, I never found out. I heard shooting and by the time I was pouring leather to my saddle pony all hell had broke out in town.

"I was maybe six or eight miles out when I saw the

bunch coming behind, strung out like beads on a string, Walker leading. He was mad when he rode up. "Damn, that was close, Bill. Ike almost got killed, maybe more of us too.'

"We trotted along as others caught up. I saw Cleve here riding close to someone, holding him in the saddle. It was Ike, that bastard.

" 'Ike ain't got the sense of a rutting bull elk,' Joe gritted out. 'Backed that woman up against the wall and tried to take her right there in the square. He had her skirts up when her man stuck a knife to him. Some of the Mex's friends kept us fellers off, but the old grizzly was too tough and too quick for 'em. He got a hold of the Mex, whirled him in the air and threw him, then started in banging heads. I take it you heard the shooting? Then some son of a bitch up on a house hit somebody in the crowd. That really woke up the place. I yelled out to you and we all waded in and got Ike out of there. Lucky for us you left them ponies ready to go.'

" 'Anybody else hurt?' I asked him.

" 'Don't know yet. We'll stop up ahead some place and count heads and fingers. There was more knives flashing in that square than you see at a skinning party when the buffalo are down.' "

Craig finished his tale. "Ike had a purty good cut but that heavy hide shirt of his kept him from getting his liver sliced into. Nobody else got hurt very bad. It's just that the boys was upset and mad they didn't get that last chance at women who was ready to play with 'em. I count myself lucky I had my time with Rosita."

"You sound like you really want to go back to her."

"Yeah, Alec, I guess I do, but you boys know how it is. You start out, something comes up and you put it off. I met women in California, some farther north, but I couldn't get shut of Rosita. After almost two years, I started out to find her and see if she'd marry me, but Indians from the south—Apache or Yaqui—raided the town, killed most of the men and took the young women and kids back south to sell as slaves or keep for themselves. So I never found her.''

"Hell of a story, Bill," Tom chimed in, "but it's purty hard for me to swallow. Now I ain't saying you lied about it, but you strung out some things don't sound right to my ears. The girls is always purty, but you leave 'em and never tell us how you stuck yer pecker in 'em." Tom smirked and spat into the fire. "That's the part I'd like to hear. We do know you was with Joe Walker, so that part can be so. But that purty girl—I'll bet she was old and wrinkled and couldn't do it worth a damn."

Craig had already gotten up and was digging into his buckskin sack. His medicine bag, as he called it, was as sacred to him as the ones kept by medicine men of the Indian tribes he had visited. When he returned to the fire, he slowly unrolled a piece of silk cloth—a bright red scarf that sparkled in the flickering light. Unfolding the scarf completely, Craig came finally to an ivory comb, its delicate filigree radiant against the scarlet.

"Rosita gave me these." That was all Craig said. Then he carefully put the comb and scarf away. Later, lying by the fire, the men lost themselves in thought—of the past, of the coming rendezvous and of the women there who might be glad to lie with them.

Chapter 4

The young man sat uncomfortably at attention. "Uncle Charlie," he said to the bespectacled, officious man across the desk, "I'm curious why you wanted to see me. Is it about a position here?"

"Not in Washington, son," Charles Madden answered, "but it does have something to do with all that. As you know, I've been appointed Chief Clerk of the Office of Indian Affairs and I have a grave responsibility toward both the government and the various Indian tribes. Up to this point, our efforts have all been focused on tribes east of the Mississippi River. Now there is a need to know more about the Indians of the far West. We have learned something about those who live along the Pacific Coast from traders and missionaries who go there, but there is a large area in the northwestern part of the nation that none of us really understands. And unfortunately," Madden sighed, "from letters I get and from tales I've heard, I've discovered there are no two stories the same."

"I see," the young man replied, not really understanding. "How can I help?"

"I want to send you to the Northwest to live with Indians, to listen to their side of the story, to find out what missionaries, priests and traders have to say. Above all,

I'd like you to listen to the trappers' tales. They've lived closest to the Indians and have had to learn Indian ways in order to survive."

"But Uncle Charlie," Laird burst out, "you know Indians killed my grandmother and that my grandfather fought them to the death from then on. All I've ever heard have been horrible stories about what Indians have done to whites. Now you're asking me to go live with them."

Madden leaned forward. He looked keenly at the young fellow before him. "My boy, believe me, I understand what you're saying and I won't send you unless you're ready to go willingly. But now I want you to understand me. Even though you're prejudiced, I would rather send you to study the Indians' ways than some stiff-necked so-called religious fellow who believes he knows it all because God told him so."

Madden rose. "Think over what I've said for a day or two," he said, "and if you decide you want to try out my scheme, we'll make the arrangements. One word of caution—and this is a direct order—do not tell anyone either about this assignment or about your relation or obligation to me or to the Office of Indian Affairs. This is to be a secret mission financed entirely by me. Do you understand?"

"You can trust me to keep my mouth shut," Laird responded. "I must say that I cannot get into my skull why you believe I'm suited for this job. I know hardly anything about the West and less than that about the Indians."

"Son, that's exactly why I picked you," Madden explained. "Everything you see will be important to you. You won't miss a thing, like some men might who think they know it all."

Laird felt confused as he left his uncle's office. He despised Indians, and here he was, being asked to travel and even live with them, to go west to lands unknown to everyone here. He entered a tavern where he could relax and analyze the situation. Over a drink he recalled an often-told incident that had occurred shortly before he was born.

Sparrow Sage, a distant relative of his who had fought in the War of 1812, had returned home after a brief absence. He found that an Indian had taken his wife and another woman captive and was heading for Fort Niagara to sell his prisoners to the British, who were in possession of the fort. Sage started after them, an axe his only weapon. He caught up soon after and attacked. When the redskin's gun failed to fire, Sage struck him with the axe. The Indian dropped both the gun and his tomahawk and tried to flee, but Sage pursued and killed him. The settler's wife, overcome by the fright of her experience, died shortly afterward.

Stories of other atrocities swept through Laird's mind, but a drink started him thinking in new directions. If he did decide to go on the mission, he might come back a hero—hailed a dauntless, bold adventurer and listened to with interest. Why, he might even bring back a scalp or two as proof that he was a man of courage and daring. The women would fall at his feet. That would certainly be worth his trouble. Damn right it would!

Before he reached home, Laird had decided to take up his uncle's request and began immediately to put his affairs in order. Affairs? Yes indeed. He meant to find more about the secret charms of Bessie Aldrich before he left. She was a tease and a flirt who always offered more than she ended up giving. So what if she refused him? He could live with that. But if she stopped her teasing and gave in, he would have that memory to warm his blood when shivering under his blankets in a strange land.

Laird met Bessie that night and got little satisfaction. If he was good, she promised, she might agree to go with him to the carriage house day after tomorrow. Trying to satisfy himself for the moment, Laird kissed and caressed her. Plump, voluptuous flesh peeked temptingly from stiff corsets and confining clothing. Laird had imagined many times how wonderful it would be if there were nothing in the way of his exploring hands. He wanted to feel, perhaps see, every hidden charm of this girl who had been teasing him for several months.

He had already enjoyed titillating adventures with barmaids in taverns and coffee houses. But brought up under the watchful eyes of his strict, religious parents, he had not dared risk being discovered. Gossips in the town might have spread tales and doomed any chance of his finding the proper girl to marry. Those worries now were in the past. Because he intended to leave home before long, he didn't need to be so careful about his reputation.

Before his meeting with Bessie in the Aldrich carriage house, Laird went back to see his uncle. Madden, sensing that his nephew would accept the offer, had already gone ahead with plans for the trip.

"You will leave tomorrow," he told Laird eagerly, "and travel under army escort to St. Louis. It's best you make your own way west from there. Here is a letter of instructions. Read the letter; then destroy it. If even the slightest suspicion is aroused, we'll both be in danger. I'll make up a believable story for your mother, so don't worry about that end of it. Anyway, it's my guess you'll enjoy traveling as a man of mystery.

"In St. Louis," Madden continued, his voice rising with excitement, "you'll meet a trader who will help you find means of traveling farther west. Money will be provided. Oh," he added, "you'd do well to send me a letter before you leave St. Louis. Do you have any questions?"

Laird was brimming with them, but because he didn't know where to start he just shook his head and grinned.

30

Madden did too, then sighed and studied his nephew's face. "Well," he said finally, "I have no doubt that either you will perform an outstanding job or your hair will be decorating some warrior's wigwam. Now let's shake and wish each other luck. I'm afraid we both will need it."

Laird chuckled to himself, thinking of the luck he'd need that night with Bessie. Later, in the carriage house, panting and disappointed once again, he wondered if the West would be a lustier place.

Chapter 5

Three great changes within a century had occurred in the lives of the Nez Perce. First, the acquisition and use of the horse changed the Indians from a fish-eating, herb-gathering tribe living in sedentary villages to bold hunters and semi-nomads who traveled great distances. Then, with the encroachment of white men on their territory, the Nez Perce began their search for new power. The final change occurred when missionaries and priests brought the Christian religion to Nez Perce lands.

At the Lapwai mission an Indian chief renamed James had been turned Christian by the Spaldings. He married and had a daughter who on advice from the Spaldings had been christened Isobel.

Isobel had grown into a beautiful maiden much sought after by the young men of her tribe. Though reared as a Christian, she had inherited ancient tribal religious dreams, and one of these shaped her life, the lives of her immediate tribe, and perhaps those of the Spaldings as well.

In the spring the grassy slopes and rolling prairies around Lapwai were covered with blooming flowers of all colors. Buttercups opened along rocky outbanks and sandy slopes where the sun warmed the ground. Next yellow bells, short-stemmed blue honeysuckle and grass pinks flowered among the prairie bunch grass. Sunflowers thrust yellow heads above the grasses and entire hillsides looked like sunshine. It was in the midst of the vibrance and promise of springtime that Isobel had her dream.

One afternoon after gathering roots and bulbs, Isobel lay down, and wondering about her future, fell asleep. When she awoke, Isobel knew the dream she'd had would shape her life. She also knew she must dream the dream again and then once more, for the magic number of dreams was three.

The second dream was much like the first. It came while Isobel was digging camas bulbs on the Weippe prairie. That day she took time to rest at the edge of the bulb grounds under the cedars where it was cool. Her dream had been so real that when she woke she looked around startled. Quickly Isobel took her basket of bulbs and returned to the smoking fires where camas were being dried for winter, but she said nothing.

With the appearance of the horse, the Nez Perce and neighboring tribes soon eliminated the buffalo from the territory west of the Bitterroot Mountains. For this reason a long trek to the prairies and hunting grounds of the Blackfoot and Crow was necessary in order to get buffalo robes and meat. Only the men who had the best ponies could join the hunting party. And each year some younger braves who went along were designated as followers; on the journey they learned the trails and participated in the kills.

A party large enough to defend itself, kill enough buffalo to provide hides and dry the meat took at least twenty or thirty warriors with extra ponies. Some women went too. They worked the hides, kept up the camps and enjoyed trade if they met friends along the way. The journey was a long one. Because the buffalo traveled also, sometimes it was a year—even two—before the hunters were successful and returned.

This year the returning party was particularly joyous. No hunters had been killed; those injured were recovering; and the ponies were loaded with hides and dried meat. In addition, the women had found a small tribe who were eager to trade beaded and quilted bags for dried fish and camas-bulb flour. A happy time again!

In the tepee that night, after feasting on dried buffalo meat and other delicious foods steamed and roasted around the fires, Isobel did not fall asleep immediately. Tribal confab and the incessant drumming still went on outside. Finally closing her eyes, she dreamed her long-ago dream for the third time.

The next day while helping work hides, Isobel spoke to her mother in a soft, low voice. "I've had a dream three times," she said, "and I do not know yet what it means."

"Tell me, my woman, my daughter."

Isobel hesitated. "I saw good things and bad things," she began. "And in every dream I saw the same man."

"Is he of our tribe?"

"No, a strange white man. I have never before seen the place where he was." To keep her dream sacred, Isobel spoke no more. But she remembered how in her sleep she had seen the strange man ride into the Indians' great camp on the edge of open grassy plains. Tall and bearded, rifle held high overhead, he raced his pony to meet the crowd.

The pony had been painted for war. On its left hip three red handprints told of three enemies killed in combat. Feathers were woven into the horse's mane and tail and various markings in green, red and yellow were smeared on its shoulders and neck. Several pack ponies loaded with furs and trade goods followed the white man's pony as he circled in front of the crowd. The scene had been the same

in each dream, and vivid. Isobel was to think of it many
times.

There were many trappers that year. At Lapwai the
Nez Perce had heard of two white men working their way
down the Clearwater River. Spies kept the tribe informed
of the men's progress toward their village.

The two trappers were William Craig and Bob Newell. On and off with two companions they had been trapping and exploring new country for a fur company in St.
Louis. The heavily wooded upper Clearwater had impressed
the men with its abundance. Marten, lynx, fox, otter and
wolves were everywhere. Elk herds and bighorn sheep
held to the higher country, but both mule and white-tailed
deer could be found in all the open areas. Beaver lived
along the streams that branched from larger waterways and
their dams made ponds where waterfowl fed and rested.

The land was in all ways unlike the eastern country
from which the trappers had migrated. But Bill Craig liked
the timber country and saw ways in which he could make a
living there.

He had often heard about the Nez Perce tribes that
inhabited the territory and he decided to find out more
about them.

Beside the fire that night he spoke his mind. "You
know, Bob, the more I see of this country the more I want
to live here. Joe Meek's led trapping parties through and
said this would be a nice place to settle in."

"He said the same thing about the valley of the
Willamette," Newell replied. "I recollect it still. Bill, we
both been in that valley and neither of us stuck. Why is this
place so much different?"

Craig leaned back against a tree stump.

"I was raised on a farm back in Virginia," he explained. "raised with a hoe in my hands and a milk bucket

I carried night and morning. The one important thing I learned from listening to my pa was to get good land as soon as I could and get enough to make a living on. Well, this land is the best I ever seen.''

Craig filled his pipe with a last bit of carefully hoarded tobacco. He lit up and puffed silently for a time, pushing his moccasined feet closer to the warmth of the fire. "If I ever want to have a family," he said slowly, "I got to begin purty soon. And if I want to live out here I'll have to pick a redskin wife. That's for sure. I can't see a white woman coming to this country now.''

"There's not much here for a white woman, I can vouch for that," Newell agreed.

"Anyway," Craig went on, "I've explored quite a bit of this territory and God alone knows how much more there is yet to see. What I find myself wondering is where to settle and when. We both know this much: Mexicans and Indians keep coming from the south. From far north, the French and Hudson's Bay are crowding down on us. We're hemmed in on all sides. I don't see settling east of the Divide nor south of the desert country nor west of these prairies. Somewhere within a few hundred miles of where we're camped, I figure to stick my axe in a tree and say, 'Here I am. This is my land.' ''

Bob Newell laughed. "You settlers are all alike. Get land, get a woman, get kids, wear out the woman, get a younger one, get more kids, get more land, raise more corn, feed more hogs, smoke more hams and bacon and make a little corn liquor on the side. Oh, in a way, I can kind of agree. In ten years or less I'll be looking for more than a winter woman. Life ain't quite as exciting as a few years back. Partner, I think we've both seen the other side of the mountain and know that what we hope for's not much better than what we already have.''

The fire snapped and smoke pitched upward.

37

"Well, Bob, I ain't quite ready to sink my axe yet, but I'll tell you this: I'm going to start looking. I hope you do the same so we can be close enough to work things out together."

"Sounds good," Newell said. "Suppose we start by getting friendly with the Nez Perce people. Joe Meek always figured he'd like living with 'em. Jim Bridger thinks so too—and if he ain't a top mountain man I don't know who is."

During the next few days the two trappers moved down the river, visiting Indian villages, talking in sign language and using a mixture of various Indian words to convey their messages. Trapping season over, they made a deal to store their goods while they explored.

The more they saw of the country and became acquainted with the people, the more they discussed the possibility of a homestead or land claim in the area. Talk with the tribes had been reassuring. Both men were convinced they could safely head along the old trade trail to the Snake River valley far to the south. And by that time they had almost made up their minds that if they did decide to settle, it would surely be along the lower Clearwater.

Chapter 6

Laird's meeting with the St. Louis trader had been well worthwhile.

"I can make arrangements for you to go overland with a party of traders and other people on their way to meet trappers at the spring rendezvous," the man told him. "While you're under their protection, you can learn the trappers' ways. One thing I want you to understand, though: this is strictly a business proposition. I can outfit you with what you need, but you'd better be prepared to make your own way and do your part in the expedition."

First on the equipment list was a .52 caliber rifle made by J. Henry; next, a pistol of the same caliber so there'd be no mixup in ammunition. Two knives were included, one for skinning, the other straight-bladed for sticking or fighting. Both had *Green River* stamped deeply into their blades. Clothing and odd articles were added, then trade goods. Bright ribbons, sacks of beads and a large package of brass tacks. Laird's eyebrows rose in question.

"You'll see how these tacks will make you friends, hold off enemies and keep you warm at night when the frost lays heavy on the ground. The Indian women love 'em," the trader said with a grin.

"What in the world are they used for?"

"Earbobs and nose spots," was the reply. "They pound 'em in their gunstocks, use 'em on their ponies' rigging—and maybe swallow 'em for pills." The trader roared with laughter.

The rifle, pistol, powder and lead, with the two knives thrown in, came to thirty dollars. Another twenty paid for the rest. A week of waiting for the party to be made up passed. Laird was impatient to be on his way but filled his time wandering the docks and warehouses in search of information.

The warehouse area was crowded with all types of people. Drunks lay slumped along streets and alleyways. Females approached any man they judged might have money, goods, drinks or even a bite to eat in exchange for their favors. Lord, deliver me, Laird thought as he thrust them aside.

A moment later a horrid caricature of a woman stumbled from a doorway. She was drunk and smelled of vomit even from so far away. Seeing Laird, she staggered toward him. Laird backed off but as he did someone shoved him from behind. The next thing he knew he was lying on top of the slobbering woman and her stinking rags and listening to the mutterings of a man close by.

"Hold him close, Maggie. Make sure the young cocksman gets what's coming to him."

Laird leaped to his feet and twisted to face the man who'd pushed him. The attacker wore buckskins. A grim sneer was plastered in the midst of his tobacco-stained beard.

Laird shuddered. The man's right eye was missing. Matted with mucus and lint, the remaining pouch contrasted loathesomely with the good eye glinting black from under its bushy brow.

"Now don't be in no hurry to get up, young scamp.

Maggie's got to be paid afore you leave her, finished or not.''

Laird knew that he'd been trapped and felt anger that was new to him. Without hesitation he backed away from the menacing figure, and pleased that he had already tried his pistol, pulled it from his belt. With the weapon cocked, he attempted to jump away but the woman caught his foot and he rolled into the street. As the pistol went off, the sharp report startled a team of mules standing nearby. They jumped in their collars with a snort of surprise; the teamster was caught by surprise too, as his dray jerked ahead.

"What the hell goes on?" he shouted as he grabbed for the tailgate and climbed aboard to stop them.

"He shot me! My God, I'm killed," the old woman screamed. As she did the one-eyed beast of a man grabbed for the scrambling Laird.

One man on a saddle horse leading two pack mules had stopped to watch the show and several others joined him. Old Maggie, still huddled where she fell, screamed again, this time for a priest. Another figure blinked and stumbled from the doorway to see what was causing the commotion.

"Young feller, hand over your weapon," the one-eyed man ordered. "You done killed old Mag. I have to make sure you don't do more bloody work."

Wishing he had never left the hostelry, Laird yelled back, "Like hell I'll give it to you! My shot didn't hit that woman and you know it."

"I saw you shoot her," the man growled, "and right here's another witness. Isn't that right, Mack?" he interrupted himself. "Now gimme that thing afore I pick you up by the heels and shake it off you." Then he lunged toward Laird, confident the young man would hand over the gun.

Laird reached for his knife. Sure that it was a bluff, the ruffian snarled, "Put that away! Who you kidding, boy?" From the doorway the other man egged the one-eyed brute to action. "Take it, Mosely. Get the gun too. I'll take his money, to pay the doc's bill for old Mag if she don't die first."

As if on cue the old woman shrieked that she was dying. Other men edged into the scene as Mosely began his slow approach but suddenly the man on the saddle horse hollered, "Mosely, you hide-stealing son of a bitch, back off afore I shoot your other eye out. Haul that sweet-smelling bundle of bones and rags as calls herself a woman back into her den of skunks. I'm warning you, I see a patrol headed this way, and I and this cub will swear out a charge that will put you away. Now get your ass in the shed."

"Jess, I never stole no hides from you," Mosely whined. "You got me wrong."

"Like hell. Get your feathers flying." And the rider watched till Mosley and his gang slunk away.

Laird sheathed his knife and tucked the pistol under his coat. With a grin he looked up at the man on the horse, then thanked him.

"It wouldn't have took much for me to shoot that one-eyed bastard," the other replied. "Out of town I would have. But enough. We'd better move along instead of sticking here answering questions."

Laird paced his steps to those of the rider's horse. "You staying in St. Louis long?"

"Day or so. Curious about something?"

"You bet I am. Like to buy you a few drinks, too. I'm due to leave for the Oregon Country in a few days."

"The hell you say! That's where I'm headed. Going up to the big doings near the Green River country with the boys and their trade goods. Come along whilst I put these ringtails away. Maybe we can chin awhile. Just call me Jess till we get going.''

That night by candlelight, Donald Laird wrote his first report to his uncle, Charles Madden.

Dear Sir:

One important fact to report is that I have met the Indian Agent, Wm. Clark, and am impressed. Of all the tribes Clark has encountered in his travels, he has thought most highly of a far northwestern people called the Nez Perce. I confess I find it hard to believe that any Indians deserve much praise but I will reserve my opinion until I meet with them.

We leave St. Louis in two days. I have already met my first mountain man, a robust, courageous fellow by the name of Jess who not only saved my life but will accompany us on the trip. I'll write again after we join the Green River Rendezvous in June.

Yours faithfully,
Donald Laird

Thomas Fitzpatrick, Ireland-born trapper, fur trader and expert mountain man, headed the party going to the rendezvous. Later this westward party was joined by Protestant missionaries: the Presbyterians Marcus and Narcissa Whitman, Henry and Eliza Spalding and William Gray. To Laird's surprise, there was a black trapper in the group. His name was Hinds. The incongruous group amazed and delighted the young Easterner and he began to realize why his Uncle Charles had urged him to make the trip west.

The Green River Rendezvous, an annual gathering of

mountain men and trappers assembled to receive goods brought up from St. Louis for trade, held some surprises for Laird as well as for the Indians who attended. The red men had come to join the roving trappers and engage in trade. Needless to say, the sight of a black astonished them, but they were even more astonished by the parade of white missionary wives who had come to the rendezvous.

Laird too was delighted to look at the women. But it was the squaws, not the white women, who attracted his attention. He remained quietly in the background watching them try to greet the missionary wives. At first the white women were reluctant to let the squaws come close to touch and kiss them. It took Joe Meek and other mountain men some explaining before they understood the ways in which Indians demonstrated affection and trust.

Accustomed to the look of Indian women he had seen in towns and along the trail, young Laird was overcome with the beauty and cleanliness of those present at the rendezvous.

Although Narcissa Whitman was lovely, with smooth fair skin and reddish blond hair piled high, Laird decided that the dark beauty of a certain Nez Perce girl he had noticed equaled that of the missionary's wife. He had watched the young Indian woman closely whenever he had a chance and wondered what sharing his blanket with her would be like.

As soon as the trappers and mountain men learned from Indian scouts that Fitzpatrick's Brigade was approaching the meeting spot, they sent a group of Indians to greet them. Eager to show off their ponies and horsemanship, the party rode down to the caravan firing their guns, whooping and hollering, racing all the way.

The second display erupted after the cavalcade reached the rendezvous camping ground. Mounted trappers, traders and Indians circled wildly around the grounds, barking

44

dogs racing among them; the noise was so deafening that Eliza Spalding covered her ears and wondered what had possessed her to leave the safety and sanctity of her father's home. But all this actually was only the beginning.

For the mountain men the rendezvous was a time of unleashed celebration; for many, in fact, the nearest approach to civilization they'd had for years at a stretch. The amount of liquor being guzzled before the feast was nothing to what was drunk later that evening and every evening during the rendezvous.

Bill Sublette and Tom Fitzpatrick passed orders to the traders and most of the trappers. "Don't give no Indian any rotgut, popskull, or anything like it. We don't want no killings nor cuttings now, specially with these psalm-singers and their women along. Meek, you see they keep order in your bunch, or by God, you'll be short in your trade stuff."

"Keep your hair on, boys, don't do no fretting while Mrs. Whitman's around," Meek adjured them, then added longingly, "That lady can have my blanket anytime she wants to crook her finger—spite of my woman."

"Don't shine your eyes too much around her if you know what's good for you," Sublette answered him. "Marcus is apt to forget his upbringing and smite you hip and thigh."

Old Grizzly Bear, Joe Meek, liked women. When he got drunk he made much of them, giving away his trade goods, hugging the squaws and kissing the young girls. That night others followed his genial example. Just about the time the missionaries had retired to their tents, he and his boys got really oiled up. All the canvas in the world couldn't have kept out the uproar that rolled and echoed across the camp.

William Gray lay alone in his blankets trying to imagine what those sons of the devil were doing. He envisioned them wrestling the willing red women wherever they fell together, and although he tried to shut out the sounds of revelry, he could not banish such forbidden scenes from his mind. More than once he got to his knees and prayed aloud.

Donald Laird wove himself through the merrymaking, thoroughly enjoying the whole show. And when Joseph Meek yanked him into the dancing and shouted, "C'mon, boy, let's me and you show this sorry-looking bunch of pups what we can do," he sensed that he was fast becoming a true mountain man. They whirled and jigged and drank as they danced. For the first time on the trip, Laird's inhibitions vanished and he opened up to the frenzy around him.

The next morning, though, everything hurt—his head, his joints—and from his stomach a bilious reminder of the evening's feast crowded into his throat. He lay still to quiet the nausea but the sun's glare hit his eyes as he tried to open them. Rolling over, his lips touched grass and he retched in agony.

Later the bitter taste of vomit remained in his mouth and throat. He wanted water but getting up seemed impossible. To test his strength he raised himself slightly, and as he did, heard someone nearby. Just beyond the stained, smelling grass near his head Laird saw a dainty pair of moccasined feet and above them, only partially covering lovely legs, a white skirt fringed with blue beads and quills. A waist girdled by a beaded belt trimmed in a curved design urged him higher, to a woman's breasts swelling behind soft doeskin. Eagerly Laird rushed his gaze to the face above the dress and he stared.

Chapter 7

An exquisite Nez Perce girl smiled down at him, her face framed by long black braids that were entwined with strips of white weasel skin. The Indian's face was not painted. Its skin glowed reddish tan. Black eyebrows arched above deep, dark eyes. The girl's nose was straight and smooth with delicate nostrils. In her ears the maiden wore tiny brass hawk's bells.

Laird kept his fascinated gaze moving over every part of the Indian girl; she giggled and walked away and at last Laird got up and headed for the stream to clean himself. He was now the possessor of a queasy stomach, a splitting head and a healing vision of someone he wanted to see again. Jess was splashing around, washing up. Expressionless, he greeted Laird. "It's a good day to die, ain't it?"

"I nearly died during the night," Laird told him wryly. "I'm not sure yet but what I'd been better off if I had."

"Well, my lad, some of us are still sleeping it off. Old Meek, for one. Still sick in the belly?"

"Sick I am, and my head's splitting. Can't see too well, either."

"Hell, you're no different than the rest. Let's look up Doc Newell, he's always got something for times like this.

Don't never ask him what it is, because if you knew you wouldn't down it. He's worse than the Blackfoot or Crow medicine men.''

Robert Newell liked to rig up potions. He'd learned the psychology of the Indian medicine men and made up his pills and potions without telling anyone what was in them. This morning, laughing at Jess and Laird, he gave them a drink of one of them.

"Just a little swallow now, boys," he warned. "Give it a few minutes in your guts and you'll be ready for another wingding tonight."

The sun-warmed liquid tasted rank and bitter and had an oily feel as it slid down Laird's throat. But sure enough, almost as soon as it reached his stomach his queasiness left him.

As he strolled through the camp young Laird recalled his uncle's instructions and decided to estimate the number of people present, try to get a feel for the relationship between the missionaries and the trappers and attempt to discover any positive effect the meeting was having on the Indians. Already he had noticed the differences in welcomes the missionaries received from the various Indian tribes. The Nez Perce were the most receptive and eager to meet the newcomers. In their group, the most persuasive tribesmen were two fine-looking warriors Laird believed to be chiefs, and he referred to them as such in his first letter to his uncle from the rendezvous.

With the Nez Perce were the two chiefs. One, a tall, stern-faced man with a dignified expression, tried to get the missionaries—Dr. Whitman in particular—to return with them to their home camp. His name is Hallahotsoot. Trappers who are familiar with this chief call him Lawyer because of the way he argues and talks.

The other chief is quieter and lets Lawyer carry on most of the conversation, but I notice he seems even more eager to have Dr. Whitman accompany them than Lawyer does. Dr. Whitman pays more attention to this man, Tackensuatis—Meek's pronunciation—because the Indian knew Reverend Samuel Parker, the man who asked that Marcus Whitman and the Spaldings come out to build missions. Both chiefs have already been baptized as Christians and are eager for others to follow their lead. They've been arguing about the direction to take along those lines; after they make their decision I will write you about it.

I agree with Mr. Clark about the Nez Perce. They are better looking, cleaner and seem more trustworthy than any tribe. Also they appear to fear no one. The wives and single women are most modest and obedient. They all dress well and I have yet to see any Nez Perce drink. The white leaders try to be strict about not allowing the Indians liquor, but their own men drink more than their share.

After the Nez Perce I rate the Spokane, and along with them other tribes of that area, the Pend Oreille, the Coeur d'Alene and the Kutenai, who have only two representatives here. All these tribes live west of the Continental Divide and of the Flatheads. They have made informal treaties so that there is little actual fighting between them. Doc Newell says that despite their peace arrangements, the Indians often raid each other's horse herds; fortunately, not much blood is shed. Actual war occurs only during the buffalo hunts, when these tribes and the Flatheads join forces against the Blackfoot and the Crow.

Here all tribes are supposed to be covered by a truce. Nez Perce are treated with great respect. Flatheads are tolerated and the Blackfoot are viewed with suspicion and constantly watched because of their pilfering. The Ute, Bannock and Shoshone are not up to the quality of most of the other tribes but well ahead of the Blackfoot. To my knowledge, there are none of the Sioux, Cheyenne or other warring nations present at the rendezvous.

When the men here talk of whether or not the bringing of religion to the Indians was a good thing, some argue that the Indians already have a pretty good religion of their own and some take the missionaries' view that because the Indians have not been baptized and encouraged to confess their sins, they are infidels and doomed to hell. The one thing all present do believe is that if the missionaries' good intentions are pressed upon the Indians without some basic understanding of the Indians' way of life, there will be trouble that in the end will lead to war.

While Donald Laird continued his report to Charles Madden that afternoon, the celebration was already in full swing. And echoing from the usual hoopla was the constant gunfire that kept every bird, animal and even the pesky mosquitoes well away from the drifts of smoke and the noise. Laird finally put aside his journal and letter, then wandered out to observe. The thought of the Indian girl he had seen that morning kept intruding in his thoughts and he looked for her in any group he passed.

50

The missionaries kept close to their tents. Laird heard Doc Newell ask the Methodist, Jason Lee, what he thought of trappers taking Indian women for wives or as winter women. The men who had gathered to listen to this conversation snickered in the background.

"It is a sin in the eyes of the Lord to lie with a woman not your wife," the dour preacher replied.

"But reverend, what if there's no preacher around to tie the knot, and she's willing, and it's a long cold winter ahead?"

"Jacob waited seven long years for Rachel before they wed," Lee interrupted. "If a grown man can't wait until he finds a preacher, he is sinning."

"Reverend, you just don't understand the problem. Every trapper needs a woman to tend camp, make moccasins and do a thousand other chores. They's a lot more women in the woods than there is men. After all, we're just taking care of the widows and orphans, like the Good Book says we should." Newell chuckled at his own cleverness.

"I say such an arrangement is a sin," the preacher shouted. "Unless you confess your evil ways and become reborn, you are doomed to everlasting hellfire."

Laird saw that the reaction of the trappers was gradually changing from amusement to disgust. This kind of talk didn't sit well with them and would cause arguments. What were women and girls for, anyway, except to be enjoyed? During the long snowbound winters companionship was as necessary as warmth and food. That's what they were probably thinking.

Moving back toward the crowd, Laird joined Joe Meek, who stood admiring Narcissa Whitman and telling her some of his tales of wild mountain life. Mrs. Whitman seemed fascinated by this great hulk of a man, and encour-

51

aged by her interest, Meek spun out the story of his encounter with a grizzly.

"She come at me and afore I could shoot she took a swipe and knocked my gun away. Then her cub come running and I'll be blamed if she didn't take a swipe at him that sent him sprawling.

"I grabs up my rifle and tried to shoot at her but blamed if she didn't get my gun and a couple fingers in her mouth. I thought I was a goner when all of a sudden she drops my gun and tears my shirt off with her paw. I reaches for my knife and when she turned her head I sticks it in clear to the hilt, but it wasn't over yet.

"She bawled and raised Old Ned with her paws. Her other cub come up and when she turned on him I picks up my gun, shoves it to her and—that was the end of that."

"Is that the hand she bit, Mr. Meek?"

"That's it. Ain't purty, is it?"

"No . . . but you were mighty lucky. Did you ask the Lord for help in that time of trouble, Mr. Meek?"

"Ma'am, I was too danged busy to ask for help, and for a few minutes I figured the Lord was helping that old bitch of a bear."

Nearby, Mrs. Spalding was trying to converse with some Indians. Through two sets of interpreters, the talk went from English to Iroquois to Flathead to Nez Perce. Practically all trappers could speak Indian language, but Laird had the impression that the missionaries didn't want the trappers in on their conversations with tribal leaders.

While at the Spalding camp, Laird heard a trapper make a rude remark concerning Mrs. Spalding and it was echoed later by another to a crowd of mountain men. A tall gaunt woman with no sign of humor in her face or appearance, Mrs. Spalding was particularly unattractive.

"Boys, it would be like sleeping with a sack of deer

horns in your bed," was the comment. "Old Whitman's sure a better picker than pucker-mouthed Spalding."

"Well, from what I've seen, the Spaldings are a purty well matched team. Maybe love will find a way. Their looks has lost the trail for certain."

The remarks continued. In the midst of them, Laird finally caught a glimpse of the girl whose loveliness had so stirred him earlier that morning. Their eyes met and held; then the girl turned away as if disinterested and not wanting to recognize the eager young man.

"Purty thing, ain't she?" a man behind him whispered.

Laird turned to see a tall brown-bearded trapper smiling at him. He remembered that Jess had said the man was a sidekick of Doc Newell's and that his name was Bill Craig. Craig had wintered with the Nez Perce while opening up the new country to trapping.

"She certainly is," Laird agreed. "You know her?"

"Don't recollect her name. She come along with the bunch from the Clearwater country. Belongs to Hallahotsoot's band. If you can't remember the name, just call him Lawyer. He's standing alongside Mrs. Spalding right now, saying she and her old man ought to come build their school near his place." He paused a moment. "Your name's Laird, I heard."

"Yes. Donald Laird from New York by way of St. Louis."

"Ain't we all. You fixing to trap for the company?"

"Yes, for at least one winter. Are you going back to the Nez Perce country when the rendezvous is over?"

"Could be. Doc Newell and I want to know more about it. We figured we ought to explore more country afore we put our traps down. You bring your own?"

"I had some traps made from a new pattern," Laird replied. "Most of the men like the look of them and want to see how they work out this season. If you like, I'll show them to you before you leave.''

"Good. Maybe I can learn something new. You try 'em for springing?''

Laird laughed. "With a stick, the leg from a dog and everything else but my own hand. Had a spring-holder made to hold the jaws open while I was setting the pan to the dog. The blacksmith said it might be a good idea.''

"I take it you're talking about double-spring traps?''

"Yes. They were made with a square pan and single dog.''

"Five pounds with chain?''

"Not quite. Smooth linked chain, though, five feet in length.''

"Sounds like you had some good advice. Have you tried it for a tight jaw close?''

"We tried everything we could think of except a live beaver,'' Laird assured him. "The smith tried them on big dogs, though. Never has had one get loose. They make good wolf traps, but most trappers I talked with like a larger size for the big wolves.''

Bill Craig grinned and returned to the subject that would interest Laird most. "I suppose you'd like to know that purty little girl's name. It come to me just now. You can try out saying it in Indian language but what it comes to in our lingo is something like Fair Morning or Sun-in-the-Morning. Her folks, specially her paw, is purty watchful of her. Make certain you move slow and easy trying to get close. Let her do the walking and when she comes around, you do the talking. Hope you win out. It'd be real nice for you to have a purty teacher help you learn the language.''

"Well, I have been away from women long enough to want to be taught a lot of things they know.'' Laird smiled.

54

"If you figure on being a trapper, you got to learn where to set the trap and how to bait it," Craig advised knowingly. "You do the same with these Indian gals. If you show 'em something to attract their attention, once they're close to the bait you can spring your trap. Works every time."

Laird asked a guarded question. "You have a woman here?"

"No, but I'm looking for one to go on the trip and spend the winter with me. I might wait until I get where there's a better choice. See you around later. And, oh—" Craig said, turning away, "make sure that gal has an even set of teeth."

Laird wandered on. Even while cutting loose and then devouring a large hump rib that had been roasting, he couldn't stop thinking about Sun-in-the-Morning. What a lovely name for a pretty girl, far better than Bessie or Faith or even Alice, who had once been his true choice. When he had dreamed enough for that afternoon, Laird returned to his campsite. There he got out his pencil and began a letter to his uncle.

Sir:

I am writing this on the second day of the rendezvous festival. I made my lunch by cutting a juicy rib from the hump of a buffalo that was roasting by the communal fire. Delicious! There were other things cooking too, but I find I am cautious about dipping into something either until I am sure what it is or until hunger impels me to try it out.

Earlier I saw an Indian woman catch a fat puppy by the hind legs, knock it on the head with a club, singe it over the fire to burn off the hair, then without any further cleaning, dump it into a kettle to cook. She put bulbs of various kinds in with the dog, then threw in a grouse with the feathers skinned off to boil with the rest. Who knows what else went in?

Most trappers have their women (always Indian) in camp with them here, and those who do not will pick up a woman to winter with them, either during the trapping season or after the season is over. What a white man looks for in a woman is someone to make his clothing, cook his food, care for furs he brings in, share his bed and be a companion.

The missionaries react strongly against this attitude. They follow a strict interpretation of the Bible and look on this use of Indian women— especially without legal marriage—as adultery. They insist that the trappers and their women will be condemned to perdition. Already this point of view is not sitting well with the trappers, and later, I'm convinced, it will be a bone of contention with the Indians.

At first I was repelled by the trappers' loud talk and boasting but now I realize it is part of their way of dealing with the Indians. Indian warriors show off their exploits and skills to attract women and if they are chiefs to demonstrate their ability to lead; the trappers act the same way. Joseph Meek shouts, laughs, tells wild tales and is looked upon with respect by those who know him. He is like a keg of powder, easy to live with but set off by a spark. His tales have the mark of truth. I have talked with men who have seen him in action.

Every man here has lost a partner or friend,

some to Indians or wild beasts. Many, too, have been lost in storms, drowned in the rivers or have fallen from cliffs. Death is known in all its forms. That's why, I guess, when the men relax and celebrate here, they really cut loose. Most of them act the same with women they meet. It will take a lot of civilizing to change men living under these conditions. Most of them will probably die before that happens.

Laird paused in his writing. A shadow had passed near him, and rather than frighten the person who so quietly approached, he wet the tip of his pencil and once more began to write. Only two lines had been added when he recognized the sound of someone breathing. Slowly he turned; the Indian maiden was standing scarcely more than a breath away.

Without taking his eyes off his lovely quarry's face, Laird pulled a piece of red ribbon from inside his jacket. Dropping it beside him—and without changing the direction of his gaze—he reached into his pocket once again and presented another treat, shining brass tacks. These he sprinkled carefully on the ribbon. The Indian girl smiled with pleasure. She bent to take a closer look, then knelt to gather her gifts. Before she stood erect once more, Laird inhaled her scent and motioned. "Sit with me." But the girl shook her head.

Embarrassed, he rose and shrugged. The girl tittered. She looked down. In a last frustrated attempt to reach her, Laird held out his hand. As he did the girl did the same with hers as if wanting him to take it. He turned her palm up tenderly and stroked the warmth. Months had passed since he had felt a woman's touch, and he trembled.

The hand was callused, yet to Laird it felt wonderful. On the surface of the palm, the lifeline was distinct and long. The fingers were straight and slender, with nails cropped short and even with the tips. Around both wrists hung bracelets made of twisted copper and silver wire that had been pierced through pieces of delicate shells. Above them sleeves had been decorated with flattened quills, both porcupine and birds' feathers.

Suddenly—almost ridiculously, Laird thought—he wanted to see the Indian's teeth. He opened his lips and smiled to show his own; she grinned. White, perfectly formed specimens met in an even line inside her reddened lips. Content, Laird laughed, and when he did the girl did too.

Her hand by her side now, she continued to stand close. Laird wanted to bring her even nearer and crush her still-laughing mouth with kisses. He pointed at her. "Suni," he said, giving her a name. Next he tapped his chest and added, "Laird." Again he said the names and the girl tried to repeat each one. "Leerd," she said, drawling his name huskily, but hers was clearly Suni.

To hold the girl's attention, Laird began to sketch her face. Drawings and designs were a familiar art to all Indians and the girl watched him closely as he worked. At last he showed Suni the penciled lines he'd drawn. As she studied the paper, he went to his pack and dug out a small round mirror.

Suni had seen a mirror before but never had held one. She peered into it then looked back at the paper. Her amazed smile delighted Laird. Braver now, he stroked her hair. Bringing her gently to him, he kissed her. Suni did not pull away and as Laird held her and felt the smoothness of her skin, he moaned, wanting so much more.

Suni rose, suddenly leaving his arms. Smiling, softly speaking his name, she collected mirror, tacks and ribbon, then turned and ran outside. Laird sighed, unsure why

Suni had left his tent so quickly. She would come back for the sketch, though. He knew it. And when she did, he would hold her softness once again and kiss her. Just thinking of that moment, Laird's heart pounded harder. What exactly did he feel for Suni? Was it love?

Chapter 8

The first fight at the rendezvous was sparked by a remark one trapper made about the way another had made love to a squaw the night before. To defend his honor, the Romeo swung his massive fist and smashed his accuser in the teeth. When, after spitting out some of his precious nippers, the victim's thoughts cleared, he roared a challenge and made a lunge for his assailant.

It was a strange sight. Two big men who had battled the elements and wild beasts for years were now engaged in a war against each other. Head to head they clashed, butting and shoving, grappling for an advantage. They puffed, growled with anger and gasped for air. They rolled on the ground and rose to the struggle again. A hand free for even a second reached for eyes to gouge, lips to tear. A huge moccasined foot stamped an opponent's thigh. Knee rose to the crotch, and once released, drew apart to strike hammer blows at the undefended belly.

The fight drew a crowd like bees to a queen in flight. Laird watched fascinated until suddenly he heard Bill Craig say, "Get a club and hit Josh on the noggin while I take care of old Carter." Laird jumped up. "Go ahead, will you?" Craig shouted again. "Knock Josh out and we'll haul 'em apart. Quick, let's cool 'em down."

The two trappers rushed toward the combatants and as if long practiced in such action, raised their two heavy chunks of wood in unison. With a whop and a grunt the fighting stopped. There were plenty of complaints.

"Damn you fellers for women. Why don't you let 'em blow off steam?"

"Hell's fire, Craig, can't we have no fun because a couple of women and their stiff-necked fellers is here?"

"Damned if I ever seen such a thing before. You afeared somebody might get hurt? This ain't much of a rendezvous. Might as well hold church right now."

The grumbling lessened and gradually the crowd dispersed. Drinking and gambling resumed; so did trading. Where the goods were displayed, men stationed themselves with ready guns and short clubs to dispel anyone's ideas about freeloading.

Craig sensed that Laird was upset; perhaps, Craig thought, because of the fight. He walked over to where Laird was standing passively to one side.

"You look about ready to fall over," he said gently. "Ain't you ever been that violent afore?"

"No," Laird answered, his voice subdued. "Would they have killed one another?"

"It's hard to tell. Trappers without teeth is apt to starve to death. They sure might have lost an eye or ear over it. Maybe one would have pulled a knife if he thought he was losing. When men like that get real mad, sometimes it gets purty bloody."

"Well, weren't those fellows real mad? It sure looked like that to me."

"Naw, not really," Craig answered. "It were just one of those tussles a bit of drinking can bring on. You'll see more of the same afore this whoop-up is over. Say, you catch anything in your love trap?"

"How'd you know I set one?"

62

"You're a trapper, ain't you?" Craig laughed. "I figured you might start a little line right here."

Laird was eager to talk about what had happened. "Sun-in-the-Morning came to see what I was doing," he began. And he told Craig about the ribbon, the tacks, the mirror and the drawing, not forgetting to mention the closeness they had shared.

Craig chuckled. "You done purty good for a young feller. What came next?"

Laird glanced at the older man before answering and saw on his face what he took to be a look of understanding.

"I never thought I could kiss an Indian, let alone want to. Was it that way with you?"

"Yes, of course it was. You'll want more as time goes on. Don't fret about it. Always remember they want it too. That's part of life, and life in this here country can be purty short and real bad. If you don't take the good when it comes, the bad things pile up on you." He paused as though surprised at his own philosophizing. "But watch your step till you learn the trail. If you're going to trap, know where you put your feet. If you're a hunter, look where you point your gun. If you want to live, then consider all the alternatives. Watch yourself all the time."

Laird waited. "What did you mean when you told me to look at her teeth?" he said at last.

"Did you? Was they nice and even, close together?"

"Yes, and so white and clean."

"Indian women's teeth get that way from chewing on hides to soften 'em. They bite off quills too, and flatten 'em. They even bite people in a tussle." Craig laughed at the younger man's expression. "Young feller, you have the makings of a trapper. One winter with a willing woman and you'll never want to go back to the prissy females in the East. This is raw-meat country and we like to take her as she is. Show me that picture of Sun-in-the-Morning some time.''

Laird nodded.

"This making pictures will serve you well in your relationships with any Indian. Don't overdo it, though,'' Craig advised. "Make 'em think it's some special treat when you sketch one of 'em or their camps.''

Laird walked to where trading was in progress. An Indian buck wanted to trade beaver furs for a small hand axe and laid out a pelt. The trader carefully examined it. The animal had been speared; there was a hole in the pelt. The trader laid out the axe and attempted to take the hide, but the Indian demanded two axes. The trader shook his head and pointed to the hole. The Indian argued but the trader was firm. The red man finally shoved the pelt forward and took the axe, then pointed to a red blanket and held up eight fingers, questioning. The trader held up ten. While his woman crouched nearby watching the transaction, the brave began to examine his pile of furs. Laird noted that the trader seemed unconcerned, as if knowing he would get all of them eventually.

Thoughts of costs and profits tumbled in Laird's head. He knew the cost of an outfit in St. Louis. What it was worth here seemed to indicate an immense profit to the trader.

"I've been watching the trading,'' he said to Doc Newell. The trapper was off by himself gnawing on a rib, and he had motioned for Laird to join him. "I saw how many hides an Indian has to give for a blanket and an axe. There must be a huge profit in it for the company.''

"Depends on how you figure the costs.'' Newell offered Laird the flask he had hidden under his shirt. "Some don't make nothing. You must know about how Nathaniel Wyeth lost his shirt dealing against McLoughlin and Hudson's Bay.''

"I do," Laird answered, his mouth stuffed with juicy beef, "but he was a long way from Boston's ways in business and at the mercy of Hudson's Bay's scheming."

Newell shrugged his shoulder and bit off another mouthful from the rib he'd been tearing into. When he could talk he mumbled a reply. "That's what I am talking about. You lose an axe here and you know pretty much what it'll cost to replace it. In where you trap, there ain't no axes, and losing one really costs you—gun, blankets, grub, even your hair. A fellow risks everything he's got, including his life, when he heads into Indian country. I'll admit some traders make money off the furs they get but nobody's going to get rich. Anyway, the red men get what they need to survive."

"What about the brigade that loads up on fur and lays out less than a smidgen of its real value in return?"

"Boy, that brigade ain't back in St. Louis yet, nor the fellers and mules and ponies that'll be trying to get it there. If they don't make it, then where's the profit? A year's work and a lot of money shot to hell and no way to balance the loss except taking a chance another year. The biggest loss, young feller, is trained men and equipment. You'll appreciate that the next time we meet—if we ever do—at another rendezvous."

The two ate in silence and Laird hurled his rib, picked clean, to a passing dog. "Doc," he began, "you have an Indian woman. Are you married to her?"

"Well, I figure I am. In the Indian way, I guess you might call it. A few words from a preacher couldn't make it no different."

"What if she wants to leave you?"

"Well, if she thinks she could find a better way to live or wants to go back to her folks, why not let her go? Right now my woman figures she has something, sticking

65

with me, that's better than she had before. As long as that lasts, so will our so-called marriage.''

"But suppose it's you who wants to take off and leave?"

Doc Newell shrugged. "Craig and me have both walked off and left women where they lived. Comes time to go. It ain't possible to take 'em along. That's the way the ship floats." He laughed. "What I think you're really asking is what you should do about that purty little thing that was watching you the other day. Curious as kittens with a ball of yarn, those red women are, trying to figure out white men so they can tell stories later on and have something to brag on. Same as men and their tales.''

"I've been wondering what would happen if she took up with me. I never planned on marrying an Indian woman or even living with one.''

"Don't fret about that kind of stuff, Laird. None of us did. Do what comes naturally and say it's fate.'' Doc chuckled wryly. "Same as running into a grizzly when you don't expect it."

"How do you get an Indian wife?" Laird asked. "I mean a Nez Perce woman.''

"Depends on who her daddy is and how much she wants you. In some cases it's easy, but I've seen a few cases where the feller didn't get the girl. The purtier she is or the better she is at keeping camp and doing chores, the more she's going to cost you. But the bigger the pumpkin you make her think you are, the easier time you'll have. Ever hear that saying, 'Fine feathers make fine birds'? Well, look at the Indian warriors when they start showing off. Biggest chief, longest tail feathers and purtiest painted pony gets the most attention.''

"Then why in hell is it that dirty, ragged old trappers smelling of bear grease and beaver castor get women hanging around them?''

"I'll tell you why," Newell answered. "Some of those old coons have brought furs and hides to swap and they're real generous with favors. Us old boys know our time is getting short. We seem to throw things away that's taken a time to get, but what we get in return we can think on all the next year. Maybe that next year won't last out for some of us. But after you've been out in the brush all those months, wintering on whatever you can find to eat and trying to keep warm, a place like this is for forgetting the hard, tough times."

Leaders Bill Sublette and Jim Bridger made a point of sizing up newcomers to the rendezvous. This applied to Indians as well as missionaries. Bridger had been in the mountains and paddled the rivers long enough to know that if he wanted to live awhile longer and have hair to comb, he'd better know who his companions were. Indians who came to the rendezvous were comparatively easy to place; he had lived with some and fought with others. They were there to trade and get acquainted with the trappers and other white people.

Missionaries were a different sort, so sure they were right in what they did and said that Bridger had begun to wonder just how long their points of view would be accepted. Although he sensed trouble in the making, the hair on his neck didn't tingle as it did when a mortal enemy was close. It was a different sense of trouble, as when before an electric storm there is an atmosphere change that predicts the approach of bad weather.

He and Bill Sublette had been keeping a close eye on young Donald Laird. Neither trapper nor missionary, the young fellow still wanted to go into Indian country. The two men couldn't figure out why, so they kept their eyes on Laird as he circulated through the encampment. They studied every move he made, even down to his daily writing and the time he made a sketch of Suni.

As each day passed, camp leaders, guides and Indian chiefs formulated future actions: the trappers, the territory they would work; the missionaries, the trail they would follow; the Indians, the buffalo hunts they would undertake for stocking meat for winter. As various reports came in, plans were altered to meet new conditions and new suggestions were considered. It became apparent that the Whitman-Spalding party would need help all the way to the Columbia or to wherever they decided to settle for the winter.

Jim Bridger, Bill Sublette and Joseph Meek threw in suggestions as though adding sticks to a fire. Marcus Whitman, already briefed by his Missionary Board, was a willing listener, but Spalding seemed to think that whatever happened, the Lord would see to it that all righteous people were saved and all skeptics were punished. Jason Lee stood fiercely independent; if no scout was present who would guide him, he would go it alone.

During the rendezvous Joe Meek had become increasingly entranced with Narcissa Whitman. He even changed his plan to trap new territory, offering to guide the missionary party clear to the ocean if necessary. And it was clear he needed every man he could find. The route cut across a thousand miles of rugged, hostile country. The mountain men agreed that although the feat was possible, it would take plenty of luck to get wagons to Fort Hall on the Snake River. How far beyond that they could go would be anybody's guess.

A large group of trappers would leave the Green River, then split off at various places on the way west. Meek was concerned who the nucleus of this group would be. He knew Doc Newell and Bill Craig had explored north and west of Fort Hall and had wintered in the upper Nez Perce country along the Clearwater, so it would be easy to start with them and a few others. A few of the Indians from Lawyer and Tackensuatis' band would go with the missionaries to the Columbia. Chief James and his band would split, hunt buffalo and take the trail over the Lolo and travel to their domain on the Clearwater.

During these planning sessions Sublette, thinking something about Laird didn't make sense, spoke with Bridger about him. "What's your idea? Is young Laird a bona fide trapper?"

"Naw, he's just along to see the country and learn about redskins. He's likable and purty sharp."

Sublette kept on. "I see him writing a lot, though. Suppose he's making a report to send to somebody as wants to know more about us?"

"Hell, Bill, I don't know and I don't give a damn. It'd be another year afore any kind of report got where it was going. Anyway, the boy's writing to some gal back home." Bridger paused. "I'm thinking we should give him to somebody who'll herd him along and teach him a few tricks this winter," he went on finally. "If he turns out like I think he might, we'll have us another good man."

"You may have something," Sublette agreed. "Give him to the bunch going with the Bible-thumpers. Meek and Doc can fix him. Craig will show him a few tricks too."

And so it was that unknown to Donald Laird, his companions on the trail were chosen.

Chapter 9

The missionaries had been invited to join up with a party from John McLeod's Hudson's Bay Company. They were going to Fort Hall. Spalding had a light wagon in which the ladies would ride. Big-hearted Joe Meek told Mrs. Whitman he would see that she could ride all the way to the Columbia if he had anything to say about it. Though all he might get out of his offer was the chance to stare a bit, Mrs. Whitman was beautiful and to an old trapper that kind of entertainment was worth a lot.

As word spread about where and when the missionary party was going, the first of many squabbles arose among the Indians. If these Christian people settled on the Columbia, it would be in lands claimed by the Cayuse. The Nez Perce weren't in favor of this plan. They wanted them to go farther north, where their own camping grounds were located. While the tribesmen were disagreeing, even their squaws argued and in some cases came to slaps and blows. Narcissa Whitman did her best to smooth things over, but it was Eliza Spalding, desperately trying to learn the language, who proved to be more persuasive.

When the missionaries moved their camp to McLeod's, Laird's opportunity came to change his own camp spot. He wasn't sure Suni would visit him but in case such an event

71

took place, he didn't want to be close to the Spaldings. Laird remembered how the supplier in St. Louis had talked him into buying a small tent. Now he was grateful.

"The brigade will have pack mules and some carts or wagons," he had explained to Laird. "When the country gets rough they'll unload the carts and pack the stuff on the mules and horses. When they come out, if the Injuns ain't burnt the wagons, they'll unload the mules and repack the wagons. With this tent you'll have a place to sleep and store your outfit. If you can get along without the tent later, you can always trade it. Canvas and cloth make good trade goods, wait and see." Now Laird concluded that the seclusion the tent would give him might well be worth the price he'd paid as well as the bother of taking it along.

Bill Craig approached Laird about going with him and Doc to trap that winter. When Sublette had suggested the idea, Craig was delighted. Years before, Kit Carson and Joseph Walker had been his coaches, patiently instructing him until he was familiar with life in wilderness and Indian country. Now it was his turn to pass along the tricks he'd learned.

"Laird," he began, "me and Doc been thinking, and that's unusual for both of us. We'd like it fine if you'd trail along with us and trap in the Nez Perce country this winter. Old Doc already has a wife but I need a winter woman. Maybe you and I could each try for a Nez Perce."

"I'll take you up on it," Laird decided after just a moment's hesitation. "I don't know about a winter woman, though."

"Start with one who's ready," Craig winked. "Sun-in-the-Morning. She's willing—"

"You think so?"

Craig threw back his head and laughed. "Let's just say don't be surprised if you find something warm in your bed tonight. If it's a skunk, don't get bit. If it's a woman, bite her. Sometimes they taste good.''

As badly as Laird wanted to be with Suni, he could not bring himself to seek her out. Staying among groups of men instead, he tasted new dishes and enjoyed fresh bread baked at the missionaries' camp. The white women there sensed Laird must have come from a good Christian home. In every way they treated him kindly, realizing they might be in need of his help later on. Besides, they liked to listen to English sometimes instead of their red brothers' and sisters' gabble.

Dark came to the prairie late that evening, the mosquitoes out long before dusk. As usual, big times were going on at the general meeting place, and although the law forbade giving any liquor to the Indians, a few redskins had somehow gotten hold of some. One warrior, having drunk too much and wanting more, grabbed an axe and began to look for a bottle. It took two red brothers who put rawhide strands around his arms and legs to convince the brave he wasn't going to get any.

As the night wore on, wrestling and fist fighting broke out in the camp. Trappers poured whiskey down their throats. As they watched and the liquor took hold, the leaders' dilemma was how to keep them from further violence and at the same time allow them to let off steam.

The Indians, especially the Nez Perce and Flathead tribes, helped by trying to keep their people under control. But a few braves who'd gotten hold of the fiery popskull were causing trouble by inducing others to drink. Around the edge of the dance circled halfway-sober Indian and white patrols seizing weapons and whiskey. Craig and a few others kept a cautious watch in the shadows, where hidden trading went on. And here and there in some of the tepees, lusty couples passionately ignored what was happening outside.

Shouts went up. By a distant campsite a trapper was on fire, his clothes blazing. As Craig ran to help, an Indian buck holding a brass cup beat the air around the unfortunate man's face. Without hesitating, Craig jerked up a blanket, threw it over the trapper's head, tripped him and rolled him up. Others grabbed the drunken buck and hauled him away. Later, onlookers told Craig that the Indian had been pushing for more whiskey and had tried to grab the trapper's drink. The white man had stumbled back toward the fire and the alcohol that had spilled on his clothes exploded into flame.

Around another fire, a drunk threw his cup of whiskey on a hulking dog sneaking in for scraps. The dog had leaped back quickly but now circled around once more to get the bone he had spotted.

"I'll teach you a trick or two, you woolly son of a bitch," the trapper snarled, and snatching a flaming limb from the fire, he threw it at the dog. With its fur on fire, the frightened animal ran yelping through the crowd. Other dogs took up the chase and the howling bunch tore past tethered mules and around the tepees as startled revelers careened to avoid them.

The mules broke loose. In their fright they knocked down some tepees, thundered past the missionaries' tents and veered toward horse herds being held and guarded on the plain. Like a great storm the uproar swelled to a volume that drowned out any shouts for order. Trappers laughed and rolled on the ground, Indians in various stages of drunkenness whooped and carried on, and in their tents the missionaries prayed for each and every wicked lost soul.

As the dog flew past Doc Newell, the trapper threw his belt axe, and hitting the animal on the head, ended its agony. "Cook him up for dinner tomorrow," Newell said in sign to a nearby squaw.

*   *   *

Laird went to his tent soon after dark, hoping that Suni would visit him. The moonlight painted the whiteness of the canvas with an eerie glow.

Except for the buzzing of an occasional mosquito, for moments at a time it was quiet. Outside, too, in the midst of all the hoopla, there were periods of silence. Laird waited impatiently. Tossing in his bed of buffalo robe and blanket, he imagined what he would do if Suni were beside him.

A shadow passed over one tent side wall. Trembling, Laird watched as it disappeared. The tent flap rose and a figure entered slowly. Not certain it was Suni, Laird remained very still, his fist clenched around his stabbing knife.

As the figure moved stealthily toward him, Laird breathed a familiar fragrance and knew it was the girl. He whispered, "Suni? Come to me here. I am Laird."

Suni moved to where Laird lay. In one fluid motion she dropped to her knees and reached out to touch his face. And Laird, pulse racing, mouth dry as sand, pulled her close. Slipping easily into his arms, Suni pressed herself against him. Laird studied her face in the dimness of the tent.

"Suni, Suni," he whispered, hardly believing she was really there. Gently he smoothed his hand across her face. Suni shivered and then in stirring rhythms returned his touch. Her fingers eagerly traced his ears, his eyebrows and lips, and through his shirt caressed his chest. So content was he to inhale the perfume of sage and summer grasses the girl had rubbed into her hair that a long moment passed before he slipped the heavy cotton off. But soon he wanted skin against him. To his delight he found Suni eager for that too. Beneath her doeskin she was bare of even the knotted maiden rope he had been warned of.

His hands hungrily caressed the gentle slopes of her breasts. Suni whimpered as he touched her and he knew that she was his. Kissing, licking, his lips moved downward to her quivering breasts.

Never before had Donald Laird been free to explore a woman's body. With girls in the East there had always been inhibitions, lack of privacy and time. Now Suni offered herself to him in ways he'd only dreamed of, and greedily, as she tugged at his breeches and his belt, he responded. Helping one another, they found the place where both their instincts led them and at Suni's invitation Laird entered with what seemed practiced ease.

The screaming of the burned man, the dog's howling, the bray of mules and pounding stampede of frightened horses failed to disturb the two who lay together. Naked, oblivious to every moment but the one they shared, the lovers clung together. Again their passion mounted and was released, and once again before light colored the eastern sky.

But as the coyotes' morning songs set camp dogs howling, Suni dressed, gave Laird one last kiss and left his tent.

Laird got up to relieve himself outside and shivered in the dawn's chill. At the stream some distance away from the camp, he washed and he realized that even deprived of sleep, he was not exhausted but exhilarated. He washed up, feeling energy he had never known. Now, he thought, he was a man with a woman to love and enjoy and though his future with her was uncertain, the present seemed gift enough.

Over the silent camp, smoke from the night's fires drifted and settled like fog on the prairies that lay beyond the stream. Far out where horse herds grazed, a stallion offered a challenging trumpet. Other horses nickered back and forth.

The coyotes had ended their morning greeting to the sun when Laird felt a faint breath of breeze stir against his face. Light from the sun grew stronger and against it a pair of ducks whipped above the stream, headed for another feeding spot. The sun's rays hit the western mountains, their peaks and crests bathed in a radiant pink glow. Snowfields glistened. With some surprise Laird realized that of all the places in the world he had seen it was this place he would rather be in than in any other. Silently he thanked God that he had been given the chance to see this paradise and resolved to write to Charles Madden even more about all that he was learning. But he would not write about Suni. That part of his life would remain his alone.

Chapter 10

Eliza Spalding had been almost hysterical when the dogs and mules were tearing through the campground. She had acted properly upset when one trapper told a squaw in no uncertain terms what he would do to her before morning came. Yet curiosity had overcome her both times, and like a child peering through spread fingers and dreading to see what might happen, she had half watched and half listened to every scene. Her husband, more honestly revolted, prayed for the sinners' souls and returned to sleep.

The Whitmans too had awakened, Marcus getting up in time to spot the frantic mules tearing through the camp, knocking down a tepee close by and heading for open country. Back in bed, he held his wife. They talked in whispers, saying prayers for their survival in this terror-ridden wild land, then slept fitfully till dawn.

William Gray was a man without a wife and fast was becoming a man without a friend. He prayed all night, calling for the Lord to teach a lesson to the infidels and the next day began a series of criticisms that would be included in his letters to the Mission Board.

*   *   *

After learning that John McLeod had decided to help the missionaries travel to the Columbia, Craig and Newell had a conference.

"Bill," Doc began, "I ain't about to spend most of the summer with them psalm-singers and Bible-thumpers. I might've done it if they hadn't swung in with that tightassed Scotch thief McLeod. But he's here to spy our country out and I don't like it. Wait and see, there's trouble cooking in the pot and afore long she's going to come to a boil. I figure to sign on with Charlie Bent for a spell. He's an honest mountain man and a good trapper, knows how to lead. He's going to set up a new camp on the south fork of the Platte, wants me to run it. I can pick four or five fellers to keep me company. We'll all make a piece of money next fall and winter."

"Who you figuring on taking along?"

"Bill New's a good one. He'll dig up the rest whilst I chew with Bent on what we need to take with us for trade."

"I'll stick with the bunch going to the Columbia," Craig decided. "Probably winter up in the Clearwater country. I figure young Laird's already made hay with that Nez Perce girl that's been shining up to him. I'll find me some woman to work the hides and keep my camp. Don't worry, partner," he said, seeing Newell's disappointed face, "you ain't lost me yet. I'll figure on meeting you next year someplace at the gathering grounds. In the meantime, keep your hair on."

Later Laird found Doc Newell loading up his pack mules. "Stand still, you swivel-necked monstrosity of a critter," Newell cussed. "Move that foot again and I'll give you a boot in the belly that'll knock the wind out both ends."

The mule snorted, then kicked swiftly. Its foot was a blur as it whipped past the packer's right leg.

"You double-crossing twisted link between a cock-eyed mare and an ornery jackass, take this to square us up!" Doc swung a kick to the mule's belly with his moccasined foot. The beast squealed and swung around to kick back with both heels. Doc grabbed a long ear, bit it and hung on. To Laird's surprise, in a minute the mule quieted down and stood still while Doc straightened the saddle and adjusted the cinch.

When he saw Laird he muttered, "You'll be cussing too, one of these mornings when you have to thaw out ropes and fold blankets covered with ice and snow. I'm guessing this hairy old bastard don't want to leave the pleasant company he's had here. Far as that goes, I don't either. How's your head this morning?"

Laird, still flying from being with Suni the night before, went on and on.

Doc grinned as he listened and turned to pick up a pack. "I know just about how you feel, son. I never will forget the first time. You got a long road ahead, but you'll never want to forget last night."

"Where are you heading, Doc? I thought you, Craig and I were going to be together in Nez Perce country."

"Hell, Laird, I don't fancy trailing with them religious folks, specially when John McLeod's along. I can't stand that tightfisted Scotchman; I think he's here intending to break into our fur trade. Anyway, Charlie Bent's hit me up to work for him. He'll give me trade stuff for the season and four or five men to help out and keep camp going. We figure on opening up a little branch on the South Fork. We'll winter in there, but I told Bill Craig we'd meet here next summer if we all keep our flowing locks."

"Sounds good to me, Doc."

"Now you're talking. You'll be a real one to tie to come next summer, that's for sure." Doc pumped Laird's hand. "Up there with Bill and his friends in the Nez Perce country, you'll have a lot better chance to keep your hair in place than any other spot I know of where beaver are trapped. If you get the right woman, her folks'll keep an eye on you too. Bill knows about that."

Doc rubbed the back of the other pack mule before he laid on the blanket. The animal humped a little when the sawbuck saddle landed on him and the cinch was tightened, then settled down. Moments later Doc rode off on his long-legged bay and vigorously waved his good-byes.

The missionaries were impatient to be on the trail; the rendezvous was getting too wild for them. Indians who had gotten a taste of the vile whiskey demanded more. Squaws used by the trappers were being traded like hides. On one occasion Jason Lee spoke eloquently at a preaching session, but to men who had lived and endured everything nature and her red children could offer in the way of troubles, threats of what might happen to them after death failed to make an impression.

"Lee can scare some folks," Craig decided, "but I know of fellers tied up, burned and then scalped alive after the squaws been at 'em. They prayed to die, those men— wanted out of this life. What a bunch of them red women can do to a man when they're mad can't be told in decent company. Lee's hell and the devil's imps can learn from them, I tell you. Even the thought of standing in fire don't fret me so much as having them squaws cut me up with their special tricks."

Marcus Whitman and Jason Lee persuaded McLeod to start the journey west with them as soon as possible, even though McLeod's trappers wanted to hang around for more fun. Soon after dawn the next morning the cavalcade headed out. Though July eighteenth was hot and dry, to the travelers anxious to be on the move it seemed a wonderful time to be leaving. Leading the way were Joseph Meek and John McLeod, other trappers alongside and following.

Laird trailed his mules with the rest of the packers. Indians darted everywhere—running their ponies, off to look for game or sometimes badgering the squaws. Almost a mile long, the parade crawled forth to the prairie like a slowly moving, struggling snake and climbed gradually over ripening grasses where cattle driven beside the wagons snatched bites as they passed.

In the light spring wagon Narcissa Whitman and Eliza Spalding talked about the Indians. Neither knew where they would live that winter but both hoped bravely that the good Lord would provide adequate shelter and food. They had already planted the seeds of their religion in the minds of the Indians; now in their packs were the seed they would plant in the fertile soil of the Columbia River country and pray over for a bountiful harvest.

Laird camped to one side that night, his mules tethered close by. Lying in his tent after dark, he heard a faint scratching on the side wall. Reaching out, he touched the canvas in answer. This time when Suni came to him there were few preliminaries. Laird had already removed his clothing. Suni quickly slipped out of hers and stood before him in the soft light of the waxing moon. Laird gasped at her beauty. Slim and straight, she stood proudly. Her long black braids, gracing her shoulders, enhanced the loveliness of her rounded breasts.

Laird drew Suni down and wrapped himself around her, his lips burning hers as they deepened their caress. When Laird eased back, Suni followed. Holding sweetly, swaying, they were unable to get enough of each other's touch. Freer at this second meeting, they made love again and again.

83

Dawn came too soon and once more the morning sights and sounds announced to Suni it was time for her to leave.

Afterward Laird went out to pack his mules. Rather than tiring him, the night had filled him with a devouring hunger. A chew on a cold rib was what he wanted. The meat satisfied him, and sticking an extra rib in his pack for later, he led his horse to where Bill Craig's was saddled and waiting.

"Mount up," Craig said. Before anyone else was up or even had a pony out of hobbles, the two companions were out of sight.

"Meek wants us to make a scout ahead to find the best way for the wagons to follow," Craig explained as they rode together. "This here's the easy part of the trip; up ahead we'll have the trouble.

"Joe's so swell-headed over that smiling blonde woman of Whitman's that he can't see dirt for dust," Craig went on. "She sure knows how to play that old goat, and I don't blame her. That woman knows if it weren't for her, the boys wouldn't give a hoot in hell whether the rest of the outfit made it through or not."

Laird grimaced. "I've been a long time now with these missionaries and I've learned that religion sure can cause a lot of trouble. The Whitmans are sincere, I think, but I wouldn't want to have to trust the Spaldings. That man's a fanatic in some ways. As for Gray—a born troublemaker if I ever saw one, all the time looking for something to criticize, picking at trivial things, never satisfied. In my opinion he's something to forget and leave behind."

"Laird, I've often used the expression 'hell on wheels,' and as sure as we're riding to where the journey ends, there's trouble in the making here. How long it takes to come out I won't venture to guess. But right now we'd better look for some meat to lay down for the noon eating. The rest will make it pretty close to where we are before they stop to rest and eat.''

Bill Craig had spent almost half of his life living west of the Mississippi River in Indian territory. He had seen some men die suddenly, others during slow torture, and because he wanted to enjoy his own life as long as he could, he was determined to know more, not only about his prospective partner's temperament, but also what his wilderness skills might turn out to be. All men in the western country carried knives; most owned a rifle and some also had a pistol. But owning didn't mean a thing unless the weapons were used well.

The two men sighted a small group of shaggy-haired beasts off by themselves, nosing the rich grasses.

"Can you slip over there and get meat for dinner?" Craig asked. "I'll wait here with the ponies. When the carcass is on the ground I'll come to help out.''

Laird planned the most efficient way to approach the buffalo. He dismounted, checked his rifle, and making sure it was ready to fire, slung the bullet pouch over his shoulder and headed out. The wind, cool to his wetted finger, blew in his direction. Half crouching, he stalked his quarry. Almost within rifle range, he dropped and crawled, occasionally lifting his head.

Bill Craig watched and measured Laird's every move against his own experience in hunting. The young Easterner's handling of this hunt was to be only one of many tests he would face before being accepted.

Laird had already hunted squirrel, rabbit, duck, quail and partridge in eastern woods and fields. But as he traveled west, deer close to the settlements were often his prey. Finding them hard to close in on, Laird learned that the first shot had to do the job.

Craig had not suggested which animal he should kill; the responsibility was his. Now, as he studied his possible choices, a cow humped her back, belched gas and turned broadside to him about seventy-five yards away. Laird steadied his rifle, settling the front sight just above the cow's brisket, back of her front shoulder. As the rear notch sight held just where he wanted, he pulled the trigger.

A cloud of blue smoke rolled. From his pony Craig saw the cow drop to her knees, then fall over, the sound of Laird's shot reaching him after the animal was down. Craig heeled his mount's flanks and leading Laird's pony, hurried through the grassy hummocks to where the buffalo had fallen.

Chapter 11

As they traveled west, the missionaries kept journals and diaries justifying their expenditures and indicating their progress in converting Indians to the faith. Mrs. Whitman, indignantly observing the treatment of Indian women, wrote in her journal that they were slaves to the men, their lives consisting of constant struggle with work never finished. To Narcissa Whitman, Indian men by contrast led an easy life. To make matters worse as far as the women were concerned, on occasion the men beat their wives for not working harder.

Laird had seen only fleeting glances of Suni in the days that passed. It was painful having to wait for her advances and he hoped that travel and additional camp duties—nothing else—were what had kept her away.

Tackensuatis prayed daily. Observing the ways of white men, he noticed that both Whitman and Spalding helped their wives in the never-ending chores of camp life, and before long he began to give his own wife some assistance. The missionaries chose to see this as a sign that Tackensuatis had accepted Christianity. They did not realize that to other Indians it was a sign that he was becoming a woman. Heeding signals an ordinary observer might overlook, the mountain trappers saw that such things meant trouble in the long run. Joseph Meek tried to reason with Whitman and got exactly nowhere.

During his rides and talks with Craig, Laird learned that men like Meek who were far from Washington were eager to hear every rumor, each bit of information, coming from the capital. Their livelihood depended not only on the Office of Indian Affairs, but on the men in charge of the army as well. Because Laird had come west from an area close to Washington and evidently knew something about the federal government, Craig questioned him casually about it.

"Bill, I really don't know very much," Laird replied. "If I had realized I was going to spend part of my life out here I might have listened more carefully when I had the chance. I suspect Marcus Whitman knows more about what you're asking than anyone else. He has to. The missionaries are quite dependent on the army's good will. Right now it seems that no one back there really knows anything about how big this country is or where the government's authority lies in regard to it."

Laird took a deep breath. "There's a policy, Marcus says, that Secretary of War Harris supports the idea of moving all the eastern Indians to the land west of the Mississippi that is now called Indian Territory. In fact, that plan is already in progress. Whitman and Spalding plan to travel ahead of those tribes that already have been in contact with whites back East.

"By being situated in the far West, the missionaries believe they gradually can convert those interested to Christianity. The idea is to open schools and teach reading and writing to willing young people, especially sons of chiefs and headmen, who will induce others to follow their example.

"There are some rumors, of course, of a plan to move the administration of all Indian affairs into the War

Department. Movement of the southern tribes is causing trouble within the government, and some members of Congress want to stop the squabbles by putting everything under one head. What do you think of that?''

''My opinion of the army heading things,'' Craig answered, ''is that it will bring everything closer to a general war. Too many bullheaded officers want to get decorated for killing off any Indian for whatever excuse they can think of. Mostly army men think of killing as a show of power.''

''Are you the only one against the idea?''

''Hell, no. Most of the trappers are. Look boy, we come out here into their territory. Oh, we get along purty well, considering we steal from the red men, kill their game, take their women and encourage people who come in to do the same. What troubles we've had so far come from whiskey, thieving and folks who think the only good Indian is a dead one. Indians been having their squabbles and wars between themselves since time began, but it's a game for them—keeps 'em strong, gives the young hotheads something to do.

''Now the army comes in, bribes some of the redskins to help 'em, knocks off the troublemakers, then works over the whole bunch. If the whole Indian kit and caboodle ever combine to fight, it'll be a bloody, long-lasting affair.''

Craig shook his head. ''I don't want to see it and I don't think you'd want to either.''

''The missionaries don't see that,'' Laird offered. ''All they've got their eyes on is the conversion of the ignorant savage.''

Craig snorted in disgust. ''And that's the beginning of the end for most of 'em. It's a long slow process, the converting, and in the end most Indians I know will never be civilized. They're a proud, independent people living in a way different than the white men. The missionaries want to make them dependent on a new type of living they don't really savvy.

"I know what I'll have to go through after the end of this fur-chasing; and there will be an stop to it, mark my words. That old Pacific Ocean is the end of the trail and if we're lucky we'll live to see it. This bunch of people we're taking in will spread the word that there's more land and better chances to make a living out here than back home. I don't want to see what happens because of it but my wishes won't stop anything, not by a long shot."

Fort Hall was the place they would separate from the missionaries. Craig and the other trappers saw growing dissension among the religious factions and were eager to get away. The rough country through which they had traveled had worn nerves raw. Whitman and his wagon had slowed the cavalcade down. Even with Indians and Craig to scout the trail, the deep canyons, precipitate bluffs and rocky stream beds continually hindered the westward march.

Ordinary people would have given up, but these pioneers were not ordinary folk. Whitman wanted the use of a wagon to prove to the Mission Board that the West was open to them and to encourage others to follow his example.

Joseph Meek and William Craig wanted to prove to the world that they knew the lay of the land well enough to get a wagon through the rough terrain to the Columbia. The Indians wanted to please the missionaries, and in trying, used all their lore and knowledge of the land to move the group onward. The women wanted the wagon to ride in.

An incident that colored the trip to Fort Hall was William Gray's illness. The missionary wanted the caravan to postpone travel for at least a day to give him a chance to recover. To his surprise and distress, John McLeod refused to stop.

"You can rest assured your heartless behavior will be reported," Gray threatened.

"Well, Mr. Gray, if you report me I guess you will have to stay alive to do it," McCleod retorted. "And if you believe my behavior is heartless, you have much to learn about what goes on in this territory." Sick as he said he was, Gray followed the caravan.

Donald Laird had his problems too. He had not been with Suni for days. Always remembering Craig's advice, he did not go out of his way to seek her out or show her attention except for a stolen glance now and then.

"Sun-in-the-Morning will be showing up at your tent the next night or two," Craig predicted to Laird one morning.

Astonished, Laird asked, "How do you know that, Bill?"

"I don't have to be told," Craig answered. "Sun-in-the-Morning's sick spell is over. When she began to camp by herself I knew that was the reason she didn't go to your tent at night. It's the Indian way. Girls and women camp alone at such times."

Laird was grateful, but added, "I wish you'd told me sooner. I didn't know what to think."

Craig changed the subject. "Suni's mother knows about you, I'm purty sure, and I suspect other Indians do too. They're waiting to see what comes of it."

"And what do you think will come of it?" Laird's face wore a teasing grin.

"Well, I don't know and I'll bet neither of you do either, you're so wound up with each other. Suni can move in with you and make it up with her folks," Craig explained, "or just ride along and split with you when the times comes. So far it's been her choice. Long as she comes to your tent her folks won't get upset, but when you start going to her camp, get your speech made up to ask her old man for her hand in marriage.''

"Is that the custom?"

"Far as I know it is. A winter woman is another thing; you'll come to that later. When we get to the Nez Perce main camp, you compare the number of women and girls with the men around. You'll see there's plenty of extras to pick a camp cook and bed partner from for the winter. Indian men get killed off hunting and fighting. The females they leave behind need someone to look after 'em.''

By August third the caravan had reached Fort Hall on the Snake River. Arguments began about who would go where with whom, but Craig and Laird stayed clear of them. They were set to explore and trap in Clearwater country. Finally Meek went with Tackensuatis and the missionaries down to Fort Boise.

Sun-in-the-Morning paid two night visits to Laird's tent during the crossing to Fort Hall. Laird was delighted to learn that her group had decided to head northeast to buffalo country for their winter meat supply. The Nez Perce were eager to go back to higher country, away from the tightly organized caravan, the troublesome cart, the summer heat and the constant bickering of the white men.

The group made its way into the Beaverhead country, Craig and Laird traveling with them. The streams offered good fishing and wild game thick in the beaver ponds and along the rivers contributed to the daily food supply. Deer were visible all along the route, but the buffalo were scattered in small herds well down from the pass and not so easy to reach. At a place on a flat where a stream ran close and the ground showed signs of use by Indian hunters in former years, the travelers halted and set up camp.

Craig pulled to the side the morning sun would strike

first. "Laird," he announced, "we'll hit the real meat here and you'll see how these fellers kill buffalo and how the women cut it up and dry it. It's a good chance to sharpen your eyes and learn to read sign. Let's pull off the packs and make camp. Let the stock rest up. Tomorrow we'll have some fun."

Once camp was set, Laird looked over the area they had chosen. Tepees were being erected by the Indian women, children gathered wood and dogs ran everywhere, kicked at by ponies and screeched at by the women. Boys herded the ponies down to the meadows below camp. Soon the first lodge was up. Smoke from fires rose slowly in the air and little girls came from the stream carrying skin bags filled with water for the evening's cooking.

The women began to arrange poles and sticks in the spot that got the most summer sun. Laird guessed that the sticks must be pegs to drive into the ground and hold fresh hides for drying and the poles would serve as racks on which to hang strips of meat. Piles of such material indicated there must have been good hunting in the past.

Further away Laird saw circular spots for heating the rocks that would be dropped into the cooking pots. Hanging from trees back of old campsites were white and weathered buffalo skulls, the strips of hide holding them now almost eaten through or slivered off by birds. On the stream side of camp he discovered established trails for water-bearers as well as flat rocks laid where they must have stood to dip the carrying pouches.

Some of the children stacked rotted wood and dry limbs on hides to use as sleds. Others cut off green sprouts, the older ones hacking away with small hatchets; all were busy, all talking, and everyone helped out.

Watching the activity, Laird felt at home, as if he could move from his former life and go on with this group from place to place, year after year, as long as Sun-in-the-

Morning shared his bed and company. He valued his friendship with Craig and Doc Newell, but he thought that now he could probably do without them if it came to that. Then he halfway wondered why Craig had taken him under his wing at all.

Far down the valley and off to one side, a boy on his pony was guarding the horse herd. Camp was not yet complete, but by the time straight blue columns of smoke rose from cooking fires, Laird had finished his explorations.

Craig lay stretched out, apparently asleep, his head resting on a rolled-up blanket. Hearing Laird's steps, he opened his eyes. "Well," he asked, "did you learn anything? How many lodges you count?" he went on, not giving Laird a chance to answer.

"Twelve, more or less."

"Not more or less. Be exact. What else?"

"Buffalo skulls hanging in the trees to the east, strung up with bits of hide."

"What do you mean, buffalo skulls? Bulls or cows? And how old was they? You want to keep what hair you have, don't you, boy? Everything you see is important, everything you hear. You're in hostile country. True, the camp looks safe, but you can't count on nothing unless you really know it well."

"But why are the buffalo skulls important?" Laird asked.

"They tell how many hunts were held from here to get meat. What's real important is to count things and soak the information into your head. It's all valuable. Learn to estimate quick by threes, fours, fives. When you look at a camp, know instantly how many lodges there is; each lodge holds so many people, so many warriors, so many lances and arrows for use against enemies and to get meat. Hone that trick of estimating so when you see a herd of buffalo, cattle, horses or a group of riders you'll know right away how to deal with the situation.''

"I never thought of it that way," Laird admitted.

"You'll catch on real quick after some Injun's arrow sticks in you or slips through your shirt. Maybe you'll count four warriors and won't see a fifth. He's the one will take your hair and ride it home on his lance.''

"How long did it take you to learn all these things?" Laird marveled.

"It took a lot of damn close calls with bad scrapes and a few scars to show for 'em. And I'm still learning," Craig said, noticing the young man's discomfort. "Every night when I go to sleep I hope to see daylight again. If we could live to be a hundred years and double that, we still won't know it all.''

Craig sat up. "Tomorrow we go for meat. I doubt that pony of yours has ever run a buffalo. You can both learn at the same time. Hone that old Russel knife of yourn and check your guns and saddle rigging; your life's going to depend on them and your horse. It's fast and furious out there when the game gets going.''

"What do you look for first?"

"Something to kill. Let the calves run. Look for a cow or bull running separate. Get mixed up in the herd and there's a chance of your pony going ass up. Keep in mind this is a meat hunt. The Indians want to get all they can as soon as possible. Course, we won't know until the scouts come in just what the particular situation here is.''

"You mean they have scouts already out?"

"Four hunters left camp yesterday morning to scout the country—see what I mean by looking and seeing? They'll come back with word where the game is, if there's any Blackfoot or Shoshone around and how the herd they got in mind should be hunted." Craig lit his pipe and puffed. "You going to have company tonight?" he asked.

* * *

Suni did come in that night to lie down beside Laird. As usual, she stayed until just before dawn.

Laird had grown used to having Suni with him; he couldn't sleep without her anymore, so when the camp stirred he went outside.

At Craig's campsite an Indian woman was starting a fire. Laird hardly knew what to say, let alone how to act. Then Craig, returning from the stream, spoke out. "Boy, we got us a cook. No more hauling wood and water, either. This Indian's name is Hawk Flying and she's willing to stick with us for a while. Let's catch up the ponies."

When the pony herd had been brought, the men selected their hunting horses—paints, bays and a few spotted whites that would later be called Appaloosas. No one seemed in any hurry. For the first time Laird counted men and ponies as the Indians mounted and estimated quickly that more than a hundred horses were returned to the grazing grounds and twenty left at camp. Ten hunters were selected to do the killing, while six older boys and one old scout went to the far edge of the buffalo herd to move them in the direction of those with ready ponies and sharpened lances. Craig and Laird were to follow and look on until they had a chance to use their guns.

Chapter 12

The sun was well up when the last group jogged down the meadow toward where the scouts had located game, but it wasn't until they climbed over a low saddle in the grassy ridge that they saw the widened valley dotted with grazing buffalo. The hunters stopped.

The chief of the party surveyed the herd, then spoke, using his hands to indicate where four hunters would ride and wait until the herd came their way. The rest stayed quiet until the chief signaled for them to follow.

Craig and Laird trailed along. Suddenly Craig motioned toward a knoll off to the right. He and his companion rode there, sat their ponies and watched.

Far across the plain they saw riders approaching, whipping their blankets, kicking their ponies and heading straight for the unsuspecting buffalo. The animals recognized danger and thundered toward the waiting hunters. When the herd was between the two groups, all riders crowded in. Their ponies raced next to the frightened beasts and the sound of hooves pounding on hard dry soil reached Craig's and Laird's ears in a rolling roar.

One brave ran his spotted pony alongside a cow, separating her from the herd. His flashing lance caught light from the rising sun for an instant before being powerfully driven in back of the ribs and down deep into heart and lungs. The cow lurched away. As she slowed and finally went down, the rider raised his bloody weapon in the air and went for another kill.

Above the sounds of the running herd, Craig and Laird heard the shouts and whoops of hunters caught up in the excitement. Their own ponies twitched with unreleased energy and the two men tensed, waiting for their chance. Craig saw the herd splitting up fast and took off after a cow whose calf was desperately trying to keep up with her. Laird rode toward another. At once he saw that a hunter attempting to spear his quarry had gotten in the way of a buffalo bull that was avoiding another Indian. The bull had hooked the pony and was lifting it, and the man as well, high into the air.

Laird arrived on the scene just as the last of the herd sped past. The pony was up on three feet, its right front shoulder and leg gashed. A gaping hole in its side was gushing blood and mangled tissue. The hunter was on the ground struggling to get his head up.

Laird leaped from his pony. The Indian wouldn't live; Laird knew that right away. Hooves digging wildly to gain traction had shattered his bones and torn his flesh to a mass of pulp.

Shots in the distance signaled that Craig was in action. Laird walked to the dying pony, shot it between the eyes and checked the hunter. He was dead.

An Indian rushed close on his sweat-drenched pony, muttering something Laird couldn't understand. He slid his mount to a stop and laid the dead man across its back while Laird held the bridle. The hunter reached out his bloody hand and Laird took it in his. A quick shake, a "Ho-hi," and the Indian rode off with his dead companion.

Laird mounted and followed the traveling herd. Along

the way he saw dead and dying buffalo. Far up ahead there was gunsmoke and then the boom of black powder as another beast was shot. Riders were returning, stopping to finish off cripples.

The approaching hunters turned their ponies to meet the two who rode with the body of the dead lancer. A gabble of words and hand signs to emphasize them meant nothing to Laird. But when the hunters turned to him, he knew they wanted him to explain what had happened. He had seen enough sign language to illustrate with his hands the buffalo running, the rider approaching with his lance ready to plunge it in. Then he showed the rider and pony, the bull coming up to hook them and the spill end over end. Both hands showed the herd trampling over the prostrate hunter. The men grunted as they listened and watched. Then each man came by to touch Laird on the shoulder.

Craig came trotting back, his pony covered with sweat. "What happened out there?" he demanded of Laird.

"The hunter's pony got hooked by a bull just as he was about to spear another one. I shot the pony; he was done for. That poor fellow got run over by at least a dozen buffalo too bunched to split."

Craig turned and spoke to the hunters, who answered in grunts and sign. Then the men gave the dead hunter's spare pony to a boy riding up from the chase and sent him back to camp. Others went to bring women, children and dogs to help butcher the meat.

Craig spoke quietly. "There'll be wailing in camp— you'll hear that soon enough—and there's an empty spot in that lodge now for a young feller wants a home and family. Hitch your pony outside. If the door flap opens, go in."

Laird was skeptical. "Have you ever tried that?"

"Not with this bunch. I don't really hanker for that

99

kind of a deal. Right now I'm getting along good with the cook and campkeeper I got. I'll soon find out how good she is at working hides. You get a buffalo?''

''No. I was riding into the edge when I saw the pony get hooked.''

''Next we'll start skinning out,'' Craig told him. ''The women will be here purty darn quick and cut up meat to haul back to camp. Your old Russel sharp enough to cut through a bull's hide?''

''If it isn't I'll whet it some.'' They turned toward the scattered carcasses; already people were clustered around each one. Knives flashed red with blood at the skinning; livers, hearts and marrow gut went into containers and pouches. Ponies drawing poles that held baskets hauled meat back to camp, dogs running beside them and barking their hunger.

Craig had downed three cows and one bull. The men went from one to another. By the time they finally got back to camp the women were slicing meat to dry in the sun, meat racks in place and girls busy hanging their slices to allow air to pass. The hot August sun put a glaze on the meat at once and in only a few minutes its surface had hardened.

Laird thought he had been fascinated by the women's skill in cutting up the meat, but what else they salvaged really intrigued him. Hot liver came first and was eaten in gulps. The heart was held up above open mouths and squeezed out in a gory stream.

Slavering dogs snatched up what little viscera had not been used. Whatever else fell was devoured too. Laird knew now that the Indians ate the dogs in an emergency, so whatever food the animals got would not be wasted.

Several squaws came to help Craig's woman cut up and hang meat to dry. They took all hides to camp and women not working with meat now stretched them flat, pegging them down with the sticks Laird had seen piled on the flat at the edge of the meadow. With his hand axe Craig chopped out the hump ribs, those bony protrusions above the animal's shoulders. Spitted with strong sticks, they now roasted beside his fire.

There was no formal mealtime this day. Everyone ate when he was hungry. Roasting ribs and tongues, bones and chunks of meat boiling with bulbs—the smell of cooking rose above that of smoke and other camp odors. The hot sun dried the meat and hides. Craig sat at his camp smoking his pipe and after hobbling his pony, Laird came to join him.

"Set a spell," the trapper grated. "Let the women do the work. Us men will take it easy and brag about what great hunters we are. The old bucks will put on a dance tonight and the widow and her friends will squall and bawl for the dead hunter. You'll see things that will give you more ideas about the Nez Perce and there will be another chance at a hunt soon as this meat's taken care of."

Warriors and the wailing, mourning women carried the dead man to the burial place. Laird stayed in camp to write in his journal. That evening the hunters prepared for the Dance of the Buffalo. They painted their faces, adorned themselves with special headdresses and bedecked their horses. Tails were looped up and clubbed, feathers tucked in manes and saddle pads trimmed with white weasel tails.

The Nez Perce Buffalo Dance was much like those Laird had seen before. Drummers beat the time and the people danced with shuffling half-steps, crouched down. The dance was still going on when Laird retreated to his tent. There, lying quietly on the robe, was Sun-in-the-Morning.

Suni had entered Laird's tent the first time in response

to his gifts and the attention he had shown her. He was different from the young Nez Perce tribesmen who had been eyeing her and had made advances but not come forth with clear-cut intentions of marriage.

Now one of the buffalo hunters had been killed and his woman had a place in her lodge for a man who could provide protection and sustenance. Suni decided she should make a move toward a closer relationship with Laird just in case the widow tried to jump her claim.

That night she gave Laird ever-sweeter symbols of her love for him and did not leave before daylight, but waited until the camp stirred, then went out and built a cooking fire in front of his tent.

Craig saw her at the fire and chuckled. His own woman was already preparing his food.

When Laird came out he made no remark, only ate the food Suni had prepared. Then he went to get his and Craig's ponies. The two intended to scout on their own today. Before he left the tent he had noticed that Suni's small store of possessions had already been moved in.

During the day Laird spoke about what had happened. "Bill, you sure started something when you took in a woman to cook and keep camp for you. Now I have one and I don't know quite how to handle the situation."

"It's up to you, boy, whether or not you chuck her stuff out the door and kick her in the rump after it. I know you're not up to that, but if you want it, that's the way it's done." His words were crude but his tone softened. "On the other side of it, if you really want camp help you've got it. As long as you permit your woman to stay there and she wants to stay, everything's fine. It's been her choice. But if you want to marry her, you have to take it up with her father and throw in some trade goods. You won't get her for nothing if she's worth a damn."

Laird hesitated. "Things have all been happening too fast," he said finally.

"What did you expect when you laid out them trinkets," Craig jeered, "free love? You bought something. Whether or not you want it now is up to you. But don't fret over it. Hell, Laird, there's a chance none of us will make it through the winter. Summer ain't even over and already the camp has lost one good hunter and fighter. A thing like that makes the squaws look sharp as to how they can keep what they have.

"Anyways, what was right back home don't always wash out here." Craig shook his head in a way that showed how well he knew. "You'll learn the Nez Perce are practical. Their ideas are easy to live with if you follow their rules. This camp's beginning to look on you as one of their people and with a little luck you'll be accepted. When you pulled out of the hunt to try and help He Who Runs, it give 'em the idea you're concerned about the tribe's welfare. Most whites would have given chase to the herd and said to hell with any Indian that got killed."

They rode in silence until Laird spoke. "Do you think you might marry an Indian woman and settle down someplace?"

"I've give it thought," Craig answered. "I probably will. I been too long away from white women and their ways. Seeing how Mrs. Whitman and Mrs. Spalding acted kind of turned me away from them and others like 'em even more. Besides, I been living free for many long years. Laird, don't make up your mind too soon. Stick around, get to really know how the Nez Perce live and try to enjoy what you can. The woman in your tent will give you what you need to live in this kind of country. I can name a few trappers who don't have a winter woman, but I've tried it both ways and having one with me's a lot better."

Laird was silent for a moment. "I like it too, Craig," he found himself saying. "I never thought I would, but it's so much better than I imagined that it makes me not want to go back to old ways at all."

"There's a chance neither of us will." Craig pulled up his pony and when Laird halted, turned to him. "Boy, so far you've camped in that little tent of yourn. That's fine for this time of year but in another month we'll get frosts, then rain and wind. You'll need more than a woman and some canvas to keep you from freezing. What say we begin to live like Indians? Make up our own family?" He saw the question in Laird's eyes. "Fold up your tent; swap it off later on. You and Suni move in with me and Hawk."

"You're not serious, Craig. Won't the women object?"

"Why should they? They share the work and we do the hunting, like Nez Perce have always done. Their women have nothing to say about things. They can only suggest."

"Won't it be kind of embarrassing . . . you know . . . ?"

"Never is for Indians. If you don't like sounds you hear at night, pull the robes over your head. Fact is, you might like being that close. Some people do, you know."

"If you want to I guess it's all right with me," Laird said slowly. "But let's wait until tomorrow. I'd like a night alone with Suni."

"Suits me. I'll tell Hawk and you do the explaining to your own woman."

Another buffalo run took place the following day. Craig and Laird had found a small bunch in a sheltered valley and they took the information back to the Nez Perce camp. This time women and pack animals trailed along to the scene of the hunt. Craig pointed out that this isolated herd could be slaughtered without a long run and suggested to the chief that he and Laird could slip up and use their rifles, killing as many buffalo as possible before animals began to stampede. Then the hunters on ponies could race in with their lances and arrows.

A council was held, the hunt discussed and an agreement reached. As soon as their quarry was in sight next day, Craig took charge of stationing the mounted hunters. He and Laird rode around the herd well away from them, hobbled their ponies and approached the herd carrying guns and bullet pouches. Craig gave Laird brief instructions.

"I'll shoot a cow through the lungs and knock her down. You have one picked out and do the same. Make sure it's a good shot so she won't run off. You want her to just hump up and fall over. The rest will stay right where they are unless you get one moving crippled or they get panicky. Leave the bulls and calves to the mounted hunters."

Craig made his shot and the buffalo humped up; then Laird shot his cow. Before he could reload Craig had shot another, and between them they had a dozen down before one tough old cow put her tail in the air and with a bawling bellow took off at a gallop.

Their faces blackened with powder smoke, the two hunters returned to their ponies. Laird's shoulder was tender from the pounding of his rifle butt but he felt satisfied that he had done well.

That's why he was surprised to hear Craig say, "Boy, if you want to keep your hair in place, there's a couple of things you ought to make a habit of."

Astonished, Laird shot Craig a look. "And what are they?"

"Before you fire make certain someone ain't slipping up on you. And learn to load that rifle a lot faster. Learn to do it in the dark, flat on your back, or even with one hand. Practice until you know just how quick you can get off the next shot. And while I'm telling you, practice loading your rifle while your pony's going at a dead run."

The mounted hunters were running the last of the herd in the direction of the waiting women and children. Laird and Craig saw some women cross the prairie with horses pulling a lodge-pole travois. Laird recognized Hawk Flying and Suni among them.

Craig went to the first animal and laid open the hide along its backbone; Hawk Flying grabbed hold of the skin and pulled it away as his curved skinning knife laid bare the flesh. When Laird started on the one he had shot, Suni appeared to help him. Others came up to slice and cut away the meat, then loaded the waiting ponies.

The scorching heat took its toll. Sweat poured from under every hat and into every eye. The hunters and the rest worked on, hands, arms and clothing bloody and sticky, but with everyone happy at the day's addition to the winter meat supply. With no water nearby, wash-up time came at the camp when all had returned. Laird and the rest of the hunters stripped and went to the river; from upstream came female squeals and laughter.

In camp hunters relaxed. Only women and older children kept working. "Don't the women take time off to lie around and rest like the men do?" Laird asked.

"Yeah. Lots of time for that next winter. Snow will be deep. Winds will be blowing, the ponies pawing for grass or eating willow sprouts. That old lodge will be a place to keep fires burning and huddle in warm furry robes drying out there on the flat right now. I tell you, then's the time to let things go on outside. All of us have had bad times in the winter, caught with no place to hole up, snow deep and no grass. Cottonwoods too big for ponies to chew bark from 'em and not much wood for fires." Craig shuddered, remembering. "Nothing to eat except ponies or mules and you make your choice: maybe eat a mule and cache the hide or wait another day for a break in the storm.

The ponies and mules chew hair from their manes and tails—anything to put in their bellies. If you don't keep your hides hid from 'em, they'll eat on them, too. Those are the bad times for the Nez Perce. They have their tales about it and know well there'll be more to come.''

Chapter 13

Spalding was not disappointed by the Nez Perce departure from Fort Hall nor by the loss of Craig and Laird. He had taken a dislike to the tall mountain trapper and suspected Craig didn't think too highly of him either. Although the mountain man had helped their party without complaining, Spalding sensed Craig's suspicion that he and Whitman would influence the Indians in ways that would negatively affect the trappers. And noticing Laird engrossed in his journal and sketch book, Spalding was sure too that the new trapper was reporting to someone events that might reflect adversely on both him and the missionary effort.

Whitman, on the other hand, gave little thought to Craig and Laird's leaving except for feeling the loss of additional help he might need to get his cart across the land. The desert, as the missionaries called the sagebrush, covered land from Fort Hall to the Boise River and proved to be a hot skillet over an even hotter fire. The August sun was relentless. With water scarce, stock tired easily. It was not until the travelers headed down into the Boise River valley that they found relief. There they camped and held another council.

Joseph Meek insisted he could take the cart ahead to Fort Walla Walla; he agreed with Marcus Whitman that such a feat would attract emigrants from the East. John McLeod was in a hurry to reach Fort Walla Walla. He was eager to let the word out that the Easterners were coming and that there might be trouble with emigrants later on. Hallahotsoot and Tackensuatis wanted the missionaries to head north over the trade trail to the Clearwater. Whitman's choice was to meet Samuel Parker to discuss the best place to locate the missions. It finally was decided to go on to the Columbia.

It pleased the Cayuse to have the missionaries travel to their home. But the decision bothered Lawyer. He would have preferred that they go up to the mouth of the Clearwater. Tackensuatis declared his allegiance to the missionaries no matter where they wanted to build their church; he was convinced that theirs was the way of life to follow if he was to become a true Christian.

Whitman promised Lawyer that after they met with Parker they would visit his homeland and perhaps would build a place there. This appeased the Indian somewhat, and with his band of followers he headed up to his wintering ground.

When the missionary party reached the Columbia they found that Samuel Parker had not waited for them. Heading down to Fort Vancouver, they sought the advice of a man named Dr. McLoughlin. Fortunately, McLoughlin talked easily with them. Although he was working for the British company, he knew the missionaries would attract emigrants into his territory, so did not discourage their efforts.

Advised to go explore the area around Fort Walla Walla, twenty-five miles upriver the missionaries found what seemed the perfect place for a mission. They named it Waiilatpu.

To keep their word to the Nez Perce, Whitman and

Spalding then rode north to look for a second building place. What they saw of the country looked barren. The soil on the open, rolling hills seemed too poor to raise crops the mission's population would need. Yet when the Nez Perce were consulted, the Indians took the party to flat bottom lands where black soil and tall grasses assured the white men of crops.

Fine timber grew twenty or more miles up the creek. The white men remembered how logs had been floated down eastern streams and knew they could do the same here. To them the stream represented water power. Spalding was sure he could eventually build a grist mill to grind the grain they would grow. And happy to have a mission located in their territory, the Nez Perce provided men to help move their supplies and families in. Building began in October.

Spalding and his helpers had found the type of timber that was needed for his dwelling. They cut logs, floated them to the mouth of Lapwai Creek, then hauled them upstream for two miles to the building site. Many Indians were willing to help, but most had no knowledge of how actually to build a structure. Spalding instructed them while laboring nonstop himself.

The fact that it was now late Indian summer lent impetus to the work. The foundation down, the men peeled logs, slabbed and notched them at the corners and began to put up walls. One room was to be for the family, about eighteen feet by twenty. The other, the same size, would be for classes. In each section of the house was a mud-daubed fireplace.

In spite of his quick temper and narrow-minded views, Spalding was a natural teacher. Both Spaldings, in fact, were examples to the Indians in the way they worked together and shared the tasks.

While Spalding worked at the house, Mrs. Spalding kept the campsite clean near the tent they were using during construction. She cooked the meals and performed countless chores at the same time she was learning the Nez Perce language. One of her accomplishments was forming an alphabet of sorts. Also, she took the time to write every lesson down so that each student could teach others at home. The Nez Perce learned quickly and often improved on what they were taught.

After the house and school building had been completed, Spalding began additional construction. He wanted a place to house milk cattle, to shelter sheep if he could get them and to store the grain he intended to raise.

Overwork and impatience made Henry Spalding's temper flare repeatedly and it took his wife to calm him down. Although he never cursed, Spalding would pound his fist against something, stomp away in frustration and sometimes scream in anger; none of these actions helped his relations with the Indians.

To make matters worse, not all the Nez Perce were happy about the invasion of their homeland by the white people. It was true that when Lewis and Clark came through their territory, the Nez Perce who had met and guided them were impressed with the honesty and compassion of the two leaders.

William Clark in particular had been effective with medicines, and his patience in dealing with the ills of Indians who came to him for help had earned him respect. He lanced boils, gave purges when he thought it necessary and used a mild eyewash, probably boric acid, to clear up inflamed eyes so common among children because of the dust and smoke that constantly blew around them.

The white man's magic was even more openly sought after Clark miraculously cured a paralyzed Nez Perce chief.

For years the chief had not been able even to wash his hands and face. After trying everything from pills to daily consultations, almost in despair, Clark had suggested the chief be given hot steam baths to make him sweat. The pain was so bad after the treatment that Clark gave the Indian a sedative, then had his father manipulate the Indian's arms and legs. To Clark's surprise, the chief soon was better and able to walk.

This one act helped prepare the way for later missionaries. If the white man had magic power, the Indians thought, perhaps they could acquire it too.

Years later, when the Whitmans and the Spaldings informed their eager listeners about the miracles of Jesus Christ, the Nez Perce remembered once more how William Clark had caused the paralyzed chief to walk. Then when Eliza Spalding read the passage in the New Testament describing how Jesus had made the blind man see, they recalled that Clark had washed and improved their children's eyes.

The power of the Indian shaman was gradually diminishing. Because his magic was no longer needed, his authority was questioned; he didn't like that.

Other Indians didn't care for what was being taught to Nez Perce children who attended school. Was it really a sin to have more than one wife? Braves who had taken in a sister of their first wife because there was no one to hunt meat and provide shelter for her were not about to throw out the women they kept in their lodges.

Young men on the verge of becoming warriors and hunters for the tribe were also having problems with the missionaries' teachings. Being told it was sinful to steal horses, kill enemies or kidnap young women and bring them back with other trophies didn't sit well with them. How could they grow to manhood and not be ready to

113

protect their people? If they decided to love their enemies—
the Blackfoot, the Crow, the Coeur d' Alene—their scalps
would soon be hanging from lances or bowstrings.

To add to the misunderstandings, the Jesuit Black
Robes began to appear. With them came conflicting ap-
proaches to Christianity that confused the Indians even
more.

Protestants seemed to want the Indians to change
immediately from old ways to new. Roman Catholics, on
the other hand, remained more tolerant and rebuked the
sinfulness of the natives less dramatically. What they would
do was threaten the Indians with fewer visits and after
building their missions say they would move them unless a
tribe came to terms with their priest. Several missions
were actually moved, some several times, and as the word
spread that the black-robed Jesuits meant business, it became easier for them to teach.

Another thing that the Jesuits did rankled the missionaries and trappers. They supplied Indians with guns and
shot for use in hunting. This was a practice patterned after
the Jesuits' success in Paraguay, where they established
colonies and in time made each village self-sufficient without further help from the European traders.

Even the way missionaries lived seemed confusing to
Indians. The white Protestants brought wives and later had
children. That was good; the Indians understood that. But
the Black Robes came as single men, never married—and
reproached only mildly natives who took several wives.
They even allowed their converts to hunt and travel and
did not insist on their living in one place to farm and raise
crops and do women's work as the Spaldings and Whitmans
did.

The Protestants built a school and church and said,
"Come to us." On the other hand, the Roman Catholics

built networks of churches and went to the people saying, "We will go wherever you are."

In the Beaverhead country the hunters enjoyed themselves while the meat and hides dried. It was a good time to be young and to have women in the lodges. Craig and his companion rode out with the hunters and Laird practiced reloading his rifle both on horseback and off. More confident, he bet Craig he could even lance his game.

"Well, it might be a good thing for you to learn more about it," Craig encouraged. "You can never tell when you might need to know how to do just that. These Nez Perce fellers are good at lancing; they have to be. They were using arrows and spears long afore guns come into this country. Some of the hunters right here in this bunch got their first guns in a raid on the Blackfoot. I've seen 'em dance and sing about it. Afore spears and arrows, they herded buffalo over the cliffs along the Missouri River or anyplace like that to break their legs and have the others pile up on 'em. That was real dangerous work. If the buffalo turned back on the braves driving 'em, there sometimes was a real mix-up."

"How long have the Nez Perce been coming to this area to hunt?"

"Probably not more than twenty, twenty-five years. That's what I been told—after Lewis and Clark come. They were just beginning to make the trips over here. Getting ponies is what made 'em spread out. They used dogs to pack afore that. It was a purty tough go because they couldn't pack enough meat back to make it worthwhile.

"When we get over into real Nez Perce country, I can show you houses along the rivers where they lived most of the time. Big houses, some twenty to forty feet long. Dug down in the ground and built up with slabs and bark walls, then roofed over with bark and bullrushes and long grass.

115

Warm in the winters and cool in the summers, those places were.

"The tribes never moved around much until they got horses and buffalo hides to build with. Horses packed hides back for lodges, clothes, moccasins and meat for the winter too, to go along with dried bulbs, berries and salmon they'd gathered. Those old camps got purty rank when things thawed out in the spring."

Craig chuckled. "They weren't able to bury their crap and after a while an accumulation of it built up, along with stuff the dogs left when something got thrown to 'em."

"Craig," Laird asked, "do you think well of the President's idea of wanting to move all eastern Indians west across the Mississippi?"

"It might work in time, but I doubt it. None of 'em will want to move, and when it comes to forcing 'em— well, it'd take guns and the army to do it. When they got here, they'd have to mix right into some other tribe's territory; neither bunch would like that. From what I've heard, none of those people in Congress know a damn thing about how big this country is or what it's really like. If they think they can move them eastern savages out here and make peaceful farmers out of 'em, they're crazy."

Craig went on speaking. "Maybe in a hundred years this part of the country will be settled. Then again, maybe it won't take that long. People want land. The only way most can get it is to move west and take a chunk. Back there they can buy and sell, but I keep thinking, if I was there and wanted a piece of land, where would I get the money to buy it?"

"I see what you mean," Laird mused. "Back home, I would have to have a job and save my money for a place of my own. And all the land would have been taken up by others long before I got to buy some. Yet I saw millions of acres still unsettled before I got to St. Louis.''

Craig got up to stretch and to gaze for a while down into the valley. Then he sprawled out by a tree, where shade eased the smothering heat. No one was moving much around the camp except women tending meat-drying racks and one or two who worked hides. Children and dogs played in the river.

"You know, Laird," Craig continued, "I've been around and about these mountain valleys summer and winter for a few years, but it wasn't till you come along and took up with Suni that I began to think about settling down. Trouble with me is I've seen too much land to make me a choice. Just thinking about it bothers me. I grew up in good country, but from what I hear it's all tied up and settled now. Those lands east of the river might look empty but I bet they belong to somebody. Move in and then see how quick somebody rides up to see what you're doing there. If a white man don't claim it, an Indian tribe will. That's why lots of folk favor moving every last one of the tribes across the river. It'll be quite a chore but I believe it'll have to be done.

"What I'm getting at is, where can this old boy settle down? Not this side of the hump, for sure. A good many scalps will be hanging in Blackfoot lodges afore things get quiet. We're apt to see something happen afore we cross the river on this trip. We're in disputed hunting country, you know."

Laird didn't. His face looked disbelieving.

"There's a few hundred miles to travel," Craig explained, "and if we don't run into scouts it'll be because they're clear east hunting. This is hunt time and the young warriors are out for any plunder they can get into. It's testing time, to see how much they've learned without losing their own hair. Notice the guard we've got around our herd? Notice how every morning there's some young fellers gone afore daylight? It's to be sure no one's slipping up on us.''

Laird had his own thoughts. ''I have never killed a man, Bill, and to tell you the truth, the thought of it makes me ill. Was it that way with you?''

''Sure. But when the time came and it was him or me, I didn't want it to be me. None of us—women, kids, men and dogs—can tell what will happen today, tonight or tomorrow. I keep the old rifle close. It's always loaded, too. Is that knife in your belt real sharp? It better be, boy. Never let the edge lose its keenness because it might be the one thing left to save your hair. Don't get squeamish thinking of killing. Think of saving your hide, my hide and the hides of those with us in this camp. Once you get charged up you'll forget about everything except surviving.''

''Do you take scalps?'' Laird asked.

''No, but I could have. It's mainly the Indians' way of acquiring a trophy, but a lot of the trappers do it. It shows the Indians they mean business and proves they actually killed the other feller.''

As they talked there in the shade, try as he would, Laird could not envision hand-to-hand combat with some of these agile, powerful people. He had seen them dance dressed and painted for war, heard them chanting, watched rugged muscles flex smoothly under skin that was greased for warfare. When they brandished axes or poised lances for attack, Laird could feel himself begin to shake and wonder what chance he would have of keeping his wits about him if he had to face them as enemies. He pictured staying far off, where he could steady his rifle and pick them off before they swept over him.

''It's best not to think too much about it,'' Craig was saying. ''No scrap I ever was in come out like I thought it might. The whole thing usually happens so quick that you just do what comes naturally, try to kill the other feller or at least hold him off from trying to kill you. You been practicing with your weapons. Don't be afraid to throw your hatchet outside camp, either. If you use it that way long enough, it'll come as second nature to use it when you have to.''

Chapter 14

Late in the fall of 1836 Charles Madden received the first letter sent by his young nephew from within Indian country. Madden had read and reread the letter, trying to absorb its descriptions of the Indians as well as Laird's conception of life on the frontier. Most of what the letter contained disturbed him. He and many others had been led to believe that people in that part of the Oregon Country were miserable ignorant fish-eaters with flattened heads and scrawny, ill-nourished bodies.

Laird's letter to his uncle dispelled misconceptions about the Nez Perce tribe in particular. Madden anticipated a second letter. To his surprise and delight, one came just before Christmas of the same year. He scrutinized carefully the package in which it was contained, recognizing that it alone told a story. The cover was of tanned deerhide, what had once been a light color but was now darkened by smoke, grease and something that looked like blood. The address on the parcel was printed in red, now smeared and almost invisible: "Charles Madden, Ind. Aff. Office, Washington, D.C., U.S. of Am." The cover was sewn with small, tight stitches, the edges sealed with pitch and tallow to make it waterproof.

Madden cut the bindings with his knife. He could

smell the smoke of fires tinged with pitch and grease as he opened the letter. From what spot in that far country had it come, he wondered. The letter in front of him was smudged and stained, crinkled by dampness somewhere along the way, yet its script remained quite legible.

10/17/1836

Dear Sir:

I am now living with the Nez Perce people and considered one of them since the time I killed my first buffalo and ate of his ribs. I killed two enemies and saved the life of one of my companions.

I will live here in this basin for the winter and trap with Wm. Craig; he is a man well known to the Nez Perce; one of their women shares his tent. Her name is Hawk Flying. My tent companion and helper is Sun-in-the-Morning. We live in a skin tepee and share life as the Indians do. From several Nez Perce who came here over the mountain pass we have recently learned that the missionaries Spalding and Whitman have found places in which to locate. The Spaldings will be close to where the Nez Perce Indians set up their winter camps.

I have learned much since the rendezvous about Indian ways and Indian beliefs. I sense there will be almost insurmountable conflicts ahead between the Indians and white people who come west to live. These problems will stem from the differences in religious views and from the white man's belief that the Indian people must live permanently in one place and cultivate crops there. Wm. Craig says trouble might be held off

for years but that it is inevitable. I agree with
him.

By the time you get this letter it will be
winter in this country; snow has already begun to
fall on the high peaks. We leave here tomorrow
morning to go over the pass and into the home
country of the Nez Perce. I am sending this letter
with a messenger who is headed for St. Louis.

D. Laird

Charles Madden read his nephew's letter twice, leaned
back in his chair and mentally reviewed some things he
and his superior, Carey Allen, had discussed regarding
Indian problems. All through the country east of the Mississippi, whites had been spreading into lands formerly
claimed by Indian tribes. At first this migration was so
gradual that when sporadic Indian uprisings occurred they
were quashed easily by the army. Now there were more
uprisings and they were occurring so frequently that there
was general clamor by white settlers either to kill the
Indians or to move them to an area where they could cause
no harm.

The army could not expand rapidly enough to keep up
with the problem. Because the primitive trails leading to
new settlements were almost impassable at certain times of
the year, it took considerable effort for a village under
attack to notify an army outpost; and by the time the
soldiers arrived, the attackers had already disappeared.

Of all the wilderness predators they had to cope with,
the settlers considered the Indians to be the worst. Even
when settlers treated one tribe kindly, they complained that
often they were betrayed by that band or attacked by
another tribe that claimed they had been physically abused
or cheated by some less considerate group of white people.

Some people had pointed to the fact that moving the

123

eastern tribes west, as was suggested, would spark intertribal warfare there. Those who favored the plan, however, gave the answer, "Let them kill each other off; then we won't have to do it." It was Harris who suggested moving only the Indians who were causing the trouble. He wanted to establish a territorial government and then civilize the natives, believing that if Indians could be kept away from the influence of whites except in schools that taught them reading and writing and a trade, a gradual transition would take place.

Because of their nonviolent attitude, Quakers might be suitable for such a project, but could enough Quaker volunteers be found? Financing the project would be difficult; Madden knew that. All whites who had suffered because of the Indian wars would be opposed to any government expenditures for it. And what did those far-off natives think of the white man and his steady encroachment into their area? How could the civilizing of the Indian tribes be accomplished without continual warfare that might eventually destroy the Indian? Madden's thoughts spun with questions.

Most of the arguments in favor of better treatment for the Indians were espoused by intellectuals who lived in the comparative safety of cities and towns. They had time to read and argue and in their discussions two opposing views of the Indians were introduced.

"The Indian of North America," said one, "presents to us man completely savage but obligated, by the nature of the forest that he inhabits and the variable temperature of the heaven under which he lives as well as by the enemies by whom he is surrounded, to employ both courage and address for his subsistence and his defense. He is of all savages the most noble in whom the unaided powers of human nature appear with greater dignity than among those rude tribes who either approach nearer to the equator or farther remove toward the poles.''

Such an environmental theory espoused the ideas that even if all men were descended from one couple, the differences apparent in the species were the result of their environment and the conditions under which they lived and that all people created equal were subject to change.

The rebuttal of the Comte de Buffon, a respected naturalist of the period, concluded that the insalubrious climate and physical environment of the Western Hemisphere contributed to the degeneration not only of the animals there, but of the people as well. He was, in contrast with those who supported the environmental theory, particularly harsh in his descriptions of the Indians.

In the savage the organs of generation are small and feeble and he has no beard. He has no hair, no beard, no ardor for the female. Though nimbler than the European because of his custom of running, his strength is not so great. His sensations are less acute and yet he is more cowardly and timid. He has no vivacity, no activity of mind. Destroy his appetite for food and drink and you will at once annihilate the active principle of all his movements; he remains in stupid repose on his limbs or couch for whole days.

Savages have no ardor for women and of course no love for mankind. Unacquainted with the most lively and tender attachments, their other sensations of this nature are cold and languid. Their love to parents and children is extremely weak. The bonds of the most intimate of all societies, that of the family, are weak and feeble, and one family has no attachment to another.

Hence no union, no republic, no social state can take place among the morality of their manners. Their heart is frozen, their society cold and their empire cruel.

American intellectuals, in defending their own enlightenment and the progress of this new country, denied the facts put forth by this theory of degeneration and attempted to prove in their arguments that the red man was equal to the white. Thomas Jefferson agreed that this was true but his treatment of Indians and his idea of what should be done with them did not always support his belief.

Debated well into the nineteenth century, the environmental and degeneration theories were superseded in midcentury by theories of evolution and racism. But used in arguments for and against the treatment of the Indian, in the 1830s these theories helped shape the policy of the Department of War.

Charles Madden was intrigued with his nephew's letters. Laird had despised Indians he had known in the East. Prejudiced, certain that all Indians were the same, he had felt they were not to be trusted and would never be civilized.

The information he forwarded now represented an almost opposite view. If the boy was really living with a Nez Perce band and had taken one of their women to live with him, he must surely be favorably impressed.

Chapter 15

On as peaceful a morning as any could be this early in September, the camp was up and active. A white dusting of frost glittered on wet grass as the light caught it. Children raced and whooped on their way to draw water for cooking pots; women chattered and occasionally brandished a stick at a snooping dog who came too close to where they worked.

Far down the prairie young men were bringing up the pony herd so hunters could select their mounts for the day. It was to be the last hunt before packing to begin the trek upriver to the wintering grounds.

Bill Craig and Laird lazed on their robes for a last talk and smoke before riding out, their ponies hobbled where the women could keep a lookout in case they were needed in a hurry.

"We'll have this last little hunt," Craig said now. "The boys have found a few head slipped away from the main herd. Frost's here and winter's headed in. Those buffalo will soon be looking to join up with a bigger bunch. How they even happened to be this far from their usual stomping grounds I can only guess at. They used to be all over here afore they got hunted hard by the Nez Perce. Now this is the closest they find 'em once they come over the pass. Used to be some over in the Snake River country, but once the Nez Perce and other tribes got ponies, the buffs didn't last long.'' There was resignation in Craig's tone.

"Do you think we'll have enough dried meat to last us through the winter?'' Laird asked.

"Well, it takes a lot. You got to figure there's others over there that been drying salmon and bulbs and other things to trade for hides and jerky. Real winter don't usually hit in that country till about Christmas or the first of the year. Course, we get snow in the mountains; that cuts off the passes and drives game to the lower country, but it's never as bad as it gets in the plains country east of here, where the wind blows and drifts the snow. January, February and even March can be rough where we're off to. Some say there's been winters lasted clear into April. That's hard on everything, specially the grass-eaters.''

"Do the Blackfoot or other tribes of hunters ever get over this far to hunt?''

Craig puffed his pipe thoughtfully. "If they do, they're not so much hunting as they are looking for longhaired scalps and plunder. That's why the chief has scouts out every day and takes good care of the ponies. Right now's the last time the scalp hunters might have a chance to take a crack at this bunch or any others come here for meat. The plains tribes already got their winter's meat dried and packed away. Young bucks looking for excitement will be scouting for easy pickings. We got hides, meat, ponies, young women and plunder, including a few guns, lances and bows they could haul off. Yep, and the hair of two white men to dangle on their lances. Laird, we can expect trouble any time, and don't think the old warriors don't know it. In Indian country, trouble always comes just when you think it won't.''

Sun-in-the-Morning appeared and slipped down beside Laird on the folded-up robes.

"Craig and I are going on the hunt," Laird explained in words and sign as she touched him. "I will bring you another hide to keep you busy."

Bed talk with Suni had helped Laird understand the language. They would whisper, ask and answer questions. By now he knew most words for the various parts of the anatomy as well as for tools and articles in the lodge. He could say the names of most people in camp. Other times Craig interpreted.

There was chatter outside. "The ponies," Craig said. "Let's get our guns and go for a little hunt." He ducked his head as he passed through the doorway.

Suni bent toward Laird and he pulled her close to hold her and kiss her. "You sure do keep me warm, Suni," he laughed. Then picking up his rifle and bullet pouch, he checked his two knives, reached under the sleeping robe for his pistol and left the lodge.

The resting buffalo herd was spread out among the cottonwoods along the river. After counsel, several riders took off to form a circle. The plan was to drive the beasts out in the open where the rest could join in the run, then stampede them back upriver closer to the camp's location. Only a few animals were in the open. Whether the entire herd there comprised fifty or a hundred and fifty buffalo was anyone's guess.

Craig and Laird stayed well back. As always, Craig sized up the terrain, the wind and the way small hollows dipped and led to the river. Long experience had trained him automatically to find places where an ambush might be in the making. Laird marveled to himself that his partner missed so little of what went on around him.

The sudden whoops and yells of the hunters startled

the resting herd and animals burst from the timber like bees when their nest is kicked. Outriders did their work well; the buffalo came thundering right up the valley toward the waiting hunters. The white men's horses shook their wild manes and with ears pricked forward watched the coming herd, waiting for the pressure of heels in their flanks to start their own run.

Laird had his rifle ready and was just about to take off when Craig said sharply, "Hold it! Look up ahead, where those trees come up the draw from the river. See that? By God, there's men and ponies in there."

Laird didn't see anything out of the ordinary at first. Then a flash of white moved within his vision, and as he strained to see what it was, the outlines of strange men and their mounts came into focus.

Craig spoke again, quietly now. "They're waiting for the run to go by. There's going to be a hot fight here purty quick. I'll get to the chief. You hang back till you can get your shots in."

The white men's ponies jumped into their run. Craig angled ahead, kicking his heels into the flanks of his straining mount. Tense, Laird watched the scene ahead: the running herd, hunters driving close, bows bent, arrows ready. He heard whoops and hollers as released arrows struck the quarry. Others rode with lances high, arms pulled back, ponies leaning into the beasts alongside them. Laird could see the quick hard drive of the lance, the swerve of the wounded animal, as well as the wrenching twist of the hunter's arm as he tried to pull out the bloodied blade. Above all the rest rose the thundering roar of hooves beating the hardened ground.

Suddenly piercing war cries shrilled and the hunters turned. Now they were the hunted. Painted, feathered riders streamed from thickets along the river to seek their human quarry.

130

Laird saw at once what the strategy of the ambush had been. Let the hunters get past, then attack from behind. "In any fight you got to use your brains or somebody will knock 'em out." That's what Craig had said one evening that summer. "Kill one at a time. No matter how many or few, make sure you get one with every shot. That's one less to try to kill you."

Laird had his eye on a big fellow riding a paint pony. The brave was trying to get close to a Nez Perce hunter at the back of the herd. The red man was so hemmed in by running animals, so intent on surviving his dangerous predicament that he did not see potential death closing in behind him. Craig had once told Laird that Indians from farther back on the plains were so anxious to make a game out of fighting that they overlooked the possibility they could get killed doing it.

Laird urged his pony forward; hot to run, it brought him nearer and nearer to the man with the bow, whose arrow was already notched and ready. As Laird moved to raise his rifle, his quarry turned and saw him. With a sideways leap like that of a startled deer, the painted Indian pointed his bow toward Laird.

Laird's bullet smashed into the Indian's chest. Slipping from his pony, the red man fell to the mercy of the pounding buffalo hooves.

The Nez Perce who had been hemmed in turned at Laird's shot and saw both Laird and a riderless paint close behind him. Laird waved and pointed to another enemy rider. As the warrior came in from the side, the Nez Perce made ready to let his arrow fly. All the while the ponies mixed at a dead run with the running cows and calves that were trailing the main bunch.

Laird couldn't turn; there were too many beasts in the way of his pony. The Blackfoot brave with the rifle now had two enemies to face. Knowing the white man's gun was empty, he felt free to head for the red man. Laird eased his mount toward the action. He saw that the Nez Perce was reluctant to shoot until close enough for a sure hit. When he finally loosed his arrow, it hit the warrior but did not stop him. Laird edged over, found a way through the calves running directly behind the enemy and urged his pony closer. The Blackfoot saw trouble coming, but sure the white man's gun was useless, decided to blast him off his mount before taking on the Nez Perce with arrows. He raised his old fusee trade gun. When he touched it off, a blast of sound and powder almost knocked Laird from his pony.

The Blackfoot would try to finish him off; Laird knew that. Rifle and reins in one hand, he held his pistol low in his other, where the Blackfoot couldn't see it. Under him his pony labored, hot with excitement.

Three lengths away from the Blackfoot, Laird aimed his weapon and pulled the trigger. The heavy pistol jerked upward as the Indian, hit by the slug, dropped his empty gun and fell off his mount.

Laird's pony leaped over the fallen rider, almost tripping on the warrior's frantic horse. As the pony swerved it stumbled. Laird went sprawling, losing both his weapons in the fall.

As the last of the buffalo spread out ahead, Laird made it to his feet only to find that the Blackfoot brave was still alive and struggling to pry his knife loose from his belt.

Laird remembered Craig's words: "If you cripple or wound one, don't stop to think about it. Just get in and finish him off."

Laird pulled his own knife. Then he ran to where the doomed man struggled, his face contorted with hate. The knife slipped easily into the Indian's belly; instantly the Blackfoot was dead.

Laird had loaded his rifle and primed his pistol by the time the wounded Night Owl came by to return his pony. Blood ran down Night Owl's side, his entire arm reddened with it, but he grinned and signed Laird to scalp the Blackfoot. Laird shook his head no and pointed to Night Owl, who slid off his pony and with one quick jerk of his knife sliced off the Blackfoot's top hair. After thrusting it aloft with a triumphant yell, he hung it dripping from his belt.

While investigating the extent of Night Owl's injuries, Laird discovered that the slug had passed through the flesh of the Indian's upper chest and arm without touching bone. All during Laird's makeshift repairs Night Owl kept urging him toward the fight.

Quickly remounting, the two men galloped toward the battle. They reached the first body, that of a Nez Perce, then two Blackfoot and a dead cow. A crippled bull buffalo stood head down. Blood was dripping from his nose, arrows driven deep into his side. Nearby were two more bodies, another cow and a downed pony, its side ripped open by a horn. A crippled pony limped toward the river. And there were two more dead men, one a Blackfoot, the other a Nez Perce, both scalped.

The herd had moved on. As the two riders reached the fighting they separated. Laird, rifle loaded, took off to the left. He saw Craig's bay pony standing and concluded that Craig must be either down or a member of the group that was fighting hand to hand. Suddenly the melee broke up. Blackfoot riders headed for the river, angling back the way they had come.

Laird and Night Owl swerved their ponies. Seeing that there would hardly be time to get a shot in before the enemy riders hit the cottonwoods along the river, Laird pulled up and leaped from his mount. With ramrod steadying his rifle for a long shot, he held it a little high and touched off the trigger. A rider and his pony went down. Night Owl raced on toward the victim.

Mounting again, Laird rode toward the fallen warrior. As other riders came in from the battle site, Night Owl raised his hatchet and clubbed down. By the time Laird arrived he had attached another scalp to his belt. Craig rode up wearing a grin.

"Get your man?" he asked.

Laird held up two fingers.

Craig nodded. "I got a couple of my own. We lost some men. Maybe we were lucky at that."

"Night Owl will be short of strength in one side for a while," Laird said.

"He's lucky to be living," Craig commented, pausing to clear his thoughts. "The braves will pick up scalps and trophies and fix up their wounded. Let's you and me head for camp for the women and more men. Them Blackfoot raiders will be hot to even the score."

Meat and hides were taken back to camp and guards stayed alert. Until they were camping at Big Hole Basin again, it was difficult for the men to feel secure. Even then, Craig couldn't relax.

"Laird," he said at the campfire, "these people think they're far enough away. They figure they're safe on home grounds. But we're going to keep our own guard at night. Take turns. And we'll do it until we get to the hot springs on the Bitterroot River."

"You really think they'd trail us this far just to get even?"

"If you figure on living with Indians you got to begin to think like one. It ain't so much getting even as getting back their honor—if there is such a thing. They lost at least ten men and some ponies plus a few weapons, but their greatest loss was the fact they got whipped. The Blackfoot, since some time back, started getting proud of being fighters like the Sioux and other tribes farther east and south. Trading had always been necessary but raiding was more fun. The Jesus people won't find that attitude easy to overcome. For generations the Nez Perce have existed under tough conditions. The ones alive today didn't just hatch out. They're all trained to survive. If the white men hadn't come west with new weapons and different ways, they'd continue to survive. What changed the course of the fight yesterday was you and me and our four guns.''

''I see what you mean.''

''And there's a little more than that,'' Craig went on. ''I got old Grey Coyote to call off the chase and look out for the camp and what we had there. The young hotheads was all for following up. But it ain't over, not until that bunch get their honor back and a little more, to prove they can whip any bunch of fish-eaters that come into their country to hunt the buffalo they consider rightly theirs.''

Chapter 16

Laird didn't look forward to the responsibility of listening to little night sounds and wondering if some scalp-hungry warrior was sneaking up. But he and Craig kept the night watches until they reached the hot springs on the Lolo Trail. There they laid over a day to wash, soak in the mineral springs and relax. The smell of the hot sulphur water was hard for Laird to take at first, but as the heat soaked into his body, the trapper's tension eased and he talked of winter plans.

"If I was alone or with Doc Newell, we would have set out long before now and already be trapping in the country where we're headed," Craig said. "But I think we'll profit by traveling along with this bunch and getting acquainted. Fur ain't prime yet, but when you trap enough hides to make a pack you can't be picky. If we plan things close to right we'll get a good haul and pay our way to the next big hooraw back in the Green River country."

"Do you think we'll be taking our women or going there alone?"

"Hell, boy, how does anyone know? Just ride along with things and see what happens. There's some big changes coming, that I know. Those missionaries will bring 'em on. They have some farfetched ideas on how they can quit these old Indians of their wild and evil ways. I sure don't hanker for the job they cut out for themselves.''

"Bill, I never thought I would see the day when any Indians would be so anxious as the Nez Perce are to get a preacher and the Bible to come and live with them.''

"They'll feel that way until the newness wears off. That'll take awhile. I don't expect trouble for some time. Whitman, being a doctor, will do right well till he can't heal somebody or makes a mistake. The medicine men or shamans don't get themselves that far out on a limb when they got to cure somebody of what ails 'em. Clark sure started something when that old chief got over his aches and pains enough to rise and walk. That made all the old shamans want in on the act too. But what the Indians are really after is the power to get stronger than their enemies. That means being able to make tools, gunpowder, rifles and everything they have to trade to get now.''

"You don't seem too optimistic about the future.''

"Things are going to happen here none of us sees coming. The Indians have no idea of how many white men there are or how big this nation is—or any other country either. Hell, even you and me only have the glimmer of an idea. Me, Doc, Bridger, Kit Carson been parading up and down and across this country—old Joe Walker, too—for nigh onto twenty year, and we still got a lot to learn.''

Laird knew he had been fortunate to fall in with Bill Craig and to have found Sun-in-the-Morning to share his life. Laird could understand now most of what the Nez Perce said if he watched their faces and body movements carefully enough. Signs conveyed the rest. Night talk helped. Hawk Flying and Suni chattered together around the tepee. When they wanted Laird to understand they slowed their speech so he could pick up enough words to follow.

It had been difficult for Laird to share a lodge with Craig and his woman. But Craig and his sense of humor changed that slowly. One evening Laird was provoked almost to the point of cursing Craig. It was still light in the lodge and he and Suni lay on the buffalo robe under a light blanket. Without warning Craig came and jerked the covering off. "Let's have a better look at your prize, Laird," he said. "I want to see all of her."

Suni grabbed for the blanket but Craig had whipped it across the tepee out of reach. Completely nude, she jumped to her feet and raced to get it. Laird's anger ebbed as he saw her profile: braids falling as she stooped, the graceful curve of her breast, thighs and slim legs firm beneath the rounded line of her arched back. His mind recorded how lovely she was.

Suni stood holding the blanket in front of her. She was angry, but the older man persisted. In her language, he told her, "Suni, drop the blanket. Let us see your body; you are beautiful. You are well named, Sun-in-the-Morning. Like the sun that warms the land, you warm your man's heart and make him happy. When you grow old and wrinkled and can no longer dance, he will not notice. Always he will remember you as he sees you now."

Craig left the lodge and pulled the flap closed behind him. Suni had dropped the blanket to the floor. A film of sunlight from the tepee's smoke hole illuminated every lovely inch of her. Laird thought he would never see anything more beautiful than her figure bathed in its glow.

The ancient trail they took wound up the creek to the crest of the Divide, now shrouded in fog. Rain had fallen the night before. The leaders had grown to manhood knowing all the turns and twists and ups and downs. On the way up from the countryside thousands of feet below, they followed special trails to avoid the cliffs and rock slides. Sharp upthrusts of jagged rock and breakoffs where a pony could fall forced them to a slow pace. Knowing which camping places lay ahead determined the miles they traveled each day.

For the first time since they had left the Green River Rendezvous, Laird made camp in drizzling rain and fog. Hawk and Suni, with Laird's help, soon made a shelter for the night while Craig unpacked and cared for the ponies. No guard or watch this night, for the tribe was on home ground at last. Fog and rain masked almost every form. But nearby lodgepole pines stood thick as dog hair in places, their downed trunks lying crisscrossed on the trail. Craig joined the leaders. Working with hand axes, they cleared the timber so the loaded ponies could pass.

Next day they descended into fir and hemlock forest and crossed down off the ridge to a flat along a stream that plunged to the river far below. At another camping place, giant cedars grew.

Laird was surprised to see several lean-to shelters. Most were made from poles covered with long strips of cedar bark. One, constructed probably by an enterprising squaw, was built from split cedar slabs. Someone had stored dry firewood. There were mainly pitch-pine sticks, some cedar and a large supply of dry bark. Heavy pieces broken up in chunks were mostly of Douglas fir. Fir burned like coal and gave off steady heat; the hot bed of coals it left was fine for roasting meat and boiling the kettle. Laird was curious about this campsite.

"The tribe comes up here to hunt sometimes," Craig explained. "They get goats and elk. Bear too, if the bear don't see 'em first. This is grizzly country. The Nez Perce like those fellers' teeth, claws and hides. You ain't seen one yet. He comes at you, teeth chomping and roaring mad. You'll have dreams for weeks that will wake you up sweating and trying to call for help. Just the thought of an old grizzly makes me glad guns and powder was invented and I've got 'em to use."

140

"Have you ever killed one, Bill?"

"Yeah, a few. Once it was him or me. I figured right quick I'd rather have it be him. You heard Meek tell Mrs. Whitman about his tussle with the grizzly? Well, that was purty much the truth. I seen the gun; it had claw marks on the butt. Joe got his fingers bit bad, but he killed the bear."

The two men stood quietly under the trees and watched Hawk Flying and Suni at the fire. "How do you like living with our Indian friends?" Craig asked.

"I never dreamed it could be like this," Laird answered. "I hope it continues as long as I live in the West."

"Take it while it's good, boy. Bad times will come soon enough. You notice the women say nothing about tomorrow. They've lived enough and learned enough to take things as they come."

"Raised as I was," Laird mused, "I still always think of what might lie ahead."

"Doc Newell and me talked about that part some time back. We'll meet up with him again after he gets through his deal with Bent. Doc ain't cut out for trading with them other tribes. I expect him to join up with us, find a good-looking Nez Perce girl and settle down somewheres in the country we're headed for. I'll probably do the same."

"Will you keep Hawk as your wife?"

"Hell, Laird, I can't say I will. She knows it. I ain't yet found the one I can't do without. When I do, maybe I'll marry her and raise a flock of mixed-blood kids. Any man worth his salt wants his blood to live after him. That's not only human nature—it's nature itself." Craig turned, restless. "Let's get fed, smoke a bit and see how warm our blankets and robes are going to be tonight. By tomorrow we might be down off this hill and catching fur. Then

141

you'll begin to see the country where we'll be spending time.''

After a night spent at the cedar-flat camp, the group dropped below the clouds. From an open spot on a ridge they saw a vast expanse of mountains and valleys covered with timber, all dipping gradually, then undulating to the west, where far away lay wide plateaus and grasslands.

Craig pointed. ''That's where we're headed. Another day and these people will be home. I don't know just where the hunters will camp for the winter, but down in the valleys there's places to set up lodges, good grass for the pony herds and rivers for fish. When the snow comes, game drops down close, where they can get it. The Nez Perce do lots of visiting during the winter. They may hole up and take it easy in bad weather, but when there's a good spell they're out playing games and trading back and forth.''

Laird breathed deep. ''It's big country, isn't it?''

''Boy, it's a lot bigger than what we can see from here. You'll see more next summer. We can trap till the freeze-up and after that's when we hit open water at the dams. The beaver hole up in cold weather but in breaks when it's warm or with a wind from the west, they come out to work the sides of the ponds for fresh bark. Whatever they've stored in the river or pond bottoms they use only in emergency. We can get beaver hides in every trap twice a day. That's where the women will help, working on the hides and making hoops to string 'em on.''

Laird saw why the campground along the river in the wide valley had been chosen. On the open hillsides was forage for thousands of ponies. Fish swam in the clear streams and wood grew close at hand for the fires. Days were mild, but nights had become cold; skim ice formed on the little ponds and disappeared during the day. There were twenty lodges in the village. When they reached the river crossing, the far bank came alive with people who paddled across to help the travelers home. As Laird helped unload the ponies and got ready to swim them across, he looked for girls to compare with Suni.

On the other shore she was embraced by two girls who started chattering immediately. He recalled that Craig had told him not to be too curious. "Just act like you ain't interested. The Indian women are curious about white men because they hardly ever see any. They want to find out what we're like, so don't worry, they'll do the exploring. It gets like kind of a game to see what they'll do to get acquainted."

Hawk Flying had found a spot to set up camp. She led the way, leading Craig's ponies. As soon as he nodded his approval of her choice the work began. Craig spoke to Laird. "Let 'em have at it. By the time we come back we can move in."

Laird saw that the two new girls and another woman were helping put up the poles and drape them with hides. Suni ordered the helpers to take care of the ponies. In the meantime Laird and Craig went to look over the village and be stared at.

"Tonight we eat with the camp," Craig told him. "We've brought meat. The camp furnishes the fish and everything else. Then it'll be storytelling time, the account of the hunt and the fight with the Blackfoot. So much has happened it can't all be told in one night's session. The story's told like part of their history; it teaches the young fellers how things are done. We played a little part in that go-round with the Blackfoot and we'll be pointed out. We can set back and look wise or raise up and give the details."

"I'll follow your lead, Bill. I'm no play-actor."

"Don't make up your mind yet, boy. You may want

to join in. Remember, your girl will be watching. She's already been bragging on what a big man you are.''

''The hell she has!''

''It's their way.'' Craig chuckled. ''She took up with you because you're rich, handsome, a big white man, enemy killer and trader.''

''I never thought of it that way. What about Hawk Flying?''

''Same thing. She wants security, pleasure and a chance to get more than she'd have with a man of the tribe.''

''You make the women sound mercenary,'' Laird objected. ''Isn't there any place for love as white people know it?''

''Sure there is. Didn't you see the grief of that woman who lost her man at the river fight? She cut her arms and chopped off a finger sorrowing. If that ain't love, I don't know what is.''

''Maybe I expected something different,'' Laird observed. ''I keep wondering about Suni, how I might have to leave her. Would she just go to another man's lodge and take up with him?''

''Laird, you fret too much. Just take it as it comes. If you die she weeps. If she dies you grieve for her. It'll be the same if you have to leave her, except you'll both be alive. You can't get too involved with what happens between you. Settle down, boy, and enjoy what you have.''

That night Laird sat back and watched the celebration; it was like an amateur play or pageant he might have seen at home. The drums set the pace, the dancers chanting to work up the audience as well as the players. Then came the pantomime of the hunt and the battle with the Blackfoot. The chief looked at Craig as though surprised at what he'd heard. Then Craig rode in, pointed his gun and fired, all in pantomime. Grey Wolf, acting as hunter, then gestured to

Laird, who moved into the circle, showed how first he had fired his rifle and killed one man, then had ridden up and downed the other with his pistol. The loud cries of "Ho, ho, ho!" increased as the drama developed.

Next morning no one in camp hurried to get up. Laird lay under the robes, Suni snuggled against him, and awakened only when Hawk Flying arose and went outside for a few minutes, then came back to kindle the fire from coals still red under the ashes. Once the flames leaped up, she slipped back into bed with Craig.

"There'll be quite a lot of this laying in after we get our hides caught and the winter sets down," Craig commented. "How do you like it?"

"Better than I ever thought I would. Is this custom the reason you picked this tribe to live with?"

"I guess you can say it's one reason. Wait till you see more of this country. That'll be another reason. Maybe a third's that things are apt to be peaceful among these Indians longer than any other I know of. The Nez Perce are intelligent, peaceful people. When they've gone to war, it was because they was attacked or their ponies stolen. Then watch out for 'em. They can work themselves up into real fighters."

"I saw a little of that back on the Beaverhead," Laird agreed. "An arrow one man shot went clear through a cow. I never would have believed anyone could have that kind of strength with a bow."

"Take a good look at the bows," Craig advised. "They're made of mountain sheep horns steamed and shaped. Best short bows of all the tribes. To get one such bow in trade takes ten good ponies. Those miserable, scalp-hungry Blackfoot jumped us for ponies, bows and meat. Lucky you and me had guns and bullets."

Under the robes Sun-in-the-Morning's soft hand had

been exploring Laird's body. He tried with great difficulty to concentrate on what Craig was saying next.

"We'll probably start trapping beaver tomorrow and take it easy today," Craig commented. "The men here will have a purty good idea where we can do some good. We helped knock off them Blackfoot, so they'll put themselves out for us. Guess I'll roll out and get to talking it over. Say, I ain't seen you write anything lately. It might be a good time to do that afore we hit out for the beaver dams."

Laird watched Craig get up and pull on his buckskins over the shirt he had on. Next he added his fur cap and knee-high moccasins. For a moment Hawk Flying lay still. Then, as Laird watched, she slowly got out of bed. Naked and exposed fully to the watching man, she found her shirt, raised her arms and slipped it over her head. Laird could not help comparing her full-breasted, sturdier body with the slimmer figure of the girl who now lay beside him.

Hawk Flying smiled at Laird. Then she pulled on her moccasins and went outside, pulling the flap closed. By this time fully aroused by Suni's touch, Laird wrapped the lovely maiden in his arms at once and hungrily made love to her.

Chapter 17

When he finally got dressed and went out to see what was happening in the camp, he found it alive with activity. Children played in the sun, men gathered where their talk would be uninterrupted and the women were busy with hides and work on moccasins and shirts. Craig was involved in earnest conversation with a group of men; their hand and arm signs told Laird they were discussing where to trap.

"Here it is, Laird," Craig said, dropping to his knees and pointing to a map drawn in the dirt. "We can trap this side stream. A few miles up there's a whole series of beaver workings—never trapped, far as anybody knows. When Doc and me was here afore, we never touched it. Found plenty closer in. The spot's a day's ride from here. I think we better move in and try it."

"How many hides might be there to take?"

"A hundred or more to start with. Depends on how close we trap. When I begin to find too many empties I move on, because time gets short and we can't stay for a few when there's more farther on. After we trap this creek, we climb over the ridge and trap another down to the river. We should have a purty good haul by then, and the weather will be getting close to freeze-up."

"When do we go?"

"In the morning. I'll tell the women. If they want to go, just watch 'em gather up plunder. We'll need dried salmon, jerky and lots of camas flour. You might be smart to trade for a couple more pair of moccasins and some mitts lined with rabbit fur. You'll need 'em."

When Laird got back to the lodge he found the two women already sorting out various articles of clothing. On his and Suni's robes lay moccasins, elk-hide shirts, mittens and a wolfskin cap.

Suni urged him to try the clothing on and nodded enthusiastically whenever something fit perfectly.

"How did you know we were going?" he asked her.

Suni explained that she knew the time for trapping was before the ice came. She told Laird that Hawk Flying had made trades for the clothing.

Well, this is how it is done, Laird thought. Craig brushed aside the flaps and came in grinning.

"Suni tell you where she's going?" he asked.

"I didn't ask and she didn't say," Laird answered. "She just fitted me out. Said you told Hawk Flying to trade off some of our Blackfoot plunder for all this."

"We won't need those ponies nor the old fusees. They belonged to us and was ours to trade by their reasoning. The women have a purty good idea what we'll need and it takes that part of it off our minds. Two things to keep your eyes on, though: your powder and lead. It'll be a long time afore we get more. If you run out in this country, your guns are useless."

Laird went off by himself to sit and think. He wanted to compose a letter to his uncle and what he had written in his journal reminded him of events that seemed important.

* * *

Nez Perce Legend

Dear Sir:

We are in the winter homeland of the Nez Perce. Mr. Craig and I move to our new trapping grounds tomorrow. Our two female companions are packing to go with us. We will trap until the final freeze-up comes, then return to spend the rest of the winter with the tribe here on the River Clearwater. Where we are camped there are miles of uncounted, unsurveyed grasslands that cover a vast plateau. Craig says this area is the home of at least five or six Indian tribes. I will ask him to draw me a map of some sort soon; in that way we can both get oriented.

Laird

Craig, Laird and their female companions left the Nez Perce village next morning, their pack ponies carrying equipment and food along with traps and extra clothing. Craig led the way; Laird followed and the two women herded the pack animals along the trail. They climbed from river bottoms across open grasslands and reached a plateau to the east. There they saw great yellow pines, miles of golden-barked trunks. Fir and lodgepole intermingled. Cedar jungles mixed with hemlock and vine maple. As they crossed meandering streams, Laird saw alder, willow and patches of thick shrubs he took to be wild currant and gooseberry.

Signs of a trail had long disappeared. Craig picked his route by his hunter's instinct. Winding here and there, dodging thickets, fording damp little brooks, circling great cedar and fir windfalls, startling elk and deer, they finally topped a slight ridge of ground and found a well-used elk trail running alongside. Laird could smell the musky odor where bulls had rubbed, then wet the ground. Their bugling could be heard from daylight until after dark; it was September and the rut was on. Off down a little hill, beaver workings were everywhere.

Looking over the flats, Laird saw the ripples made by swimming beavers. Some were out on their dams. While Laird watched them, Craig looked for a campsite that would get first morning light and sun throughout the day. A few ducks flew overhead, disturbed by something.

"You ever kill a moose?"

Startled, Laird reponded, "No, are there moose up here?"

"Just beyond that clump of willow brush there's a cow and calf." Craig turned Laird around and pointed. "We'll leave the ponies here and take our guns up to where we can get an open shot. It'll be the best meat we'll have this winter."

"You want me to drop the cow there where she is?"

"Hell, no. She's in water up to her belly. We'd be all day getting her out of there. If you shoot her through the lungs she'll get out to solid ground. You ready?"

It turned out just as Craig said it would. At Laird's shot the cow reared, swung around and plunged through the water and mud, spraying it around her in great bursts as she made for shore. Behind her came the frightened long-legged calf, big ears pointed straight ahead.

When the calf reached the shore, Craig's shot knocked it down and for a moment Laird felt queasy, almost sad. "The cow won't go far," Craig said as they reloaded. "She'll lay down and wait for the calf."

Suni and Hawk Flying made camp. The two men skinned and cut up the moose carcasses and made ready to set out traps next morning. Laird was impatient; he wanted to start that evening, but Craig held him back.

"Plenty of time," he advised. "We'll be out there all day just taking beaver, resetting traps, making our stretching hoops. You'll get your fill of the smell of alder and beaver grease by nighttime tomorrow.''

The next day each man set six traps. By noon each trap held a beaver, drowned where it was caught. After traps had been reset, Laird, having learned a little about how it was done, began to work alone. Craig told him that when making sets in shallow water he must check them often because a beaver would sometimes try to free itself by chewing off its own leg. The best way to make water sets was to use a slip pole or large rock fastened to the trap to give it weight.

The job of skinning and stretching the skins was shared by everyone. Hawk Flying ran the camp; Suni helped. Both women saw to the ponies and got wood for the fires. Craig and Laird had already cut down a dead fir, but mostly the women used limbs and thick pieces of bark to feed the flames.

Indian summer came and was gone with the fall rains. Soon heavy white frost lay on the ground and ice collected on the edges of the water; when they skimmed over, the ducks left. The elks' bugling had tapered off and only occasionally a young bull squeaker could be heard trying out his voice in an imitation challenge. The trapping party moved camp into new country and the furs piled up. Laird's clothing became slick with beaver grease.

Time passed quickly. One day crowded the next, with little difference between them except that each seemed shorter and colder. Sometimes snow fell, but where the men trapped along high-country streams and ponds, its depth was never more than a few inches. On overcast days with no perceptible air movement, everything was held in readiness for a quick departure.

Laird checked his traps and headed for camp with his

load of beaver. Once as he approached he saw the women loading up while Craig hurriedly skinned his catch.

"Drop your load, Laird, and go pick up your traps. A weather change's coming. We better get to lower country. See all the meat moving downhill? When they move down, so do we."

"I can be back in an hour. Will that be time enough?"

"Go get them traps. If you can't skin the beaver here, we'll tie 'em on whole. In the meantime we pack. We'll chew jerky on the way and hope we hit open country by dark or afore the storm hits."

As he trotted the line picking up traps, Laird saw game moving west, seeking lower ground. There was no panic but all moved deliberately in the same direction. The one fresh-caught beaver and the empty traps made a light load. By the time Laird returned the rest of the party had packed up.

Picking a well-used game trail, Craig took the lead and the rest trailed behind with the pack ponies. Traveling ahead was a herd of elk. Occasionally deer stood still to watch the travelers go by, moving onto the trail once the human beings had passed. There was no sign of wind but a few flakes of snow drifted lazily down. On flats or gentle slopes where the going was good, Craig kicked his pony into a trot and Laird sensed his eagerness to reach safe harbor. Before they reached open country, snow was falling heavily.

"Think we should keep on going down or make camp and wait?" Craig queried.

None of them had been over this stretch of country before, so all shared in the decision. Hawk Flying, seeing plenty of wood as well as trees to break the wind, wanted to camp where they were. Suni wanted to go on. She said if they could reach open slopes there would be feed for the ponies. And if they could manage to get down off the bench to the river bottoms and camp there, the snow wouldn't bother them even if it lasted for weeks. There the ponies could feed on the willows after snow covered the grass. Laird contributed little.

"We'll camp here," Craig decided. "Getting off the hill in a snowstorm with loaded ponies would be tricky even in daylight. Pick your spot, Hawk," he went on. "It'll be dark in an hour. We'll hole up till the storm breaks."

The two men cut poles for the lean-to while the women pulled off packs and tied the ponies under scant cover of bare-limbed trees. Snow fell thick and fast. Hide coverings, stretched over the poles and down the sides, made a shelter to hold the sleeping robes. When Craig struck sparks into punk and the fine frizzled shavings Suni and Hawk had gathered, a glimmer of fire appeared. Soon the blaze caught larger pieces. This site would be home not only for the night but perhaps for days to come.

When the ponies had been checked to make sure they would not break loose, Craig squatted under the shelter's overhang. "We might have been purty smart to stop here," he said. "We've got grub and a couple of packs of fur and it's a good place to camp with good company. Laird, the talk time I been telling you about has arrived. Nothing to do but hole up, feed the fire and lay in the robes. The ponies will get a mite gaunt-looking, but until they have to start eating each other's tails and manes they'll stay in purty good shape."

Laird lay back on the soft piles of robes while Hawk busied herself sorting out things to cook and Suni crouched down and slivered wood for the next fire. He had noticed that everyone in the Nez Perce tribe stayed well prepared for anything that might happen. Always the women stocked plenty of food and wood. They were forever patching

153

garments, making new moccasins and shirts and in spare moments decorating whatever they had made.

Craig and Hawk Flying went scouting during some of the days they were snowbound. Luckily, they found a patch of alder and willows where their hungry ponies could feed.

Laird made the most of the time he spent inside the dimly lit shelter snuggling Suni against him in the fire's warmth and questioning everyone about the Indian ways.

Craig knew of Lewis and Clark and the young Indian woman who traveled with them to interpret. Hawk Flying told how her people had gone with Lewis and Clark to the coast and described the place Sacajawea had been raised as a girl.

"She was a Shoshone, Laird," Hawk explained. "Some call Shoshone Snakes. They live on upper Snake River about Fort Hall. You remember fork in trail after we left the fort to head for buffalo country? If we'd take north fork over a little pass down a valley into upper Salmon country, we see where Sacajawea's people made their camp."

Craig talked about the Blackfoot as he knew them. "I've run into those people here and there in their own country," he began. "To me they're the trickiest of the lot.

"The Blackfoot come down from the north a long time ago. Since the time they got ponies and a few guns they began spreading out fast, but they never crossed into Snake country till lately. Now they come to raise hell and hair. Some of these old trappers who worked their way up to Canada and met Frenchmen there told me what the Hudson's Bay people say about the Blackfoot.

"They come out of the bush country, where they hunted buffalo that lived in the timber," Craig continued. "Then they got guns from Hudson's Bay, raided farther south and got horses. One thing different about the Blackfoot, they always play for keeps. They seem to breed faster than other Indian tribes; either that or they're healthier. There will be plenty trouble from 'em unless they're slowed down." Craig sighed. "I don't see the missionaries doing it."

"What do you see in the future for mixed-blood children?" Laird asked.

"Us who have lived with Indians and Mex have talked about that. Most of the men don't give a damn. I'd say Walker, Sublette, me, maybe a few more look at it differently. But what can we do about it? Here we are, holed up in this country where it takes two to keep each other alive.

"Anyway, we ain't looking too far ahead, just sticking here where we can survive as long as food holds out. We can't travel because we're blind and helpless in snow. Once it clears, we can start out again from one point to another."

Laird and the two Indian women watched Craig's expression, his bearded face solemn in the firelight. Craig sighed, then kept on talking.

"Remember them lodgepole jungles we come through on the trail last fall? Well, there's one hell of a lot of 'em in this country. You get in one in fog or rain and you'll never get out unless you have the right savvy. Now what I'm leading up to is something me and Doc Newell argued about last year. Where do we go from here? Both of us would like to see the end of this running all over looking for hides to skin and swap. It ain't such a great adventure anymore. We've seen a lot of country, hair skinned off a few of our friends. We both decided the end's coming."

The trapper turned to Laird. "Boy, I come back up here to try out these Nez Perce people, see how they live. If they turn out good and I like the country well as I did last year, I might stake me out a claim.

"Only reason Doc ain't with us is Bent made him a good deal to open new country and cut him in on the profits. Bent's sharp but he's fair, and he'll let Doc get a taste of honey just to whet his appetite. I believe that when it's all set up, he'll ease Doc out. That's the way it's done. But if I send word this here's the good way to go, Doc and others'll follow."

Suni stirred the fire, then returned to Laird's side.

"What about the missionaries' work?" Laird asked.

"Oh, us old boys have sized up Whitman and Spalding," Craig bragged. "They'll lead us and the Indians will follow along but I look for trouble with both of them. They're too starry-eyed and sure of their ways.

"In the past," Craig went on, "the old chiefs listened to their shamans for years till one made a mistake and got 'em in a mess. Then the shaman was done for, sometimes killed right on the spot. The same thing could happen to the missionaries."

At the questioning look on Laird's face, Craig explained, "Don't mistake me; there could be a future in what they're doing. But they aim too high and when they fall they'll have to start over again or find somebody to take over. I can guess your next question, Laird. How long will it be before these men get their comeuppance? It could happen any time, I imagine, but I give 'em two, three years before the chiefs and shamans wake up to the fact they're losing their grip over their people. I hope I'll be squatted someplace by then so I can ride it out."

Laird sat pondering his own future, at that moment in no mood to think very far ahead. Good companions, food, shelter. When the storm was over they would move to lower country and be back once again with friendly Nez Perce people.

Chapter 18

Laird was developing increasing respect for William Craig. Here was a man he would like for a neighbor if he ever settled in the West.

"I suppose you've thought about where you might settle in," he said, moving closer to the fire.

"In a way, yes," Craig replied. "If the company down below looks good and we winter like the old people say, it might well be down there in Butterfly Valley."

"Butterfly Valley? Is that what their village place is called?"

"That's right. Butterfly Valley, or Lapwai. Wait till you see the hillsides in bloom in the spring. I seen flowers wild on the prairies; I seen the poppies in California after the first rain hit the deserts; I seen sights along up the big river; but to me, this country for a hundred miles north and south and west is more beautiful than anything I've seen before. Yellow, blue and red hillsides. Benches above the rivers thick with miles of waving grass and flowers. Butterflies of every kind, big ones, little ones, all looking for whatever they can get from the blossoms. Bumblebees and hornets aplenty—but no honeybees, though. Someone told me once that all the honeybees was brought into the nation from outside. That must have been real early, because we had bees back where I come from. If I settle out here, I sure as hell will get me a swarm. This is a honey-making country if ever I saw one. Wish we had some now.''

"But how would you support yourself and a family?'' Laird questioned. "You can't trap forever, you admit that. Where could you sell what you'd raise?''

"Doc thought of that,'' Craig replied. "When Whitman brought that little wagon along and it got made into a cart, he and Meek introduced an idea that will work. People, especially women, ain't going to move much unless it's on wheels. When that long-ago feller found out he could roll a round rock better than a flat one, and hooked two together, he started something.

"The Nez Perce are smarter than a lot of the other tribes. When they first seen horses, they got the idea quick and begun to raise 'em. They not only raise 'em, they breed better ones, cutting most of the young studs, keeping the best for breeding. Wait till you see some of the young stuff they're training.

"After the tribe got horses they used 'em like they did dogs, only the ponies could pull more. Didn't take long afore they begun looking at that wagon. First thing you know, they begun talking about how much wagons could haul in some parts of their country. Whitman and Meek didn't know it, but the Nez Perce wanted to pull that blasted thing clear to Fort Hall too, and on down to Fort Boise, just to get it to their country.

"Now, let me finish. Whitman's smart, but Spalding sees further ahead in spite of his ornery ways. He's talked of farms, growing crops, raising grain and stock. He wants a grain mill and a sawmill. And that's what I been talking about, things to feed people and things to build with. Once folks back in the States hear there's free land and a wagon can fetch them and their women too, they'll come swarming like those bees I want to get. That's when I can make a living on the land I've staked out and settled on.''

"You've told us everything except when that will be, Craig. How long before you can pick your place and settle down?"

"I think in four, five years we'll see people moving in. I'm already looking for a place. Where last year I was just thinking about it, now it's more a possibility. But I got to see how the missionaries get along with the Indians and how they'll grow crops. If they grow what I think they can and at the same time get the local Indians settled down to where we ain't afraid of having white families scalped and butchered, then I'll plant my feet and my land."

The storm stopped late on the fourth day. Craig looked at the bright western sky. "It looks like we can move out of here in the morning," he said, "afore more cold weather comes. Tomorrow night I hope we can set up camp low enough so the ponies can dig for grass."

The next day longhaired ponies wallowed through snow just above their knees heading west toward open country. The Indian women knew exactly where they were and how to find a route out of the high lands. From the first opening in the trees Laird saw the lower, pinecovered lands and grass fields. Where in this vast land would a person find a certain place where he could put his axe to a tree and say, "This is the place for me"? Perhaps when he saw Craig's choice he would like it too, and want to settle there. Sun-in-the-Morning would have some ideas about that, he thought, for he had no other woman in his mind for marrying than this Nez Perce girl. If he knew anything about love at all, he was in love with Suni and would continue to be.

The loaded ponies made headway down the slopes, often stumbling into trees, squatting to slide on their haunches or sinking into holes blanketed with snow. Out of the hills there was some relief. Snow cover dropped to less than a foot. The four companions began to see game trails and the first of the elk that had drifted down before the storm. Lower still they saw mule deer, and when they hit the creek and river bottoms, white-tailed deer were feeding in willow and alder brush. Laird expected Craig to kill one for fresh meat but the trapper kept his pony traveling steadily toward the lower country where Hawk Flying and Suni had said they would reach the first of the villages.

In late afternoon they were welcomed by people in Chief James' little encampment. The villagers were curious to see the white trappers and their women. James himself came out to ask them to stay and visit. He knew Craig before and wanted to exchange news with him. While the women unpacked and set up their lodge, Craig and Laird went to visit with the Chief and a few of his men.

The hunters were interested in the trappers' luck, where game was wintering and if they had seen bear. Craig told them they had seen no sign of grizzly but that several black bears kept eating the carcasses of the beaver. Craig had killed one of them and brought the hide and grease back with him. These Nez Perce had already collected some furs and would get more when a crust formed on the snow. Then they would trap along the ridges for marten and get lynx with their snare sets. Rabbits were plentiful, they knew, and that meant more cats to prey on them.

When Craig and Laird left James' lodge they went back to their own, now up, a fire burning inside and the packs off and cared for. Hawk Flying and Suni had been helped by other women, who questioned them about the two white men and about how they had treated their Nez

Perce companions. Evidently all reports to the curious squaws were favorable, because after that exchange of information, Craig and Laird were shown great respect by the people in James' village.

Often during Craig's stay at Lapwai, Chief James asked his opinion about what might be happening in times to come.

"White men will live in this country with their families," Craig predicted. "Your children will need to learn their ways. With Eliza Spalding's help they are already learning to read and write the white man's language."

"That is good, I know that," James replied. "But the black-robed missionaries say not to kill, but to love our enemies. How can we love the Blackfoot? They steal our women and our horses; they take scalps and do many other bad things."

James smoked slowly, content to talk, also to listen. His concerns were ones Craig had heard many times before. "The Nez Perce," the chief went on, "are an old people. We have lived here a long time and get along with our friends and those who live near us. But if our neighbors steal we punish. If they kill we hunt them down and kill them too. When the Blackfoot come, if we do not fight we die."

Craig was scarcely able to counter this view without taking sides, and to do so would be to stir up trouble that was bound to come soon enough on its own.

"The Nez Perce are a peaceful people," Craig began after much thought. "I have lived with you and you have taught me much. The Flatheads and the Shoshone are peaceful too, but all your young men are warlike now, for they must fight the Blackfoot and sometimes the Crow. Once the Nez Perce lived only on the rivers and ate fish and camas. Then the horse came and the Nez Perce could go far to hunt the buffalo. The Blackfoot did not want you to hunt their food so they fought you.''

''Ah,'' the chief interrupted, ''but the Blackfoot came from the north and stole the horse from us and from the Shoshone and he had guns to kill us. Now we need guns to kill the Blackfoot and other bad Indians who steal our horses and take our women. The trappers here do not trade us guns, but the Blackfoot get guns from trappers to the north and the French traders give them guns and powder and bullets. Why do not your people give us guns?''

''James, traders who do not know you think that your young men will use the guns against the white man. They believe that if they give you guns, they will have to give your enemies guns too, and war will go on all the time. Someday you will have the weapons that you want, but only when you have the white man's tools and live as white men do. I want to stay and live here with peaceful people, but I cannot give you guns nor get people to give them to you.''

''Craig, you are a good man,'' James offered. ''Your friend is good. You stay with us. We will always be friends.''

Chapter 19

While the trappers secured furs in the upper country, the missionaries were kept busy establishing their missions. By Christmas the Lapwai mission had been far enough along to have its first celebration. The look on her listeners' faces inspired Eliza Spalding as she translated the Christmas story from English to the Nez Perce language, their eyes studying her every movement.

The Spaldings had learned that the two white men, Craig and Laird, and the band of Nez Perce who had left the party at Fort Hall had gone into the Clearwater country to trap beaver and take other furs.

Henry Spalding recalled that William Craig had seemed skeptical of the missionaries' work, and he was concerned that Craig's influence might direct the Indians away from his teachings. He also viewed Laird with suspicion because of his unexplained writing and sketching. Needless to say, he was distressed to hear that these two men had openly taken up with Indian women and were living with them in sin.

Sure that the two trappers could mean trouble, Spalding was upset to learn that the two had showed up at Lapwai. He remembered the drinking and frightful orgies that had prevailed at the rendezvous, the obscenities mouthed by the drunken trappers, the demon whiskey they consumed and the trickery they used on natives. In his mind he associated Craig and Laird with all rendezvous activities he detested.

Among the missionaries themselves there were problems. William Gray had grown so dissatisfied with Whitman and Spalding that he decided he must have his own mission. To accomplish this goal he made plans to go east to the Mission Board, explain the need for a mission among the Spokane and while there tell them the truth as he saw it about why he believed the other missionaries would not be able to accomplish their present aims.

But first he had to find a possible site for his proposed mission so that he would have details and facts to support his arguments. For that purpose, Gray went north to meet with Spokane Garry. There he got the information he wanted, and in the spring of 1837 was ready to travel east.

He had convinced Spalding that if he took horses east to trade for cattle he would be able to secure enough stock both for the mission at Lapwai and for the mission that he would establish among the Spokane. This plan made sense to Spalding. His own Nez Perce had shown great interest in white men's cattle at Waiilatpu and wanted some of their own. After some discussion Whitman agreed with the plan. He would send ponies from the Cayuse tribe.

Hearing of Gray's plans, once again James asked Craig and Laird to come to his lodge. He liked the idea of trading horses for cattle but was doubtful that Gray was the one to carry out the mission.

"Craig," the chief began, "I would let the white man have horses if I were sure he would bring back cows, but I think he will not get cows. I have bad feelings. The white man Gray is not wise. Do you think, as I do, that he will get into trouble?"

"I would not stop Gray," Craig advised, "nor would I urge any of my men to go along. If Gray needs horses to trade let him have three or four—you have many horses but no cattle."

"Craig," James replied after only a moment's hesitation, "I will do as you say."

Later James decided to stay at Lapwai and not go to the rendezvous. He wanted to keep his people close at hand in order to maintain his position as chief. A major concern was that if he took some of his people to the rendezvous, those who remained at Lapwai might be pulled into the power of the mission and lose some of their respect for him.

But without Chief James' knowledge, four young Nez Perce agreed to go east with Gray to help tend the horses and the returning cattle, also to interpret in conversations with other tribes. The four were Ellis; Big Ignace, an Iroquois who traveled with the Nez Perce; Blue Coat, so named because of the cast-off blue coat he wore; and The Hat, named because of a tall silk hat that was given to him by a mountain man.

Gray's plan was to start out by himself, go north to the Spokane country, where he would join up at the Flatheads' Kalispell House on the Clark Fork River with a Hudson's Bay Brigade that was on its way to the rendezvous on the Green River plains.

At Big Hole Basin Gray preached to the Flatheads and told them he might establish a mission for them in their country at a later date. Four Flatheads joined his travel party, and impatient to move ahead of the slower-moving Brigade, Gray pushed ahead.

Craig decided that he and Laird, with the two women, would take a few Nez Perce braves along with them to the

165

rendezvous for added strength in case they met Blackfoot and to help with the furs and the extra horse.

At the Snake River they met up with Andrew Drips and his party and then all joined Ermatinger, Gray and company, also on their way to the rendezvous. With the four Nez Perce and the horses for Gray's trade, the long line of ponies, men and dogs stretched out like a great snake curling along the river that bore that name.

Gray had not greeted Craig and Laird with enthusiasm, but Craig, with his perverse sense of humor, had introduced his group, including the two women. Trying to keep a straight face, he told Gray that the women were along to cook and take care of the camp. Gray knew very well what Craig really meant, and his imaginings kept him awake until he could pray himself to sleep.

When their party arrived at the rendezvous on the tenth of June, hunters were already beginning to gather. The past winter and trading were the main topics of discussion. And when the talk turned to Gray's proposed expedition to the East for cattle, there were disagreements.

"It's the end of hunting beaver in the West, mark my words. Once cows come, women and kids will follow. When Whitman took that cart to Fort Hall I seen the end. Fur prices are already shot to hell. We trap and hunt all winter, come on in here, and not one of us knows what we'll get—except screwed."

"Aw, shut up, Weaver. Let Russell tell you what he knows. He's lived with the Indians and has a feel for this country."

Russell shook his head, unconvinced. "I don't know anything more than you fellers do," he said. "But I agree that times are due to change and change fast. I covered a lot of country last winter and found less and less fur. In the next few years the settlers will come and the game will go. Isn't that the truth, Craig?''

Craig nodded. "It's happening. I wintered in Nez Perce country and heard the stories. Spalding's building mills, one to cut timber into boards, one to grind grain.''

"Where in hell's he going to get grain to grind? Don't tell me he's going to get them tame Indians of his to plow and plant it?''

"That's his plan. He's got them to help build his house and sheds. Now he's getting cows and he's planting gardens and sowing grain this spring. By fall he figures to be able to have his own flour. If he carries out his plans, he'll be purty self-sufficient in another year or so, specially if he gets cows.''

"Speaking of tame Indians, somebody ought to tame them Bannocks killed trappers awhile back and stole their outfits. That bunch is getting purty snotty, it seems to me.''

"What's this about killing two trappers?''

"Ain't you heard about that, Craig? The Bannocks killed a couple fellers sometime this spring, took their horses and everything they had. Jumped 'em in camp. Took their hair too, and real proud of it.''

"You know where they are, Russell?''

"Yeah. They're camped downriver three or four miles on a flat.''

"Who were the trappers?''

"Hell, I didn't know 'em. I heard it from other fellers. I know the Indians stole horses and outfits from a couple French trappers on Bear River along in April.''

"Has anybody faced 'em down, taken the stuff back?''

"We just come in. We're waiting for somebody with enough gumption to go with us. You and your chum want in on it, Craig?''

"We'll go. Get your shooting irons and sharpen your knives. How many in the Bannock camp?''

167

Russell spoke. "I counted sixty lodges. It's a full bunch that comes here to trade and hunt. There will be real trouble if you brace 'em."

"Hell, Russell, there's already trouble, and a lot more to come unless we nip it in the bud. You let these troublemaking red bastards get one up on you, and the next thing you know there's a knife at your throat and one skinning your topknot. Craig knows what I'm talking about."

Craig, Laird and three trappers followed by four Nez Perce rode downriver, where some Bannock, a warlike and treacherous branch of the Shoshone tribe, were camped. Like the Blackfoot, Bannock always looked for easy pickings among small groups of trappers or neighboring Indians. Mountain men had found out early that to display weakness to a Bannock could be disastrous. Stealing horses, plundering camps or killing must be punished as quickly as possible, even if it cost lives.

As luck would have it, most of the Bannock braves were away on a hunt when Craig and his men rode up. Still, it would have been dangerous to enter the camp unprepared for trouble. Craig laid down the rules.

"We go in ready for anything might come up. Laird, stick with me and watch my back. You other fellers take the edges. Nobody's to shoot unless to protect himself or one of us. The Nez Perce can stay close and watch the lodges. We keep together. If anyone's hit, we take him with us. I'll do the talking."

The men rode directly into the village, rifles lying across their knees, knives thrust securely in their belts, hand axes tied but ready to be jerked free if a man's gun was emptied and a warrior tried to close in. The chief's lance stood before his lodge. When Craig stopped there, a squaw stepped out, fear and hate mixed on her face. Craig spoke in the squaw's language and at the same time made signs so she could not mistake what they had come for.

Almost immediately the men were shown to where the stolen horses had been tied, no good to the Bannock hunters as yet because they had not been trained in the Indians' style. The white men led away the seven mounts while the rest of the raiders kept their circle, watching the entire camp for signs of danger. When Craig and Laird found the murdered trappers' belongings, the plunder was laid out, packed and loaded on the horses. This done, Craig spoke to the assembled Bannock.

"If your warriors do not stop killing trappers and other white men, we will kill Bannock braves and take all they have. If they want to be our friends we will be their friends, but if they want to fight we will raid their camps, we will fight and we will kill them."

By the time Craig's party had returned to the rendezvous encampment, Jim Bridger and his brigade had arrived with supplies. And later that afternoon the scout on watch, spotting thirty Bannock warriors, called out, "Here comes trouble, look to your guns!"

By chance Bridger had one of the stolen horses by the bridle. At that moment the Indians rode close and demanded the return of the murdered trappers' plunder. Bridger refused, saying it hadn't been theirs in the first place. Sign language and Indian talk crossed back and forth. A Bannock warrior was heard to say, "We came here for the horses. We take them or we take your blood."

"Watch yourselves, boys," Russell warned. "Here comes the action."

The Bannock braves stormed like thunder back and forth across the camp. One reached to grab the bridle reins from Bridger's hand. As he did, two men shot him. Other rifles fired. Indians fell from their ponies dead or wounded. When the fight was over in a few minutes, twelve Bannock were dead and the rest had fled. One of the Bannock arrows had killed Joe Meek's wife.

Many trappers mounted and went after the marauders, shooting as they rode. Following the Bannock to their camp, the trappers plundered everything they could lay hands on. For the next three days the whites kept on the Bannocks' trail, killing when they could and capturing every loose pony or piece of camp booty they could find. On the fourth day the Bannock made peace and swore to keep it. Later, when some new trappers encountered the same band, they reported a peaceful greeting.

After the battle with the Bannock another supply brigade came in. Tom Fitzpatrick, called Broken Hand by Indians, led the caravan, which consisted of twenty carts pulled by mules, a number of pack ponies and forty-five men to hunt for the travelers' meals and supply necessary protection.

With the rendezvous encampment now enlarged, the carousing began in full force. To the men who had spent a year in the mountains what money they got was to be spent; what whiskey there was available was to be drunk. As usual, once their fur cache was disposed of, their money and trade balance rapidly disappeared and it wasn't long before the troops found themselves in debt for another year.

This year was to be different for Craig. He took his trade balance in goods and left himself some credit on the books. Laird too traded his share of furs for goods and a few gold pieces. In the country they'd just come from, money was of no value, but Laird had plans for the future in which money would play an important part. The goods he took included equipment to carry him through another year of trapping, also some things Sun-in-the-Morning could use to decorate herself and show off her wealth.

Chapter 20

Gray was particularly displeased that Craig and Laird, Nez Perce braves and others had gone into the Bannocks' camp and brought back the stolen horses and goods that provoked the eventual bloody battle. He would have preferred to go to the Bannock camp himself and negotiate the return of the stolen goods. That, he pointed out to anyone who would listen, would have avoided bloodshed. At this the trappers called the indignant missionary a "damned prissy, pigheaded fool."

"How in hell would you have gotten the hair back on the heads of them trappers they killed over on Bear River?" Craig demanded.

"That was an unfortunate occurrence," Gray replied. "But we are here to teach the Indians it is wrong to fight and that it is especially wrong to kill and mutilate their enemies' bodies."

"Well, Preacher," Fitzpatrick put in, "a grizzly ain't our enemy, but by grabs, if we don't kill him and take his hide for robes and his meat to eat, he'll chew off our arms and legs, claw our faces and eat us to build up his winter fat. When the blasted Bannocks started giving it to us, the only way we could stop 'em was to kill off a few, take their camp and run hell out of their women. Let that happen a time or two more and they'll stay clear of white trappers for good.''

Gray was about to demand that Fitzpatrick put an end to that violent kind of talk when he saw a look in the leader's eyes that changed his mind. Rather than pursue the matter he asked instead if the rendezvous could be speeded up so he and his Indian friends could be on their way to the States to trade ponies for cows.

"Hell, no, it can't be speeded up, Gray! These men have gone and spent a whole year trapping and looking forward to this like kids to Christmas. There's no way I'll cut this party short just to please you or any other Bible-thumper.''

"But Mr. Fitzpatrick, the men have done their trading. Now they'll just get drunk, get the Indians drunk, abuse the women and carry on a series of orgies and debauchery. That's wrong. If you ever read your Bible, you know it's wrong.''

"Mr. Gray,'' Fitzpatrick yelled, "you may be big potatoes in the sack you come from, but I run this ragtag outfit for what it is, and I'll continue to do so until somebody better or bigger than me comes along. If you're so all-fired impatient to go, don't bother me with your bellyaching. Go back to your trusting natives and tell 'em the sad story that we're not leaving till the last dog's hung. If you don't know what that means, ask one of the trappers.''

This confrontation convinced Gray that the best thing he could do would be to leave the rendezvous. Like a pestering mosquito he avoided Fitzpatrick but kept buzzing around the other mountain men, trying to persuade them to get their revelry and trading over with; in that way, Gray felt, the brigade chief would give in and travel with him.

The plan failed. The mountain men were far from eager to go along with what the missionary wanted. For months they had frozen, starved and barely managed to stay alive; to deny themselves now would be ridiculous.

Yet however fed up with Gray's self-righteous badgering the trappers were, however eager they were to see him leave, they were also willing to caution him. His party, they felt—especially with the horses—was too vulnerable to hold its own against raiding tribes to the east. But the more the trappers talked against Gray's leaving without adequate protection, the more certain Gray became that they were wrong and concluded he'd start out anyway.

The Hat and Big Ignace agreed to accompany him. Ellis and Blue Coat decided to go back home. Gathering up the rest of the Indians willing to travel as well as three French Canadian trappers, Gray headed east.

In the midst of all the goings on, Laird managed to find some time for writing letters.

Rendezvous
July 1837

Dear Sir:

We are at the rendezvous, camped with the supply train from the States. The missionary William Gray has just left for the East with a band he's leading. The purpose of his trip is to trade horses for cattle so that the Indians can start their own herds.

I have managed to stay alive and am actually in better health than ever before, thanks to William Craig. Without that trapper's patient teaching of Indian ways, I would have been lost long ago.

I have not yet been at Mr. Whitman's place. It is called Waiilatpu and is located not far from Fort Walla Walla on the Columbia River. Because he is close to Fort Vancouver and the Hudson's Bay Company supply depot, Whitman has ready access to supply trains and news of the East. Those of us farther north on the Clearwater (a river that the Nez Perce call the Kooskoosky) are not quite so fortunate.

The Whitmans have started a school and are trying to learn the Nez Perce language. I hear they are attempting to Christianize the natives of the Cayuse tribe rather than teach them the white man's way of living.

I've learned that the Whitmans built their place on Cayuse lands, not believing it made any difference whose territory they settled on. Apparently it did make a difference to the Indians. The Cayuse chief asked for payment, which Whitman refused to give. Of course this refusal caused resentment. The Cayuse argued that they shouldn't have to suffer, that they had not sent people east to ask the missionaries to come. Many of us new to the country think it is open and that anyone is free to move in. We forget that the situation could be compared to similar ones back home in settled territory, where land claimed by the owner is his to sell, rent or give away rather than let an outsider move in and occupy.

At Lapwai, where the Spaldings have located, much is happening. Mr. Spalding is a hard-driving, ambitious man. His religion stirs him to attempt the impossible. He has built his house and a school, is breaking land for crops and plans to dam the stream for a sawmill and a grain grinding flour mill. The soil around that mission is rich, black, deep and very fertile.

The grass on the open plateaus and hillsides is lush, and I saw no sign of gravel or rocks. The Indians' great horse herd roams out all winter and comes in fat in the springtime. No buffalo live nearby, but there are deer of two kinds and elk in great numbers.

In the mountains wild sheep and mountain goats live among rocks. There are black bears, as at home, as well as the great fierce grizzly bear of which Mr. Lewis and Mr. Clark wrote.

All Indian tribes respect the grizzly. It is as great an honor to count coup on him as it would be to fight a warrior enemy. Joe Meek attained his reputation for outstanding bravery by facing a maddened grizzly and hitting it on the head with his ramrod three times before shooting and killing it. This fight was witnessed by other men and is true, though to some unbelievable.

The utter disregard for death or injury displayed by many of these trappers cannot be appreciated by those who live in civilized places. Bravery among Indians is honored and that is one reason the white trappers feel they must always avenge crime committed by the Indians against any of our people.

Recently I went with Craig and a few others into a Bannock camp of some sixty lodges to recover horses stolen from the friendly Nez Perce and to avenge the murder and robbing of two trappers. The Bannock are a part of the Snake or Shoshone tribe.

For an hour Laird wrote of the battle with the Bannock warriors and concluded:

After the shooting was over, we found that one Bannock arrow had hit Joe Meek's wife in the breast and penetrated her heart. Mr. Meek was almost beside himself because despite his

175

infatuation with Narcissa Whitman, he had truly loved this woman. She was a Nez Perce and had been the wife of the former leader of the brigades, Milton Suttleton, Old Milt, as the trappers called him.

When Suttleton lost his leg, he was forced to go east and wanted his wife looked after. Meek volunteered. According to his story, he had always been in love with Lamb-of-the-Mountain, so much in love that he had once killed an Indian in camp for hitting her with a quirt.

Bill Craig told me he saw Meek's wife dressed up once after Meek had given her a lot of presents. The way Craig tells it, he had never seen a prettier woman on a finer horse. She was described as wearing a skirt of bright blue broadcloth; bodice and leggings were of brilliant red of the finest material. A headcloth of bright silk adorned her braids. Her moccasins had been painstakingly embroidered. She rode astride and to show she was ready for either peace or war carried a war axe on the right side of the saddle and on the left a peace pipe. Shells, beads of cut glass and small hawk bells that tinkled when she moved decorated her entire outfit.

Because it was late, Laird stopped writing for the night. Early the next morning he continued:

Also, I hear more and more that the army will be the authority chosen to intercede between Indians and whites in case of trouble. If that happens, I predict there will be more of it than the present military forces can handle. This is a large country and the tribes that inhabit it are nomadic, not grounded by any real central city or town. Constantly migrating Indians follow the herds and for many years various tribes have claimed their right to hunt and fish in these vast western lands. Any who come west must be prepared to deal with people here who live differently.

When I left you, Uncle, I had planned to stay west no longer than a year, but I find that I like the life here and I intend to stay longer. My friend Craig plans to return to the Nez Perce country by a different route to see if beaver have been trapped out of the area through which we will pass. We are beginning to hear that there will be an end to the supply before long: the catch this year is down and there are many additional trappers in the field. Prices have declined too and more and more trappers are talking about settling.

Rumors concerning the Indian Affairs policy of moving all Indian tribes east of the Mississippi River to areas west of it are causing considerable resistance here. There will be opposition from whites living in this territory as well as from native Indian tribes who, when they hear of it, will prepare for war.

Another thing now becoming a problem is smallpox. The disease is beginning to spread west from the Mandan villages on the lower Missouri River. When the Sioux accused Mr. Bridger, saying that white men were responsible for the epidemic, Bridger replied that it was not white men, but a half-breed Crow chief, Jim Beckworth, who gave to the Sioux two blankets that had been used by people sick with the disease. As for myself, I feel fortunate that Mr. Clark had me inoculated.

Your last letter to me had been opened before I received it and I suspect this one of mine will be opened also unless I take precaution. I have reason to believe that some members of the Hudson's Bay Company consider me a spy. I plan to ensure this letter's safe delivery by paying one of the returning men to hide it until he reaches a place from which it can be safely delivered to you. I will tell the messenger he will be rewarded if this communication reaches you still sealed.

Hoping to write more soon,

Yours respectfully,
Donald Laird

After Gray left with his brigade—as he liked to call the small party—the rendezvous camp settled into a routine of unrestricted revelry. Naturally there was room for discussion about what might happen to Gray's group.

"That damned fool missionary will get his topknot cut short, wait and see," an old trapper at the evening fire declared. "If he tries his high and mighty ways with Blackfoot or Sioux, his locks will dangle on the lance of some warrior what don't like his snotty talk."

"Naw, he'll give 'em a song and dance about his special powers," another put in. "They'll ask for him to prove what he's talking about. Then will come the time."

"Nope, you're both barking up the wrong tree. The old coon will come out of it alive even if he has to skin hair off other fellers' heads," countered a third. "I've seen that kind back in the States. The towns are full of 'em. Every place with a sharp-pointed steeple has a psalm-singer like Gray always passing round a plate or a hat, taking the biggest piece of chicken in the pot on Sundays.''

And so it went. All agreed that Gray's obnoxious, superior ways, his endless faultfinding, would cause Indians and any white man he met to view his project with suspicion. Exactly where trouble would evolve into disaster no one could predict, but it was bound to happen. And happen it did.

Gray's brigade made it to Fort Laramie without too much trouble. By this time Gray was more convinced than ever that he could make the entire journey safely. However, continuing on, he encountered a band of Sioux out after scalps and whatever plunder they could find. On the North Platte River at a place identified as Ash Hollow, a fight ensued, Gray and his group managing to get to the top of a bluff where they believed they had a chance of defending themselves.

After the first flurry had died down, a French trader who was a member of the Sioux band made it known to Gray that the Sioux were after the Indians, not the whites. By this time Gray had a couple of minor head wounds from clambering up the bluffs—also fear in his soul—and he began to parley.

During the process of negotiation, Gray agreed to lay down his arms. With the three French Canadians he sneaked into the open, leaving his Indian companions behind.

The opinions of Big Ignace, The Hat and the others would never be recorded. As soon as Gray and the rest left the bluff, advanced into the open and were taken prisoner, the Sioux warriors, hot for fresh blood, tore up to the top of the bluff and annihilated the almost defenseless Indians there.

At the Sioux camp on the North Platte the prisoners were treated with contempt by their victorious captors. The

French trader among them, however, was still convinced that the chief would keep the bargain he had made; it would be risky for them not to. The trader was proved right. Finally the prisoners were freed.

Gray's defense later was that if he had not left the group, then everyone would have been killed and his mission in life—to convert savages—would have been prematurely aborted. As it was, Gray's mission ended anyway. By his maneuvering he lost not only the respect of all Indians who eventually learned of what he did, but of missionaries and trappers as well. To the Indians, power and honor were worthy of deep respect. Gray had surrendered both. As stories about him spread, all white men, by association, began to be looked upon as weak and untrustworthy.

Before Gray and his remaining companions made it to civilization, trouble had already begun in the West. When Ellis and Blue Coat returned with horses but no cows, Spalding became incensed. Certain that Whitman would rebuke him for the trip's failure, he vented his self-righteous fury on the two Indians.

Spalding had had Indians whipped before. Now he decreed that as punishment, each of the two men would get fifty lashes and have to give up a good horse.

The two Nez Perce were proud warriors. Their training made such punishment unacceptable; they were men, not women or dogs. According to those who heard the story from Indians, Ellis walked away and went back to Kamiah, where he lived.

Blue Coat, however, certain that Spalding would relent, went to the prayer meeting the missionary was holding. There, instead of forgiveness he met Spalding's insistence that he be tied up. No Indian volunteered, so Spalding gave a direct order to a young Nez Perce brave.

180

Blue Coat, not resisting, stood calmly. When he had been secured, Spalding told the brave to whip him.

"I do not do the whipping," Spalding explained. "Others do it. I am like God."

"You lie!" the Nez Perce exclaimed. "God does the punishing." The Nez Perce pointed to a picture of two men. An image of God stood behind them holding a bundle of rods. "See there," the Nez Perce said. "God has the rod, ready to punish. You take the whip and whip Blue Coat or we will tie you up and whip you."

With quiet fury Spalding gave the silent captive fifty lashes, and later Blue Coat gave the missionary the horse he had demanded.

As yet no one at Lapwai had heard what had happened to Gray or about the deaths of The Hat and Big Ignace. If the Nez Perce had known of Gray's disgraceful surrender and the massacre, the downfall of the mission might have occurred right at that moment. As it was, some of the younger Nez Perce braves at Lapwai had begun to listen to the shamans, who all along had scoffed at the white man's ways.

Even friendly Tackensuatis was fed up with promises. Believing that others were being treated more fairly than he was, the Indian quickly became disenchanted. In no time he had gathered his belongings and moved farther up the Clearwater.

In the East, meanwhile, Gray was describing what he would accomplish if more people and funds were made available. To the Mission Board, which reproved him for making the trip east without their permission, he glibly explained away the loss of Indians and horses at the North Platte and in the process glorified his role in the escape. So convincing were Gray's arguments that eventually he was awarded aid. But Gray wanted more than that.

He'd noted the respect and gratitude that Marcus

Whitman had received when he doctored Indians; he had heard stories of how William Clark had helped a paralyzed chief to walk. Gray too wanted the respect associated with the title of doctor. Needless to say, he was delighted when the Mission Board agreed to let him study medicine. After that all he needed was a wife. At a church meeting held in Ithaca, New York, Samuel Parker introduced Gray to a likely prospect, Mary Augusta Dix. Mary was twenty-eight years old. About ready to give up the idea of finding romance, let alone a famous husband, she imagined she had found both in Gray. The missionary responded to this adulation by proposing immediately. Then he wrote Mary a letter confirming his intentions and said he needed her to help him with his Indian converts. Six days later they were married.

The party heading west comprised the Grays and three other missionary couples—Cushing Ellis, Elkanah Walker, Asa Smith and their wives. An unmarried man of twenty-three by the name of Cornelius Rogers also went along, all of them quarreling and complaining every mile of the way.

Chapter 21

It was early fall. After the rendezvous, Craig, Laird, their women and a few Nez Perce were headed back to Nez Perce country, Craig breaking away for a few days to check for beaver. Returning to the site where his party had been camped, Craig sensed trouble and moved in slowly, armed with a caution that years in the mountains had taught him well. What greeted him were the still-smoldering ruins of what had been his temporary home.

Bloodstains attested to the killings that must have taken place—stripped bones too, where ponies had been killed and wolves and vultures had descended to feed on flesh. Remnants of a dozen lodges were strewn about the campsite. From what he saw Craig concluded that the attackers had not killed everyone and that the survivors must have been the ones who hauled away the dead.

Not knowing who had been killed, trying with every fiber of strength not to succumb to sentimental imaginings about whether he ever again would see those close to him, Craig turned to study the distinct trail left by the raiders and their stolen horses. He was not sure exactly how large the raiding party had been, but after examination believed their numbers were not small. With a last look at the devastated camping spot, Craig spurred his horse down the survivors' trail as it wound its way toward Nez Perce country across the Bitterroots.

As he rode Craig investigated every possibility for reprisal; if not undertaken, the Nez Perce would lose face. The trapper was aware that Chief James must be advised of the raid as quickly as possible so he could make plans for an attack before winter set in and the pass over the Lolo was closed. So far Craig had seen no sign of pony tracks. Knowing the possible campsites the survivors might use and estimating how fast they could travel, Craig pushed his horse to get as far as he could before dark.

He caught up with the survivors' rear guard the next morning and they told him as much as they could of what had happened. One group of Blackfoot warriors had struck in the night, which was unusual, and run off their pony herd. At the same time another group attacked the camp and killed the ponies that were tethered. The Blackfoot fought with and slaughtered many of the Nez Perce warriors, through surprise and weight in numbers overcoming them. The few men who escaped had broken through the ranks and given the women and children an opportunity to scatter and hide. The Nez Perce told Craig that Laird and Sun-in-the-Morning had not been found among the dead and must have been captured. Hawk Flying had been killed with several other squaws who had taken up axes and knives to fight with the men.

As Craig had done before many times over the years when comrades and friends had been killed or failed to return from a hunt, he now tried to put out of his mind thoughts about how the tragedy might have been prevented, also hope that Suni or Laird might be alive. There was no room in a life like this for unharnessed emotion. To be most effective now he must focus on his next move. So while the rear guards stayed back, Craig went ahead to talk briefly with other sorrowing travelers. And he gravely discussed what must be done next with Tall Elk and Lame Bear, who were now the leaders.

"I'll ride to Lapwai and talk with James," Craig offered. "We will return quickly with many horses and warriors, also horses for the women and children and food for them. But most important, we will trail the Blackfoot and get back the horses and the people they took captive. Have some of your men trail the Blackfoot to their camp at once, for I believe they do not think the Nez Perce will strike back this late in the year."

"Craig, we will do what you say," Tall Elk agreed. "You come fast and we will go with you and get back what is ours."

Lame Bear spoke. "Craig, I think Laird was shot and taken with his woman. We found no place where the two of them could have hidden or blood where they might have died. The Blackfoot will hold your friends to trade next year; that is, if they do not kill them when they get back to their big winter camp."

Craig was pleased to hear again the news that Laird and Suni had not been killed. But he didn't stay with that thought long. There was no time.

From the food that they had grabbed and managed to take along, the Nez Perce woman supplied Craig with enough dried meat and meal so that he would not have to stop and hunt. If he did kill game, he would hang up what was left for those following. The men had bows and arrows and some lances, but their dismal journey back to their homelands stripped them of all desire to hunt.

When Craig reached the Big Hole Basin, he startled a group of Flatheads camped there after a hunt. Fortunately the Indians were friendly; Craig had met some of them at the rendezvous in former years. When he described to the Flatheads what had happened, they were upset to learn that Blackfoot had made war on friendly Nez Perce. Immediately they sent ponies and men to meet the survivors, and their leader told Craig they would stay where they were until he and the Nez Perce warriors returned. At that time, they said, they would accompany the Nez Perce on the warpath.

James, advised of what had happened, was enraged. A powwow soon followed that made Craig feel things would turn out badly for the Blackfoot if the Nez Perce warriors ever caught them. James grieved especially over the loss of Laird, his woman and Hawk Flying. Sorrow would not get them back; he knew that, but the chief also knew that if his men could kill some Blackfoot and retrieve the horses and possibly the captives, they would regain prestige that now was lost.

Preparations for the trip began immediately and the day after Craig's arrival a war party took to the trail.

Laird remembered little of the trip from the Nez Perce camp where the fighting had taken place to the Blackfoot camp where he was now held captive. When he revived enough to listen to Suni, she told him what had happened.

They had both been awakened by a tremendous commotion at the far side of the camp. Laird had snatched his rifle and stepped from the door of the lodge. As he did, he was hit by a Blackfoot warclub, knocked to his knees and then hit again. Moments later he was trussed up and tied on a pony's back.

Suni had grappled with two men while Hawk Flying had slipped out the back of the lodge in an attempt to fight with the Nez Perce braves. Hawk Flying was speared and died soon afterward. As Suni scratched and kicked, she too was knocked on the head and tied up. Within seconds she came to but played unconscious. By daylight the fighting was over. The victorious Blackfoot warriors, having lost only a few men, gathered their loot and their captives.

Six horses had been killed and the rest, more than one hundred, stolen. Almost all the lodge coverings had been taken, most of the stored dried meat and pemmican, Laird's two guns, his knives, the bag that held his journal and personal things and the trade goods he and Craig had carried with them. Besides Suni and Laird, the Blackfoot took four young women captive.

Because the raiders had no women of their own along, the captive Nez Perce women quickly became slaves to the Blackfoot and were told they must or be killed. All cooking and camp chores fell to them.

Laird's head was covered with a mass of clotted blood. Even over his left eye it had dried to a crust so thick that he was unaware if he'd been blinded. So tightly had his arms and legs been tied that no feeling remained. Off and on, Suni said, he had returned to consciousness, only to swoon and faint again.

Suni and another woman brought water and tried to clean Laird's wound. He partly revived, but his throat was parched and he asked for something to drink. While Suni held his head and tried to help him, a tall painted Blackfoot strode into the lodge and kicked her in the side so hard she fell and almost rolled into the fire. Then with one hand the snarling warrior grabbed her by the hair and jerked her erect. With the other hand he slapped Suni's face, knocking her sideways, then back and forth till she was almost senseless.

With her hair in his hand, the Blackfoot pulled her head back until she groaned in pain, then commanded, "Forget your white dog of a man until you care for me. If not you both will die—and slowly."

The other girl had slipped out of the lodge. Laird had passed out, then awakened again during the scuffle, but was too bewildered really to know what was going on.

Once the warrior had been fed, he lay back and

smoked some of Laird's tobacco. Then he directed Suni to feed and care for his white captive. Suni made no effort to untie or loosen Laird's bonds and no attempt to speak to him; she knew it would only bring more punishment. After she gave Laird water and pemmican and felt satisfied he was as well off as he could be under the circumstances, she arose, about to leave the lodge.

"Stop!" The Blackfoot spit the word. "Come stand before me."

When Suni went to where the Blackfoot lay, he told her to strip off her dress. "I," he announced, "will show the white dog how Blackfoot men treat their women. Blackfoot warriors are strong, not sniveling half-women who let their squaws tell them what to do."

The lounging brave sat up. Pointing his pipe at Laird, he sneered, "You white dogs take our women, but we do not even get to look at yours. Now I take your Nez Perce she-dog and show you our way."

Laird could make out little of what the Blackfoot said, but as he grasped what the Indian had in mind, a violent fury rose within him and he strained futilely to be free of his bonds.

"Tell that white dog that I have taken his gun, his ponies and his medicine bag," the buck told Suni. "I have counted coup on him and now I will use his woman. After I am finished with her, I will let my friends come in and use her as many times as they wish. Tell the lousy white dog that I will have him watch and that if he closes his eyes for even one moment I will have sticks put between his lids to keep them open. Tell him, go ahead! If you do not, I will kill your white dog slowly and you will watch."

Suni knew there was no point in trying to tell Laird anything different than what the brave had told her. She knew she must accept the way of the Blackfoot now; she was with the Nez Perce no longer. Besides, if she complied she might hope to stay alive and keep Laird alive. Perhaps the God that Laird believed in would save them.

In broken English and signs Suni talked to Laird. She spoke slowly, giving him a chance to ask questions. Was she all right? Suni nodded. Was Craig alive? Again Suni nodded. Did she think they would be killed? She shook her head no. Then she told him what was to happen to her and that if she allowed the Blackfoot to have his way, it would be easier for them.

Laird listened, hardly believing what he heard. The information was too painful to absorb. Picturing even part of what Suni had told him made him want to retch. But rising to the strength of his magnificent Indian woman, he overcame his nausea and steeled himself.

"Enough," the Blackfoot ordered. Grabbing Suni by the arm, he pulled her to him. Another command. Then slowly, as the Blackfoot's eyes seemed to consume her, Suni took off her clothing and dropped it to the ground. For a moment, the brave did nothing. Suni stood before him innocent and completely naked, waiting. Despite her knowledge of what was to happen next, she stood proud and erect.

The Blackfoot made her turn toward Laird. A moment later he wrenched her down beneath him. As Laird watched, the red man, grunting cruelly, punished Suni, took her and when finished called in two others who did the same.

When the ordeal ended, the prisoners were left alone. Suni crept to where Laird lay weeping silently in frustration and sorrow. Gently she kissed away his tears, then loosened his bonds and retied them less securely.

As Suni tended him, ignoring the whole time what must have been her intense pain and shame, Laird vowed that if it took him all his life, he would have revenge on the Blackfoot tribe. All that night he thought of what he might do. The next morning he asked Suni to call their Blackfoot captor into the lodge. When the warrior finally appeared, Laird gave careful instructions to Suni.

"Tell the Blackfoot he is a brave man; he fought the Nez Perce and captured us. But also tell him he is a foolish man. He has abused the white man's woman and for this he will surely die. Tell him, too, that his woman and his children and all of his people will die, that the white man's God will punish the Blackfoot for what they have done and that all this will happen before the snow comes.

"After the sickness the Blackfoot people will no longer be great. They will no longer be able to fight the Nez Perce or the white trappers. Make sure this Blackfoot understands that all this will happen because he harmed you and other Nez Perce people who came only to trap and hunt. Tell him that."

The Blackfoot had concentrated on every word that Laird was saying. He knew the words must be important because of the way Suni stood still and listened.

Suni had Laird repeat his message several times until she was sure what he wanted her to say. Then she turned, walked to the tall warrior and told him forcefully, in short distinct sentences, what Laird had said. Laird studied the Blackfoot's face while this was going on; he saw the warrior's eyes close to slits and his mouth tighten.

Almost immediately the warrior responded, angrily waving his arms and striking his fist repeatedly into the palm of his hand. Suni too responded, not relinquishing a step. Then she told the brave to call in the others so they could hear what the white man had said would happen to them and their tribe. The Blackfoot brave—Laird had yet to hear his name—relented and called in warriors to hear what the Nez Perce squaw had to say. The men ringed the fire, and Suni, standing stiff and defiant, translated Laird's prediction once again.

There were questions. Where did the white man get his power? How did he know all this would come about?

Sun-in-the-Morning decided she would answer for Laird. She knew that the Blackfoot had seen the white man's book in the hands of priests far to the north and had heard of the powerful God the Black Robes worshipped.

"The white man gets his power from the God who made the book. He talked to the Great White Spirit last night and felt great strength, as you do after you fast and learn what the Blackfoot Great Spirit has in store for you. But the white man does not lie, as the Blackfoot often do. And he has power greater than your medicine men and he makes messages to the Great White God where the sun comes up in the morning. I tell you true, you and your people will soon become sick and die. The white man says it will come soon after the first snows. If you dare to kill him or me it will begin soon after we are dead."

A storm of frenzied talk broke out. Sweating, Laird prayed that his promise of death would be accepted as truth. Suni stood calmly as the arguments raged, the bruises on her arms and face ugly and dark. One of the newcomers walked over and spat a stream of saliva at her mouth. Suni said nothing. The spit dribbled down and dripped from her jaw. The Blackfoot who had captured Suni jerked the arm of the spitter and spoke harshly to him. Then Suni spoke again, this time to the brave who had insulted her.

"The white man has seen that you have insulted me, his Nez Perce woman. He will swear that you and your woman and all your children shall be the first to die in agony."

For a time no one spoke.

Then: "We still do not believe that what you say is true."

"You will know it when you sicken and die," Suni replied.

191

"Can the white man stop this curse?"

"I do not know."

"Ask him what we can do so that our people will not die."

Suni spoke to Laird and made him understand the questions and the Blackfoot's wish for negotiation. Laird answered that if the Blackfoot untied him he would agree not to run away. And if he and the other captives were treated fairly, when they reached the main camp he would ask the God who made the book not to punish the tribe badly and allow some to live.

Suni explained his words to the waiting warriors and then stood silent, awaiting the end of the discussion. The atmosphere was quieter now; there was little shouting or waving of arms. Abruptly the leading warrior walked to Laird and cut the thongs on his hands and arms, then handed Laird his knife. The captive shook his head weakly, refusing it. He was unable to move his fingers.

Suni watched the warrior in disdain as he freed Laird's feet. "Go," she said to him, pointing to the open flap of the lodge.

Once the lodge had been cleared, Suni rushed to Laird and rubbed his limbs until feeling flowed painfully back into them. As she cried and tears moistened the dry saliva on her cheek, Laird reached to wipe them away. Then he pulled Suni close and kissed her again and again.

Later Suni went outside. Seeing that the camp was packing up, she returned at once to inform Laird and to prepare for the trip they must make. No one objected when she untied Laird's pony and led it to the lodge. She found another loose pony at the lodge, her captive friends helping her get ready and pack the horse. All the while their Blackfoot captors watched.

Laird felt shaky and ill, but as his mind cleared he thought back to the attack. If he had been the only white man in camp, why had the Blackfoot captured him and held him prisoner instead of killing him and taking his scalp? Was he to have been traded for some advantage they had in mind? But who would they trade him to, and why? Finally Laird wondered what Craig had done after discovering the siege. One thing he felt sure of: his friend would want revenge.

Chapter 22

Craig and the war party made their way up the tortuous Lolo trail to the summit, then down past the old Hot Springs campground. Up the Bitterroot River across the Divide they went, and entered the Big Hole Basin, where the Flatheads were camped. The party from Kamiah had met the survivors at Hot Springs and were gratified to learn that the Flatheads were awaiting their arrival.

But here Craig and the Nez Perce encountered a setback. A party from Flathead House had arrived and having finally heard what had happened to the Indians accompanying Gray, they advised the Indians not to go with Craig against the Blackfoot. Craig tried to reason with the chief but was unsuccessful.

Spalding too was opposed to any of his people joining the war party, especially because it was being led by William Craig. He quoted words from the Bible, "Vengeance is mine, saith the Lord."

When the Flatheads withdrew, Spalding's arguments took on added strength and finally there were only twenty men left who were pledged to rescue the captives. Craig was disappointed. He had planned to have at least a hundred warriors and now had only one fifth of the manpower that he needed.

He looked over the men willing to go. Those men he did have were determined braves. Each had lost relatives and supplies to the Blackfoot and were hungry for revenge. Craig knew each one and they knew him as a man they could trust. With these braves Craig decided to undertake the chase.

When Laird announced that the Blackfoot would die because of what they had done to her and the others, Suni wondered how he could accomplish the feat, and if he did not, how they both could avoid the terrible punishment that would certainly be meted out. Suni believed in Laird, but hardly to the extent that he could call down fire from heaven or lay a curse of death on people and have it materialize.

She alerted the four other Nez Perce women to what she had told the Blackfoot. If asked they could tell lies of the powerful things Laird could do. It was essential to stay alive as long as possible in the hope that there soon would be a rescue.

The raid and capture had taken place in early September. Now late September lay on the land. Cottonwoods turned gold along the rivers and the days grew short. Visitors from the east came to camp—a small band of Blackfoot, their ponies and shaggy dogs pulling the loaded travois. The whole camp greeted them, then at the river trail held a meeting that seemed to go on and on. There was no great rejoicing among the returning crowd. Laird and Suni stood outside their lodge and wondered what was happening.

Their Blackfoot captor, whose name they learned was Young Antelope, came to speak with Laird. Suni interpreted.

"Young Antelope says the people who have come here have a sickness. In the camp they left many have died. He asks whether you know about what happened.''

Laird looked straight at the warrior and spoke in even tones. ''I do not know of these people or of their sickness,'' he answered. ''I only know what I have told you: that when the snow comes, some of your people will begin to die.''

''You say some. Who will live?''

''I cannot say. Maybe none of you will live. Maybe all of you will die before the snow is gone.''

''Can we leave this place and hide from the sickness?''

''Can you hide from the bad things you did to us? No, you cannot hide. The sickness will follow you.''

Young Antelope stopped to talk with other Blackfoot, then entered a lodge with them to smoke and discuss what Laird had said. There was no celebration that night. Laird told Suni not to eat from the common food bowls nor drink water from the common carrier. He warned her to stay away from the newcomers and explained that he was concerned she might get the sickness from them.

Late that afternoon dashes of reddish clouds patterned the western sky. No frost lay on the ground the next morning and a high overcast hid the sun. The usual chatter of women and boys going to fetch food and water was not heard. Suni felt strangely subdued and said little. At noon a misting rain brought no splatter of drops to the buffalo-hide lodges. It was a gloomy day that seemed it would inspire little to go well. Even in the lodges, the evening fires failed to draw smoke up through the cones. Cold air chilled the campsites. Before morning Laird had drawn the furry robes tight around his shoulders and pulled Suni in closer to snuggle in his arms.

After the morning meal the next day, Suni left the tent but came back soon.

''Laird, children are sick.''

''Those who came with the people from the East?''

197

"Yes. Young Antelope and the others know of it and are waiting."

"What do you mean?"

"The one who was sick first, they gave him sweat baths and they will wash him in the river."

"Suni, the child will die before tomorrow morning," Laird told her. "And the other sick ones will also die. That is the way it will be."

All that day the sky remained overcast. A cold drizzle fell and the camp was silent until evening. Then a wail of sorrow came from the lodge of sickness, followed by the wolfish howling of dogs. The wailing persisted. One woman after another took up the mournful sound.

After still another day of miserable drizzle, gusty winds kept people inside, where they did nothing but talk in low voices.

The Blackfoot had given the Nez Perce girls the freedom of the camp when Laird told them he would not try to escape. They were still captives but treated more like guests. This act of kindness was a great concession for the Blackfoot; because of it they had had no chance to put on a great war dance and display their contempt for their enemies and the white trappers. The Christian religion was already having a slight effect, it seemed, with the Indians now torn between God's power and the religion of their own shamans.

Laird had long ago given up praying, but after the capture he went back to it. His own life as well as those of all the women in the camp was at stake in this game. And always in the back of his mind lay the desire for revenge on those who had humiliated Suni. Laird's prayer was for snow on the mountains and for the sickness to strike his enemies.

To relieve his mounting tension he brought out the little Bible from his bag and began to read it. Not long afterward Young Antelope came into the lodge. He saw Laird squatting by the flickering flames, trying to read the Bible's fine print, and watched awhile in silence before slipping away.

That night the drizzle stopped; the air grew even colder. When Laird got up in the night, stars were blazing in the sky. Later, just at morning light, coyotes howled far away on the bluffs. And in the clearness of the day, miles across the prairies, mountain tops gleamed with ice and snow.

Suni brought water for the kettles and said in a low voice to Laird, "Lone Bull, who spit on me, is sick. He will take his sweat bath today to kill the evil."

Laird considered what his next move should be and decided to wait. Young Antelope, he sensed, would take the initiative; some reaction would be coming very soon.

"How many others are dead?"

"All the children," Suni sighed. "And all the new people are sick, too. Will they die?"

"I think so," Laird told her, "but say nothing until Young Antelope comes to talk. Then tell him only what I say."

Later in the day Young Antelope and three braves came to the lodge and waited for Laird to hold open the flap so they could enter. This was the first time Antelope had shown such courtesy, but it was not surprising because today he had come to bargain for a favor. The pipe was lit and slowly passed. Finally the young warrior spoke as if neither Laird nor the others were present.

"Bad times have come to my lodge and my people. The white man's sickness is here. Laird has said that the reason it would come is because the Blackfoot have been bad. We have fought the Nez Perce and killed their women and children and stolen their ponies. We took Laird's woman and made him watch us use her. Afterward Laird said we would be punished for it, also that when the first snow came the Blackfoot would begin to die—that all winter long we would die. He said we would want water but not be able to drink, that we would be hungry and not able to eat. He said we would burn with heat that water would not cool. He said all these things we did not believe. Yet now snow lies on the hills and ice forms on the rivers, for winter is near. And my heart is sick because many have died already and soon my people's turn will come—my children's.''

Young Antelope paused to look at Laird. "We have come to Laird and his woman to say the Blackfoot are sorry we have done bad things. We say to Laird and his woman that we, the Blackfoot, ask them to help us. What can we do but ask?''

The Indian remained motionless for a moment and then went on. "It is true that we are a strong people. But though we do not fear death in war, we know not how to fight this sickness that comes to us so suddenly. Our children burn with inner fire; they whimper in pain in the night; water does them no good. We wash them clean and still they die. What is this thing that we cannot see? That we cannot fight? Does it kill the white man too?''

Laird gathered his thoughts. His words, he knew, must be carefully chosen. "Yes, it does kill the white man. But it will not kill me. I will live to see you all die unless—''

"Unless what?" Young Antelope was angry. "You have already told us we will die. Do you speak from both sides of your mouth?''

"No, I only said that you will die and your people will die. As I have said would happen, the snow has come to the mountains and your people have become sick. I can do no more for you—except one thing.''

Young Antelope's eyes asked a question. Then he

spoke and Suni translated to Laird. "He say, 'What can Blackfoot do now?' "

"Tell him if he lets us go, I will read in the book and say to my God not to let all his people die."

When Suni repeated Laird's words Young Antelope looked at Laird, then turned to his men sitting nearby and spoke to each in turn. When he had finished he spoke to Suni. "Tell Laird we will talk about what he has offered us and come back. It is for us all to decide and will take time."

When at last Young Antelope appeared at the lodge again and Suni let him in, he did not seem quite so self-assured. Seating himself beside the fire, he spoke quietly.

"Tell Laird we cannot do this thing. Our wise men have said they do not believe in the power of his book. We will try the old way, the way they have told us."

Laird had already picked up the gist of Young Antelope's words. "That is not good for your people," he declared. "It is not good for you. More people will sicken tomorrow and more will die. By this time tomorrow you will know I speak true words."

Antelope heard Suni's translation in silence. After a moment he asked, "What will we have to do? What do you want to read from the book? How many of us may live? Can you tell us that? How long will it be before the sickness is gone?"

Laird knew that to answer immediately would not serve his purpose. He opened his sack, took out his pipe, filled the bowl ceremoniously with what little tobacco he had left, lit the contents, puffed and took much time before speaking. Many smoke rings wavered around his head before he said through Suni, "It will be three moons before the sickness leaves. After the chinook wind takes the last of the snow, those who still live will never suffer from the sickness again. But if your band steals from the Nez Perce or continues to fight them unfairly, the Blackfoot will be plagued with a far worse sickness than the one they are facing now.''

"Can you tell us how many of my people will not die?'' Antelope persisted.

"When the Great Spirit tells you the hunt will be good, does he say how many hides you will take? When he says it is a good time to make war, does he tell you how many scalps will hang in your lodges? No, I cannot count the deaths. I only know that some people will live if you let us go. Tell your wise men this—let them think— for tomorrow the worst part of the sickness will begin.''

Antelope tried to sort out what Laird had told him. That this sickness would surely kill his people was impossible to believe. Nothing in all the stories handed down by his elders had prophesied such a thing. He sat in silence while the two watched him, Suni standing, Laird squatting by the fire.

Suddenly a stick of green wood, sap hot within, exploded. Heated gas broke from one end. A stream of hissing red-blue flame gushed forth, brightened and grew larger. As the gas diminished the flame flickered down until only a tiny red glow remained.

As Young Antelope watched the burst of flame, Laird took advantage of the diversion. "Young Antelope, behold a sign. The fire that came from the stick is like your tribe. It was small, but it grew larger. Then it began to die. After the sickness there will be as little left of your people as the flicker that remains here. Tell your wise men what omen you were given.''

Within an hour Young Antelope and several others were again at the lodge entrance, waiting to be invited in. They seated themselves around the fire. Laird lit the pipe, puffed on it and passed it to Young Antelope. Once the

202

ceremony had been performed around the circle, the pipe was put aside and Young Antelope spoke.

"Laird, I saw the fire. I now believe what you have said. Lone Bull is dead. My son is sick. Say again what you will do if we let you go."

Again Suni repeated Laird's offer.

After talking with his men, Young Antelope asked, "If we let you go, what will you take with you?"

"Whatever your people took from us. Our guns, our supplies, our women, our ponies—nothing more. Bring the ponies into camp, pack our goods, lay the guns in the lodge where I can see them. I want the powder that is left and the lead. We will take nothing that is not ours. If we have not been allowed to leave before this time tomorrow, we will stay and see you all die. Then we will burn your camp, scatter your food and supplies and let your ponies go. Forever this camp will be called the Bad Place where Young Antelope's people died."

Suni translated sentence by sentence, often repeating what Laird had said. The Blackfoot silently watched the white man, intent on his message. Finally, followed by the other warriors, Young Antelope got up and left. Laird felt sure he would get away but was not certain about the fate of the Nez Perce women. If they had been exposed to the sickness or began at ths point to sicken in any way, no one would believe his powers.

Minutes later Laird heard Suni gasp. Startled, he looked up and saw her surprise at the sight of guns and bags of powder and lead being placed inside the lodge.

"Laird, you are wise and strong," Young Antelope offered. "We know you are good. Say to your God that the Blackfoot will do as you say. We will give back all we took and when that is done you will leave. We will stay here and help our sick people. We ask only that you read the book and ask that some of our people live."

Laird opened the Bible to a familiar place. Suni translated as he read. "Yea, though I walk through the Valley of the Shadow of Death, I will fear no evil, for Thou art with me."

Laird bowed his head and prayed that some of the tribe would be saved from death. Suni repeated his words.

When the pony herds had been delivered to the camp, Suni and the other women began to pack them with the growing pile of supplies and goods intended for the trip back to the Kooskoosky country and home. Next day, far down the trail, the newly liberated travelers recognized Craig and his party coming to meet them. Laird told Suni to stay with the women by the pony herd and packs until he motioned for them to follow. As the gap between him and Craig's band narrowed, he held up his hand and shouted to his friend, "Keep your men back until we talk. We have been exposed to smallpox."

Craig was concerned. "You all right, Laird?"

"I'm all right—and I won't get it, I hope. I was vaccinated in St. Louis by Mr. Clark before I left the city. I don't know about the women and Suni, though. They've probably contracted the disease. I expect to see signs by tomorrow or the next day. Why don't you take the horses and packs ahead and stay clear of us. Don't open anything until we see what happens to the women. Have you had the pox?"

"A long time ago," Craig replied. "I'm clean. Don't worry about me. What's next?"

"If you want to stick with us, let your men take the horses and lead the way, but stay out of our camp. I believe that if any of the women come down with it, they all will." Laird looked intently at his friend. Their first words to each other had been brief and to the point. Now he said, "By now you know what happened to Hawk Flying and the rest of the camp."

204

"I know everything but what's been happening to you. How the hell did you get the guns and everything else back?"

"Lucky guessing and foretelling the future. Let's get going. We can talk in camp tonight. I want to get settled in before the women get sick. We'll have to camp until it's all over."

Craig went back to his men. He told them what had taken place in the Blackfoot camp and that none of them should get close to Laird's party at any time, just ride ahead and herd the ponies.

At a campsite close to water and wood, a lodge for Laird and the women was set up, another close by to hold supplies. The two white men sorted out materials to make sure that nothing contaminated be placed where it might spread the sickness to others. Items like blankets, robes and cloth goods that had been exposed were piled separately. Neither Craig nor Laird knew how long contamination might last and they took no chances; the risk was too great.

After Craig had heard Laird's entire story, he went to the Nez Perce camp and repeated it. Then he spoke directly to Lame Bear, who was leading the party.

"Lame Bear, the sickness may come to the Nez Perce women who were held captive. They might all die. You and your men go back to Lapwai and tell Laird's story to James and his people. Laird and I will stay with the women, bury them if necessary and burn everything in their camp so the sickness cannot spread. Tell James we will not see him until next spring, for our hearts are sick and we will go somewhere to trap. Most important, tell James the Blackfoot will fight the Nez Perce no more; they have promised that to Laird. We will take Hawk Flying's pony with us—and Sun-in-the-Morning's too, if she dies—

and give them and others to their people in the spring when we return to the Kooskoosky country.''

Suni knew that when Bright Flower spoke of a warmth she felt, they would all get the sickness soon and she asked Laird several times if he would not get it too. She could not comprehend why he and Craig did not fear the disease and until Laird explained, Suni attributed their fearlessness to the book.

When the fever came it burned, almost consuming her, and Suni knew she would die. For the other women, too, the burning came and the pustules broke; the women cared for each other while they could. After that Craig and Laird bathed their hands and faces to help reduce the fever.

The calmness with which Suni faced her inevitable death reminded Laird how proud and dignified she'd remained even when Young Antelope had cruelly raped her in the lodge. Often during her sickness Suni smiled and said, ''Suni loves you, Laird.'' When she spoke these words he wept.

As one by one the women died, the men dug graves near a stand of trees. Burned robes and branches were strewn across them to disguise the scent of what lay beneath. Despite the earlier promise to save the ponies, Laird suggested killing them so the women could follow custom and ride to the happy hunting grounds.

''No, Laird,'' Craig countered. ''Let's do it the white man's way, the way the Nez Perce now believe in. I think the women would have wanted us to save the ponies. Change is coming; the old ways are fading fast. We'll burn most things here, then take the ponies and only what supplies we need with us. Let time and the wolves and the birds take care of what's left.''

Saddling up, the two friends rode north to Flathead

country. Trying not to think of Suni, Laird focused on the late September beauty of the afternoon. He and Craig were alone now. There was no need to hurry; winter had not yet locked them in.

Chapter 23

The two trappers stopped at Flathead House to exchange news and information with the Hudson's Bay Company trader there. Surprised to hear that the smallpox had spread so far west, the trader wanted to know how the two men had escaped it.

The factor at Flathead House had little knowledge of the smallpox spreading swiftly among the Indians. He had heard, though, that the disease had completely wiped out villages along parts of the Missouri below the great falls. Thank heaven, the Flatheads so far had escaped contamination. The factor hoped that when cold winter stopped travel between various villages, the disease's spread would slow. In truth he seemed more interested in the coming of Protestant missionaries to the area than in the spread of smallpox. The disease could die out, but the religion of the whites was certain to make even deeper inroads.

Laird found traveling without camp-keepers difficult, and he missed the attention and warmth Suni had given him more than he could have imagined. Craig kept silent concerning Hawk Flying; nevertheless, Laird sensed he missed her.

Both men had learned that life was short in the wilderness and that death came too soon to most in the West.

They thought more often than usual about settling down and about building on a plot of land, wherever it might be. As they traveled down Clarks Fork River to the land of the Pend Oreille, both men eyed the valleys and fertile lands they passed through. But no matter how beautiful the ones they found, none could compare with those seen in Nez Perce country.

Traveling through Hudson's Bay Company trapping territory, Craig and Laird were cautious; they knew any intrusion there by strangers from the south would be discouraged by drastic means. But if they were to do winter trapping of beaver anywhere, they would have to start the work soon. With this in mind, whenever Craig met Indians, either Flatheads or Pend Oreille, he swapped information. At the beginning of a valley opening west of the gorge in the river they came to a small village of Pend Oreille staging a hunt for the deer and elk that now were coming down from the mountains.

In the village were two hunters who had killed one elk and badly wounded another day before. While following the wounded cow elk, the Indians had been attacked by a grizzly. Before they managed to kill the enraged animal, it had battered them into bloody caricatures of themselves. Their women had tried to clean and bandage the wounds, but when Craig saw what damage had been done, he thought he'd better help.

"Want to play doctor, Laird?" he asked. "I can sew 'em up if you want to help me."

"Sure. Just tell me what to do."

"Stick around close. You can keep the skin together while I sew."

Holding his curved needle and thread, Craig made signs and spoke a few words. The Indians nodded and agreed to let the white trapper do what he could. One brave's torn scalp had been flimsily patched with pieces of cloth and soft doeskin.

Craig's patient showed no sign of pain when Craig poked his needle through one side of the cut and pulled it to the other edge. Once the scalp had been sewn closed, Craig stitched together several other nasty cuts and tears, then washed his hands and rethreaded the needle.

The second brave's right arm had been broken above the elbow and the skin above it raked open by the bear's claws. Although the arm was already splinted, the deep cut had not been closed. It took both trappers to set and resplint the arm so that the bones would join, then pull the skin together enough so it would heal; each trapper was puzzled as to how the Indians had stopped the bleeding.

At the fire that evening Craig told Laird, "I've seen lots worse things, old Peg Leg Smith for example. He got his leg bones broke so bad he tried to cut his leg off with his knife and passed out. We finished the job, took hot knives and seared the end, wrapped him up and put him on a sling-stretcher between two ponies. Then we hauled him along with us. In one place the ponies fell in a river.

"After we straightened that mess out, we wound up at an Indian camp. The squaws and kids chewed up leaves and twigs of a weed I'd never seen and had a spitting contest to see who could spit the most on old Smith's leg. Anyway, it quit bleeding and begun to heal up. Pieces of bone kept coming loose the whole time, though, so old Smith pulled and we got pincers and pulled until all the jagged pieces come out. By golly, it finally healed over. Smith whittled out a peg leg, made a pad of hair and hide for the stump and a harness to strap it on, and to this day he hops and stumps all through the mountains. Amazing things a feller can do if he's tough enough and wants to live."

After seeing to it that the hunters were healing properly, the trappers shared their camp meal and asked the usual questions about the country. Where to trap beaver? Where might they find an area that would still yield enough furs to warrant going there?

Before long maps had been drawn on the sand. One sketched with charcoal on white doeskin showed how the river ran to the lake of the Pend Oreille. The old man drawing the picture pointed out that they were camped just west of the river's gorges and he drew in a river system that ended in a lake on the south side of the mountain. The lake ended and emptied into a river. As he showed the river running west, the old man marked a tepee and said, "Spokane House." The lake above it he dubbed Coeur d'Alene and let his finger trace back up the river system he had drawn.

On the upper end of the river and on its tributaries the old Indian put the sign for beaver and traps. This could be their winter hunting ground. An Indian woman came by and stood close until the chief drawing the map looked up and saw her. "Squaw Spokane," he said to Craig.

The Indian woman spoke in broken English, expressing her desire to show the trappers to her homeland.

Craig asked in surprise, "You want to go Spokane place?"

"Home is there. I was sold to Blackfoot in fight. These people trade for me. You buy?"

"Now what do you think of that?" Craig marveled to Laird. "We come up with a cook. Now all we need is a helper who can take care of your side of the lodge, and we'll go trapping in style."

Soon afterward Craig spoke to the chief, who saw a profitable trade in the making right before him. "You sell this Spokane to me? Want winter woman to cook," the trapper began.

"She goes for trade," was the reply. "What do you have?"

The woman interpreted for Craig as he asked if there were another woman or girl in camp who could go along. The Spokane woman, not old but certainly no longer a girl, nodded her head, went away and to Laird's astonishment came back with three other women.

Craig and the Spokane talked. All of the women, Craig learned, had been captured in a Blackfoot raid while a band of Spokane and Coeur d'Alene were holding a buffalo hunt in their territory. The Blackfoot had traded the women to the Flatheads, who had sent them along to Flathead House with a party of trappers. There they were swapped for supplies and powder and lead; the trader in turn dealt them off to the Pend Oreille for ponies the chief had stolen from some other tribe and wanted to get rid of. Now the Pend Oreille chief intended to get something in trade for the women.

"Hell, we don't want four women," Craig protested. "It'll keep us busy hunting just to feed 'em." He turned to Laird. "What do you think?"

Laird steeled himself. The thought of other women in the lodge where he and Suni had lain still grieved him. But Suni wasn't coming back and there were realities to face. "Can't we take at least two and trade them to the Spokane when we get to the trapping area?" Laird asked in a voice so steady it surprised him.

"Now that's an idea," Craig roared. "You're beginning to think like an old trapper. Anything you catch can be eaten, sold or traded if you work it right. Let's deal for the works, take 'em with us and let 'em help us trap and work hides. When we end up in Spokane country, we can be the great white men who brought back the stolen women and collect our own reward. We might end up with something besides a fat-puppy supper. Ponies, hides, furs, clothes—anything to help us pay for the trouble of getting slaves to work for us for free board and room.''

The men named the four women Spokane, Bit Chest, Flat Nose and Long Hair. The first woman got the name of her tribe and the name of each of the others indicated her special look. The chief and his bunch wound up with awls, gunpowder, lead, a bullet mold, four knives and some red and blue cloth for their women. To sweeten the deal the trappers gave the chief two plugs and a small tin of fine-cut tobacco.

Before Laird and Craig left the camp the braves they had mended with thread, needle and splint came to shake hands and make the sign of friendship. The one with the worst cuts and claw marks turned out to be a brother of a Pend Oreille chief who bore the name Plenty Grizzly Bears. Craig laughed at that and said this fellow's name should be Too Many Grizzly Bears.

After helping his visitors swim the river the chief led them to the old Indian trail that connected with the Coeur d'Alene river system. Then he gave them the map as passport through Coeur d'Alene country to Spokane House.

The winter hunt began. Craig and Laird had plenty of help in camp and out. Laird chuckled at the trade but after a while he got to wondering if the women had lice. He calmed down only when he noticed no unusual scratching.

Once they were on the trail, Laird felt better than he had for many days. The chatter of the women cheered the men, and the ease with which the Indians drove and handled the ponies relieved Craig and Laird of the burden of handling the mounts themselves.

They crossed the Divide. Four inches of snow spread over the vast upper reaches of the watershed. The area was heavily timbered, but on one clear, cold November day during their crossing they glimpsed the rugged Bitterroot

Divide blocking the way to the east. The river and its tributary fingers lay before them, a gradual ridge dropping down to the tiny valley that the Spokane chief had marked "beaver country" on the map.

There the trapping party came on an old campground, lodgepoles still standing. It would be theirs until they had trapped out the local beaver workings. How easy it was to drift into the way of life of the trapper, Laird thought. Then he slept while the coyotes' night song echoed from the hills. Later the wolves overwhelmed the sound with their deep-voiced howls.

In the lodge the next morning Laird heard the ponies snort outside as if trying to break loose. Both men, out with their guns, found an old sow with two half-grown cubs scattering the horses. The she-bear, head up, looked at the oncoming trappers.

"Take her, Laird, right in the chest," Craig coached. "I'll be ready if your shot don't stop her."

Laird fired. The old bear dropped, raised her head and bawled a few times, then slumped down dead. While Laird reloaded Craig watched the cubs. When he saw Laird's ramrod shove down the rifle bullet, he raised his gun and killed the closer one. The second cub made a loud gravelly sound. With teeth chomping it walked stiffly to its mother, then stood looking at the two men, its lips drawn back, its hair bristling on its neck—all fight. Laird shot it.

Later, with the ponies gathered together and the bears skinned, he and Craig were happy. They had good meat to their credit, not to mention fine furs. The day had been truly an auspicious beginning to their season.

The days after passed quickly. With four women now to do the skinning and other work, Laird and Craig had plenty of time to trap. First they cleaned out the ponds, then moved on over the Divide for a few days and into the flats where another part of the stream branched. Soon they made another move and then another.

With meat of bear, elk, deer and fish to eat, the travelers lived well. Snow held off and the weather remained clear and cold. Soon ice began to cover the ponds and trapping became more difficult. As the weeks passed, sets were made in narrower channels, the strange scent of castoreum the trappers had brought with them attracting the beaver almost immediately.

Carcasses were placed where wolves and coyotes could feed and the men shot a few of these beasts for their thick, glossy winter hides. The women, left so often in camp, made snares of fine brass wire for Craig and Laird to carry in their packs and set in thickets to snare white snowshoe hares. Heavier wire snares were baited with rabbit and hung on bent saplings. Many foxes were captured by this method as well as lynx and three bobcats.

Gradually weather changes came. An overcast sky one morning accompanied unusually warm air. When they went outside, Spokane and the other women looked at the sky and Spokane told Craig they must move camp.

"That's fine with us, Spokane," Craig agreed. "We eat and pack up."

In a short time they left the place where so many Indians had camped before them, and following an old trail down to the Little North Fork, climbed over the Divide. Camp was made late that day and there was no time to set out traps. Great cottonwood trees grew along the flats close to the river and beaver ponds were everywhere. Ponies would be used to cross to the ponds farthest away.

The weather stayed warm. After a few days in the new spot Craig was ready to move again. "Laird," he urged, "let's get out of here. All I'm catching is half-grown beaver cubs. This country's been trapped before."

"Where will we head? Lower country?"

"You bet. We'll get to Spokane House, swap off the women there and go see what the Nez Perce are up to. Stop over with James and his tribe, see some Nez Perce women for a while."

"What will James think of us when we come back? We left two of his women dead in Blackfoot country."

"What can he think? Leaving them sure wasn't our fault. We'll swap these women for what we can get and donate the booty along with the Nez Perce women's ponies to James' tribe or to the women's folks. That way the families will come out ahead and be happy about it. They'd probably written off the two girls anyway."

"You're sounding a little tough, seems to me."

"Oh hell, boy, forget your civilized upbringing. That's the way it is here now and always has been. Don't try to cover it up with preacher talk. I remember when old Parker and Whitman first come to the rendezvous, Parker held out against hunting, gambling or doing anything except praying and preaching on Sunday. The men stayed in camp more to please the women than the preachers. But when some feller hollered, 'Buffalo coming, get your guns,' we all jumped and run for ponies and guns handy and made a good kill.

"Old Parker takes his knife, whacks off a chunk of roasting hump ribs, squats to eat, then had the guts to tell us his praying caused the Lord to send meat to our camp. Me and old Doc figured the Indians might swallow that, but the trappers sure didn't. They called Parker old Mealymouth from then on."

Laird grimaced in laughter, thinking how inappropriately the word "old" was often used. Craig wasn't old, but he, Meek and some others were always called old Craig, old Meek, old this one and old that one at rendezvous. There were other expressions, too, like "old hoss" and "you old bastard;" some, in fact, were clearly obscene.

Laird recalled how pleased he'd felt when after the fight with the Bannock one trapper had commented, "That old boy with Craig is a son-of-a-bitching good feller to have along."

Now that all seemed long ago. Laird's attention turned once more to Craig. First he agreed to go with his friend to Nez Perce country; then he teased him.

"I'll bet you've been thinking of some woman or girl in the Nez Perce camp you've had your eye on."

"You've guessed it," Craig chuckled. "I won't say who she is till I see her again. I have the feeling I might have to marry her, though; they're all for doing it the missionary way nowadays. But if that gal's what I think she is and I decide I can make it a permanent deal, I'll shoot the works and marry her for good.

"You know, Laird," he went on, "we'd got to be like a family traveling together. You to talk to, Hawk and Suni to cook and sleep with us. I swear I never had a better time than in the mountains, all of us together. I feel real bad at times, wishing I'd been there to kill a few of them red bastards that attacked you."

Feeling a new surge of grief, Laird urged, "Well, then, Craig, let's get the hell out of here. I don't want to spend the winter in this snowbound hole with these four Spokane women. I want to look over the Nez Perce situation too and try to make it up to Suni's folks."

The journey down to the lake was not easy that late in the year. Water froze on the horses' legs when the party splashed across the river, and it decked their tails with icicles. Packs got soaked, then hardened. Ropes stiffened hard as iron.

Fortunately, north of the lake were flats frozen solid enough for the travelers to make good time crossing. They reached a small inhabited camp on the flat bench above the lower end of the lake. There they were given a fine welcome. Spokane told the Indians there that she and her companions were on the way to Spokane House, where she would rejoin her people. Craig traded a few presents and two slightly lame pack ponies for a pair in better condition.

Winds blowing snow and cold hit them the last few miles of their trip, but the Spokane women were in familiar territory now and led the way to the big camp sheltered from the winds on the banks of the Little Spokane River. The trading post lay only a few miles farther on, but the two trappers decided to stay and visit with these Indians. They would be happy to see their missing women and might give information concerning the post.

The factor there might be curious as to why two trappers had shown up with Spokane women after having lived with a Nez Perce band. He would also want to know why they had crossed by the northern route and come down the Coeur d'Alene River instead of using the well known Salish trail. Trapping and trading competition increased yearly and the Hudson's Bay Company would not be left behind if it could prevent it.

Craig and Laird kept on the lookout for a man Laird knew only as Toom. Laird had not forgotten what Young Antelope had told him, that he and Suni had been captured and not killed because a Hudson's Bay Company man had wanted it that way and had promised to bargain for them later. What Toom was planning he hadn't said.

Craig thought the name Toom, as Young Antelope said it, meant Tom. He knew of Tom Hill, a half-breed; Tomahas, an Indian; a white man called Thompson; Tom McKay; and a flock of others with that name. "We got to try to match one of 'em up with what the Blackfoot said," he told Laird.

They stayed in the Spokane camp for two weeks until

weather cleared and travel became easier. While there they met with Spokane Garry, who recently had become chief of the Spokane.

Receiving cloth, knives, shears, beads and little bells for the furs they had taken pleased the Spokane women. Normally Indian women who traveled and trapped with Hudson's Bay Company men lost title to furs of animals they caught. Craig and Laird had given them more than the women could have received at the post, and still the men would receive many times the value of the trinkets when they traded the furs at rendezvous.

Chapter 24

Moving on at last, Craig and Laird came to the first Nez Perce winter village and stayed there a few days to visit and get the local news. The village was situated near the mouth of the Clearwater. The Nez Perce knew the two trappers from the year before and gave them the welcome they sorely needed; their friendliness reminded Laird of Sun-in-the-Morning.

He and Craig saw girls and women available in the village, but neither man offered one the chance to share his lodge and robes. James' camp was not far away and both wanted to see what women were there and what welcome James' people would give them.

The Indians' almost instantaneous communication of news and events always amazed the white men. James and his people already knew much about what Craig and Laird had been doing. Returning warriors had told of Laird's ultimatum to the Blackfoot and his prediction of the sickness and death of the Blackfoot people. These Nez Perce warriors spoke highly of the two men, reporting that the trappers had cared for the dying women and buried them in a Christian way before traveling north to Flathead and Pend Oreille country.

The story of Craig and Laird's purchase of the Spokane captive women also had spread. The Nez Perce knew that the trappers had returned the women to their people and had given them goods in fair trade for their lynx and fox furs. James had learned of the friendly meeting with Chief Garry and knew that now the trappers had returned to the Nez Perce because they wished to live with the tribe for a part of the winter.

When Craig came to James to shake his hand and call him by his Nez Perce name, Hin-mah-tute-ke-kaikt, the chief was impressed. Craig's gesture indicated a respect not often extended by whites to Indians, whose names the white men usually found too hard to remember, let alone pronounce.

"My friends, I am glad to see you again," James intoned. "My people are happy to see you. Our lodges are your lodges. Our village is open to you."

"James," Craig began, "Laird and I are sorry to come back without your women. Our hearts were too heavy to come at once. We took the long trail here in order to mourn our women's deaths properly and to heal the wounds we suffered because of losing them. With us we have their ponies and trade goods. Will you see that each family receives what is its due?"

"My friends, it will be done."

To Laird the welcome they received was truly a homecoming. The Nez Perce had taken him in and he felt one of them. They laughed easily at his attempts to speak their language and he laughed warmly at their English. Before accepting James' invitation to smoke and talk he met with Suni's parents and gave them a sketch he had made of their daughter as she sat crosslegged working on a shirt. The portrait seemed so close to reality that when he handed it over, tears welled up in Laird's eyes. Those watching knew that his Nez Perce girl had not been merely a winter

woman, but one whom the trapper had cared for deeply—
his love woman.

Later James told Craig and Laird that news had fil-
tered back about a massacre at Ash Hollow. The two men
were horrified but not surprised, having heard about the
incident from the Flatheads.

"We were at rendezvous and saw him go," Craig
replied. "Gray was not wise. He had no judgment. We
may not see him again."

James disagreed. "I think we will. Some fools do not
die. They do things we would not dare, they hurt others
and yet they live."

At the meal the men all ate first and had their bowls
filled often. And that day Craig saw Isobel. He had seen
her around the camp before and thought about her. Now he
realized how she had changed, maturing from a pleasant-
looking girl into a beautiful woman. To Craig this daughter of James excelled all others—even Suni—in grace and
beauty. Seeing her, he felt struck as if by lightning and
was determined to know her better.

Neither the girl nor her mother had told James of
Isobel's dream regarding her future husband. James wondered occasionally why his daughter had not chosen a
young man to share her blanket, but so many other concerns filled his mind that he had given the matter little
thought. Now that the two trappers were here, however,
James had noticed how steadily Craig's attention was focused on his daughter. Would she respond to this rich and
powerful white man? Craig was respected among all the
Indians, their opinion of him overshadowing what they
felt for any of his trapper associates.

James hoped Isobel was waiting for some sign from
Craig that he was indeed interested. He asked Isobel's
mother if her daughter had ever spoken of marriage.

"She spoke of a dream she had. It said that her

husband will be someone not from our tribe. Where he will come from I do not know. Isobel has never seen the place.''

"We will go to the rendezvous to trade," James told his wife. "I will say to Craig that we will meet him there and that he can camp with us. He and Laird are strong men. They do not lie or cheat us as other white men do.''

William Craig had grown to have great respect for his trapper partner. Never had he openly questioned him about his background and why he had come west to take up the difficult life of a trapper. But why was Laird here? True, after leaving the Blackfoot and while caring for the Nez Perce women before they died, Laird had spoken a few words about his past and in doing so had mentioned his written documents.

"Craig, if anything happens to me—and we both know it could—please see that my journal and letters reach the man they are addressed to. Make sure the letters are sealed and waterproofed and pay someone to make certain they arrive safely.''

"I'll do that, Laird," Craig had promised. "Are they real important?''

"I'm not sure, but I don't want to take chances. My writings are mostly my impressions of the Indian tribes we meet and how they trade, the way they live, what they believe. My trip and supplies were financed in return for such information.

"My mother would have been greatly distressed if she had known where I was going. The man I write to covered for me so she wouldn't hire someone to try to find out where I was. I had committed no crime, merely drifted into a situation that might have created a scandal at home.''

"Don't fret about it, boy. I think I understand. Most of us fellers out here aren't who we were back home. But what makes you think your letters might not reach the person you sent 'em to?''

"Letters I received at the rendezvous had been opened and read. Whether that invasion of my privacy was accomplished in St. Louis or earlier I don't know. But that's off my mind now I have your word that my letters east won't be destroyed.''

Laird wondered aloud what he and Craig would be doing next.

"James says his people will go to the rendezvous in late June,'' Craig replied. "We can meet up with 'em there. Let's cache our packs with James' band, take a couple pack ponies and swing west through the prairie country to see what the Palouse are doing. I've been wondering how they're feeling about the missionaries. We'll wind up down among the Cayuse and stop over with the Whitmans. If you want to see other tribes and learn things about 'em, there's no better time than now.''

"You're sure you don't want to take in a spring hunt?''

"Naw, I'm kind of camp stale. I got to see more of this country before I decide where to sink my axe. We'll sure see purty landscape this spring. I don't know what the Garden of Eden was like, but I can show you the purtiest flower gardens on this green earth. If I was one of the old boys grew up here, I'd do everything in my power to keep out the white men's plows and fences. This is the ancient people's land. There ain't no better place.''

Laird smiled. "You kind of go off the deep end when you talk about this country, you know that, partner?''

The trappers took the Indian trail downriver to Fort Walla Walla and visited the Whitmans at Waiilatpu. It was like meeting old friends as they greeted one another and exchanged information. Marcus hadn't changed much since the Green River meeting, but not having white men around to admire her looks, Narcissa was showing signs of being fed up with Indians.

With all her beauty, she had not been nearly so successful in her missionary work among Indians as had Eliza Spalding with her plain looks and hard work of everyday teaching. The Indians, used to close observation of men and animals, must have sensed what she was feeling. Both he and Craig felt that like an unmatched team of horses pulling a heavy wagon, the Whitmans were not matched well for the work they had come to do.

At the Hudson's Bay post the two trappers sensed the coming of more trouble. The factor, Pierre Pambrun, welcomed them cordially and invited the travelers to have dinner and relate news of their travels among the tribes. Not really caring about Craig and Laird's religious convictions, he spoke openly of how he was teaching the Roman Catholic religion to the Indians who loitered at the post. The Cayuse and some Nez Perce were particularly eager to learn, he'd found, and were curious about the contradictions in white men's beliefs.

Pambrun was not the only Hudson's Bay employee who had successfully spread the Roman Catholic view of religion. French employees had been doing the same. They were good trappers and had come west following the river with their companions, the Iroquois.

From Pambrun the two trappers heard again about the incident at Ash Hollow and about how Whitman and Spalding had been treating the Indians. According to the factor both missionaries had used the whip at times, not only on boys but on grown men. Pambrun warned that the Cayuse especially would not put up with such treatment.

The initial Cayuse complaint, Pambrun explained, was that although Whitman had come supposedly to work with the Nez Perce, he had settled on Cayuse lands. Another trouble spot was that Parker, who first came with

226

Whitman, had promised that the missionaries would build houses and a church for the Cayuse and compensate the tribe; to hear the Cayuse tell it, there had been little compensation.

Pambrun, trying to be fair, had suggested that Parker had been referring to the church school and the missionary teaching as the compensation. But the Cayuse weren't convinced. They were certain that he had promised to buy the land from them with money, goods or horses.

Another complaint was that Whitman worked all the time and that no Indian man could ever be expected to do that. Other problems stemmed from the fact that Whitman feared no man on earth, only his invisible God. Also, he never bargained, stopped to talk or parleyed; that attitude was indeed contrary to the Indian way. Finally, Whitman had no sense of personal dignity and no manners either, the Indians reported. Parker, at the rendezvous, had been ashamed of the way Whitman speared his food, then chomped away with little concern that grease and blood were smearing his face. Even the mountain men tried more than Whitman did to show the red man they had some sense of propriety.

"What do you hear about Mr. Spalding?" Laird asked.

"The best thing about Spalding is his woman," Pambrun answered. "She really means well and shows it. She's not stuck up, she doesn't complain, and although she's homely as a stick fence, she has a purpose and serves it well. In the process she is learning the Indians' language and is composing an alphabet for printing. When that's done, the Indians will have a Bible in their own language to carry around. I tell you, one good woman can save more souls in this country than ten men armed with their black books and what they call the word of God."

"Purty strong words, Pambrun," Craig observed. "Many other people think like you do?"

"Who knows? My opinions are pieced together from the crumbs of conversation I pick up, the talk and whispers. There have been troubles in this river valley many times since the first white men came. These people have different ideas about the missionaries' intentions. I was here when Dr. Parker arrived. I saw how they listened to him. He saw something that the new people do not see. Most Indians—Nez Perce, Cayuse, Umatilla, Yakima and any other tribes who want the men with the book to come—are actually seeking the power, guns, horses and all the trade materials we have and they don't."

"You are Catholic, Pierre, but are you prejudiced because of it? Does it make any difference to you that these missionaries are Protestants?"

"I hope not, Laird, but I see that like others, your missionaries make too big a fuss over little sins instead of trying to change the Indian ways gradually."

"How do you think Whitman will get along here, where four or five tribes come together?" Craig asked.

Pierre Pambrun shook his head. "Trouble, Mr. Craig, big trouble. You see, all along here several tribes have fishing rights, which in past times they traded to other tribes for hunting rights on their lands. These weren't landholding rights, mind you, just the right to fish or to trade. Nez Perce, Cayuse, Umatilla, Walla Walla, across the river the Yakima and even the Palouse tribes come down to fish. There are other minor tribes that come occasionally too, and all this time we have had no warring. If—and I say if—Parker and Whitman had made sure who owned the spot they settled on and then carried out some sort of specific purchase instead of infringing on Cayuse land, this area would have been assured a peaceful place to meet with most interior tribes at one time or another every year. Now I don't know; it could be a real trouble spot."

*   *   *

After the visit with Pierre Pambrun the two travelers stayed on for a night and a day at Waiilatpu. Marcus Whitman, enthused about his missionary activity with the Indians, complained they didn't have much heart for physical work—just as Pambrun had predicted he would—and asked Craig for information about the Nez Perce and various other tribes Craig knew.

Narcissa Whitman cornered Laird, wanting to know about his life in the East, when he might return there and why he had come out to this wild country in the first place. Laird parried her questions with a few of his own to see if Pambrun might be wrong in his assessment of these two. His conclusion was that Narcissa Whitman was a fine-looking woman whose religious upbringing and desire to teach and spread the gospel had gotten her into a place she was not prepared for. Laird sensed her aloofness from the Indians. He noted how she ordered them about with no respect, in the same way he had seen Indian women do to those under their command.

Later, on the trail to Fort Boise, Laird remarked to Craig, "You know, old Pierre might have hit pretty close to the mark with his comments on the Whitmans."

"You said it, Laird. They'll never work out there. I'm glad we're heading for the rendezvous. Before long there will be trouble and it'll spread into a war like a knife with two edges, cutting deep both ways. Both reds and whites will suffer, the reds most."

"Won't that affect you if you take up land in the Clearwater country?"

"Course it will. It'll make noises clear to the East. After seeing what Whitman and Spalding are doing and what's going on up at Spokane House, there's one thing I'm sure of: this country will begin to settle up and the Indians will have to get used to seeing land plowed up and things to eat getting planted. We saw what the gardens

229

produced up where Spokane Garry lives. Things have already begun to change. The Indians were against plowing till they saw what good stuff come from planting seeds. Now they want cows, first for prestige over other tribes, second for meat and hides and lastly for milk and butter. What they don't yet see is the care and feeding those animals will take.'' Craig chuckled. ''Those women and kids will have quite a job to handle; these old red men will see to that.

''Fencing always upsets things, too,'' Craig went on. ''There will be squabbles over lands once open to anyone and everyone. The whole way of the hunting, root-gathering tribes will have to turn around, and no matter how soon the changes come or how slow, they'll cause trouble for everyone in this territory.

''To settle squabbles and try to keep things on any even keel, the army will move in and wear out men and horses running back and forth over the country. Then, to justify all this expense to the people in Washington who ain't got no idea of tribes, territory, climate or anything else, they'll have this thing mapped, divided up, split sixteen ways from Sunday. Every white-collared stiff-necked do-gooder what comes here will want to get some of the honey on his fingers to lick off. Hell's fire, Laird, we're here too, and try to get along peacefully, but when it comes to fighting and killing, there's only one side we can be on—the whites'.''

''My God, Craig, what a dismal future you see,'' Laird burst out. ''Maybe I ought to keep right on going east and settle down there.''

''Did I sound that bad?'' Craig laughed to himself. ''I was thinking out loud and couldn't stop once I got started. I'll tell you something, Laird. Even though it all begins to add up sour, I'm going to stick here and I think you will too. Back East things ain't no better than out here. They'll

squabble and fight there, too. Watch and see. If I read the wind right, Eastern folk will have their own war to fight before long, and to hell with us out here.''

"Now what are you talking about? War back there? What war?''

"The war over keeping slaves.'' Craig was solemn. "The South ain't going to put up with people from the North telling them it's a sin to keep slaves. Them folk from the South considers it a matter of economic necessity and won't listen to nothing different. Everyone was talking about slaves when I was a boy, and from what I hear they're hotter than ever about it now.''

"What does slavery have to do with us out here?''

"Next time we set in with the Indian chiefs in a powwow,'' Craig replied, "try to pick up their thoughts concerning missionaries and others who come here and put Indians to work with no apparent compensation. I know and you know that Spalding and Whitman believe it's for the Indians' own good that they work for religion, but the natives ain't grasped that concept yet. They'll work like hell against their own beliefs for food they learn to raise— they can see that—but to give up their lands, then be made to work 'em and see others fed without gaining money and power themselves—that will sure go against the grain.''

"But what can we do about it?'' Laird queried. "The two of us don't have the power to change the pattern, do we?''

"We just might be the threads that can hold the blanket together. You can't never tell what influence you have on other people's actions and lives. Someone has to stave off trouble, turn it another way. I ain't seen anyone among the missionaries capable of understanding the Indians here. This bunch ain't war-crazy like the tribes farther east, but if they're pushed there will be blood running down some streams and rivers here too. Years ago these

people settled land claims with blood and war; now again they're facing the chance of being taken over, being forced to give up what they rightfully own and watch Mother Earth being torn up by a plow. The old men like James will counsel and try to work out a plan, but there ain't no way they can win this one.''

"I begin to see what you mean," Laird mused. "I suppose this has come on since Whitman asked you to help Joe Meek bring his cart to Waiilatpu."

"That's sure correct. Even then I could see Whitman speeding up the whole procession of emigrants to follow. History, of which I've read some and listened to others tell, shows that ease of travel, like water running downhill, will spread people around over the land faster than you can count. Long time ago the Indians walked. Then they got ponies. Now the Indian will be seeing wheels headed across his land. The white people will move their families and their plows here, bring in seeds to plant. When those eastern folk hear about that two-wheeled cart reaching the Columbia, there will come a string of people like ants following a trail of spilled sugar."

After a while of thinking this over, Laird changed the subject. "Have you seen the woman you'd take a shine to yet?"

"Maybe, maybe not. I can sure see the missionary influence already. I'll bet this year they'll put the price of marriage on the sleeping robes. You're not apt to have another girl like Suni come slipping in with the knotted rope left in her lodge. Things are changing."

Craig's mention of Suni reopened Laird's memory of her.

"You know, Craig," he said hoarsely, "I thought Suni's folks would blame us for what happened, me more than you, but all they talked about was all the odd things I had done for her. Are all the Nez Perce that forgiving?"

232

"If you do your best and level with 'em, they are. James' people and the other tribes don't blame us for the deaths. They all know the Blackfoot. They feel we done the best we could and that you was lucky to come out of it all alive, let along bring back stolen goods and ponies.

"You'll hear things said about Gray now that will do him no good if and when he ever returns—that's for sure," Craig continued. "That fool went east without the protection of force of arms, got two Nez Perce killed and two sent back smack into trouble with Spalding and Whitman. That little action of Gray's will have repercussions for years."

Both men felt themselves woman-hungry. They began to talk about the rendezvous. Laird knew well by then how important it was for mountain men to have something to look forward to. He remembered when during the winter after coming into camp at dark, he had entered the lodge and been greeted with smiles and eager help in pulling off his frozen moccasins and wet clothing. He had stood naked while being warmed by the fire and drunk hot tea or coffee the women had handed him as they provided dry buckskins and a wool blanket to warm him.

One night in particular a storm had hit. Laird was a mile from camp, loaded with traps and beaver, stumbling along, hardly able to see through the whirling, cutting flakes of snow. Suddenly, riding an icy gust of wind, came the sweet smell of smoke. He had known then that he was close to camp and had staggered on until he saw the delicious glow of the fire Suni and Hawk Flying had made outside to direct their men home. That night Laird realized more deeply than ever the importance of women to trappers who spent their lives in this land of mountains and uncharted rivers.

* * *

When Craig and Laird visited Fort Boise, they swapped information and learned from the factor there that the Sioux had bragged to French-Canadian traders about the killing of Gray's people at Ash Hollow and had warned other tribes the same thing would happen to them if they tried to cross Sioux land. The trader declared that the white missionaries were cowards who were afraid to fight and would sooner give up Indians to be killed than to die in combat themselves.

"That damned fool Gray, he sure upset the keg—everything we're hearing tells us that," Craig exclaimed. "I guess we should've stopped him at the rendezvous, but no. That dad-blamed missionary was too bullheaded. All we could hope for was that he might get through without trouble. Now no Indian will trust his judgment and that lack of trust will reflect on every white man in the territory. I'll bet all hell breaks loose out at the rendezvous this year when the story gets around."

Chapter 25

Although Craig had tried to get Isobel's attention in camp, the Indian girl continued to ignore him. Craig was reluctant to show his feelings openly by giving her presents; he preferred that she show an interest in him first. But Isobel remained as aloof as a nun.

When she didn't even attempt to attract his attention, Craig's curiosity became aroused. Why would Isobel act that way? Not knowing how to approach James, the trapper could only wait and see—and the waiting was uncomfortable. There he was, thirty-eight years old, desiring to settle down with the woman of his dreams, and she wouldn't give him a tumble.

Laird was having his own problems. After looking the camp girls over, hoping—but doubting—he would find one as beautiful as Suni, he concluded that the only Indian woman in Suni's class at all was Isobel. Not aware of Craig's feelings, he had made a sketch of the girl, and was disappointed when she'd shown no sign of interest in him. "The girls are not so anxious to make up to us now," he complained to Craig. "What's made the difference between this year and last?"

"Religion. Old Spalding's threatened the women with hellfire and damnation if they lie with a man afore they're

married to him. Now they'll back off unless they find we're serious enough to offer taking 'em as wives. There ain't going to be no easy woman from the Nez Perce tribes from now on except those who think easy come and easy go and like the old ways best.''

"It's hard to believe the change would come so fast."

"Well," Craig temporized, "give us a few days on the trail and see what happens. I have a hunch your bed might be warmed some night, specially in June, when nights are warm and blood runs hot."

But though they traveled with James' entire village to the rendezvous, not one Nez Perce girl invaded their lodge. Craig was especially disappointed for Laird. He knew how the young trapper had hoped for some easy love to entertain him during the difficult trip.

This year they found another type of enlivenment at the rendezvous. Gray was there and with him more missionaries he hoped would be able to convert the Indians to the white man's religion. Over and over again, Gray gave his version of the Ash Hollow fight, as he called it. And over and over again, the trappers and mountain men spoke of the incident as "Gray's lack of guts."

The missionary had insisted there had been no option but to capitulate to the demands of the Sioux. If he had stayed on the spot and fought, he said, even more would have been killed. As it was, the Sioux had let the white men live and given back their ponies and goods.

The trappers were furious. In times past they had fought against far greater odds to prove that when attacked, white men fought back to the death. Now they argued about what really must have happened and about what could have been done to avoid the fight and the needless loss of friendly Indians.

*　　*　　*

At the rendezvous Craig made no progress at all in attracting Isobel's attention. In a moment of frustration he mentioned his predicament to Laird, who now knew for certain Craig's choice of woman. To Craig's surprise Laird offered him advice.

"Bill, do you remember when I was looking for a way to attract Suni, you took the time to tell me how?"

"Yes, I remember that."

"You told me how the young braves dressed up their ponies, painted themselves for war, put on their finest buckskins, took their lances with scalps and coup sticks and rode at parade in front of the women they wanted to court. Why don't you do the same? Put on a front, show off for once. In all the time I have known you I have never heard you brag or boast. Do it now. Let's see what comes of it."

"If I ever heard crazy talk from anyone!" Craig seemed to dismiss the whole idea. But then his curiosity overcame him and he asked, "What makes you think that might work with Isobel?"

"It will surprise Isobel and the others; she will certainly have to recognize you. Who knows what will happen after that, but it seems worth a try."

Craig had a drink or two to work up enough nerve to go through with what Laird had suggested. Finally he brought up his best pony, one he had gotten in trade with the Nez Perce, wound and braided strips of bright red, blue and gold cloth into its tied-up and clubbed tail, then painted three red bands on the pony's left hip and stripes of red and yellow on its withers. He stuck feathers in mane and forelock, draped the saddle with a red blanket and hung bells wherever there was a place to hang one.

Laird watched as Craig dressed in his best shirt and buckskins. He suggested that Craig's pack ponies, loaded

with plunder and hides, be allowed to trail along with him. Craig protested.

"Craig, you have got to be the conquering hero," Laird pointed out. "Let the girl see who and what you are. I'll bet Isobel thinks you are just another trapper. James knows better; he and other chiefs listen to your advice, but Isobel doesn't know that. When you come tearing through camp shouting war cries and showing off your horsemanship, I'll bet her attitude will change."

Craig relented. "Will you take your pony and herd the loose pack ponies along behind me so they won't tear through the lodges and raise particular hell?"

"Yes, I'll do that. Now get ready to make your move."

Craig prepared himself. It was a good time to show off. In late afternoon the camp was in action—missionaries getting ready to preach, traders busy short-changing the trappers, Indians looking for whiskey. Squaws were eyeing goods they hoped their men would trade for and little kids and dogs ran squealing everywhere.

Taking an extra swallow of liquor to steady his nerves, Craig climbed aboard his painted war-horse. With a last look at the grinning Laird, he lifted his loaded rifle in the air, pulled the trigger and gave a loud war whoop. As Craig's startled pony leaped into action, Laird fired off his own rifle, kicked his pony into a run, and herding three loaded pack ponies ahead of him, watched as Craig went wholeheartedly into his show. Trying to keep from running into lodges or cooking fires, Laird whipped the doubled rope against the ponies' flanks and slashed at dogs. Young Indians released the tethered mounts. Then, whooping their own ear-piercing cries, they jumped on bareback and jostled their way into the procession. Trappers with loaded guns handy got into the act by firing until the panic-

stricken missionaries retreated to their tents and prayed for quiet.

Three times around the camp riders urged their ponies on, then slowed as Craig headed his directly to James' lodge. There Isobel stood in front with her father and mother, watching as Craig slid his pony to a stop, dismounted and handed the girl his pony's picket rope. He strode up to James.

"I ask for your daughter as my wife," he declared. "I will marry her the Christian way if she wishes it."

"Craig, my friend, if she wishes it, you may marry her," the chief replied. "I am glad that it is you who ask."

When Craig came racing through the campgrounds, Isobel recognized him as the man she had dreamed of and knew her dream had become reality; she would marry Craig whenever he wanted her. By not returning the picket rope, she indicated her acceptance both to her father and to Craig.

James was pleased. He realized he could form with this courageous white man an alliance that would not only give him prestige among Indians, but act as a shield against his white enemies. This marriage was a good thing.

Later, at their lodge, Laird asked Craig when the preacher would marry him and Isobel. "Back home," he commented, "the groom has his best friend make all the arrangements for the wedding and pay the preacher. Do you have a ring somewhere to put on her finger?"

"Hell, no. What makes you think I'd carry a wedding ring around with me?"

"I'm surprised you don't. Half your misguided life you have been looking for a woman to marry, and now when a good one says she'll have you, you have nothing to seal the agreement. Oh well, I'll find a ring and make the

arrangements, even to paying old Mealymouth Gray to marry you. By this time tomorrow you'll be an old married man with more problems to solve than catching beaver.''

Laird went first to the traders. They had the usual assortment of shiny gilded junk jewelry, but nothing appropriate for the daughter of a chief and the wife of a boss trapper. A blacksmith standing nearby asked if Laird had a ten-dollar gold piece on him.

''Yes, but I figure on giving it to Preacher Gray to perform the ceremony.''

''To hell with Gray,'' the blacksmith scoffed. ''Give me the coin and I'll make a ring to fit Isobel's finger. Get me the size with a piece of string or something. I'll be at my anvil and forge.''

When Laird told Isobel what he wanted, she held out her hand. As he took it he recalled the first time he'd held Suni's hand and remembered how soft and small it had been. He looked up to see Isobel smiling at him. He thought how lucky she was to have Bill Craig for a husband and how fortunate Craig was to have this pride of the Nez Perce people for his wife. After he measured her finger with string, he lifted Isobel's hand to his lips and kissed it. James, watching, said to himself, ''This friend of Craig's is also a good man.''

At first Gray showed opposition to the marriage. But Laird told him it would be a great honor and privilege for him to marry the daughter of a chief to one of the noted mountain men in a Christian ceremony, that it might lead others to follow Craig's example and Gray would gain more converts among Indians and white trappers.

This approach made Gray agree.

Laird had another idea. ''My friend,'' he told Craig, ''if you and Isobel stay here in camp after you're married, your trapper friends will make your life miserable. I have already heard some of their rowdy plans. Believe me,

you'll want to be far away from here with your new bride."

"I'm listening," Craig said.

"While the trappers are getting drunk after the ceremony, you and Isobel slip out to where I'll have one pack pony loaded and two others for you to ride. Take off on the trail that we've chosen to head out on and we'll all meet later."

In the missionaries' camping spot there were mixed emotions. The Elkanah Walkers both believed it was a good thing for Gray to marry the white trapper and the Indian girl, but the Asa Smiths differed with them.

"They're both infidels and savages," Mrs. Smith raged. "How can you, Mr. Gray, an ordained minister of the Lord, permit such a marriage, let alone perform it? I do not understand your reasoning and I am sure the Mission Board would object to it."

"The Mission Board is not here, Mrs. Smith," Elkanah Walker put in. "I am sure Mr. Gray has thought the matter over carefully. Surely it is better to have these two bound in Christian marriage than living in sin as the rest of the trappers do."

"I say it is a sin, marriage or not," Smith thundered. "For a minister to perform such a marriage is totally and absolutely unacceptable."

The argument went on until Sarah Smith became hysterical and Asa retired to his tent with a headache. Gray himself appeared after conferring with Jason Lee, who had come in from the Willamette country. Lee agreed with Gray that the marriage was a good idea; it would keep the trapper and Indian from living in sin and thus save two lives from the devil.

"Mr. Lee has lived with the Indians. He has performed several such marriages as a way of converting

savages to Christianity," Gray reported later to the Smiths.

"But Mr. Lee is a Methodist. I think we should follow our own denominational training."

Gray closed the silly argument by suggesting that Mrs. Smith had not asked the Lord for guidance and perhaps she would feel better if she did. Once the Smiths bowed out, Gray got out his Bible and studied details of how the marriage ceremony should be performed.

Laird found Doc Newell and told him the plan to get Craig and his wife away from camp before the trappers got too drunk and playful. Doc, in a happy mood after a few drinks, agreed to help.

"Shoot, boy, that's an easy one for us to handle. Give me some money and I'll get a keg to open after the ceremony. Then I'll tell old Craig and his woman to get on their ponies and ride through the camp to give us a show; you can have the pack pony tied out where they can get him easy after they ride through camp. Next I'll holler out there's free drinks for everyone, including missionaries. That will keep everybody's eyes off the newlyweds till they skin off with the pony."

"Doc, that's great, but will one keg do the trick?"

"It'll do to start the fireball rolling. By God, there will be a hell-raising time in this camp by nightfall."

"Drunks and swelled heads all over the prairie by morning," Laird chuckled. "Doc, you better have a cure ready for the hangovers."

"Hell, boy, I'll just bust in the kegs and let those sorry drunks lick the staves." He chuckled. "I'll bet them greenhorn missionaries will see and hear things that will keep 'em awake all night praying for lost souls. Old Yellow Belly Gray will think there's a scalp dance going on. Some of the boys would like to see his hair on the end of a lance anyway, the dirty, gutless bastard."

The ceremony went off the next day, not as planned

but fairly close. Interruptions by well-oiled trappers at times drowned out the preacher's voice. But once the knot was tied, Craig kissed Isobel and then Laird moved in to try it, with Doc pushing him aside to be first. James, dignified in war bonnet and trailing feathers, came to shake hands with Craig, whom he called William from then on. He shook Laird's hand while Doc squeezed Isobel and sang, "Oh, she's the sweetest girl in the mountains."

Not long afterward, Doc called for free drinks and everyone toasted the health of the newlyweds before cheering his suggestion that the two mount their ponies and show off their rigging. While Craig and Isobel dressed their ponies for the show, Doc and Laird measured out the liquid fire. Indians were not included in the whiskey handouts; there were too many guns and knives handy that drunken braves might misuse in settling arguments.

Once the two riders had made a circle of the camp and Craig had shaken hands with friends eager to help with his woman if he needed it, the couple rode off at an angle, picked up the pack pony, then departed the camp at a gallop. An old half-drunk trapper, batting bleary eyes to watch them go south, puzzled over it. "Craig must be drunk and don't rightly know where his lodge is," he said to himself.

The missionaries in their tents listened to the raucous sounds outside. Doc Newell got pleasure out of the concern their rowdiness gave the prune-faced mission woman.

Joe Meek got so liquored up that the new Nez Perce wife he had taken shortly after his first wife's death abandoned his company and went to the lodge of friends. When Joe found her gone, he took a snort to celebrate the fact, lay back to enjoy it and didn't wake up until the next day, his jug beside him still containing enough firewater to make him feel quite unconcerned about the whole affair. Meanwhile, the missionaries and the cavalcade had packed

up to go west and Meek's wife had packed up and gone with them, leaving her husband with his jug and horse close by.

Two days after she had gone, Meek found himself out of drink and grub and company. The camp split up. They all went their separate ways, and with no good reason to stay put, old Joe climbed on his patiently waiting pony and followed the trail west.

The next day, traveling without grub or liquor, he saw some waiting figures far ahead of him on the prairie. As he came closer, he recognized the woman who was standing beside a form that lay prone on the ground. It was Sarah Smith. Asa was either dead or dying.

"What's the matter here?" Joe asked, pulling up.

"Asa says he's sick and can't go on, Mr. Meek. And the others just rode on and left us." The woman had cried piteously and she was so thirsty she could barely speak.

"Hell, if he's that sick, we won't worry about him," Joe answered, and unstrapping his water jug, handed it to the thirsty woman. She drank. Then she bathed her face, which had burned brown in the sun and was streaked with dust and mud. Meek jumped down to where Asa Smith lay moaning. When the trapper poked him with his boot, Smith grunted in protest and opened his eyes.

"You going to stay here for the buzzards?" Meek asked. "They're up there making circles right now."

"I'm too sick, too tired to travel anymore," Smith wailed. "All I can do is lie here and pray for strength."

"Well, I don't see as we can help you much. Here, Mrs. Smith, I'll put you on your pony and we'll try to catch up with the others afore some of them blasted Sioux catch up with us, maybe. I'm afeared they're purty close on our heels right now."

"Don't leave me here, Mr. Meek. If Indians come, I'll be helpless."

"Rightly so, Mr. Smith. First the scalp, then the knife—unless they got women along to pick you to pieces first."

Not waiting to say or hear another word, Meek seized the protesting Sarah—she weighed not much more than a half-pack of hides—and he swung her easily up onto her pony. Tying the lead rope to his pony's tail, Meek said his farewells. "Smith, take care, now. We're leaving you to your friends, the Sioux and the wolves. Adios."

When he'd traveled with Smith's wife some way down the trail, Meek heard a horse behind them, getting closer. There was Smith, sagging from the saddle of his trotting pony. Meek didn't stop to greet him. Instead of slowing down the trapper urged his mount to a faster pace.

Smith never forgave the missionaries and Meek for leaving him to die on the lonely prairie. In letters back East and in stories he told to those who would listen, he raged against his treacherous companions and boasted how only because of his own strength and God's help did he manage to keep up with them and survive.

At the rendezvous Jason Lee had told Gray he was going east to recruit more missionaries for the fruitful fields in Oregon valleys. Gray replied that Roman Catholics in St. Louis were sending priests to the Flatheads and the Kutenai. A race to convert the savage Indians seemed to be under way among all religious groups. And though many missionaries saw trouble ahead, no one realized how uncontrollable it was to become.

In February Father Francis Blanchet and Modeste Demers arrived—to the surprise of the Indians there—at Fort Walla Walla. Word quickly spread among the tribes that the Black Robes had come to help them know Jesus.

Not knowing that the priests were coming, Spalding previously had told the Spokane and the Coeur d'Alene that he could not spare a missionary to help them. When the Indians greeted the Black Robes, therefore, it was with open arms.

While the priests were at Walla Walla they met a Cayuse headman, Tauitau, Joseph's half-brother who had helped attack Pierre Pambrun several years before. Since then the factor had played up to other Cayuse and undermined Tauitau's influence until the chief saw his error and became friendly. After the reconciliation, Pambrun built a house for Tauitau on the Umatilla River, where he and Five Crows lived. Pambrun saw a chance to convert Tauitau and he convinced the Cayuse to have one of his children baptized by the priests.

As the mountain trappers might have said, "This was *something!*" The Indians marveled at the rituals, the garments, the old pageantry presentation; in fact, their reaction to the ceremony was the beginning of the conversion of many Cayuse to Roman Catholicism.

If Whitman was perturbed when he heard about all this, Spalding was furious. He saw conflict in the making and began to denounce the black-robe religion as the work of the devil. So vigorously did Spalding condemn the Jesuits that if ever there had been confusion among the Indians regarding the white men's religion, there was confusion now and it grew rapidly.

News of the Cayuse baptisms flooded the tribes in the Columbia Basin and each wondered when its own people could receive the sacrament. As the two priests traveled to the Willamette Valley and performed more ceremonies, Toupin, their interpreter, told the Indians this new religion was stronger than that of Whitman and Spalding, that indeed it was the only true religion.

A letter describing what the Black Robes were doing

was sent to Spalding by one of the Methodist ministers. It informed him that the two priests were now remarrying couples who originally had been married by Protestant preachers. Spalding and Whitman realized that nothing they could do now would stop this troubling conflict. Their only solace was believing that for some unknown reason the Lord had given them extra burdens to carry.

Another conflict arose because of the priests' practice of baptizing any Indian who said he wanted to be saved; this practice went contrary to the views of Whitman and Spalding, who insisted that converts be prepared properly for the rites. But Spalding had baptized only two Indians, Timothy and Joseph, in all the time he had been in the West. Also the priests were telling the Indians that the Protestant religions were not true, for the Protestant missionaries took wives, lived ordinary lives and did not dress or act like men of God.

During the summer of 1840 another menace arrived from the buffalo country. A priest, Father de Smet, came upriver to begin a mission and preach to the Indians. As if one priest wasn't enough, Father de Smet found such a need that he sent East for more; and if the pot was not hot enough then, more fire was added when the fur-trading companies disbanded, leaving hundreds of trappers to wander the West looking for ways to survive and get together another stake. Whenever and wherever mountain men met they talked about it. Most of them by then had taken Indian wives; a few had children.

Chapter 26

In July 1840, at the last rendezvous ever held, Andrew Drips showed up with the usual caravan of supplies from St. Louis. As one trapper said, "He brung along a new set of educated animals too."

There were more missionaries determined to lead the Indians to Jesus: three couples, a single man and the Joel Walker family with five children. These individuals were the first real settlers to make the trip across to Beulah land, and their caravan westward marked the beginning of the emigrant invasion.

Drips left the group at the rendezvous. Soon afterward Doc Newell came up with the idea of guiding them to Fort Hall. Craig and Laird agreed to go along; they shared a lodge with Isobel. Meek joined the caravan later and at Fort Davy Crockett the four men had a smoke-talk together.

Old Meek, the happy-go-lucky, take-her-as-she-comes trapper, wasn't so frustrated about problems with the fur trade as he was about his new Nez Perce wife. She no longer wanted any part of him and his drunkenness. But no matter how perturbed he got, Joe could always throw in ideas.

"You know, Craig," he suggested, "I think we should

start a little trading post of our own. We've got a little stuff cached away. To hell with the big haul, like the brigades tried. Suppose we find a place, build us a fort, then pitch in and divvy up what we have to stock it? You can run the show and the rest of us will hunt fur and trade stock. I just have a crazy coon's hunch we might do all right. Hell, we know every hole in the mountains and every trapper who hunts 'em. We know all the tribes and we all have Indian wives with all their begging relations. What do you say?''

Craig said nothing but continued to smoke.

"Let's vote on it," Meek urged. "We might do all right. Course, I have to find me a new woman first.''

"Another one? Hell of a chance you have," Doc said. "You've got a woman now, and you know as well as any of us that the missionaries have put new ideas in Indian women's heads; I don't know of no tribe will let you have a woman till you get rid of the one you got.''

"Oh, I'll get around that," Meek guffawed. "But afore I do, I want to locate a better woman, get lucky like you or old Bill, here. Bill, ain't old James got another girl like Isobel?''

"If he has, it's news to me. But take a look at the sister of Doc's woman, why don't you? She's young and good-looking and she'd be right to home in this bunch. For gosh sakes, though, get shed of the one you got unless you can persuade the chief that a bully boy like you needs two wives. You've started to preach, somebody told us. Well, read up about Solomon; he had a thousand wives, more or less. Find out the names of others that gathered 'em in like a rooster runs down hens. The old chief might be impressed enough he'd give you the girl and his blessing to boot.''

"Bill, them's the sweetest words this old coon's heard in a long, long time," Meek enthused. "Maybe you got a

few brains after all.'' He turned to the young Easterner. "Laird, you know the sister of Doc's woman. What do you think of her?''

"She's all Craig says from what I have seen. There's really only one objection—''

"What's that, young feller?''

"She is just too damned good for you,'' Laird declared, laughing. "She's really more my style. You're too old for such a beautiful girl.''

"Aw, you young pups are all alike,'' Meek exploded. "I've plowed more ground in my life than you and two others could harrow. Just to show you I can get this thing licked, I'll start on it soon as we figure out where old Bill's going to set up our fort.''

All at once Laird was unhappy. The talk about women had again stirred memories of Suni. In his grief he sensed how much he needed her to make life seem like old times.

Time passed. Somehow Laird managed to collect himself and compose a long-overdue letter to his uncle.

Fort Davy Crocket
July 1840

Dear Sir:

I have wintered well. Actually, I am lucky to be alive. While we camped far north in the buffalo country we were attacked one night by Blackfoot Indians. I was captured along with five Nez Perce women. I soon learned that the women were to be sold as slaves or wives to the Crow. I realized I might be held for ransom or perhaps killed for sport. Neither fate appealed to me.

However, we had learned while at the rendezvous that summer that the Mandan Indians had smallpox and it was rapidly spreading to the

Blackfoot as the two tribes traded back and forth.

At their main tribal camp I took a long chance and told a Blackfoot chief that the sickness would come and destroy his people; I said they were already doomed because of the deaths in the raid and the atrocities they forced on the captive Nez Perce women. This held the Blackfoot back from further bad treatment; they are a superstitious people. Then I promised the chief I would not try to escape because I knew he and his tribesmen were going to die anyway when the snows came.

The Indians wanted to see if what I predicted was going to come true. They let us live with them not as captives but as guests. As luck or the Lord would have it, we were visited by the remaining inhabitants of a village that had suffered the ravages of smallpox. Within a few days the disease hit the camp and we were set free to take all our possessions and go. We were even allowed the horses that the Blackfoot had stolen from the Nez Perce camp during the raid. In return for our freedom I had to read from the Bible and pray that some Blackfoot would be spared.

All the captured women took the disease and died. We gave them Christian burial. My partner, Wm. Craig, escaped the raid and sought help in the Nez Perce country. We met up with him and the Nez Perce war party shortly after we were released.

Laird went on to describe the trip with Craig, including visits to the Flatheads, Spokane and Nez Perce, as well as the problems the missionaries were having with each

other and the Indians. He mentioned the fur-trade difficulties and the need for organized military authority to quell the uprisings that would surely come. Finally he discussed possible routes west, travel options and land resources.

Mr. Meek, Dr. Newell and William Craig have often discussed a wagon route from Fort Boise (now called Fort George) on the Snake River through the mountains they call the Blues clear to Fort Walla Walla. I have listened. Some say it may be possible sometime in the future to create a wagon road from there up a valley and through some mountains to come out near Oregon City in the Willamette Valley. Up to this time, of course, there had been no need for one.

One question always arises: why not follow the Columbia down to Fort Astoria? The reason is that inland the river passes through an immense gorge, many miles long and full of great rocky cliffs and waterfalls that are formed by streams pouring into the river.

You asked about the natural resources of the area. From what I have learned there is an unbelievable amount of timber, soft white pine as in Maine, a yellow-barked pine suitable for building lumber and harder wood from the fir trees. All could be used as building material for houses, barns, etc.

Timber of the white pine along the western slope of the Bitterroot Mountains would make excellent ship masts if the trunks could be gotten out whole. I have seen many trees six feet or more in diameter and one hundred or more feet tall. Their wood is white, soft, workable, and the Indians say very durable.

253

The land varies. Some places are broken by rubble from ancient rivers and covered only lightly with soil. In other places deep, rich, dark soil grows grasses that could feed millions of cattle and horses.

Since the coming of the horse, buffalo formerly living in these valleys and prairies have been mostly killed off. Western horses are not large but possess great strength and endurance. They seem more intelligent and easier to work with than the highstrung racing animals at home. (Of course, I generalize because I am acquainted only with the Nez Perce ponies.)

You also asked about river travel here in Walla Walla country. The Indians use canoes to cross the rivers, or quickly construct bullboats, tanned hides sewn together and stretched over willows, their seams covered with pitch or fat to keep out water. Large boats can come up the Columbia to the falls called The Dalles. For a distance of several miles above them, the river smooths out and one can boat all the way to the Clearwater. The Snake River above the confluence of the Clearwater can be navigated for a few miles by small boats propelled by steam. The Indians say that the river from that point is impassable by men, boats or horses.

If the men I am with decide to travel to the Willamette River country, I plan to go with them. I may be able to get another report to you from there. It will go by boat and you should hear from me sooner that way. There is more and more travel back and forth across the western land now. Soon, perhaps sooner than we think possible, I expect to see a road that wagons can

safely negotiate from one coast to the other. Oh, a fact you should know: Wm. Craig has taken a wife, Isobel, the daughter of Chief James of Lapwai.

Yr. ob't servant,
D. Laird

Chapter 27

Doc Newell and Craig led the party with Joe Meek across to Fort Hall, where they split up. Meek could not yet forgo trapping or living the wild life but took off on his own to hunt and trap near Bear River. He had been only two days on his way when a Nez Perce scout caught up with him to say that he was desperately needed back at the fort. Suspicious as usual, Meek questioned the messenger and finally decided that Doc and Bill had something going they wanted to cut him in on.

"What in hell is going on here?" he stormed at Craig when he arrived. "I spent time coming back. That feller said I was desperately needed."

"Joe, we've decided we're going to the Willamette Valley. Do you want in on it or are you so bullheaded you can't see a good thing with those bleary eyes of yourn?"

Meek was taken aback. "Well . . . who all's going to the valley? Just you fellers?"

"Hell, no. Men, women, kids, horses and cattle—everybody. We'll take the wagons we traded for and show old Marcus Whitman and Bushy-beard Lee we can do it."

Meek squinted his eyes for a moment. "You really mean to try it, Doc. How about you, Bill?"

Craig laughed. "Sure thing, Joe. I say get busy, pack

up and light out. We'll have lots of help. Some of the old boys and their wives and kids will go along too.''

"What all you fellers taking besides the wagons?''

"Whatever we think can go. Look, there's three good wagons to haul the kids, grub and some of the women. We'll take the pack mules and ponies. We make trail and the kids and women bring along the stock.'' Craig smiled. "One good thing about this trip, we won't have to fight off hostiles like we did in Blackfoot and Crow country.''

"What kinds of plunder you got loaded up, Doc?''

"Everything we could beg, borrow or steal. Saws, axes, chains, ropes, shovels, picks and grub. If you think of anything else speak up, because we leave in the morning, ready or not.''

As planned, the party left the next morning. At Fort Boise they stopped for four days to readjust their loads and make ready for the stretch across the Snake River and into the distant Blue Mountains. Several trappers had been in the country before, but Joe Meek was more familiar with all the routes than any of the others.

Every day men rode out to scout the best way of passage. Those in the group who had never seen the country before could scarcely imagine what the task of finding the best route through was like. The easy decisions were made while traveling stretches of upland prairies where grass grew tall and domestic stock had never fed. Difficult decisions were the ones that involved which stream or river to follow to a pass that would lead them to another stream or river that led eventually westward.

Scouting ahead, shoveling gullies, picking through rocks, crossing rivers, felling trees, chaining and doubling up the wagons, cutting through windfalls, pushing and pulling the unwieldy vehicles, whipping the horses, shouting, cursing—through the constant exercise of sheer will power and bull strength, the caravan climbed and then

crawled slowly down over grassy benches to Waiilatpu in late October.

When finally the procession reached the mission, there was great excitement. Indians who had been expecting the arrival had from time to time joined the party and followed along, amazed to see women and children in the wagons pulled by heavier horses from the East. Mules they had seen before, but the oxen were a source of wonder.

The Whitmans were particularly pleased. Now they had company and the help they desperately needed. Things were not going well at Waiilatpu; the Cayuse Indians, more than ever, were demanding payment in return for the mission's use of their lands. Whitman's life had actually been threatened and he knew he could expect more violent reaction. But so sure was the missionary of his work with the Lord that he bragged he would continue regardless of the consequences.

Joe Meek was again enthralled with Narcissa Whitman. In his ingratiating way he persuaded her to keep his half-breed daughter Helen Mar with her and to educate the girl as a Christian. The Whitmans were happy to assume this responsibility, believing Helen might take the place of their own little girl, who had drowned in a river accident.

For a long time Isobel and Craig had discussed finding a woman for Laird. Isobel suggested using the excuse that she wanted to see James, her father, to travel to Lapwai. There or in a village nearby she would see what she could do to find someone suitable.

Craig also had a suggestion. Before going to Lapwai he thought they might visit some relatives of Isobel's who lived with the Nez Perce in Wallowa country. Having been to that area only once, Craig wanted to strengthen his friendship with the old chief there as well as show Laird

that part of the Nez Perce domain. Isobel readily agreed with Craig's plan.

An ancient trail led them up through gradually rising prairie and bench lands where grasses grew thick and tall. Back to the river valleys, as far north as the eye could see, no mountains obstructed the view. Higher up, the travelers marveled at the timbered side valleys. When they reached the pine and fir high on the mountain, they crossed the Divide. Now the trail followed a spur ridge to the south, and from the highest place they saw far away to the east the dim but rugged outline of the Snake River canyon cliffs. Farther on their way, the deep gorge of the Grande Ronde River stretched glistening like a thin strip of silver wire far below. The trail led always down, saddle and packs sliding forward on the ponies' withers as they descended.

The path below was broad and easy to follow as it crossed and recrossed the river; it was late summer and the water was shallow in places. Joseph's village was nearby. Hundreds of horses ranged there, the majority white with black or red spotted hides.

Joseph, a wise and thoughtful man, seemed glad to welcome his guests. He was anxious to hear news of the mission at Waiilatpu. Wagons had reached it—he knew that—and in them was the first complete family to take that route to the valley.

Parker had come to the Nez Perce chief's village and had impressed Joseph with his sincere desire to help the Indians. He had told Joseph and his band about the Bible and the white man's God, assuring them that other white people would come to build missions and schools. Privately, though, he thought Joseph's people too far away from a suitable site. When Whitman and Spalding came and Joseph tried to persuade them to build in his area, he again was refused.

Laird, Craig and Isobel stayed in the remote Nez Perce village for two days before they returned to Lapwai to visit James. In the meantime Laird had been struck with the looks and grace of one girl in Joseph's band who seemed a bit older but in some ways reminded him of Suni.

The Nez Perce girl had been interested in the strangers too, and with several other girls had asked Isobel about the white trapper who accompanied her and her husband. Was the white man looking for a woman? Did he already have one? Had Isobel known him long? Did he live in her village?

One girl seemed especially attracted to Laird. Isobel learned that her name was Dancing Leaf. Someone said that though she had become the most skillful dancer in the tribe and had been eligible for several years, Dancing Leaf had not yet chosen a mate.

Isobel wanted Laird to meet this girl. But he was still so filled with memories of Sun-in-the-Morning that he put aside all thought of other girls and women. Could she change his mind?

She asked Dancing Leaf if she would like to know Laird better and whether she was interested in having him as a husband. Dancing Leaf's answer was direct: yes, if he was a good man. She also asked, "Is he rich? Will he stay in Nez Perce country? Does he have a woman now?"

"Laird is a good man," Isobel answered. "My father thinks of him as a son and of my husband as his brother. We are a family. You will be one of us if you marry my friend Laird.

"Once he had a woman. Her name was Sun-in-the-Morning. The sickness from the Blackfoot killed her. Suni was a Christian, as we all are. Since the day she died, Laird has not looked at any other woman as I saw him look at you yesterday."

"You think Laird might want me for his woman?"

Isobel was pleased at the girl's interest. "I will ask your father and Joseph if you can come with us to visit," she offered. "If you will ride with us, Laird may take you for his woman before long. He is lonesome."

"If my father and Joseph say I can go with you, I will go," Dancing Leaf replied.

"Your father will take us to Joseph. I will tell him you will be happy with us and with Laird, for he is a good man. Even the trappers say that. Laird does not lie. He does not get drunk. He will marry you forever."

Dancing Leaf's father was a chief by the name of Jason. When he heard Isobel's proposal, he asked Dancing Leaf if she wanted to go to Lapwai. Seeing that his daughter was eager, Jason went to Joseph, who agreed that the decision was an acceptable one. When Isobel asked both chiefs whether they would object if Laird wanted to marry Dancing Leaf, both men smiled. They could see that Isobel and Dancing Leaf had already been making plans.

Laird looked puzzled as the ponies were collected for the trip. Two fine horses among them were new to him. One gelding, a four-year-old almost white, had a few black, dollar-size spots over his rump; the other, an older mare, had small red dots over most of her back and red hairs showing in her short mane and tail. Craig and Laird were impressed with the quality of the ponies and learned they were Dancing Leaf's and that the girl was going to be visiting people at Lapwai and Kamiah.

Chief Jason told the trappers that his band had well over six thousand horses grazing in this valley and more in another valley beyond.

Laird wondered why Dancing Leaf, the girl he had found so attractive, was accompanying his travel group. Craig explained away her presence: "Leaf goes with us to visit Lapwai because her father wants her to see how it's

run and to learn if Spalding will accept her in his school. Isobel liked the idea of having female company along.''

"Will we share the robes or sleep single?''

"Hell, I don't know. Let the women figure it out.''

Laird spoke modestly. "Just thought I'd ask. I wouldn't want to cause Dancing Leaf any trouble.''

"Well, I'll be damned. Here you been living with Indians day and night, trying to be one, and you don't yet realize it's the woman's choice. Just ride along and see what happens.''

"Bill, I'll still curious why Dancing Leaf and Isobel teamed up all at once.''

"Well, don't get your fire hot, boy. Just ride along. I don't know what the women and the chiefs have in mind. I'm just glad we only got one more along. I've been on a few trips when we was so slowed down with a bunch of relatives that we were days late getting where we hoped to be.'' As they rode out of the village on their way north, Laird sensed that good times might once more be coming.

Craig and Isobel took the lead and Laird and Dancing Leaf followed after the pack ponies. It was late in the year: short days and cold nights. While the ponies were fresh and strong they pushed rapidly on, hazing the laggard pack animals. Each night the travelers stopped at another village; on this ancient trail the camps were approximately a day apart.

As time passed and days grew shorter still, Craig pushed his group relentlessly in order to compact a day's travel into half a day and prove to Laird what high-quality ponies could do when hard pressed.

All stops at villages were cut short by Craig's explanation that the four were on the way to see James and give him a message from Jason and Joseph. Every village had heard of Laird and his recovery of Nez Perce supplies and stolen ponies from the Blackfoot. Craig, of course, was

known to all and Isobel and Dancing Leaf were Nez Perce people. The two white trappers cemented relationships that would endure for years to come.

At Lapwai mission, Spalding was not happy to see the group arrive, but his wife welcomed the women and showed them her school.

That night Spalding wrote in his diary, ''I have seen enough of mountain men.'' He was fed up with white men corrupting the morals of his converts and unaware of the positive effect two of these men later would have both on his personal life and on the history of Idaho and Washington. He was glad to see Craig and Laird and the two Nez Perce women go on upriver to James' village.

At Lapwai there was a welcoming feast and a lodge was erected for the newcomers to use. After the feasting and revelry eased, James asked Isobel if Laird would want Dancing Leaf as his woman.

''Father, I do not know,'' Isobel replied, ''but it is important to Leaf that he be sure.''

''Jason and Joseph are strong chiefs. Laird is a strong man,'' James declared. ''The three of them and Craig can help us keep peace as other whites come. It would be good if Laird married this woman.''

''Laird is a Christian,'' Isobel replied gently. ''When the matter is decided, he will do the Christian thing.''

During the trip from the Grande Ronde to the Clearwater Dancing Leaf studied Laird closely. She observed that he treated Isobel as a sister and a good friend. She saw that Craig respected Laird's attitude and that all three seemed bound together by respect and understanding.

Laird displayed no overwhelming affection for Leaf, as they all now called her, yet his consideration of the young Indian woman grew as they traveled. Several times, too, he brushed against her, and once when she had slipped and fallen, he helped her up. For a fleeting moment they

were in each other's arms. Thinking of that moment, Leaf often trembled and felt her body flood with warmth.

Laird also remembered the incident. Had Leaf deliberately fallen? He liked to think so and was alert for another chance to hold her.

That night Laird warmed his feet in the lodge by their flickering fire. Full of food, tired from the long ride, he listened to the patter of rain on the lodge covering and the sound of wind ruffling the smoke flap. Longing for Leaf's company, he fell asleep.

Isobel and Leaf had gone off to a quiet place. There Isobel plaited Leaf's hair and rubbed sweet grass on it, then laughed and whispered how its scent would please a man.

"Maybe Laird will not want me."

"If he pushes you away, go back to your own bed."

"Shall I put on the maiden rope when I go with him?"

"Yes, that would be a good thing. If he wants you, he will feel the rope. Be sure to let him ask to marry you before you give yourself to him. If he wants to do that, then it is your choice to take away the rope. Do not fear Laird. I think he wants you but waits to know what you want."

Laird stirred as Leaf gently touched his robe; then he awakened but lay still. Heart pounding, scarcely able to breathe, he felt the girl move close and tenderly caress him. Lying there, feeling her soft probing hands, he inhaled the sweet scent that clung to her hair and controlled the impulse to turn and clasp her to him. Her exploring fingers found his shoulder, then his face. Next his beard was gently stroked, his lips and eyes; he felt his eyelids flutter. Eagerly, then, he shifted to one side and touched Leaf's doeskin shirt. She sighed, and touching Laird—faster now, deeper—felt him want her.

265

Chapter 28

The Spaldings and Smiths felt at odds with the Nez Perce and saw no improvement in their relationships with the Indians now that Bill Craig was back. They knew that any advice Craig gave the Indians would likely be contrary to their teachings. Spalding particularly disliked the trapper because he was James' son-in-law.

At one time Spalding was convinced he'd had the Nez Perce chief converted, but James returned to old ways as soon as he'd seen the results of Spalding's teachings. Another thing that rankled the chief was his loss of power over his land.

Craig sympathized. It seemed impossible to anyone familiar with Indian ways and traditions that the missionaries could overlook Indian ownership of the lands where they had dwelt for centuries. They owned them by virtue of possession and use and perceived newcomers as guests only, with no right to force them from their ancestral homes.

The Smiths, even more ignorant of Indian ways than the Spaldings, soon saw no way out of the problems with the Indians; they wanted to leave. The pair had not planned to go west in the first place, expecting instead to be sent to Siam. And now it haunted them that Joe Meek, a drunken

mountain man, had been the one to save their lives. All the Indians were aware of the embarrassing rescue and because of this knowledge had lost all respect for Asa Smith's power and beliefs.

Up to this time there had been numerous threats against the missionaries but no actual violence. The threats persisted, the Nez Perce now threatening to burn and destroy the Spaldings' buildings.

Eliza Spalding had been driven almost to tears by the taunts and insults that were hurled at her; she felt she didn't deserve them and asked her husband for help. But Spalding found he could make no headway at all with the belligerent Indians. He sent for Chief James and asked the chief to call off his young men, but James refused to leave his lodge. The incident became a battle of wills until at last Spalding capitulated and agreed to send away people not of James' band who were claiming his territory as theirs. After making this concession, Spalding left James' lodge defeated, frustrated and unable to understand why the chief could not see his point of view.

Around the time of this incident, missionaries began labeling as heathens Indians who opposed them. As a result Craig entered into the discord. When asked his opinion, the trapper told the truth as he knew it, that James was right about his ownership of these lands and should be compensated for their use. Many Indians were beginning to support this view with action.

Asa Smith had taken a place and plowed a field for grain. While he was working down it with a harrow, two Indian brothers who were headmen in the village confronted him. They asserted that the land Smith was working was theirs and that they wanted Smith to pay them for its use; in doing so the Indians aroused real fear in the missionary.

*   *   *

"Nothing good'll come of this fighting," Craig predicted to Laird and Isobel. "There's too big a difference between the missionaries' ideas and the Indians' upbringing. Whitman and Spalding are trying to change things too fast." He shook his head. "I don't know what to do. Hell, I'm caught in the middle with no place to jump except into hotter fire than there is in the skillet. If I advise James and his people, I'll get hell from Spalding. If I take Spalding's side of things just because I'm a white man, I'm going against my own idea of the way things should be done. Right now I'm all for moving farther up the creek to make another start. Let the devil take over his own handiwork."

Laird was pleased with that idea. He had heard and seen enough to recognize that a wedge had been driven between the missionaries and the Indians and that from now on each time they met to counsel, additional blows would drive it deeper. Isobel and Craig were caught in the vise. And Dancing Leaf, an outsider, had been brought to this place of dissension by a love now so strong that she and Laird planned to marry. There was no use asking Spalding or any of the others to perform the ceremony, so Laird decided to continue life with Leaf in the Indian way until a more amenable preacher came along. Maybe they would take a ride up to see Walker and his wife. Those two bore some resemblance to sincere people who were trying to untangle what was happening. Or if worst came to worst, they could leave this dog-and-cat fight, visit Whitman's mission and have him do the job.

Isobel was glad to talk privately with her husband. She agreed with what Craig had said, that they should move farther away and not live so close to where both the Indians and missionaries could come running for advice. There were better places than this, she said encouragingly. They could find one, build a house and stay there. Her

father would give them all the land they wanted and the Spaldings would have nothing to say about it.

"What do you think, Laird?" Craig asked his friend later. "Would you and Leaf go along with us? We could pick us a spot up the creek and make a go of it together."

"Right now I'm all for the idea," Laird replied. "But let's look for a place for you first. I'll help you build your house and then decide what Leaf and I will do. We might visit Jason for a while."

Craig smacked a fist into his palm. "Then, by God, let's go. I want to mark a spot I can sink my axe into. Then I want to have it settled with both James and old Spalding that it's mine so Isobel and me are in the clear. You can act as witness. I'll get one or two others too."

William Craig found his place. It was four miles up the valley and with Laird looking on he marked the spot. Both men cheered triumphantly as Craig swung his axe into the trunk of a giant pine. Later they stepped off and measured what they believed to be one square mile of ground and Craig marked sites for barns and a house.

"I'm going to make peace with Spalding, although it sure goes against the grain," he declared. "I'll see him about cutting lumber for the buildings and in exchange help him get timber out. Laird, if you want to keep in Spalding's good graces, why don't you throw in with me till this thing's cooled off. I can get James cooled down by seeing him about land up here. He's apt to be easier to deal with; after all, there's a grandson on the way."

Fortunately, both Spalding and James were not against the site Craig chose. With that issue settled, Craig and Laird decided to take a trip to the Willamette Valley to see how old friends Meek, Newell and others were getting along. It was no surprise to find out they were having their own troubles with the missionaries.

"I can't figure out how these fellers can eat on Sunday

but won't sell anything to them as needs it,'' Meek grumbled. "When I tried to buy grub from one of 'em, he wouldn't sell me nothing because it was Sabbath Day. So I says, 'Shall I tell my growling guts they got to wait till Monday?' I tell you, hell's full of preachers."

Strongminded Meek had strongminded followers. Newell was fed up both with wet weather and the attitudes of the settlers, missionaries and priests.

"Boys," he forecast, "troubles here are on their way even faster than I'd thought they'd be. Do-gooders from all breeds of religion are splitting things apart. They all think they have the word straight from God and they intend to prove it. We have Anglicans, Catholics, Methodists, Baptists, Presbyterians and freethinkers here along with half a dozen Indian tribes plus know-nothing drunken trappers—all squabbling for their rights above everything else."

"Any worse than trying to trap in muddy water with the Blackfoot or Crow trying to stick you with an arrow or blow off your hat with a blunderbuss?" Craig teased.

Newell was too upset to laugh. "I can't rightly say," he replied. "I had a chance to fight back them days. I can't now. It's like finding yourself caught half-naked in a brier patch. Every move I try to make, I get hooked, scratched, cut or caught. We got whiskey, rum and wine being brought in by boat and skull-bust being cooked by moonshiners from the hills back home. I'll bet you fellers ain't had that to fight over yet."

"No," Laird agreed, "but it's coming. Spalding is grinding grain and growing corn on his mission farm. He and Whitman have fruit trees. If we get one or two men who know how to make firewater, we'll have our scalp dances and lodge decorations too. I'm sure of it."

"We have another problem coming up," Meek went on. "There's a do-gooder here beginning to like red meat

271

in his bed every night or two. Mark my words, that's
going to raise eyebrows and purse lips among the rest of
the Bible-thumpers. He'll get kicked out, but he'll be
back.''

Meek's crude reference was addressed to the missionary
Dr. Elijah White, an aide to Jason Lee. White differed with
Lee in so many ways that Lee had asked that his aide be
recalled. But White beat Lee to that request by leaving for
the East to set himself up there as an expert on western
Indian affairs.

Soon afterward he began a series of lectures and
convinced the Mission Board and others that he should
have more to say about dealings with western Indians. He
applied for appointment as Governor of Oregon, but with
two factions claiming the territory, failed to receive it.
Next White tried for the position of Indian Agent in Oregon. What Dr. White had in mind was the acquisition of
everything in that area he could get his grasping hands on.

Having no money to work with, he set out to persuade influential people that Oregon should be settled by
the United States before any British group decided to do it.
The fur trade was disappearing, he explained, but the land
remained available.

Before too long White found one branch of the government ready to spend money secretly. What White planned
was to draw on Secret Service funds to move emigrants to
Oregon. In that way he could influence the Indians if
necessary.

At a regular meeting of the missionaries at Waiilatpu,
Whitman and Spalding argued bitterly. Whitman had not
only laid down his version of the law and rules to Spalding, but had openly accused Spalding of working against
him.

The quarrel between the two upset the other mission-

aries so much that finally six-foot-four Elkanah Walker spoke his piece and sobered the two men till they withdrew to talk things over. At last they decided to reconcile their differences and both men made apologies to the other missionaries. Fortunately for everyone, the priests and their interpreter Toupin had not been present during the disagreement. As it was, some Indians did hear enough to relate portions to others and thereby further inflame the situation.

In the meantime, Indians at both Waiilatpu and Lapwai had begun to rebel against being whipped by Whitman and Spalding. At Waiilatpu Whitman was confronted by angry Cayuse, his hat torn from his head and thrown into the river. Indians brandished a gun and threatened to tie him up. Whitman showed no fear, and his religious training, like that of the rest of the missionaries, kept him from using violence to protect himself.

At Lapwai Spalding heard of the incidents at Waiilatpu and went there to see if he could help Whitman. The two men had a conference, after which Spalding returned to his own mission. Later it was discovered that it had not been a Cayuse who had instigated the trouble, but instead a half-breed Iroquois who hated whites and had egged the Cayuse on.

Craig and Laird learned what happened and hurried upriver to help. On their way they stopped at Fort Walla Walla, where a fire, at first thought to have been set by Indians, had partly burned some buildings. McKinlay assured them it had been an accident.

"Another time it'll be on purpose. These Cayuse want blood," he told Craig. "If they jump me, I'll get some of theirs. Those Indians seem to think they can get by with anything since their attacks on missionaries, and they did come down here to teach me a lesson, but I read the book to them as to what I'd do, and it kind of settled them down."

"But what'll you do if all these hostiles join up and go looking for blood and hair?" Craig demanded. "Hell, Mac, they can burn this old rat trap down easy and roast you fellers out."

"Oh no, they can't. I'm going to build up the fort with adobe bricks like we've seen other places. Adobe stops bullets and fires won't burn it. And we've got a few more tricks to keep them in their place if they get nasty."

"Well, I wish you luck. From what I been seeing and hearing, some of us are apt to need it."

At Waiilatpu, Craig and Laird were reassured that the ill feelings of the Indians there were only temporary and not so severe as reported, so the two men moved on to Lapwai. And to prove that he held no animosity toward Spalding, Craig went to work for him.

The fall of 1841 and the next spring were perhaps the best of all times for the Lapwai mission. The Indians harvested their first crops. Spalding wrote that they were bringing in grain to be ground into flour. Attendance at the church school rose rapidly and success in the whole venture seemed assured.

Up the creek, Craig was also doing well. Laird had stayed through the winter to help him build his house and mark the boundaries of his land. When warm winds took the snow and brought flowers, Dancing Leaf suggested that they visit her parents. She did not press their Christian marriage, for Laird had told her he wanted neither Spalding nor Gray to perform the ceremony.

In May, with travel easy, they started on their way. At Waiilatpu Whitman married them. Laird told the Whitmans that things were going better at Lapwai since Craig had moved somewhat away from Spalding and had not joined his father-in-law in his arguments with the missionary.

*　　*　　*

Dr. Elijah White had finally recruited a large group eager to settle in the West. He started with more than one hundred people and their horses, cattle and nineteen canvas-topped wagons on the long trek to the Columbia River. White carried a letter from the Mission Board recalling Whitman and a document showing his own appointment as subagent to the Indians in Oregon; the official paper furnished the power that he needed.

The group gradually abandoned their wagons and by the time they reached Fort Hall were either walking or riding horses. This decision encouraged Indian plunder of later trains. As the first wagons were seen traveling west, Indians discovered within them things they formerly had to beg, buy, trade for or steal. Each year, then, as settlers followed the Oregon Trail Indians grew bolder. More and more they ransacked abandoned wagons.

From Fort Hall the emigrant group followed the trail across the Snake River to the Grande Ronde and across it to Waiilatpu. Here Dr. White delivered the unwelcome letter of recall to Whitman and didn't stay long enough to find out the result, hurrying instead to the Willamette Valley to submit his letter of authority to those in power.

The Methodists in the valley were shocked to learn that the man they had found guilty not only of misuse of money but of sleeping with Indian women now had been authorized by the United States government to share charge of Indian affairs, a position of importance and considerable power. Until he actually saw the document, Jason Lee was sure it must be a joke.

Now Joe Meek felt more certain than ever that hell was full of preachers. He expounded along those lines to whoever would listen. "When I first met old Mealymouth Parker and he wanted us to pray instead of kill buffalo, I seen the end of the good life for us fellers. When I come on over here and wanted to buy grub and the preacher

wouldn't sell us any because it was Sunday, I knew we was in trouble. Then they sent a crazy preacher here from up on the Kooskoosky—Munger is his name, or was afore he played Jesus Christ and nailed himself to the wall and burned up. Now they've took a feller kicked out of the church for stealing money and sleeping with squaws and made him a high muck-a-muck to handle all the Indians in Oregon. He'll handle 'em, all right, starting with giving the girls a tumble every night—and by hiding away money he steals from wherever he finds it.''

The letter from the Mission Board delivered by Dr. Elijah White to Dr. Whitman caused great consternation among all missionaries. Forgotten were the various complaints each had made in the past. Now it was necessary to band together. After much discussion a series of letters was written that Dr. Whitman offered to deliver in person.

A large group of adventurers and farmers calling themselves the Bidwell-Bartelson party arrived at Waiilatpu just as Whitman was leaving. The missionary was pleased and hoped to use the presence of the group as evidence to the board that missions were in fact necessary and should be kept functioning.

Asa Lovejoy, a thirty-four-year-old lawyer, had been urged to accompany Whitman; the journey was too dangerous to make alone so late in the year. On October third the two men left and made their way through hostile country to plead with an equally hostile Mission Board. Once there Whitman was confronted with damaging letters from Gray, Smith and others. The missionary refuted most of the charges against him by handing over favorable letters from Elkanah Walker, the Ellises and the Spaldings. In doing so he was able to convince the board not only to keep the missions functioning, but to recruit more missionaries.

Only one person was available to accompany Whitman on his return trip to the West—his thirteen-year-old nephew Perrin. Undaunted, Whitman proceeded to Independence, Missouri, where to his great joy and surprise he found more than a thousand emigrants, a hundred twenty-five loaded wagons and well over three thousand head of cattle, horses and mules ready to head out. Not only did Whitman become the travelers' advisor, counselor and doctor but with his abiding optimism, their inspiration as well. When they pulled into Fort Hall, that optimism was tested.

"You fellers are crazy to think you can pull them blamed wagons to Walla Walla," local people told them.

"Mr. Whitman told us it could be done," one emigrant retorted. "He comes from there."

"Oh, Whitman's one of them consarned preachers thinks he can educate Indians, make 'em civilized. Hell, you fellers don't have no idea what that country's like. You better leave them wagons here; figure on packing just mules and horses."

"How do you suppose we got this far?" another farmer protested. "If we'd listened to people like you we'd still be back there arguing."

But the farmer had not completely convinced himself and he went to talk with Whitman. The missionary was not surprised. He had been plagued with pessimistic opinions before.

"Did the man you talked to say who he was?" Whitman asked.

"All he said was he knew more about that country then any damned Bible-thumper. Excuse my language, Doctor, but that's what he said."

"There will always be people who'll say you can't make it through," Whitman exclaimed. "If you people really want to go west—and I know you do—then I will

277

take you. Now, let's get the caravan together. We start in the morning.''

By nightfall word had spread through the camp that the captain of the wagon train did not intend to go any farther. He had heard of the Cayuse Indian trouble at Waiilatpu and Fort Walla Walla through representatives of the Hudson's Bay Company, Pambrun and Toupin the interpreter. News of Spalding's troubles at Lapwai was also being tossed about and the captain was doubtful they could make it across the Blue Mountains without encouraging real trouble.

There were other rumors that added to the skepticism. One was that if the British realized that emigrants from the United States would be appearing in the West in droves, they would be disturbed that no territory would be left for them and there would be trouble.

Trappers were another issue. Disgruntled, unsure of their own future and seeing the type of people they thought they'd left behind now coming to settle among them, the mountain men were not at all pleased about the emigrant invasion.

But Whitman persisted. Finding another man to help him lead the caravan, he led his group west. And not only did the wagon train make its way safely through, but in many places straightened and improved the road as each wagon's wheels laid down tracks that others could follow more easily.

Men, women and boys cut, shoveled and pushed aside obstacles that impeded progress. Hundreds of turning wheels flattened grass and pounded rock and gravel into sand and soil. Thousands of hooves did their work. Because of these efforts, the Oregon Trail became a reality. And each night at evening prayers, Whitman said gratefully, "Lord, You have led us safely this far. Lead us on tomorrow."

They did meet Indians; Whitman expected that. Nez Perce of the Grande Ronde and Wallowa valleys came across white people arriving in a long procession of wagons and cattle, just as the missionaries and trappers had told them they would. Indians in the villages on the upper Grande Ronde and the Wallowa spread the word downriver that the settlers were in the territory. Some went to see for themselves. In the village where Laird and Dancing Leaf were then living, Laird was asked what he thought of the migration.

"I think more people will follow," he said. "Many in the East want land, a place to raise their cows, a better place than the one they come from. When they come here they will build schools and missions. They will plow the ground and plant grain to grind into flour. Houses will be built from pieces of the trees like those you once built along rivers where salmon come each summer. The settlers also will plant crops; remember the camas bulbs you planted for winter eating? They will raise hay for their cows and ponies. This is the way these people live. Some things about them will be bad, but most things good if you allow yourself to see them that way."

"But can we keep the Easterners away from here if we don't want them? This is our home. Our people have lived here for so long we do not even know when they first came. No one has told the story of the first ones."

"The Easterners might not stop right here," Laird replied. "Most will probably go on to the valley where their people are and later stop at Waiilatpu and Lapwai."

"Should we fight to keep them out if we don't want them?"

"You can fight them as the Blackfoot and some Crow and others do who hunt in the buffalo country, but no matter what you do, they will still keep coming, for that is their way."

279

The older men sat silent, smoking while others talked. They had accepted Laird as one of their own and listened well to his counseling, just as James and others now listened to William Craig at Lapwai. Younger men of the tribe did not like to hear what Laird was now saying; they could not believe so many white people would come to their country. But the old chiefs had seen many things happen that their wisest men had not predicted. They knew Laird's words must be carefully considered.

Yet even some of the older men of the tribe were not convinced. Many felt it would not be impossible to stop the white emigrants; they began to voice their arguments.

"Laird, you know white men. You have come from the place where the Great White Chief lives. We believe you tell us only the truth, that there are many people that live there. You say more will come here than all the Indians in all the tribes. We believe this may be so. But we ask what power we would have if all our people—the Nez Perce, Cayuse, Yakima, Spokane—make war. Wouldn't it be enough to keep out the white men and their women and children?"

Laird searched for a way to explain why their numbers would make little difference. "My friends," he began finally, "I have seen your young men and women go to the winding waters when the salmon come up the river in the summer. I have seen them build dams of sticks and stones to stop the fish and force them into a place to be caught for winter food. Day after day the salmon come and day after day your people take them. Even in the darkness they come. And when the dam and all the sticks are gone, the fish still appear. This happens in all the rivers. So if all your people and all the white people and all the birds whose feathers you wear in your bonnets ate their fill, still more salmon would come from the sea.

"Think of the coming of the white men as like that of

280

the salmon. Even if you kill all of them as they appear, as well as those who live in your lands now, they will not be gone from your land for long. From the north where the Hudson's Bay trappers live, others will come to settle. They will send even more of their Black Robes and other missionaries to preach and teach.

"My friends," Laird went on, "when your hunters go to the land where the buffalo come from the north in the summer, have you not seen that their herds number many more than all the people in your tribes and that it has always been so? If all your hunters tried to stop the buffalo, they would run over you and your ponies and pound you into the dust. But because you ride along with the herd, in many ways they serve you. That is the way you must live with the white men."

There was silence and then a younger man spoke. "We have heard Whitman and Spalding say it is bad to make war. But if we do not fight, we lose our strength, grow weak and die. We believe this. Besides, when the white people come as we have seen them come this time, in wagons and with cattle, will they live with us as you and William do? Will their women live with our men and come into our lodges? Tell us these things, for we do not know."

"Rabbit Runs, I am not a wise man," Laird countered. "I know the white man's ways and I know those of your people. I think they will live in villages where there are others, for this is their way. The people who come now will go to where others live while their men look for a place where no one lives, and then they will take their horses and cattle there. They will plant in the ground, build trails for their wagons, build new villages and spread like water over flat ground until they wash higher and higher into the hills. It is their way."

281

Chapter 29

After Whitman left for the East there was trouble at Waiilatpu. For a long time Cayuse men had been wondering what white women looked like under their strange clothes. One Cayuse brave became particularly excited during a discussion about it and bragged he was going to find out for himself. Whether or not the brave took whiskey to inflame himself even further was a matter of speculation. What was clear, however, was that the Indian had been determined to satisfy his curiosity.

Believing themselves under the Lord's protection, the missionaries had taken no precautions against attack—this had caused trouble before—so when the brave stole into Narcissa Whitman's bedroom on one still, moonlit light, there was no lock on her window, no loaded gun by her bed to turn him away.

Hearing someone near her, she called out; there was no answer. Frightened, she called again and was seized by strong hands. The smell of her captor and the grip of his fingers let Narcissa know that he was an Indian. What she also knew—instantly—was that her attacker was naked.

Narcissa had been clothed for sleeping as modesty required. The Indian, angry because he had thought she

would be naked, had ripped the bedclothing from the terrified woman, then pulled her from the bed.

"Get out of here! Leave at once," she ordered. Her husband had warned her that in case of attack, she should never show fear as that might lead to further violence.

There was no answer from the Indian except his heavy breathing; then, a second later, he tried to tear off her filmy cotton gown. Narcissa jerked his hands away— she was a large, strong woman—and pushed him back. Once more she demanded, "Go! Leave me!"

Her captor whirled her around. His arms pinioned her. He pushed himself against the whimpering Narcissa and as she bucked against his body she felt him straining, pressing down on her. Certain that the Indian would not heed any command she might make now, she screamed, but foolishly, the Indian did not let her go.

He wrested the ragged remnants of her gown from her body. As she struggled, Narcissa's long blond hair fell unbound across her breasts. His passion rising as he looked at her nakedness in the dim light, the Indian explored her, fondling areas he had only avidly imagined before.

The exploration lasted only a moment. Narcissa's scream had awakened others. They came running from their quarters, but not in time to prevent the Indian from seeing and touching enough of the white woman to feed the stories he would spread about her. Now he could tell his friends how she was shaped—much like an Indian squaw but a lot bigger than most—and that she had more hair in places where their Indian women had little. Hearing the stories, the Cayuse were far from being concerned about possible retaliation. In fact, the warriors cheered the courage of the Indian who had invaded Narcissa Whitman's bedroom; they had only dreamed of doing it.

Although she had been saved that night from what she believed to be "the ultimate shame," she never fully

recovered from the terror. And because of the incident, for the first time the people at Waiilatpu could not wash from their minds the increasingly real possibility that the Indians might revolt.

When McKinlay, the Hudson's Bay factor at Fort Walla Walla, heard what had happened, he cursed in frustration. He had feared an event like this, and wise to Indian ways, felt it to be a harbinger of ill fortune.

Retrieving Mrs. Whitman from Waiilatpu, McKinlay escorted her to the Dalles mission, where he believed she could be safe until her husband returned. But as if relations between Indians and whites weren't under enough strain, the Cayuse became further incensed hearing of the transfer. So infuriated were they, in fact, that they set fire to stored grain and burned several hundred bushels of precious wheat and corn. So great was their terror that the settlers did nothing to punish the Cayuse men for burning the grain; previously, no action had been taken against the impassioned Indian brave because his identity remained unknown. In no time word of both events had reached other tribes and missionaries.

When Craig heard the story he shook his head sadly. Several white settlers and workers at Lapwai came to confer with him, respected as he was in his relations with the Nez Perce.

"Hell's fire and damnation is all I can say," he burst out at their query. "Now we can expect trouble up here. Ever since white men came to this country, they've always hunted down and killed any man who started trouble. The missionaries let trouble start and do nothing about it. I say somebody ought to force the chief to turn over that buck, then shoot him. Better yet, hang him."

"But that'd cause an uprising. Them Cayuse been trying to start something since Whitman built his place on

their lands. Kill one and they'll use that as an excuse to murder and burn till we're wiped out.''

"It could happen, I'll grant you that," Craig agreed. "But those missionary folk are living in the clouds. They think God's going to protect 'em without their lifting a finger. But they're wrong, I tell you. Look what happened to Mrs. Whitman. If she'd kept a loaded gun handy, she might have blown that Indian apart. That sure would have discouraged another attack on a white woman.''

"You've got something there, Craig," one settler commented. "But do you think such a thing could happen up here with the Nez Perce?"

"I can't really say," Craig answered. "I'd be lying if I said the Nez Perce aren't getting upset with people coming in here to settle without asking old James first. This here's his land, after all, and his warriors are beginning to ask him why he don't kick a few asses out of here. Believe me, they're ready to do it if he gives the word. I've tried to stay out of the argument between him and Henry Spalding, but mark my words, it ain't finished. I think that woman-crazy Cayuse has started something. Keep your guns loaded and handy. You might need 'em.''

The Spaldings were shattered when they heard news of the attack on Narcissa Whitman. Immediately they got word to the rest of the missionaries and all of them met to discuss the affair. Hearing the story, most shared the Spaldings' reaction. They had felt secure with the tribes they worked with and had never imagined for a moment that any white man—let alone a white woman—would be set upon violently. It was true that eastern tribes they'd heard of had assaulted and abused whites they'd captured, in many cases even taking white women as wives. But now that these practices might expand and sweep the West, it was a matter of intense concern.

*   *   *

News of the troubling incident at Waiilatpu reverberated all the way down the Columbia to the Willamette Valley. Dr. Elijah White saw in the situation a chance to use his newfound authority as subagent of Indian affairs in Oregon.

He recruited a group to investigate and quell any uprising among the Indians that might be in the making. Hiring several armed guards, he persuaded Cornelius Rogers and Baptiste Dorion to become his interpreters.

Baptiste was a Roman Catholic half-breed, the son of Pierre Dorion, who had been killed in the massacre at Boise River in 1814. Baptiste's mother had then married Pierre Toupin. He also was Roman Catholic, as well as an interpreter familiar with life at Fort Walla Walla and Waiilatpu.

Baptiste, now an interpreter like his stepfather, held tremendous power. And later many who questioned the outcome of various investigations believed that Baptiste's translations had not reflected the true meaning of the Indians' words. Other rumors spread as well. One was that he had told stories among the Indians that were damaging to Protestant missionaries.

White's investigation contingent reached the Dalles mission on November 24. White questioned Narcissa Whitman about her ordeal. William Geiger and the Littlejohns were in residence, William Gray having hired Geiger to look after the mission until Marcus Whitman returned from the East. Both men went back with White to Fort Walla Walla to confer with McKinlay. When the group now including McKinlay reached Waiilatpu, White and the rest were shocked at the damage to the grain supply and asked to confer at once with the Cayuse Indians. Because the few under interrogation had been too frightened to call the whole tribe to a meeting, White gave orders that they get

their chiefs together and be ready to meet with him on his return from Lapwai.

At Lapwai White was greeted by Spalding and the Nez Perce who were eager to meet this man who proclaimed himself a leader, yet was neither preacher nor army man. In discussions among themselves they had finally agreed that his authority must be like that of Lewis and Clark, who had visited them many years before and were well remembered by some of their old people. As a result of this attitude White was received as one who had come to help them prepare for the arrival of more whites in their country.

White was delighted; the Nez Perce acceptance of him offered added stature. In his parleys he flattered the Nez Perce chiefs and brought forth a new set of rules that he promised would not allow white men who harmed Indians to go unpunished. These rules would stand as white men's civilized laws; therefore, any white man who hurt or killed an Indian would be punished by his own laws.

Already the Indians had two sets of laws. One was God's laws as taught them by the missionaries. The second set comprised their own laws. Confident that he could devise a third set of rules, both workable and lawful, that would satisfy Indians and missionaries alike, Dr. White returned to Waiilatpu to confer with Dr. Whitman. Again he met with the Cayuse and again they were suspicious.

News of the attack at the Whitman dwelling reached Jason's Grande Ronde village. It was Dancing Leaf who first brought the news to Laird.

"Laird, men say that a Cayuse man wanted to see Narcissa Whitman without clothes, that he went to her place of sleeping and ripped them off her. Mrs. Whitman fought the Cayuse, the story says, but the warrior stared at

her and put his hands all over her body. Could that be so, Laird?"

"I think it might be. Did the Cayuse do more?"

"No. Mrs. Whitman screamed. Others came and the brave ran off, but no Cayuse will betray him to the whites. Will there be trouble when Mr. Whitman comes back?"

"Yes, I think there will be. What do our people say about this?"

"My father will talk to you. Wait until he asks. My mother heard him tell what he had learned to other men." She was quiet a moment, gazing at Laird. "We do not like this thing."

"Nor do I, Leaf. It is not good for any of the people."

Although Laird had been accepted by the tribe, the Indians felt differently now, wondering how this white man, no matter how well he fitted into Indian life, would react to the present situation.

Laird had learned much from Craig about taking time to answer questions and make decisions. Because of his new understanding, he had not taken sides in any argument concerning relations between whites and Indians. Now questions would be asked to test his ideas and beliefs. As much as he realized how precarious his position was, he looked forward to the meeting with Jason and other leaders. Anticipating what they knew and what they might propose was pleasurable to him.

"Laird, we have heard of the bad thing at Waiilatpu," Jason reported later at a meeting. "We think things may be done to hurt our people. We have talked. What are your thoughts?"

"My chief, of the thing done at Waiilatpu I would first like to hear what you know. What do the whispers of the wind bring?"

"I hear that a bad Cayuse boasted he would learn about a white woman's body. He went to see in the night

289

and entered the house where the women slept. The story said that the brave did no more than look and touch. The woman was not harmed, merely frightened. She fought him away and he ran as whites came to aid her. Later the Cayuse told others he had seen the white woman and how she was different from our own. Now we hear that the woman has gone to stay at the place where salmon are caught and will remain there until her husband comes back from the East."

Laird had taken to smoking a pipe, as Craig did, when in a council meeting; it seemed to add dignity to his speeches. He did not want to know who brought the stories of what had happened at Waiilatpu; it was better to say the wind whispered them.

"Like you, Jason, I do not like this thing," he agreed solemnly. "There will be trouble at Waiilatpu. This trouble will spread, for white men will be angry."

"White men have looked at our women," Jason said at once. "They have taken them. Some wives have gone to lie with white men who join other tribes. The Nez Perce do not like this. Nez Perce do not live like the Blackfoot or others who trade with trappers and buy their firewater whiskey. Now a crazy Cayuse frightens one white woman and we hear there are bad things to come."

"My friends, my people, I think the same." Laird puffed a moment. "Whitman once said, 'Do not strike back.' I do not know what he will say or do now, but men like Meek and other people from the far valley will want to punish the Cayuse. You remember how Meek once shot and killed a brave who struck his Nez Perce woman. They will think that if they do not act, the Cayuse will do more bad things."

Noises from the camp were muted by the lodge's covering of skin. The fire settled into greying coals. An aged chief spoke, a chief whose memory of times past was clear.

"We will wait and see. We will live in peace. Laird, we know you and Craig are of our people and we will listen to your counsel."

Nothing more was said of the matter in Jason's village until close on the heels of the attack on Narcissa Whitman, word came that the Cayuse had burned the grain. Again there was more talk and again Laird was brought into the council.

At this meeting, the council elders urged the Nez Perce to remain quiet, not to interfere even if the white men punished the Cayuse.

Soon came word that Dr. White had arrived at the mission with the Hudson's Bay factor, McKinlay, and that White was in charge not only of all Indians and all missionaries, but of the Hudson's Bay Company as well. Hearing the news, Laird was astounded. It could not be true, he thought. The United States, to his knowledge, did not own the lands where trouble had arisen. And if White took charge of all Indian tribes within the Oregon Country, then the British would have to fight or back down, perhaps leaving the lands they had claimed north of the Columbia River.

When another council was called, Laird sat and listened until asked a direct question. Was it true that Dr. White had authority over the missionaries and all the Indian tribes?

"I do not know this, my friends," Laird answered. "Where I come from, many things new to me are taking place. I have not met this Dr. White. I do not know if he has the power that is spoken of. I do know that if he calls for a meeting and wants the Nez Perce there, some of you—not I—should go. Your way of life is yours to keep, not mine, but I will help here in whatever way I can."

Chapter 30

After Whitman had returned from the East with new emigrants, White met with Spalding and Whitman at Waiilatpu and called in the rest of the missionaries to discuss the stirrings of revolt among the Cayuse. It was said that the Spokane and the Yakima too had begun to talk of running the white invaders from the country.

To counteract this possibility, Dr. White proposed eleven laws for governing the tribes:

1. Whoever willfully takes a life shall be hanged.
2. Whoever burns a dwelling house shall be hanged.
3. Whoever burns an outbuilding shall be imprisoned six months, receive fifty lashes and pay all damages.
4. Whoever carelessly burns a house or any property shall pay all damages.
5. If anyone enter a dwelling without permission of the occupant, the chiefs shall punish him as they think proper. Public rooms are excepted.
6. If anyone steal, he shall pay back twofold; and if it be the value of a beaver skin or

less, he shall receive twenty-five lashes; and if the value be over one beaver skin, he shall pay back twofold and receive fifty lashes.

7. If anyone take a horse and ride it without permission, or take any article and use it without liberty, he shall pay for the use of it and receive twenty to fifty lashes, as the chief shall direct.

8. If anyone enter a field and either injure the crops or damage the fence so that cattle and horses go in and do damage, he shall pay all damages and receive twenty-five lashes for every offense.

9. Dogs may be kept only by those who travel or live among game: if a dog kill a lamb, calf or any domestic animal, the owner shall pay the damage and kill the dog.

10. If an Indian raise a gun or other weapon against a white man, it shall be reported to his chiefs and they shall punish him. If a white person do the same to an Indian, it shall be reported to Dr. White and he shall redress it.

11. If an Indian break these laws, he shall be punished by his chiefs: if a white man break them, he shall be reported to the agent and punished at the agent's insistence.

The Indians brought Laird these new laws verbally. When he heard them he questioned the bearers. "Does Dr. White say he has power to enforce all this?"

"He only said it will be done. That the 'Bostons' will see that others will come and that this is the way eastern white man says we must all live from now on."

"Brush Rabbit, does White say he will write these

laws onto a paper to send to all tribes, or that he will talk to the people?''

"Laird, White said he would put his words on paper so all not there could see and know what his rules are.''

"Then we will wait. When we have the paper I will tell you what the words mean to our people.''

The document containing the eleven laws was printed on the little press at Lapwai. Before the paper came Laird wrote a letter to his uncle Charles Madden in Washington.

Chief Jason's Village
December '43

Dear Sir:

I am far from where I last wrote you. This place is in lower Nez Perce country. It is south of the Columbia on a small tributary of the Snake River, which flows from the Blue Mountains. The people here raise the finest horses in all the West and often have to fight off Shoshone raiders, who travel in a long, roundabout way to steal them. My companion here is the chief's daughter.

We came to this area because of troubles at Lapwai and Waiilatpu. The natives had become confused by the teachings of the several different Protestants, and a Roman priest came to confuse them even more. Now a Dr. Elijah White comes with strong laws he says will be applied to all tribes in the Oregon Country. He gets his authority, it is said, from the Bureau of Indian Affairs in Washington.

Things are changing rapidly here. When Dr. White told the missionaries and Indians he now had charge of all Indian tribes in the region, it took away much of the missionaries' power over

the tribes they had been teaching. Soon after Dr. Whitman went east to protest the closing by the Mission Board of the missions at Waiilatpu and Lapwai, a Cayuse Indian broke into the Whitmans' dwelling and attempted to assault Mrs. Whitman. Shortly after that the same Cayuse Indians burned the mission's store of grain. Among all whites in both this area and the Willamette Valley, these incidents have caused great fear of a general Indian uprising, but what the Indians now fear is the coming of more whites.

Yours,
Laird

Soon after Laird wrote the first part of his letter, an Indian brought the printed declaration of the laws to Jason's village. The chief asked Laird to read and interpret the laws to the tribal council. Each law was read repeatedly and the meaning of each word discussed until the whole had been clarified. The first few laws were fairly easy to understand and readily accepted. Number five, however, troubled the Indians; they argued about whether or not the schoolhouse dwelling at Lapwai was a public house.

"We helped build it. We have gone to school there and have held meetings there," one Indian asserted.

"That is true," another answered him. "But the Spaldings live in the part that is not a meeting place. We were always told to make a sound or ask permission to go in there. Spalding did not even want us to come in the school unless he invited us. Laird, what do you think?"

"I would ask the council to say whether or not it considers the schoolhouse a public place. If the chiefs or Spalding's people say it is public, that will do."

Number seven also caused disagreement. Thousands of horses ran loose in various ownerships, some hard to

identify. There could be real arguments as to the payment of rent for their use. This concern brought up land use, as Laird knew it would. The usurping of land by whites at Waiilatpu and Lapwai had always angered the Cayuse chief whose tribe claimed ownership. James also disputed claims with Spalding.

The laws concerning use of the whip were not overlooked either. None of the Nez Perce, young or old, liked them. Some said they would never tolerate whipping as punishment. Indians, they argued, were not dogs, horses or women.

"We do not whip our children. We are grown men, warriors. When a man strikes another, he counts coup."

"Then do not do these bad things if you do not want to be whipped," Chief James counseled. He too saw that the laws would cause much trouble, but he wanted to make sure all present expressed their beliefs while Laird was there to answer from a white man's point of view.

They argued also about the keeping of dogs; bitter words were uttered during that discussion. No Nez Perce could remember when a lodge did not have several; dogs were as necessary to their life as shelter or clothing. Many times they had served as beasts of burden and their flesh provided food when other meat was gone. Their hides could be used as clothing, too. To have no dogs would be a very bad thing.

Laws ten and eleven caused dissension. To expect Indian chiefs to punish Indians committing a crime against white men, and when a white man did the same to Indians, to have Dr. White decide his case made no sense to them.

White men had different laws than the Indian. They punished those who broke the laws by putting them in jails that took away their freedom, by hanging them or if caught in the act, by shooting.

Indian laws had been created primarily to deal with

incidents arising from the buffalo hunt, the transgressions punishable by the destruction of the offender's possessions or by public disgrace. Besides, no matter what a white promised, white men were often not punished at all for crimes against Indians.

The Nez Perce council concluded that while Dr. White's laws might have been a legitimate attempt to bring the Indians and white men to agreement, it had not succeeded. Many chiefs, in fact, left Jason's lodge puzzled. Why and how could one white man alone judge all other white men's crimes, and how could he alone decide their punishment?

Laird realized right away that the last two laws were unworkable. Their stipulations gave the white man freedom to do almost anything he wished in Indian country. According to the laws he would be responsible neither to Indian laws nor to the laws of decency. Indians could not punish him; only Dr. White could. It would be only natural to expect that all the whites would stick together to protect one of their race against the natives.

Dr. White ignored the complaints of those unresponsive to his laws. On the contrary, he reported to the Mission Board that the Indians had accepted his laws willingly and in their entirety, happy to have a guide to live by. What he neglected to say was that he had substituted his laws for the very laws of God that the missionaries had encouraged the Indians to obey. And now he was proposing something else, a more upsetting plan than anything he had yet devised.

He boldly declared that in order to make sure his laws were obeyed and all tribes were treated fairly, there should be only one leader to rule over all Indians.

This was unheard of. The Indians were as close to being a democratic society as was possible under the conditions by which they lived. Each unit had a leader who

was responsible for his own group. The leader gained his status by accomplishing an admirable deed in war or by assuming responsibilities that proved his ability to lead and direct. Now it was proposed that one man was to make the laws and say what must and must not be done. The prospect was unthinkable.

Laird knew any explanation of White's actions he could offer would have no effect on what the Indians concluded. He decided to visit William Craig at Lapwai. He himself needed counsel now and Craig was the one to give it. After informing Dancing Leaf and Jason of his intention, he made ready to leave.

Chapter 31

"By God, Laird, it's good to see you. What brings you to this godforsaken neck of the woods?"

"I figured White might be up here with Spalding."

"I should have guessed that was your reason," Craig sighed. "No, White's not here, but we can chew that matter over later. Put up them miserable spotted ponies and come on up to the house. Isobel will sure be glad to hear your news. How's Leaf and her old man?"

After some preliminary talk the two men settled into a discussion of Dr. Elijah White's eleven laws. Craig maintained that if a general Indian uprising did not occur before long, the lack of one would indicate that the chiefs still had control of their people and that it would be some time before that authority broke down.

"I tell you, Laird, this thing will raise more hell than anything else that bastard's done. He supposedly made those silly damned laws to protect the Indians, but all they do is protect the white riffraff coming into his country. There was always one or two of them among the trappers but they didn't last long afore the Indians or some trapper knocked 'em off. Now if an Indian has a complaint, he can't do nothing except turn it over to White, and for all

his bragging that bastard's as helpless about what to do as a cat in a sack of rocks at the bottom of a well."

"What's to come of it then?"

"Just what we expected. Murder, plunder, rape—that's what's to come of it. Any kind of hell-raising you can think of. Regardless of their faults, old Spalding and Whitman was doing their darndest to help the Indians; the chiefs admit that. James here, ornery as he can be sometimes, says the missionaries were on the right track, if they'd only had just a little patience and used a little sense. Whitman should have made sure he was on Nez Perce lands or had a clear agreement with the Cayuse chief to buy or rent Waiilatpu. But no, he and Spalding both figured any western lands was free for the taking, and they took 'em. Now they and a lot of others are going to pay for it. It's a sorry thing." Craig thought a minute and then began to laugh.

"Here's something for the book, boy. My father-in-law, old James, been claiming this whole valley and a lot more for himself and his tribe since many years and generations back. Now he's offered to give me all of Lapwai if and when Spalding leaves. The Nez Perce tribe wants me to take over the mill and granaries, run the whole shebang for 'em.

"Spalding got wind of the offer from his tame Indians and he thinks I put James up to it. Hell, I don't even want the outfit. I have enough to do. This kind of thing getting around raises all kinds of trouble. Nothing's like the days when me and Hawk and you and Suni was camping over in buffalo country. We'll never see those times again." His face softened.

"Bill, how will these things White proposed affect you and Isobel?"

"I'm not sure," Craig answered slowly. "I mean, we're purty safe here among friends, but I suspect I'll be

making some enemies among whites who move in. They'll doom anyone who cohabits with an Indian woman to hell and damnation, you know that.''

He paused. ''Laird, it's my turn. Let me ask you something.''

''Sure.''

''You know some higher-up in Washington. I know you write to him. Would you take it on yourself to go back and give him our side of things here? Hell, Whitman's made his trips. White went there and come back loaded with money and power. But nobody's ever told our side of what goes on. Maybe you write it in letters, but face to face is a hell of a lot better.''

''I have thought of it,'' Laird mused. ''I just don't think now is the time or that I'm the one to do it. If Joe Meek, yourself, even Doc Newell went and saw the right people, it might help. You have to know the right people to get anything done.''

''Meek knows the right people, I can tell you that,'' Craig exclaimed. ''Didn't I ever tell you he's related to some big bugs back there?''

''No!'' Laird was startled. ''Who does Meek know in Washington?''

''He's related to the Walkers, the Knox family and the Polks, to name a few. All of 'em know somebody who married somebody else's sister or brother or slept in the same bed. Old Joe would be some hombre to deal if he ever got to his kinfolk. Newell ain't so bad off, neither. He's got relatives who can swing the gate when it's needed.'' Craig chuckled. ''But I got a blind sow's hunch you can find acorns under the leaves if you go back there and start rooting around. You know this country, the Indians, some of the trappers. You was educated to hate Indians and now you've married one. If anyone can do the job right now, you can. But if you go, Laird, don't let nobody

here know what you're up to. Somebody's got to beat old White to the punch or he'll ruin us.''

Laird hesitated.

"It'll make a hell of a lot of difference, Laird, it really will." Craig's voice rose. "A few years back, when I was loose and snorting around after beaver and whatever I could find to make life interesting, I could say the hell with it, but no more. I've sunk my axe in a tree and I've planted my seed. This here's my land and the Nez Perce are my people. I will fight for both and I will live for both and do what I can. Once I was butting heads with Spalding. It didn't work.

"Like paddling against the current or bucking the wind, you have to work the way I told you to drive buffalo. They're not like cattle. You don't push them big old curly-headed brutes; you ease in on your pony from the side and act like you intend to cut 'em off. They'll push against you and you keep easing 'em along to go in the direction you want 'em to go.

"Here's how to work old Hanging Jowls White. You slip back East soon as the weather breaks and talk sense with whoever you're sending letters to, just like we talk with the chiefs. Hell, anybody hears our story will at least give it some thought."

"Craig, you really believe that my going will help the situation?"

"Boy, I do. You're the best suited. Laird, you always make sure them reports are sealed and waterproofed but I seen the name of the man they was to be delivered to. Others seen it too, boy, you know that? You told me yourself that when you and the women were in Young Antelope's hangout he said somebody named Tom or Toom wanted you alive."

Laird nodded.

"Well, I figure that somebody probably seen one of

them letters, thought you was a spy and wanted to put a stop to what you was doing. I been trying to find out who. I discovered there's a half-breed set up the whole affair, but after the pox hit camp and cleaned out most of the tribe, the matter was dropped. Some think Tom McKay was back of the Blackfoot raid; others disagree.

"This Madden you write to must be someone you trust. If you've wrote him about the Indians, how we get along with 'em and how we can beat the British getting title to this country, the sooner Madden gets some straight talk, the better for us and the United States."

"Bill Craig," Laird confessed, "this Madden is my uncle. He swore that it was important for me to come west. Now you say the same thing about my going east. I'm caught and hardly know where to be now."

Craig pushed. "I say go east soon as possible. You can't leave right now because of the chance of getting snowbound somewhere between hole-ups. But," said Craig, beginning to conjecture, "you might make it to Fort Hall fairly easy. Now, you'd have to lay over there or fight your way up to Bear River and over the hump. Stay put. Leaving now won't do. If you lay around till April, you'll make faster time. On the bad side, though, creeks and rivers will be up then and you'll have the damned Blackfoot, Sioux and Crow to worry about."

"Would going overland be better than going down the river and around the Horn?"

"That's thinking. By the time you got on the boat, word would be out and everybody from here up to Fort Vancouver would be dead sure you was a spy or a thief. You're not a mountain man nor a trader neither, you know, and there would be speculation as to where you was headed and why."

"You wouldn't think of going along with me, would you?" Laird put in. "You could go as far as the Platte,

then lead in a bunch of emigrants coming this way. From what Whitman said, there's sure to be more on their way this year.''

"No chance. I'll stay here to keep the kettle from boiling over; the fire's getting hotter every day. Did I tell you about the young bucks getting worked up and deviling Spalding a while back? A dozen or more went down one night and tore up his rail fences, made a fire in the fields, began a war dance and whooped it up. Spalding came to see and begun giving 'em hell. In the middle of it a couple of redskins grabbed him and they had a real tussle that ended up with Spalding getting thrown in the fire. It was only that old buffalo coat he wears saved him from getting cooked. As it was, he got his hands and hair scorched afore some older braves come down and read the riot act to the bucks.''

Laird gave a whistle. "Things are sure getting wild," he exclaimed.

"Something else took place," Craig went on. "Ever since that crazy Cayuse got a look at Mrs. Whitman, there's stories going round among the wild-eyed young bucks about how Mrs. Spalding might look naked. Half a dozen of 'em got stirred up, and while the old man was away and the kids was out in the fields, they slipped up on Eliza painted for war, nothing on, not even breechcloths.

"Well Eliza has spunk. She faced the whole bunch down and tried to talk 'em out of whatever they had in mind. They danced around and let her see what they had to offer but her cool head and the way she looked at 'em stopped the trouble. If they'd gone ahead after her, there sure would've been a lot of killings." Craig paused a moment, then added, "When White said he had new laws for Indians and white men, he sure started something. What he did took all the power away from the missionaries. Up till recently they had purty good control with the

fear of God and His punishment to help 'em, but that's about gone. And it didn't help that the Black Robes come and claimed to have the only real religion. That kicked over the kettle for sure.''

"Have you heard the story that Tauitau wants to give the Whitman mission to the priests?'' Laird asked.

"There was some rumors. James told me the Cayuse were purty upset about Whitman bringing all them people back with him, and of course James is still rankled about Whitman not paying rent for the use of his lands.'' Craig shook his head. ''I can't see the reasoning of the missionaries and priests when it comes to taking possession of Indian lands.''

"If the Roman Catholics really move in, I guess there will be even more trouble,'' Laird added. If he went to explain, would his uncle be able to do anything? Madden couldn't control the priests or the missionaries, but he might be able to prevent Dr. White from getting more political power. That would certainly help. And maybe he could persuade Washington to favor increasing the army gradually by establishing posts in carefully planned locations.

As Laird saddled up to leave for home, Craig repeated his warning. ''Don't let on to Leaf, Jason or any other Indian if you plan to head east. You're white; they're red. It'll be a good while afore you're really trusted. If the rumor gets out where you're going and what you're up to, you just might not make it.'' Craig slapped Laird's pony on the rump. ''They might think you're skipping out on Leaf, like most every other trapper's done to their squaws afore you. Some will figure you're going to lead more whites in here; that won't set too good either. Then there's the few who will think you're a spy. They'll believe you're trying to upset the Hudson's Bay Company and bring people here to run the British to hell back where they belong. All things considered, you'd sure better think of

some farfetched reason for taking a trip to Fort Hall.''

Troubled, Laird went back to Leaf and her people. The prospect of a trip to the distant capital to see his uncle did not bother him as much as leaving his beloved Indian woman. There would be a child later in the spring and he would not be there to see it, tiny and snug in its mother's arms. But as Craig had insisted, he seemed the logical one to make the trip. There he could talk with a person who had the influence to shape a new and better United States policy toward the Indian tribes of the West.

Laird thought of reasons he might give to explain the trip. He had learned from living among the Nez Perce and from Craig that Indians had a built-in sense of danger and of things to come. Chiefs had attained their positions through acts of bravery and leadership that through the years proved their ability. To mislead the wise and shrewd Jason could be serious error; it might cause the chief to distrust whites even more than he did already.

Nez Perce Chief Jason listened to his son-in-law Laird, who squatted facing him from the other side of the fire. He knew Laird had visited Bill Craig and Whitman and perhaps other white men to the north, and was aware, since he had seen Dancing Leaf sewing moccasins and packing them full of pemmican, that Laird had been preparing for another trip.

''My father,'' he now heard, ''bad things have happened since the man named White came and forced his laws on our people. White has too much power and that is not good. I will go to where he got his power and say to the men who gave it that it should not be so. White does not know the Indians. He does not know their religion. He leads our young men in ways that will hurt them.

''My father, I do not know if I can do what should be done but I must go and try. It will be like hunting wild

sheep in the mountains or buffalo on the prairies. I must go where there are many dangers and where bad things may happen. One white man knows what I am thinking and he is Bill Craig of James' village. He said it would be good that I go.''

Jason sat in silence. So, he thought, this is what Laird has been preparing for. He knows White's laws will cause trouble. He wants to stop him in some way. Laird is a good man. Like Craig, he speaks the truth. Laird has much to learn, but he is brave and strong. Perhaps he is the son of a great chief, for he thinks of his people. If he does this thing he plans, he will help the Nez Perce.

Jason turned to the white man. ''Laird, my son,'' he announced, ''I have listened well. You must make this journey you speak of. My daughter will bear your son while you are away. I do not know that we will see you again and that saddens me. Still, we will live in our way here and care for your child and your woman; many things may happen on the long trail you take through the lands of the Blackfoot, the Crow and the Sioux. I will say nothing to my people about where you go.''

Laird acknowledged Jason's approval. ''I will go as if on a buffalo hunt, but alone,'' he said. ''I will leave some money with Dancing Leaf and take only two ponies, my guns and food. My heart is sad that I must leave our homeland.''

Chapter 32

In the Willamette Valley homesteading trappers were encountering tough times. Joe Meek, Bob Newell and others who had taken up land claims had become fed up with the French-Canadians moving into the valley. The new emigrants proved less liberal than mountain men and the missionaries were even worse. Used to the relaxed atmosphere of good times—drinking bouts to cement friendships and brawls to loosen muscles and dissipate boredom—the trappers now found that such activities did not sit well with the God-fearing newcomers.

Worst of all, the wet drizzly rains of winter contrasted sharply to the high dry mountain air they were used to. In the valley mountain men found hunting difficult and game scarce because there were so many hunters hot after anything that had meat on its bones.

The trappers' Indian wives were looked on with disfavor, their half-breed children eyed with suspicion and treated poorly. White children were forbidden to have anything to do with the so-called half-breed brats.

Spring came early that year. It was still February, but winds blew soft and warm; the land steamed under the spring sun. Grass greened and as ground was cleared, the valleys filled with the soft blue haze of fires from burning

logs and stumps. Days were longer; more work could be done in the sun's light instead of by candle and lantern. Travelers got the itch to move about. When Bob Newell told Joe Meek he planned to head east and bring back a bunch of plow jockeys and woodcutters so he could come up with money enough for plunder, Joe was all for it.

"Hell, Bob, take off now. Get over the trail upriver, stop and see what Whitman's doing and visit old Craig to find out how he and James is making out. Ten chances to one you can get a line on what them fellers need and take some letters back or news to pass along. Whitman may have something to tell you that could make your trip worthwhile. I want to get more white people in here instead of them half-blood French Canucks what think they own the blasted country just because the Hudson's Bay Company was here first."

"Why don't you take off too, Joe?" Newell asked.

"Don't tempt me, old hoss. You make the first trip. I'll stick here and keep the settlements entertained and watch over your tribe of kids and women."

"I think you ought to pull stakes and go with me," Newell persisted. "We'd travel like we used to, see what's going on over at Fort Hall and hear what new ideas old Elijah the Prophet's put in the Indians' heads."

"Well, I can tell you what will happen to old Elijah White and you can call me a prophet or a darned fool; they're both the same in my book. If he ain't run out of the country, somebody's going to cut his throat or drown him. I never saw or heard of such a fool thing as that set of laws he expects Indians to live up to. Hell, Bob, that's going to raise more hell than a bunch of Blackfoot with a keg of white mule piss and a bunch of skinning knives. To cap it all off, the priests have to come in and cozy up to old Tauitau, who ain't above turning 'em on the missionaries. I sure wish we had some feller to go back and put a stop to

having White handle Indians in a country he don't know nothing about. When old McLoughlin heard of them laws he had a fit and I don't blame him.''

"Joe, you're a worthless old drunken scoundrel, but once in a while you show sense," Newell agreed. "Anyway, I'll go see Bill and maybe get other ideas. That is, if you'll see nobody moves in on my place or my woman while I'm gone.''

The early spring made Bob Newell long for the prairie benches near the country where Bill Craig lived. Maybe, he thought, he'd find a place to squat there after he got rid of his claim on the Willamette.

The Whitmans were glad to see Newell. They remembered that he had helped them move in and later had brought their wagon to Waiilatpu. Right away Newell noticed on Narcissa Whitman's face what must have been the effects of the Cayuse Indian's assault. She seemed afraid to let her husband out of her sight. Whitman, finally alone with Newell, spoke of her fears.

"Mr. Newell, Narcissa is still suffering.''

"Was the feller who attacked her punished in any way?''

"No. No one could prove who he was. The one who we're pretty sure came in and attacked Narcissa denied even being on the property. Their chief acted smug about the thing too, and gave us no help. He still insists I ought to pay for the land we built on. I don't understand his attitude after all we have done for him and his tribe. I really don't.''

"Hell, Marcus, it's all easy to understand if you know this tribe. You come to help the Nez Perce, yet you set your mission on Cayuse lands. Old Tauitau ain't never going to get over the fact you didn't ask him if it was all

313

right for you to settle in. How you getting along with Father Blanchet and McBean over at the fort?"

"I have met them both. I like and respect Father Blanchet, but McBean will stir up things because he is a strong Catholic and throws his weight behind the priests. The real troublemaker, though, is that part Indian, Tom Hill. That half-breed's against all whites. He's already begun trying to unite the tribes in a general uprising—says all whites should leave or be killed."

"Tom Hill," Newell mused. "Yeah, I know the feller. So he's the snake in the grass. What's he done besides talk?"

"He tried to get guns and whiskey, I guess to stir up the young men. I have even heard it suggested that he was behind the Blackfoot attack on the Nez Perce party in buffalo country when young Laird and the women were captured."

"Well, so it was Tom Hill. We heard it was Tom McKay. I'm going to see Bill Craig and I'll tell him to keep his eye on that shifty-eyed skunk. It's a wonder he wasn't shot or knifed a long time back."

"Violence begets violence, Mr. Newell," Whitman said primly. "Merely killing Mr. Hill won't prevent what's coming."

"What are you talking about?"

"I can't help believing that my work here is about to end." Whitman's tone was somber. "Too many things complicate what I came here to do. The very people we came to help now turn against us; some are on the verge of physical violence against us here at the mission. I am not afraid to die, but I do fear for my wife and the others. Dr. White substituted man's law for that of God and brought confusion to our converts. I fear that those laws will also cause trouble with the priests, who say that their religion is the only true one."

314

Newell felt sorry for the missionary. "Whitman," he said as sincerely as he could, "me and some of the others, including Craig and Meek, thought you was on the wrong track when you and Mrs. Whitman come here to build this mission. But even if you was wrong, you sure have done a lot of good. You and the Spaldings and others that work with Indians teach 'em and set examples. Whether the people believe and follow 'em or not, they'll pick up something to think on and that will help 'em live with whites later. When you brought that last bunch of emigrants over the Blues into this country, you started the real building of this country, you know that? Even old Meek admits it was the biggest thing you done yet."

"No, Mr. Newell, I can't accept that. Mr. Meek insisted there was a way to bring wagons across mountains and I clearly recall you also insisted it could be done. Both of you, with Mr. Craig and others, brought them. I merely followed your road. Others will follow it too. I can safely say I expect a larger number this year and every year as people write back and send word to friends and relatives about this bountiful land."

"But the natives are bound to resent strangers coming in to settle, Whitman. They don't want people killing off the game they been living on for centuries. Not only that, to plow up land goes contrary to all their beliefs and training."

Whitman was silent for a moment. "Yes, Mr. Newell," he agreed. "I can see that. But I want to suggest that the Indians will have to change. They will have to learn to exist with the white man or be obliterated. There is no place for them to hide or to flee. Just look at all the eastern tribes represented in this country, the ones pushed out by the French, the English and their enemies; they were encouraged and armed by Americans who wanted their lands and I suppose the same thing will begin here

315

before long. What will you and your Indian wife and children do then?''

''Same as always,'' Newell told him. ''Get along and hope things get better. I'll be heading east soon as I see Bill Craig. Anything I can do for you, like taking letters or putting in a good word if I meet some influential muck-a-muck along the way?''

''I would appreciate that,'' Whitman replied. ''I will make ready a few letters for delivery and have them for you by the time you leave.''

''Want me to tell somebody about how well your fellow missionary Elijah White is organizing the tribes of heathen Indians?''

Whitman frowned. ''I wish you wouldn't joke about Mr. White. He means well.''

''Whitman, open your eyes. He's making your job impossible. Where does White get the power he talks about? People who know the old goat and the reasons why he got kicked out of the valley wonder what strings he pulled back East to get the power to tell Lee and the rest of you what you can do and what you can't do. He's dangerous, that man. What I want to know is whether he can be stopped in any way.''

''I don't know. The problem you describe is one I have wondered about too. We may find out some answers in time, but that time may be too late. Take that trip, Mr. Newell, and meet new people. Perhaps you'll get answers to some of your questions soon enough to do some good.''

''Maybe . . . and maybe I'll just run into more swell-headed people like old Elijah,'' Newell jeered.

Craig was surprised to see Bob Newell come riding in. He was more astonished to learn that Newell planned to go east to lead emigrants back to Oregon Country. When Laird came in again on his way east a day later, the three

talked and each was certain that scattered uprisings would break out as more whites moved into Indian lands. Craig said he had heard that a group of braves were planning a trip south into California, taking many ponies to trade for cattle that the settlers in the Sacramento Valley had allowed to expand into vast herds.

Instead of joining the annual buffalo hunt, the Indians would bring back tame beasts to graze on their own grass lands and range with their horse herds. Tauitau, Garry and others of influence would be with them. There was talk that perhaps a trading line would be established from the south up through central Oregon; that would benefit all the tribes. As the three trappers discussed this trip, someone mentioned Tom Hill.

"Tom Hill," Newell said. "Laird, that half-breed Delaware is the one put Young Antelope up to grab you and the women to hold for ransom. If it hadn't been for the pox, you might have been dead and buried long afore this."

"Who told you that?" Craig demanded. "We thought it might have been Tom McKay; I never thought of Hill."

"Whitman said he'd heard rumors, that's all," Newell offered, "but he seems purty sure it was Hill. Laird," he said changing the subject, "I'll ride along with you till we meet an outfit I can bring west. When I do, you can keep on going east and find out where Elijah White got his so-called letter of power over this whole blasted country. No one with an ounce of brains would give that man authority to ride herd on Indians in British territory."

Laird had been thinking of the half-breed. "I'd like to meet up with this Tom Hill some day," he declared. "Quite a few people got killed along with Hawk and Suni. If Hill was responsible, he should pay for what he did with his life."

"Laird, you getting involved with Hill right now

wouldn't help things one bit. If he jumps you sometime and you have to protect yourself, that's one thing, but if you kill him it's just another case of a white man killing an Indian and that will cause the missionaries to catch even more hell. You can be sure White with his blasted laws will see that his kind of justice is done and that what you're starting out to do now will have to be forgotten, maybe for good.''

"But I can't let him get away with what he did," Laird fumed.

"The hell you can't," Craig put in. "If you do by any chance meet up with him, for God's sake and ours too, don't kill him; just beat the hell out of him the best you can. Then the bastard will lose face with his red brothers. And don't forget to count coup by slapping his face first."

"Not much chance of running into Hill this trip," Newell said. "Whitman told me he's stirring up the Yakima into making a trip for cattle along with Garry. I hope you never run into the hook-nosed thief, but if you do, watch yourself; remember, he uses a knife."

Early spring had melted some snow off the pass over the Little Salmon River summit. What drifts Laird and Newell encountered were few and easily navigated. A group of young riders anxious to be on the move joined the pair and helped break trail through snowpacks the sun had not yet touched. When they reached Fort Boise, Laird heard more about Tom Hill from the trader there.

"That half-breed and a couple of Cayuse braves come through here a day or so back, heading for the Shoshone around Fort Hall. The slippery son of a bitch is stirring up trouble, you mind my words. He sure wanted whiskey, but he didn't get none from me. A few drinks and him and the two fellers with him would blow the guts out of the first

white men they seen. As it was, Hill was saying they ought to put a price on whites' hair like the British put on Indian hair back where he come from.''

''Wasn't there any white man around to shut him up?''

''Nary a one. 'Tain't like it was a few years back, Newell. Things are getting touchy. Nobody wants to start a killing spree with these rules White laid down. I think Hill would like to start trouble, though, then see if White can enforce the punishment us whites might have dealt out to us. It all seems logical, knowing Tom Hill. Hell, he's always been for running us out of the country, keeping it just for Indians. It won't work now, but he's giving it a try anyway.''

''If he starts his boasts around me, I intend to coax him to shut up,'' Laird declared, sneering.

''Well, if you run into Hill, keep your eye on them two Cayuse bucks traveling with him. Them fellers look mean as a saloon-keeper's mutt. It'll be three on one, that's for sure, and those boys are real handy with knives and hand axes.''

Laird and Newell left Fort Boise and made their way across the sagelands to Fort Hall. There they stopped overnight, leaving in light rain the next morning to head toward Bear River and the distant passes. It wasn't hard for Laird to learn that Hill and the Cayuse were a day's ride ahead; but where they were going was anybody's guess.

Laird couldn't shake Hill from his mind. He wanted to find out from the Indian who had set him up to get captured for ransom. Despite his priority of traveling east as quickly as possible, Laird was determined to confront Hill with the deaths he had caused. Though Laird knew he was taking chances even thinking about revenge, he thought about it anyway and allowed himself to hope that he and Newell would catch up with the party ahead.

When Bob Newell let Laird be the one to go ahead, he noticed their pace increased and knew that Laird was trying to overtake Hill's party. At a camping place used by trappers and Indians near Sheep Rocks, they met a small band of Shoshone braves from the village of Sleeping Thunder. Once Newell had traded the leader an old fusee trade gun he had taken from a dead Blackfoot in a shootout, and the two men recognized each other at once. The warrior needed powder to tamp in the ancient, rusty barrel of his gun.

Laird learned that Hill and his companions were trying to encourage the tribes to plunder articles from oncoming emigrants, steal their horses, cattle or oxen, frighten women and children and in any way they could, try to discourage whites from settling on and stealing Indian lands. Hill, the Shoshone warrior said, did not talk of killing, but suggested that the half-breed must have known it would be inevitable when the white men tried to protect their caravans.

Later, when Newell and Laird caught up with him and the Cayuse, the Indians were eating and drying meat from a buffalo carcass that lay nearby. Their ponies had been picketed and were grazing on short grass. The three did not seem alarmed as Newell and Laird rode up; evidently Hill and his companions took them for innocent travelers, not men looking for trouble.

"Well, Tom, we meet again," Newell grated. "Long ways from The Dalles. How's the ribs going down?"

"Try 'em." For a moment Hill's face registered surprise. "Get down and cut yourself some for you and your friend, Newell. Plenty for all. Where you heading?"

"Going east to meet company somewheres on the trail."

"I'm making the rounds afore the country gets so full of wagons and whites there won't be no game for us who live here. Who's your partner in the Nez Perce shirt?"

"His name's Laird. He's been with Jason's band this winter. Guess you know about him and Craig and the mixup with the Blackfoot over on the Beaverhead awhile back."

"That's right, I heard about it. Him and his woman almost lost their hair, so I was told. Go on, cut yourself some ribs, boys. While we eat we can talk a little."

Newell climbed off his pony, his rifle in hand, seeing Laird do the same. The two men by the fire were close to their weapons but seemed not to be alarmed. Laird saw that Hill's weapon was not within his reach. Another fusee gun lay off to one side, two bows and their arrow quivers close by. The Indians near the fire were using their knives to cut meat. A throwing axe lay beside the flames, another near the buffalo carcass.

Because of Bill Craig's painstaking instruction, Laird had remembered to size up a situation and take advantage of whatever it offered, especially where danger was involved. He handed his rifle to Newell and muttered, "Bob, hold onto this for me while I have a talk with Hill. If those two bucks with him try to interfere, fire away." Laird's voice sank to a hoarse whisper. "I can handle the half-breed gut-eater."

Hill looked up in surprise as Newell began to speak to the two Cayuse in their own language. Laird walked directly to the half-breed and began to speak.

"Hill, some of your friends have said you tried to kill Bill and me while we were camped with Nez Perce on the Beaverhead. Your Blackfoot did kill several men and women and they caught me and four others who died in Young Antelope's camp. I owe you and now I'm about to make the first payment. What I'm going to do right now is beat the hell out of you. You are not a man, but a sick squaw who bleeds and goes to her lodge. In your own country you are a disgrace. Men will shun you, for you have

321

betrayed your people and the white men as well. Once I
am done with you, if you do not leave the lands of the Nez
Perce by the time I return, I promise to kill you.''

Hill reached for his axe as Laird kicked the fire. Hot
coals, ashes and chunks of wood scattered over the Indian
as he scrambled for his weapon. Laird leaped and landed
on Hill, his force and weight pinning the Indian flat to the
ground. But like a tightly wound spring the half-breed
burst away, still clinging to the axe he had managed to put
his hands on.

Laird sensed his opponent's next move. With the
accuracy of a winging Nez Perce arrow, his right hand
grasped the half-breed's wrist so tightly that his fingers
could not keep their hold on the slender axe handle. As
Hill bucked and twisted, Laird rolled with him toward
where a meat-cutting knife lay and Newell stood, rifle at
ready, watching to make sure the two Cayuse did not join
the fight.

There was no need to worry. The two Indians were
enjoying the battle. Although they traveled with Hill, they
seemed more interested in seeing what the white man
could do in this hand-to-hand battle than in their companion's survival.

Laird had inherited a grip of unusual strength. Ten-
dons ran down his arms into his fingers strong as piano
wires, their steel-clenched hold like that of the bald eagle's
talons, grasping his high crag so not even a hurricane wind
can blow him away. Hill desperately flung himself toward
the knife he knew was near. At the same time he brought
his moccasined feet up to kick.

Anticipating this move, Laird turned his head aside,
but not before Hill took a mouthful of long hair and beard.
As his head was jerked back Laird almost lost his grip on
Hill's leg and as he straightened up he felt Hill's right
hand reach for more hair. In a lightning-smooth motion

Laird banged his skull against Hill's. The impact forced the half-breed's head to the ground; it jarred his teeth, but Hill's quick hand reached to gouge Laird's eye.

In response Laird's knee jerked up into Hill's unprotected crotch. Pain flashed through Hill's body. The advantage in the fight switched to Laird. Twisting Hill's arm, he threw him flat on his back, dragged him a foot or so, then pitched him into the scattered embers of the fire.

There was plenty of life left in Hill, but Laird grabbed his flailing legs, swung him in a circle and let him fly into the two Cayuse, who were standing close by.

Still charged with energy, Laird lunged toward the Indians' quivers and grabbed them before the startled Cayuse could recover. Then he dived for Hill's knife and rifle. As the three men untangled themselves, Laird spoke panting.

"Hill, I've let you live for one reason: so that Indians will know you were whipped by the man you persuaded Young Antelope to capture. What you did hurt others, not just me. Nez Perce women died of the pox caught from the Blackfoot who captured us. When I come back to Nez Perce country, the Nez Perce will tell me where you are and I will hunt you down and kill you. Because of the bad things you did to me and the Nez Perce and because of what the Cayuse have done to the missionaries, a new sickness will kill their children and many of their people. If more harm is done by the Cayuse, the Umatilla, the Yakima or any other tribes, sickness and war and bad times will come to them too."

Hill stood sullen and defiant, his left arm and hand paining him and useless now. The two Cayuse braves moved back. Their black eyes watched this wildcat of a white man lay his curses on Hill and they had caught enough of his talk to know that his warning was also a threat to them. Now he spoke in their language.

"We go on now. I take your bows and arrows and

your guns. You stay here, but before the sun goes down follow our trail and find where I leave your weapons. Tom's gun I keep, for I do not trust him. Leave Tom. Go back to your people. Tom is a bad man. If you follow him you will be like rotten meat that only starving dogs eat.''

Laird gathered up Hill's axe, knife and rifle and tied them on his pack pony. Then he looked at the charge and cap of his own rifle to make sure it was ready to fire. Feeling for his knife, he caught up his pony and mounted, the Cayuse quivers in hand. With his rifle pointed at the three men, he waited until Newell had mounted. Pack animals in tow, the two rode east.

Two miles farther on Laird threw down the bows and arrows and the old fusee. Bob Newell grinned.

''I always knew old Bill saw something in you, boy,'' he chuckled in relief. ''But I never expected such a wild whirlwind of a mixup as took place back there. Why didn't you kill the bastard? He'll only cause more trouble later on.''

''I was mad enough,'' Laird acknowledged, ''but if a white man kills an Indian or even a half-breed, it could cause other trouble. White's decree that a white man would be tried under white men's rules would cause the Indians to think of Hill as an Indian and me as a hated white enemy. As it is, White may now lose some of his influence with the Cayuse and others who want war.''

''I don't doubt your sincere intentions,'' Newell observed. ''We'll wait and see what Hill does to get even, because you can bet your greasy old shirt that right now he's scheming how he can kill you, steal your ponies or poison your drink. A half-breed renegade can be meaner than a stepped-on snake.''

''The hell with Hill and his meanness. If I get back and find him slinking around where I live, I'll have more of his hide.'' Laird drew a long breath. ''Let's keep going,

find us a camp. I'm starved. Why didn't we throw on some of that meat they were roasting?"

"Because you was too damn interested in roasting a skunk named Tom Hill," Newell replied laughing. "Kick your pony and I'll try to keep up."

Chapter 33

The two men pushed through wet camps and dry camps, rain squalls and snow flurries, eating well when they found game handy to their trail, not so well when there was nothing to kill. Until they approached Fort Laramie they met no one.

There they encountered a troop of twenty soldiers on a scouting trip, the lieutenant in command so surprised to see just two men traveling that he halted his entire troop to ask who they were and where they had come from.

"We're just a couple mountain men from the west side of the Rockies," Newell replied, "from the Willamette Valley and the Nez Perce Columbia River country."

Anxious to learn more of western country he had yet to see, the lieutenant led the way back to the fort, where Laird and Newell unpacked their ponies and ate with the troops that night. No emigrants had yet arrived at Fort Laramie that year, but a train was on the way and the lieutenant had gotten word there were more to follow. Plenty of men could lead wagons this far, but there were none who could pilot them past Fort Hall and through the Blue Mountains to the Columbia. If Newell and Laird wanted to hire on, the lieutenant told them, they could wait here at the fort or keep going until they met the

emigrants; the first train was not more than sixty or seventy miles east.

Tom Fitzpatrick and William Sublette, who had built the fort years before, were now at the post. Doc Newell had once been their trusted companion. It was Sublette who had suggested Bill Craig take Laird to the Nez Perce country.

Fitzpatrick asked the first question. "Doc, you and Laird seem in an all-fired hurry to go east. What's up?"

"Tom, it's this way. You ever meet a preacher by the name of Dr. Elijah White?"

"Hell, yes. He come through here going west a few years ago, then come back in a couple years going clean east. Once he got there he gathered some missionary people and a bunch of cattle and emigrants for the return trip. Said he had orders to take charge of all the Indians west of the Rockies. Said he had it in writing from Congress."

"Well, boys, since this old goat with big ideas got back out there, he's raised holy hell and he's about to set fire under it," Newell explained. "He's took over and made laws for both Indians and whites. McLoughlin and the Hudson's Bay Company's mad enough to declare war and unless White's slowed down there will be hell among all the tribes. We've told the troops here that we're on the way to meet emigrants and pilot 'em to Oregon. But Laird's going clear on back East to see the higher-ups who run things. And he's in a heap of a hurry."

Sublette smiled. "I never thought much of that highhanded bastard White. He always had his nose in the air and his hand on a woman's rump. Laird, you mind letting slip the name of one or two of them relatives of yours?"

"Sage is my family name, quite common in New York. Fact is, I was born in Sageville."

"You ever heard of a Rufus Sage?"

"Why, he's a cousin of mine."

328

"Well, he come through here with George Bent. Then he and five others went south, to where Bent's about to open another post."

"Bill, what are you going to do with this one?" Newell broke in. "And what's that troop of greenhorn soldier boys doing here besides eating?"

"Don't be fooled, Doc. These fellers are on a scouting trip. Wait and see, the army will dicker to buy us out afore long. Want to guess the reason why?"

"Emigrants and Indians. They don't mix, do they?"

"You're dead right. I hope to make a few dollars in this trading post over the next few years, selling what travelers need. Doc, you coax 'em in here and we'll shear some sheep instead of beaver. I'll put out the word that you, Meek or any of the old boys can lead the innocent through any and all of the Indian tribes. Meek and Craig still have their Nez Perce women? Maybe a mess of kids by now to fetch water and carry wood?"

"Yeah," Newell replied, "and Laird here got the daughter of the old Nez Perce chief, Jason, to make his shirts, round up his ponies and keep him warm at night. Tom, we all figure to stay and live in that country. Craig and I talked about it years back while we was scouting where Spalding has his layout now. Craig always was looking for a place to sink his axe and plant some seed. Now me and the rest are doing the same." Newell's voice rang with intent. "We'll build that country yet by living there and raising kids—you'll see. And if we have to get help from Congress and the higher-ups to do it, we will."

"Don't get worked up, Doc; it ain't like you. Things are bound to work out all right."

"No, they ain't necessarily. I used to think so, but no more. And us old boys got too big a stake in that country to set on our butts and smoke. We want American

laws and rules, not the Hudson's Bay Company and the English to tell us what to do.''

''Hell, none of us want that,'' Fitzpatrick agreed. ''Well, take it easy, boys. Go your way and if we can help, call on us. I don't see us moving in your direction, though. South to Santa Fe and Mexico is where the company wants to trade.''

The two travelers left the next morning, having spent half the night exchanging news and ideas. Much of the talk centered on how to get rid of Dr. Elijah White and keep him from influencing the Indians.

When they met the first emigrant train, Doc said his farewells to Laird, then turned west with the line of wagons and cattle. There was no deal yet, for this group already had a captain who knew something about the trail to Fort Laramie. Doc was patient. He knew that the train leaders would talk with Sublette or Fitzpatrick at Laramie and learn how much assistance they would need beyond that point. Then he'd have himself a job.

Laird pushed on, driven by his desire to see Charles Madden and tell him of the problems with White. In St. Louis he saw the Indian Agent, William Clark, and thanked him for suggesting he get inoculated against smallpox. Then he explained briefly why he thought White should be removed from western lands and steps taken immediately to prevent an outbreak of Indian warfare.

After he heard what Laird had to say, Clark wrote a personal letter to Charles Madden asking that he consider Laird's request and that his letter to Madden be destroyed; Clark wanted no evidence that he had so much as thought of getting White fired. Finally Clark made the necessary arrangements for Donald Laird Sage to proceed to Washington under army escort.

''General Clark,'' Laird protested, ''I need a change of clothing and some pocket money more than an army

escort. It took whatever little I received from the sale of my horses and outfit to get me this far.''

''Mr. Sage, let an old fool advise you. Clean up, yes, but wear the buckskins you have on now. Let people in Washington see what a mountain man looks like. Men in the capital live so far from reality, they need to be presented with what goes on in the West. Dressing as you are will add emphasis to your words.''

''I will do as you say,'' Laird agreed, ''but I question the need for an army escort.''

''We have brigands and ruffians around here who would rather steal than work,'' Clark replied. ''I want nothing to happen to what you carry in your pouch and in your head. Four troopers to ride along will ensure safe delivery of both you and your dispatches.''

In Washington Laird was received by his uncle and his cousin, Congressman Sage, who listened with great interest to Laird's stories of life in Nez Perce country. Tales of Laird's travels and his meetings with famous mountain men intrigued the congressman, but always the discussions brought him to the question of whether this territory was ready to become part of the United States and whether such a decision would bring on war with the British.

Laird had his own viewpoint. ''Gentlemen,'' he declared, ''all I can do is guess based on the stories of people I know and trust. If more emigrants go west before the British get word of what is happening, and if the settlers in the Willamette Valley vote favorably, then the power will swing to the States. But right now many French people who worked for the Hudson's Bay Company want to be on the side of England and the company. These people are devout Roman Catholics and friction is growing between them and the Protestants, even more intensely since

Dr. White brought forth his set of laws. Unless White is removed I see bitter brush-fire wars breaking out between whites and Indians, with priests and missionaries on opposite sides according to their beliefs. Believe me, gentlemen, when White was given this authority he was given the power to stir up a batch of trouble.''

"Laird, in the order of their importance, list a few things you think will help the situation."

The man from the West looked at his two relatives and studied their faces. They were men of importance, thinkers and doers who he believed would accept as truth what he told them and work quietly to help him and his friends, both red and white.

"The first thing," he suggested, "is to get rid of Elijah White. Next find someone to head Indian affairs who knows the West and who has more than hearsay knowledge about Indians and trappers. As both of you know, my ideas about Indians changed once I actually lived with them and the mountain men.

"I slept, ate and fought with the Indians. I've married into a Nez Perce tribe. My wife Dancing Leaf is the daughter of a Nez Perce chief and has probably borne our first child by now. The Nez Perce are her people; now they are my people. The same goes for William Craig, Robert Newell, Joe Meek and many others. We want protection for ourselves and our families, not for just a few months, but permanently. The third thing that should be discussed and planned for is army protection for us and those traveling west, so that large-scale plundering by Indians and whites can be prevented. As of now, a few strong mountain men from the Hudson's Bay Company and the American fur companies have done a good job of stopping trouble.

"Lastly, we need representation back here, people to work for us and our future, and I'm not talking about some

mealymouthed priest or preacher who has ideas of heaven on earth and the life beyond but doesn't know how to look for a trail or travel one.''

"Laird, your people already have representation here if you'd just realize it,'' Madden pointed out. ''Mr. Meek has close ties with President Polk. Robert Newell has relations in state office with influence he can call on whenever it is necessary. We can't perform miracles. The only miracle I'd like to see happen is for Congress to forget the idea that merely spending money will make things get better.''

Congressman Russell B. Sage smiled at his cousin. ''But I think we can promise him a few things, don't you, Uncle Charles? For example, I know that Dr. White is quite likely to be relieved of his position with the Indian affairs office. We hope to find someone who knows more about western Indians than he does.

"Bear in mind that the religious folk have much to say and do about who gets appointed. They have a strong voice with Congress; rightfully so, for they have used their own people, money and time to begin settlements out west. Most of them are conscientious people who serve in the best way they see fit, though I'll grant you there are many who think more about heaven and getting there than of trying to make a better place for themselves and others here on earth.

"The army's presence in western territory will have to wait till after we have a legal right to send troops. There is a need now, but as I see it, none of such importance that we dare risk trouble with England or the Hudson's Bay people. Dr. McLoughlin is a bulwark of good in his little kingdom. I can't think of a better person to administer their interests and some of ours too. Let us think more about your problems, have more discussions. In the meantime, rest up, visit friends and bring yourself up to date on what's been happening with the family.''

Chapter 34

Some Nez Perce had been loafing around Fort Boise with a group of Shoshone, Umatilla, Walla Walla and unidentified half-breeds. No war was going on; it was too early to steal horses and not yet time to catch salmon or hunt buffalo; and when Tom Hill and the two Cayuse returned, these troublemaking Indians had made the usual inquiries about what the three had been doing. Hill and his two companions told and retold elaborate stories about how Doc Newell and Laird had jumped them from ambush and taken Hill's weapons.

Tom had lost some of his brashness, though. Now he needed desperately to buy a rifle and a knife as well, to fit his empty sheath. A suspicious trader was curious about what had happened to his weapons. "Where's your gun? It's a little too important to be losing, don't you think?"

"I lost it." Hill didn't explain. "That shouldn't make no difference to you. I want one of them new rifles you got in for the trappers, and a Wilson Green River to go with it."

"Not so fast, Hill. You know the law of the company. You got your name on the books here?"

"If she ain't there, put her there. I'll pay part right now and the rest when I come in with some fur."

A lot of dickering followed, but finally the two men came to an understanding, and to show there were no hard feelings on the part of him or his company the trader gave Hill a couple of drinks of whiskey and one to Hill's Cayuse friend. The trader knew what he was doing was forbidden by the company, but he made an exception, hoping that what he found out from the men might offset his risk of being caught for violating rules.

"Lame Horse, if you tell me how Tom lost his rifle and knife, I will give you another drink," he promised.

The Indian's craving for whiskey made his mouth water and desire overcame loyalty. In order to make certain of the biggest drink possible, he told a whopping story of what had happened on the trail when Newell and Laird found them camped by the dead buffalo and dramatized the event with hand and body signs. After repeating the curse Laird had put on Hill, Lame Horse got his drink.

That drink stayed with him and prompted the repetition of the story to Nez Perce friends at the fort. When the Nez Perce learned how Hill had lost his weapons and how Laird, a friend of the Nez Perce tribe, had counted coup on the Delaware half-breed, they went back to Lapwai to see Craig. Mixed with their account was a request for powder for their fusees and lead to make bullets.

The message that Laird had really whipped Hall was good news and worth, Craig felt, all the ammunition he would give to the Nez Perce. But Craig knew that the half-breed, running loose like a rabid coyote, would continue to thirst for revenge on Laird, his family or any other whites.

Spalding, in the meantime, was having troubles with his tame Indians, who were kept edgy by fellow tribesmen wanting to oust him and all other white missionaries. Whitman had the same difficulty and when a group of

mixed-blood Indians took off for California to trade for cattle, Craig breathed a sigh of relief. He hoped the rest would wait for the others' return before stirring up more conflict.

Influential men in the California-bound trading party included Spokane Garry, Elijah Heddings, Tauitau and Kipkip Pahlekin of the Kamiah group. They had taken the old trade route up the John Day River and across benchlands and had raided a few Klamath and Shasta Indian villages. In California there were more adventures. Looking for excitement, the group went after a tribe of California Indians from whom they stole horses, just as they had in old times taken ponies from the Shoshone and Bannock. Now they had a better herd to trade for cattle.

Settlers in the Sacramento Valley spread the word that murderous Indians from the north were headed for Sutter's Fort and raiding horse herds. Immediately, all unfamiliar Indians were regarded with suspicion.

When they arrived at the fort, the trading party was welcomed with caution. Many suspected they were spies and scouts looking for an opportunity to raid the fort and surrounding ranches or to provoke a general uprising among the California tribes.

Grover Cook was at the fort. He was a white settler and Indian-hater who boasted of having killed many Indians for the simple reason that he hated "any damned stinking redskin." It didn't take long before Cook claimed that some of the horses in the Indians' herd belonged to him. At once he demanded their return and when the Indians refused to give in he shot Elijah Heddings. Outraged, some of the group almost started a battle right there, but cooler heads prevailed and the disappointed party went back north without cattle or ponies. While they lingered in the midst of nowhere, raiding for horses and plunder, the word was spreading to ranchers the entire

length of the Sacramento Valley to be on the lookout for a bunch of renegade Indians. Spokane Garry and Tauitau kept their party at a quick march, planning to report the outrage to Elijah White and see how he would handle this business of a white man killing an Indian.

White was astounded to hear the news. He had not anticipated such an event when setting forth his eleven laws and saw no way of meting out justice. Futilely he tried to mollify the aggrieved Indians. But they wanted action, not talk. And when action was not forthcoming, the Indians talked of organizing a war party of several thousand men who would head south and even up the score by killing white men and come back with even more horses as well as cows.

Dr. McLoughlin calmed down Peopeo Moxmox, one of the leaders. Moxmox had come to ask for supplies to make war on the whites in retaliation for Elijah Heddings' death. McLoughlin countered by explaining to Moxmox that such an act would turn into disaster for all Indians, that they could not hope to mount and win a war against the whites. Certainly the Hudson's Bay Company would not help the Indians in any way, he assured Moxmox. In fact, they too might turn against the red men in spite of their long association. McLoughlin urged that Moxmox confer again with Dr. White and let him handle the problem. Another conference, McLoughlin hoped, would allow tempers time to cool.

Some tempers wouldn't cool down. Tom Hill soon organized a mixed group of warriors who were hungry for revenge. They headed south to get satisfaction and were never to be seen again in Nez Perce country. Hill remembered well Laird's warning and kept away. Later, when he met old friends in California, he joined up with those who led the Bear Flag Revolt.

*   *   *

White's letters to the East had gotten him nowhere. Feeling pulled from every side, he finally decided to go east himself, wangle a promotion and get more money. With him he took a resolution from the Willamette Valley settlers stating that Oregon should be declared part of the United States under the jurisdiction of Congress.

When White arrived in Washington, however, he encountered so many embarrassing questions about affairs there that he suspected someone had been before him. Blind to his own weaknesses, he forged ahead, asking for an Indian affairs position with more pay. Congress turned him down. To make matters worse, Polk eliminated White's position altogether, forcing him to abandon all thought of ever returning to the West.

When Bill Craig heard that the Cayuse planned to hold up the next wagon train crossing the Blue Mountains, he felt sure that the action could spark open warfare and sent word to warn Dr. Whitman of danger.

Whitman had been having troubles of his own at the mission and put Craig's warning aside. The priests had been talking with Tauitau, who was still furious about Elijah Heddings' murder and wanted Father Blanchet to establish a mission on lands he owned. It was only when word reached Whitman that a wagon train had reached Fort Hall and was advancing across the Snake River plains that he gathered a band of Nez Perce and rode to meet the caravan in order to escort it across Cayuse lands.

When they saw that Whitman had outwitted them, the Cayuse had still another grudge. Some of the tribe, in fact, were more determined than ever to have Whitman move out of Waiilatpu and Father Blanchet move in.

Mose Harris, the old mountain man who had guided the emigrant party, left word that Doc Newell would lead another group west later on. That was good news to Whit-

man. Newell had always been wise in handling Indians, especially the Nez Perce and Cayuse. The missionary hoped he would be able to forestall trouble and handle the Cayuse situation until Newell arrived.

The Nez Perce near Lapwai, learning that priests were about to build on Cayuse lands near Waiilatpu, feared that the Black Robes might next choose a location near them. Chief James became alarmed. He went to talk with Craig, who tried to keep James and his people from taking an active part in the mix-up.

"William," James began, "the Black Robes think of buying Waiilatpu and starting a mission there. It is still in my mind to give you all the lands Spalding has taken. If I do that, then you, a white man, can say yes or no to the priests."

"James, Spalding and the others will not like that plan. All white men will be with Spalding."

"William, the priests come," James urged. "They are already at the Whitman place. Tauitau will give them land or take back the Waiilatpu House. If he does that for the Black Robes, they will come here to Lapwai. This land is mine; my father gave it to me and his father gave it to him. All Nez Perce know this. How then can Spalding say my land is his? If he believes it is he will say so to the priests. That cannot be allowed to happen. William, I say to you today that the land where Spalding is now belongs to you. Go and say to Spalding, 'This land is now mine, for my father James has said so. I will come to live here.' "

"James, Spalding believes he has paid for the place by helping you and the Nez Perce people. Dr. Whitman believes the same about his mission at Waiilatpu. You and Tauitau want money for your lands. The priests will come and talk to you. I have heard they will pay for your lands but I do not believe that. It is not their way. Do nothing

until I talk with Spalding. He will not like what I have to say to him but I will tell him your words.''

Incensed at Craig's proposal that Spalding buy the Lapwai mission, Henry Spalding responded vigorously. "Mr. Craig, you amaze me. This land belongs to the Lord. I cannot sell it. I built this place in His name to help these Indians. What audacity prompts you to propose such a thing?''

"Well . . .'' Craig hesitated. "I just wanted you to know how James feels about this land. He was born here; his father and grandfather and their fathers before them all lived here. Nobody ever had a deed to this land, but the Nez Perce people have lived here for so long that there's nothing within memory except legends to tell how they came or from where.''

Craig continued, "As far as James and the Nez Perce are concerned, the earth is our mother. We can't sell it; it belongs to all of us. We only use the land for what it produces. It wasn't till the white man came and brought the idea of buying and selling land that it ever occurred to the Indians. I take it you or your pa owned land in the East? How'd you get it? Somebody give it to you? Did you buy it or just move in?''

"Why, we owned it. We bought it and when we left we sold it,'' Spalding stuttered. "But that has nothing to do with the mission here at Lapwai. Why bring it up?''

"Because you ain't seeing James' viewpoint. He believes this land is his and always has been. He already thinks of you as trespassers, and now you deny him the right to collect money for the use of the land and the timber and the water to run your mills. To the Nez Perce, this is contrary to your own teachings, and if you stick with it it'll be too bad for you.''

"I know there are problems,'' Spalding conceded.

"In fact, they're already upon both me and Whitman. The presence of priests doesn't help either."

"Well, I can't say as to that," Craig said, "but they feel they're doing the Lord's work too, so I'm not surprised they want missions here. We can't stop that, can we?"

"No, I suppose not," Spalding replied sheepishly.

"Well, you can't sell this land. You say it's the Lord's and you can't give His house away. Suppose the priests come and want your houses, the land and the mills here; they're religious folks, aren't they? And suppose James and his people say, 'Spalding, we want the Black Robes to have this place.' What will you do then, Mr. Spalding?"

"I will pray night and day that such a thing will not happen."

Craig shrugged. "For my part, I hope it never does," he agreed, "but Whitman's up against such a thing right now and I don't think praying is going to stop it. Unless a miracle happens, the priests are going to move in and take Waiilatpu over. You still have a chance, though."

Spalding did not take Craig seriously. "And what might that be, Mr. Craig?"

"That I move in and take over the lands, buildings and mills and say they're mine because they set on my father-in-law's inherited lands and he's give 'em to his daughter, my wife."

"Why, that's absurd," Spalding exclaimed.

"With all due respect, I think you're the one a mite confused," Craig countered. "It's you that's taught the Indians the white man's buying and selling land and houses and all the things white men put on 'em. And supposedly, in your religion, people who take lands and timber and put the real owners to work without pay and tell 'em it's for their own good are thieves and slaveholders. But what

have you been doing? And when the Indians don't like it, you can't understand the point of view your own religion taught 'em."

There was little more to be said on either side. Henry Spalding could not believe Craig had been thinking along such radical lines. He returned to his house and prayed for guidance, then talked with his wife Eliza, who tried to calm him. Eventually she advised her husband to confer with Dr. Whitman. Whitman's troubles with the Cayuse, she reminded him, were similar.

Dr. Whitman purchased the Methodist mission at The Dalles and established his nephew Perrin there to help Indians who came periodically to fish for salmon. Congress declared all territory south of the forty-ninth parallel to be American. Hearing that decree, settlers poured into empty country and took up whatever land they wanted. So much of it was fertile and fairly level that many westbound travelers talked of stopping earlier than they'd planned. Only previous commitments to reaching the Willamette Valley—as well as the advice of their captains—kept most members of wagon trains from pulling out to set up claims.

It was a time of despair for many Indians who lived along the migration route. Little concern was being shown for their rights. The Cayuse and Nez Perce were still surprised that so many white families would want to come to their country, and Jason, Joseph and other Nez Perce bands began to think seriously in terms of boundaries around their lands. "This land is mine," they wanted to say to the white man. "It was given to me by my father, who got it from his father, and I have marked it off."

The previous winter had been a devastating one for stock that ranged all through the grassy plains and sheltered valleys; bad weather had hung on until warm chinook winds swept in from the Pacific. By the time these breezes

finally melted ice and snow some Cayuse had lost most of their horses and farther to the north, the Yakima had lost even more. Nez Perce and Cayuse bands attempting to build cattle herds were also disappointed. Many they had owned were found dead on the moist, glistening grass.

And when summer came, still another tragedy affected happenings in the West, this one stirring further talks of violence among the Indians. One wagon train heading west carried children sick with measles; the illness spread to over half the Cayuse tribe. Over the centuries white people had built up some resistance to this childhood disease, but the Indians had no immunity and were vulnerable. The curse Laird had placed on Tom Hill and the Cayuse had come to pass.

Chapter 35

Joe Lewis, another half-breed, had taken over troublemaking where Tom Hill left off. When he saw his chance to foment a really bad batch of it, he started in at once. Lewis hated whites, Dr. Whitman in particular, in spite of what the good doctor had done for him. He began saying to the tribes that white men got their hands on Indian property by killing off those who lived there with famine or disease.

Lewis was a persuasive talker. And because so many of the Cayuse horses and cattle had died and measles had killed Indian children, the tribesmen listened and believed his stories. Lewis implied that he'd heard Spalding and Whitman discussing how they could poison the Indians and blame the resulting deaths on the disease. The whiskey the Indians drank, the rumors they heard, the bad fortune and despair they had suffered all combined to magnify angry feelings. Lewis advised the Cayuse to do something.

"Get rid of Whitman," he urged. "Kill this poisoner of your people. Kill him; kill his woman and anyone who tries to stop you. When he is gone your friends the Black Robes can move in at Waiilatpu. You are not women; you are warriors. Plan the time and place to act. After you kill Whitman and his woman, go up and kill the other preacher at Lapwai. Kill them all and take back your lands!"

The more the Cayuse talked and planned, the better Lewis' idea seemed, and those of their tribe who might have held them in check were not there. This late in the fall travel to and from the mission had almost stopped. The time to act would be as soon as Whitman returned from The Dalles.

Spalding and his ten-year-old daughter arrived at Waiilatpu from Lapwai to confer with Whitman. It was agreed that little Eliza would stay with the Whitmans to study and become a companion to Jim Bridger's daughter and Helen Mar Meek.

Henry Spalding kissed his daughter good-bye. He promised to stop and see her on his way back from visiting some sick Indians near The Dalles, explaining that Dr. Whitman had persuaded him to go along. They would confer with his nephew Perrin, who might have some information about the Cayuse. Rumors of war had been circulating all through the basin. The Yakima, Spokane, Nez Perce and Umatilla, all formerly peaceful tribes, were restless after the winter kill of their livestock and resentful that the dreaded sickness finally had struck their people too.

Before Whitman and Spalding reached the Cayuse villages, Spalding's horse stumbled and fell, pinning him down. Badly bruised, the missionary could ride but needed help getting on and off his horse. After some consideration Spalding decided to stay behind and rest at the family lodge of Stickus, a Cayuse chief who had remained friendly to both missionaries.

Whitman went on tending sick Indians and then visited now-Bishop Blanchet, Father Brouillet and several other priests at their new mission. One topic discussed was the possible sale of Waiilatpu to the Roman Catholics in case the Cayuse no longer wanted the Protestants there. The priests invited Whitman to dine with them but he declined,

choosing instead to return to Stickus' lodge. Because Spalding was still not able to travel, Whitman rode on alone.

It was late November, the weather along the Columbia miserable as it always was before real winter set in. A cold wet wind blew up the great stream, bringing with it drifts of fog heavy enough to dampen clothing. As the day lengthened almost into darkness, a feeling of dread seized Whitman. The good doctor tried to think of Waiilatpu, his wife's welcome, warm fires and food, but as he rode it seemed to him that all the work he had done, even the work Spalding had done, was coming to an end. Narcissa had never recovered from her fright at the hands of the Cayuse brave. Even now she would be distressed, worrying.

It was true. Mrs. Whitman had worried about her husband's safety more than usual that day. She dreaded the coming darkness; the fog and chill seemed to forbode evil. Even the children were more subdued than usual. It wasn't until Whitman finally rode in that they were all relieved; Eliza Spalding, however, grieved about her father's accident.

In spite of hints of impending revolt the Whitmans made no effort to prepare for trouble. The seventy-two persons at the mission were all considered loyal friends and Christians; they were completely trusted.

Morning came, and with it more fog and drizzle. It was a day to feed fires and talk. At the noon meal, where laughter usually prevailed, the mood was one of silence, broken only occasionally by Narcissa's attempts to talk cheerfully about Christmas. They could sing songs, she suggested, have a Christmas play to celebrate the birth of Jesus. Little Eliza Spalding liked the idea, but not enough genuine ehthusiasm followed to dispel the strange premonitions they all were feeling. Dread continued to build as they got up from the table and went about their routines.

About two o'clock that afternoon a group of Cayuse Indians appeared and calmly asked to see Dr. Whitman.

He invited them into the house. A Cayuse chief, Tilaukait, asked for some medicine for his children. While Dr. Whitman's back was turned to get it, another Indian struck the doctor on the head with his tomahawk.

Marcus Whitman did not give up his life easily. His attackers had to strike him time and again until finally he fell. Once down, he was shot, then dragged outside, still alive.

In the meantime other Indians were shooting members of the mission and attacking them with axes and knives. Screams and pleas pierced the air. Narcissa, shot in the arm, managed to run to where her husband lay dying in the mud. Pleading for his life, trying to comfort him, she was shot again, dragged away from her husband's body, then flung face down in the mud and beaten with clubs and leather quirts until merciful death relieved her pain.

Among the seventy-two persons the Cayuse planned to kill or capture, some managed to escape and sound the alarm; for the rest the killing and beating went on for several days. Eleven people had been killed and many more injured, and those who lay unattended died of their injuries. The Cayuse took forty-seven captives.

An immigrant named Canfield then living at Waiilatpu had been shot in the hip as he ran to escape the murdering Indians. Two days later he showed up at Lapwai and described the massacre to Mrs. Spalding, who was alone with her three small children, her brother, another white man and a girl who helped out with mission chores.

"Mrs. Spalding, I am not sure if your daughter is dead or captured, but I say you'd better pack up and leave this place," Canfield warned. "Those Indians sure intend to murder your husband and all the rest of us. For God's sake, don't tell the Indians around here what happened; they're mixed up with the ones near Whitman's mission. If they hear what's going on, none of us will be left alive."

"Mr. Canfield, please, I'm only human. You've just told me that my little girl may be dead—who knows? My husband may be too. And you expect me to forget all that and do what you say." The woman's body shook with sobs.

"That's right, Mrs. Spalding, that's exactly what I expect," Canfield answered quietly.

Mrs. Spalding sighed, collecting herself. "Rest and eat, Mr. Canfield," she offered solemnly. "I will send a message to Mr. Craig. He and his father-in-law will protect us."

Canfield was skeptical; he felt sure that even the Nez Perce at Lapwai could not be trusted, but Mrs. Spalding sent a messenger on horseback to the Craig farm with news of the raid. Craig acted at once. Grabbing weapons, he mounted, rode down to the Lapwai mission and sent word to James. When the chief and his loyal Nez Perce appeared, Craig told them what he expected of them.

"My people, the Cayuse have killed our friends Dr. and Mrs. Whitman at Waiilatpu. Their attackers are on their way here now to kill the Spaldings. They may already have killed Mr. Spalding—he was traveling with Dr. Whitman—but I am not sure of that. Some young men of the Nez Perce are said to be with these Cayuse. We must be ready to protect our friends here and save them from these bad people. I say that even if we have to fight to save them it will be a good thing; such killing must not spread. If it does, the white men will bring their soldiers, and white people from the Willamette Valley will come with their guns. James, I ask all your chiefs to stand beside me to protect these white people who are our friends."

Chief James spoke. "William is right. We must not let our wild young men and the Cayuse kill the Spaldings and their children. I say let us be for peace. War is bad. When the white soldiers come, they will surely kill all

349

those who have done bad things to the white people here."

The group was none too soon in getting organized. The Nez Perce and Cayuse who had participated in the bloody affair at Waiilatpu arrived shortly afterward at Lapwai and demanded Spalding. When the missionary did not appear, the Indians accused William Craig of hiding him.

"I ain't got Mr. Spalding," Craig responded, "but even if I did, I wouldn't give him to you. You have done bad things," Craig told them. "If you don't stop killing, you also will be killed. White men and their soldiers will come. They will kill you and all your people.

"Now we go to my house. We will stay there on that land. It is mine, given to me by Chief James, who goes with all of us who want peace."

Craig and his party mounted and escorted the women and children to his home, where Isobel waited. By now Canfield's hip had been cared for and he had calmed down enough to tell Craig and the others exactly what he had seen and heard.

At Lapwai Cayuse and Nez Perce braves had worked themselves into such a state of uncontrollable fury that it was almost impossible to reason with them. Some chiefs tried anyway, and one by one the Indians desisted from further attempts to destroy buildings. At last they were content merely to stand by the burning buildings for warmth and boast of what had taken place at Waiilatpu.

But where was Henry Spalding? The warriors knew he had left with Whitman. Disappointed not to find the missionary at Lapwai, the Indians began to search.

Through a set of lucky circumstances Spalding was still alive. He had rested at Stickus' lodge, recovered from his accident, and because no word of the massacre had reached him, had finally set out for Waiilatpu.

*   *   *

Father Brouillet had ridden over to Waiilatpu the day before to talk again with Whitman regarding the purchase of the mission. On his way he had stopped to visit Chief Tilaukait. To Brouillet's horror, Chief Tilaukait bragged to him that the priest could now have the mission without paying for it because he and his warriors had killed the Whitmans and taken captives.

Brouillet tried to act unconcerned. He realized how vulnerable he was and knew that if he showed outrage and anger over the missionaries' deaths, his own life might be taken. That night, sleeping in Tilaukait's lodge, hardly closing his eyes, Brouillet dreaded the visit he must make to the mission the next day.

He was never to forget the sight that greeted him there. None of the bodies had been buried. Rain had fallen. The partially stripped, mutilated corpses of Narcissa and Marcus Whitman lay in mud and water.

Hours later, the frightful task of burying the bodies completed, Brouillet rode back to Tilaukait's lodge and told the chief he must now return to his own mission. Before he left with an interpreter, Tilaukait insisted that his son Edward be an escort on the journey.

They rode a short way downriver. Edward and the interpreter, pausing along the trail, dismounted to relieve themselves. Lost in his gloomy thoughts of the ghastly tragedy behind him, Brouillet rode on ahead. All at once through the mist and rain he glimpsed an oncoming rider; in a moment he knew it was Henry Spalding.

The priest kicked his horse to a gallop, hurrying to warn Spalding that those who had killed the Whitmans were now searching for him. Angrily Edward rode up behind him; he gave every indication of wanting to kill Spalding on the spot. But Brouillet pleaded for the missionary's life and the undecided Eward turned his pony

and traveled back at a dead run to tell his father that Spalding still lived.

The moment the Indian was gone the priest urged Spalding to ride for his life. He handed over what food he had with him, then took charge of the missionary's pack horses. With not a moment's extra conversation, the fugitive turned his horse and galloped back downriver.

Soon Edward reappeared, this time with three Cayuse warriors. Furious to find that Spalding had gone, the four men wasted no time in talk. They tore after him, whipping their already-lathered ponies into a reckless run.

The lateness of the day, the rain, fog and drizzle all contributed to the desperate man's escape. Spalding lashed his fairly fresh horse to top speed, but instead of going on to Fort Walla Walla, now not many miles distant, he thought of his wife and children and turned onto a side trail that led to the mission some sixty miles away.

The pursuing Cayuse had not expected this decision; they overran the turnoff. But the leader's sharp eyes soon missed the track of Spalding's horse running on the muddy trail and back they rode. Following the less-used trail, they tracked Spalding through the fast-approaching darkness.

The missionary desperately whipped his tiring pony. He looked for a place where he might elude the pursuing savages, certain they were close behind him by this time. When darkness fell he left the trail and cautiously continued to make his way through the night. At dawn he found a place to rest and hide, but his bruised body and his bewildered, worried mind prevented him from sleeping. And as if conditions weren't already bad enough, the next night as he lay down to rest, his horse wandered off in the darkness. Limping on, his shoes in shreds, Spalding arrived at his trusted friend Timothy's village.

As he painfully walked in among the lodges, Spalding heard the talk of war and murder. Confused, he thought

everyone had turned against him. Finally an Indian woman who recognized his bald head called out her name to him and he responded. Timothy and other Indian friends came at once to feed and care for the beleaguered missionary, then took him to William Craig's, where he found everyone but his daughter Eliza safe.

When word of Spalding's whereabouts reached the rebelling Cayuse and Nez Perce, they banded together to demand that Craig turn the missionary over to them. Craig refused.

Every Indian in the Nez Perce country knew William Craig. He had lived among them for many years, married the chief's daughter and built this log house, where he and his wife were raising a family, close to a Nez Perce village. Craig was a strong man, that they knew, one who had killed and would kill again, but who was always fair and had advised the Indians well.

In spite of their anger at Spalding and Whitman, the rebels would neither attack Craig nor harm James, Timothy or the other chiefs who stood with him. That fact, that this one white man and his Indian friends, without force of arms, had stood off hostile Indians, would later set Craig even more apart.

Chapter 36

As news of the Whitman tragedy spread, white settlers grew ever more alarmed and infuriated. The priests sent word to officials at Fort Walla Walla, who requested men and arms to defend the post. From there news ricocheted to The Dalles, down to Vancouver and then to the Willamette Valley.

So far information had been collected only from the priests, and most of the whites distrusted them. That the priests' lives had been spared was a major cause for suspicion. Now all settlers, religious or not, knew that something must be done to keep the interior tribes from banding together and exterminating them.

Peter Skene Ogden headed upriver from Fort Vancouver with sixteen men to rescue the Waiilatpu captives. Ogden had lived among the interior tribes for thirty years and thought he knew their ways. At Fort Walla Walla Ogden learned that the prisoners were still alive. He asked to see Cayuse chiefs and they agreed to meet. With them were Peopeo and two Nez Perce braves.

Ogden spoke bluntly. "For thirty years I have trapped and traded in your lands. I have smoked and slept in your lodges. I have eaten at your fires and given you tobacco and lead for your guns. Now you have done bad things to

people who came to help you. Now I ask you to deliver your prisoners to me and my company before war comes to our people. If you refuse, you will no longer be my friends.''

The Indians were shocked and surprised. The man who had befriended them for so many years would not approve their war with the Bostons, would not now even remain neutral. Frustrated, the Indians argued that they owned the people they had taken captive. The chiefs bragged that they could sell or trade them as they pleased.

Ogden heard them out, then said, ''It is true you have taken captives for many years in your own wars. But the Bostons are not your people. They came to help you and meant to be your friends. I say to you that if you do not give these people back, men with guns will come from the valley to make war. They will send for the white soldiers to bring more guns and more men. They will destroy you and all your people. There will be no more Cayuse. There will be no more Nez Perce.''

''Peter, you have been our friend,'' Peopeo replied. ''We have known you many years. We have sold you horses and furs, traded you pemmican and moccasins. We have smoked with you. Some of our women have slept and lived with your men. We know you. Also we know Craig at Lapwai. You both say war will come if we do bad things. Now tell us what we should do. Tell us what you will do.''

''I know you, Peopeo, and I have heard you. I am telling you to bring all your captives to Fort Walla Walla at once. I will pay for them there with blankets, guns, powder and lead.''

The Indians discussed this proposal among themselves. How many guns and blankets? What else could they get?

It was like the old days, when traders had things Indians wanted and Indians had articles of value to bargain

with. Each chief had something he desired in exchange for the captives, and eventually a list was completed. In six days, the three Indians told Ogden, they would bring the prisoners to Fort Walla Walla in exchange for sixty-three cotton shirts, sixty-three three-point blankets, thirty-seven pounds of tobacco, twelve guns, twelve flints and six hundred loads of ammunition.

For a time during the parley the chiefs had insisted that Ogden promise not to make war on them. They also wanted him to persuade the Bostons not to. Ogden, always the trader, promised them nothing but said if they brought in the captives, negotiation might follow. Knowing the Indians, Ogden felt this arrangement would speed up the return of the prisoners. The Cayuse knew that regardless of their anger and frustration, they would lose out if both the company and the Bostons joined forces against them.

When word of the massacre came to the Willamette Valley, meetings were held to discuss the sending of men and equipment to Fort Walla Walla. Joe Meek wanted to ensure the safety of the captives and make certain that the murderers were punished. His daughter had been with the Whitmans and now he didn't know whether she was alive or dead.

A party was organized to go upriver immediately. It included Meek's old friends and companions. Meek himself was named as a possible delegate to go to Washington and appeal for help from the federal government.

Many new settlers in the country had secretly scorned the rough-looking, loud-talking mountain trappers, but they listened to them now. And though earlier the emigrants had looked on the natives as being too lazy to work and too cowardly to fight, that view too had changed.

More and more the emigrant women had seen bands of half-naked warriors in war paint and feathers wheel their ponies in wild races as they approached the wagon

trains. Their gestures with tomahawks, guns and lances were frightening; no one could deny that if all Indians banded together, white settlements could easily be wiped out.

Although Meek, Newell and others including the French-Canadian settlers were angry, they cautioned against rash moves that might instantly unite the Indian people. Luckily, the entire story of the massacre did not reach them until January. It was then that Ogden brought three boatloads of captives down the Columbia; the Spaldings, the family now together again, were among the group.

Even during this time of rejoicing, the whites were furious about what had happened. There was a series of inflammatory meetings. Declare war on all Indians, peaceful or not! Wipe them from the face of the earth!

There was one story that was particularly disturbing.

A young woman by the name of Lorinda Bewley had been forced to stay at the lodge of the Indian called Five Crows. The Methodists were outraged that the priest who advised her said she would be safe there.

Lorinda had been sick at the time of the massacre, when she was taken captive. As one of their rights of war, individual Cayuse men could claim a woman prisoner for themselves. Five Crows, baptized by Spalding, had taken on the white man's way and he desired a white woman for a wife. At this chance to get one he sent word to the Cayuse to save one of the white women for him. Lorinda was the woman he'd been allotted.

Bishop Blanchet had been in a tight spot. He was only one man among hundreds of still-bloodthirsty Indians. Thinking Five Crows might protect Lorinda during the trouble, he suggested she go with the Cayuse warrior on the Indian's promise he wouldn't touch her till they had been married in a Christian ceremony.

Still weak, Lorinda was cared for during the day at

the priest's house, but each evening Five Crows came and demanded her; Blanchet could do nothing but give in.

Lorinda testified at the hearings in the valley that Five Crows treated her kindly at first. But soon, she said, his desire for her took priority over her objections and he used her as his woman.

People hearing Lorinda's testimony were upset even more on hearing that many of the priests had laughed at Lorinda's complaints about Five Crows. Like coal on smoldering embers, Lorinda's words ignited an already explosive situation and demands were made that the Roman Catholics be thrown out with the Indians.

Earlier, at Lapwai, Craig and James had seen to it that things were pretty well under control. It was the first time Craig, having taken charge, was trusted by the Spaldings. Once Mrs. Spalding was in Craig's house, she poured out her grief and fright to Isobel, and Chief James' daughter soothed and comforted her until the exhausted Eliza Spalding gave up her tears and slept.

Isobel, the beautiful Nez Perce maiden who had dreamed long ago of the man she would marry, soon became an inspiration to many. She was a woman who believed in the ultimate triumph of good over evil, and just as she comforted Eliza Spalding and her children, she stood near and consulted with her father and William in their talks. White men as well as red listened when she gently advised them. And when doubts plagued Craig during disagreements with Henry Spalding and in arguments with James and his Nez Perce braves, Isobel always assured him that the situation would turn out well.

Once, holding her close in the quiet of the night, Craig had asked, "You stupid Indian woman, how do you know all this? Why can't I see things as you do?"

"William," Isobel answered, "I told you long time

ago I had dreamed about you. The dream came true. You are here with me. The dream was good. It told me all will be good for you and me. Do not worry. The dream does not lie. Good things will come to you that you do not yet see. I can say no more or the dream will die.''

William Craig never brought up Isobel's dream again. He knew of the belief she had inherited from her people, that a dream completely revealed might die. But what Isobel said that night stayed with him and gave him confidence to carry forward what his conscience and instincts told him.

William Craig swiftly rose to a position of true authority among the northwest settlers. The Lapwai mission had been deserted, perhaps never to exist again. Other missions closed, but Willaim Craig remained to guide and direct the Nez Perce people and protect any white person venturing into the territory. At the appropriate time he went to Fort Walla Walla with eleven chiefs of the Nez Perce tribes to say that these tribes would not join the Cayuse war. This pledge eliminated a great threat. If the Nez Perce with their thousands of mounted warriors had joined the war, neighboring tribes like the Spokane, Coeur d'Alene, Yakima and lesser bands would also have joined. Before Meek went east to deliver the message concerning the massacre to the President and Congress, he and Craig had a private talk.

''Joe, young Laird's back there now to see his uncle, who's something or other in the office of a highfalutin feller who's got a lot to say about the Indians. Laird went up to put the kibosh on old Elijah White, who won't be back to stir things up, I'm sure. Tell Laird what's happened here since he left. Let him know while you two are alone what happened to Tom Hill, that he's no longer here but set Joe Lewis on to stirring up trouble.

''Tell Laird his curse fell on the Cayuse. They and

360

some of the Nez Perce caught the measles, and that I'm really sorry to say Dancing Leaf, Laird's baby son and many others of Jason's tribe died of it." Craig drew a long breath. He wished he didn't have to make his next request.

"Joe, will you also tell him the Cayuse blame the Whitmans for this sickness and if he comes out here it'll spook 'em into warring with his family's outfit until he's tracked down and killed? That's how I see it, and I think Laird should know how things stand. It's going to be rough here for years."

"I'll hate telling the young feller all that, Craig, but I'll do what you ask. Who is this feller Laird's going to see?"

"His name is Madden. He acts as kind of an advisor if he has the right information." Craig paused and sighed, his mind on his friend's grief. "I don't know what Laird will do when he hears about Dancing Leaf. He's lost two women out here and he sure loved both. That's hell for a young feller. Do the best you can, telling him. I wish you luck back there. Too bad Bob or me can't go along to side with you."

Joe Meek took others with him to help break trail through the deep snows of the Blue Mountains and for protection against Bannock Indians they might meet on the way. Some travelers broke off from the party at Fort Boise, others at Fort Hall. It was May before Meek arrived at the capital.

Meek had connections from President Polk on down to Thomas Hart Benton, who was all for opening up the West, to black servants who had known Meek as a boy. With several bigwigs vying for his attention, it was several days before he reached Laird, now known as Sage.

In Madden's home, where they could talk undisturbed, Joe Meek broke the news.

"Laird, some of us old boys lost our children in the

361

killing at Waiilatpu. I lost my daughter Helen Mar, old Jim Bridger lost Mary Ann and Henry Spalding almost lost his Eliza. When the measles hit the tribes, it got to Jason's bunch, and a lot of his folks caught it. Your woman Dancing Leaf and your baby boy took sick and died.''

Laird stared disbelievingly at Meek, his eyes filming with tears.

''Hell, boy, we all lost something and it ain't over yet. Bill Craig wanted me to tell you myself. Him and Isobel's weathered the whole thing well so far. Old James is getting power now that Spalding has left. Between him and Craig I think they can control most of the upper Nez Perce country.''

Laird grieved silently for Dancing Leaf and the son he'd never seen. He remembered how he'd hated to leave Leaf, knowing as he did that trouble was coming. He had hoped it wouldn't come so soon nor affect Jason and his family. With that family now gone, Craig and Isobel were Laird's only ties to the West.

The usually garrulous Meek smoked his cigar and waited for Laird to speak. But no words came, so lost was Laird in his thoughts. Meek cleared his throat.

''Boy, it hits hard when it comes. I'm living with my third wife, and you know, I had to turn Christian to get her. She's a good woman, made me a better man, same as Isobel done for Craig and Leaf for you. You ain't never going to forget Leaf, but you got a big job to do here; I see that. If you can't find a woman here to take up with, wait awhile; then head out where you can still piss out the door and spit on the floor. These dandy dudes with their stuck-up women are sticking in my craw, and soon as I can put the bite on old Polk for more of his contingency cash, I'm heading where living is hard but where a man can be free.''

Listening to his old friend run on, Laird began to

recover from his shock. His time with Dancing Leaf was over. Somehow he must plan a new life as soon as he finished with his uncle's work.

Meek was talking again. "Now if you'll take an old fool's advice for what it's worth, I say stay clear of Nez Perce and Cayuse country for a while. Them crazy Cayuse remember what you told Tom Hill. Joe Lewis took it up and got them all riled up at old Whitman, who's now dead and gone.

"Spalding's taken his family and left the country, so they can't take the blame out on him or his wife or kids. If you show up, hell will be raised again and some will stick a chock under it. Nothing can go back to where it was afore the killing."

Meek leaned forward and looked intently at Laird. "Your name's now Sage. West of the river or on the upper end of the Missouri, those who ain't never seen you will take you for a new hand. Me and others will put the word out you've done gone under, and afore long you'll be forgot."

Laird spoke at last. "Joe, you're right. The advice is what I'd expect from you and Craig. When I left Dancing Leaf, I think she knew she'd never see me again, but she never let on. Are all Indian women like that? I've kept wondering what the baby would be like, if it was a boy or a girl and what Leaf would name it. Now they are gone and as you say, I must keep on going, but I'm not going back. My life out West is finished."

Before Joe Meek left Washington several things happened. Elijah White was rejected. The Bear Flag Revolt had taken place in California.

Meek went before the President asking for help for Oregon. While Meek waited Polk made his appeal to Congress. Soon afterward the legislators stopped arguing

about whether Oregon would be a slave or free state and voted that as of August 14, 1848, it would be a territory. Afterward money was made available for the new government in Oregon and for the settlers to defend themselves.

President Polk appointed General Joseph Lane of Indiana Governor of Oregon. Lane was ordered to accompany Joe Meek back to the new territory and take charge at once. Meek was appointed United States Marshal.

In Oregon City in the meantime, the interim governor, Abernathy, had appointed Joel Palmer Superintendent of Indian Affairs and put him with Robert Newell and Major Lee on a peace commission to go to Walla Walla and settle the war with the Cayuse Indians.

In May 1848 Palmer, Newell and Lee met at Fort Walla Walla with William Craig, who said he could bring in the Nez Perce from Lapwai to talk peace and discuss their problems. Craig was promised a council. Later Joseph came to the fort, carrying a New Testament in one hand and an American flag in the other. Two hundred and fifty warriors accompanied their chief.

Palmer, impressed with the Nez Perce chief's sincere efforts toward peace, agreed that William Craig, who had lived among them for years, be their representative in any future problems with the whites. Palmer then appointed Craig as Indian Agent in charge at Lapwai.

For the first time since the white men had come to live in Nez Perce country, the natives had a white man they could trust to represent their interests. William's wife, one of the most beautiful of Nez Perce maidens, was a Christian judged worthy not only by Indians but by the white trappers as well.

James took over Lapwai, the lands that had been his in the first place. William had already selected his own land and marked it so all who lived there knew its bound-

aries. It became the first legal land claim in the State of Idaho.

Many things of importance happened to Craig after Joel Palmer gave him public recognition. As his influence became known he sat in on many meetings to discuss policy and bore witness to various treaties and agreements. Having been appointed a lieutenant colonel, he acted as guide and military advisor. The mountains behind his home were given his name and a town was named for him.

Joaquin Miller told of a time when on a trip with Craig he saw the morning sun shine off the top of the mountains. Craig had said that the Nez Perce called the sight I-Dah-Hoe, meaning Light on the Mountains or Gem of the Mountains. When Miller sent this report to a Portland, Oregon, newspaper later, he spelled the name as Craig had pronounced it—Idaho.

Epilogue

William Craig sat in his easy chair and looked over the lands he had claimed. By title given by the Nez Perce and the United States government, these acres now were legally his. Craig remembered how he had lived before sinking his axe into the great tree that now spread nearby. He thought of the time he told Laird, "This land will be mine," and recalled every detail of building this home for himself and Isobel. Chuckling to himself, he thought of many of his former comrades; they had also chosen Nez Perce girls as wives. But of all of them, Isobel had been the best.

There was no doubt that Isobel had made his life what it was. From the time he first saw her he had sensed what her influence might be. Even when the Whitmans were killed, Isobel had kept a quiet faith that he and she would be all right no matter what happened to others. He remembered her serene smile when he called her a stupid Indian. Had she really seen in her dream all the things that had since come to pass? Well, that didn't really matter.

After William Gray had married them and they were alone that summer evening on the wildflower-covered prairie, Isobel had whispered to him words that as a Christian

Indian she had learned from Eliza Spalding. As Craig thought of them now he smiled.

"Surely goodness and mercy shall follow me all the days of my life and I shall dwell in the House of the Lord forever."